DAVID BROWN

A BELL RINGING IN THE EMPTY SKY

The Best Of The Sun

VOLUME I

A BELL RINGING
IN THE EMPTY SKY

The Best Of The Sun

A Collection of Writings
From The First Ten Years
Of
The Sun, A Magazine of Ideas,
Published in Chapel Hill, North Carolina

EDITED BY SY SAFRANSKY

MHO & MHO WORKS   1985   SAN DIEGO, CALIFORNIA

This book is published by Mho & Mho Works
and was manufactured in the United States of America.

The entire contents of this book first appeared in THE SUN, 107 North Roberson
Street, Chapel Hill, North Carolina 27516.

Library of Congress Cataloging in Publication Data
Main entry under title:

A Bell ringing in the empty sky.

    "A collection of writings from the first ten years
of the Sun, a magazine of ideas."
    I. Safransky, Sy. II. Sun (Chapel Hill, N.C.)
AC5.B385 1985   081   85-10462

ISBN #0-917320-24-7 (Softcover volume I)

ISBN #0-917320-23-9 (Softcover two volume set)

3 4 5 6 7 8 9 10 J Q K A

Table of Contents

Foreword

When I started **THE SUN** in 1974 — peddling the first crudely-printed issues on the street for twenty-five cents each, the "office" fitting neatly into my knapsack — I had no more idea where it was going than I do now. Which is to say, I've been as consistently surprised as any of its readers by the magazine's unpredictable turns, its unusual marriage of the sacred and the profane, its many changing faces — mystical and harsh and honest and funny — and its extraordinary evolution from a local oddity to a national "magazine of ideas."

Each monthly issue is an amazement to me, shaped by invisible currents I know better than to try to name; the people who write for the magazine and the people who read it startle me with their passion and intelligence, their faith in the power of love, their acknowledgement of the great mystery and the great truth in each of us, which words can only hint at, but oh such lovely hints. . .

This is a book of the best of those hints, in essays and interviews and poems and stories and photographs and drawings, published during the first ten years of **THE SUN**. Some of the authors or people interviewed are well-known, others are unknown. That, too, has been typical of **THE SUN** — to mix, without reference to anyone else's formula, such diverse voices as somehow feel right together, like a cook, without regard to recipe, reaching for a little of this, a little of that.

Bent over the simmering stew, I'm the head cook and chief bottle washer. I love it back here in the steamy kitchen, all these strange fragrances in the air, friends dropping in, sun streaming through.

As before any meal, a few words of thanks: to Lorenzo Milam of Mho & Mho Works, for his generous support and razor judgments; to Doug Cruickshank, Lorenzo's partner in Mho & Mho, for the book's handsome design; to John Cotterman at Lunar Graphics here in Chapel Hill, North Carolina, who typeset the articles; to Carol Logie and Jan Bellard and Lisa Holm of **THE SUN** staff who, along with me, proofread the book, though I suspect a few errors slipped by us; and certainly to all the people whose work appears here; and also to those whose work doesn't, but whose contributions are just as deserving of praise.

—Sy Safransky

I.

Sy's Spac

In the first **SUN** I came across, there was a funny, wise speech by Richard Alpert/Ram Dass, which resonated with my many memories of two decades before. There was also a fine interview with O. Carl Simonton on our bodies as metaphors for our minds. I immediately sent founder/editor Sy Safransky a check and a long letter. I told him to mail me all his back issues. I also asked him what the hell he thought he was doing.

I've since had a chance to read all the past issues of **THE SUN** twice. Once, shortly after I received them, for my own edification. And again — a year or so later — when Sy and I decided to put together an anthology, the one you are now holding in your hand.

I had moved to Tijuana by the time the second reading came about. I was suffering from a broken heart; in keeping with the American artistes' tradition of running away from our country of origin, I moved to TJ, which made me as close to an expatriate as I could wish. I rented a house in a Tijuana *barrio* river valley and lived there in splendid, broken-hearted squalor.

I kept the issues of **THE SUN** in my bedroom, or, on occasion, in my outhouse (no running water in Squalorville) and as I dealt with insomnia, or adjourned in the company of various flies and spiders homesteading in the outback Shangri-La, I would attack another issue, marking the copies, folding down the corners of the pages containing the articles I liked. I started to compile a list for Safransky, a list which represented one fan's version of The Best of **THE SUN**.

A house with no heat or water connects you with the earth. I had then (I have now) a certain fancy for show birds (chickens). They — the Belgian Bearded Bantam d'Anvers, or the Barred Cochins — would fairly often join me in my bedroom (or, on occasion, near the throne). Me and the chickens and the skinks and the noise of the Tijuana water-trucks. **THE SUN** was my only intellectual companion and my only love in those days. And I have never lost my love for **THE SUN**.

It was there I met the aptly named Patricia Sun — whose picture and words quite swept me off my feet. It was there I was first introduced to Pat Ellis Taylor, a master, obviously, out of my generation. It was in those dusky rooms that I first met Peace Nigger — whose writing must surely match in joy and in existential passion the long journey of Juan Ramón Jiménez and his wise donkey Platero. . . . Jiménez travelling in poverty through the plains of Spain; Peace Nigger and pack-laden goat Iowa marching bravely, wordlessly, through the infested swamps of Mississippi.

It was there I could journey with Peg Staley as she fought the cancer that had invaded her own sweet breast — the same breast that had once fed her babes, that now was feeding something far darker. Peg, the brave, the desperate; in anger, in sweetness, in grief, in endless journeys, seeking — what? — relief, spiritual nourishment, hope, understanding, some answer. Caught, trapped, on the cruel point of the worst question one can ever ask oneself, lost in the gloom of a life-destroying disease: did I do this to myself? If I did, why? If I didn't, why do these so-called "helpers" keep telling me I'm responsible for my own suffering? It was a potent, scary, hideous, somewhat hopeful, ultimately hopeless, journey, and I think that you and I might have done much the same. . . .

It was there that I met Dr. Stephanie Matthews-Simonton, who taught cancer patients (like Peg) to try to visualize their cancer. It was there I met Ron Jones and David Spangler and David Koteen and Rufus — Rufus, certainly as wondrous a dog as anyone would want to spend the day with. It was there I met poets like Christopher Bursk and David Childers and Hal J. Daniels III and Adam Fisher and David Searls and Sparow and Name Withheld. And Safransky.

For he is *the* regular of regulars, isn't he? He's the one that is always there, typing, pasting up, taking the stuff to the printer, selling the ads, cutting the articles from inchoate down to genius size, nibbling all the while on yet another cup of coffee. I can see him now sitting at his bestrewn desk, wiggling his toes, scratching the unruly Hasidic beard, muttering Hasidic wisdom to himself, worrying, always worrying, always worrying. Thinking, as many of us do, of the very early days, him and his sandals, apologetic on the streets of Chapel Hill, selling copies of **THE SUN** — "Won't you buy one? Would you be interested, let's see, it's a new magazine, about, uhn, well about energy, and work, and friends, and community." He's a little embarrassed, and yet — after all, it's the first thing he's done on his own. Except quit *The Long Island Press*, run away to Europe, worry. Like Blake, the perfect all-in-one writer/printer/distributor; unlike Blake, always fussing: "Am I doing the right thing?" "What would my father think?" Sy's mind the busy bee, fretting endlessly, making honey.

In snippets — over the years — he has told us much about himself. We have had a chance to experience, with all the grief, worry, acceptance (worried acceptance, at that), his marriages, his loves, his father and mother, his doubts. "You're a *mensch*, but you're too mushy," Dass once told him, straight on. How wise that Dass.

We got to share in his fussy paternalizing, stewing over **THE SUN**. "Am I doing it right?" "Is it worth it?" he would wonder, *sotto voce* — especially during the early days. "Am I wasting my time?" he would fret, and we could hear his mother, his father, two thousand years of Judaic heritage, wrangling in his ear. "Are you blowing it, Sy? Not *again* Sy. . . ."

Ah Safransky, you are something, aren't you? Keeping on keeping on. Getting out yet another issue. Dealing with the advertisers, the subscribers, the landlord, the typesetter, the crabby writers, the lawsuits, the occasional burst of beautiful publicity (*CoEvolution Quarterly*! National Public Radio!) and always another issue to get out. Always. It never quits, until you're dead, or until it's dead, or until you retire — which might be the same thing.

We are there at the birth of his child, taking the bloody sheets to the laundromat. We are there with him when he moves into the office — after the breakdown of his second marriage. We are part of his family, *nu*? And the day his mother comes to visit; as always — sigh — such a troubled visit. Does she like **THE SUN**? Does she understand what Sy has done for so many of us, the loving, worried, always worried, sons and daughters of the spirit-sun. Is he too much

V.

i' th' sun? We know she asked him, didn't she, if he was eating properly, getting enough sleep. . . .

And the day his father died. It was a heavy occasion for all of us — in no way lessening the pain and the questions and the memories: a long weekend — the trip to New York, the hospital. New York: from lovely Chapel Hill. A long journey — in every sense of the word.

And then there was the day when he and Priscilla (and you, and I, and countless others) travelled in the snow all the way to that ashram, in frigging Pennsylvania, or was it upstate New York, and the car broke down, and there was a spectacular wreck, and we were late, and the baby started crying, right in the middle of the Meeting with The Master, and someone had to take her outside, but we had to go on, no matter what — because we wanted some answers, and we had to figure out if Muktananda had the answers, the answers we were seeking, the answers all of us are seeking, always. . . .

I guess that is the word, the one that most belongs about the corona of **THE SUN**: "seeking." It should be emblazoned there. Not "Endure Burning." No. God, no. Rather: "Endure Seeking." To never be satisfied, ever. Never sure if these new-fangled/ancient ideas out of the East can mean something, can do any bloody thing for us. Especially to those who live (god forbid) in the winter/snow summer/humid/sweaty wastes of North Carolina. The Dark Enduring Sun of North Carolina!

From the ash-ridden, paper-littered office on Rosemary Street (there is a couch with straw weeping out of the bottom, isn't there?) — to those of us adoring fans in Washington, or California, or Maine, or Illinois, or Texas (or Colombia, Vancouver, Tijuana). We are all there, rooting for it, aren't we? **THE SUN** has filled a special place for us, hasn't it? There is no other magazine I can think of that fills those two disparate needs: one for straight, good, honest, artistically deliberate writing, classical interview and reportage. And the other: for writing that addresses itself to the suspicion that many of us have — that there is a spiritual being there somewhere (perhaps without, perhaps within) who is available to us if we try, if we are honest enough, if we quiet our blabbing brain, if we give ourselves a chance at peace, and silence, and honest searching: the God of Answers, some very important Answers. If we are ready to listen. If we are willing to learn, put down our Western either/or. What is it they tell us? It's not either/or; no, it's either/and/or. . . .

□ □ □

"You know what I want to put in *A Bell Ringing in the Empty Sky*," I say to Sy, as we start on this project. "I want to put in the very first essay you ever wrote, the one in Issue #1." "But why?" says Sy, no little ashamed. "Because," I say, "it's prototypical you, pro-totypical Safransky." From the very first issue, the folded 8½ x 11 sheets, grainy and poorly printed, dated January 1974, typed up on one of those portable Royals, with a picture-cartoon by Mike Mathers of some big fat guy with a tourniquet on his arm, shooting a big syringe in his arm, the syringe marked "ALASKA OIL."

And on Page 15 there's "Sy's Space." That's what he called it. A page long, a few hundred words, with printing so off-center (he couldn't do that now, not in a thousand years, even if he tried) it comes out as SY'S SPAC, some 21st Century Spac opera by this Martian guy in the rolling hills of Chapel Hill:

"A CLOUDY (emphasis his), dreary day, sick with a cold, yet I want to mark the day, the year, to settle old accounts and begin something anew. It is what I am always up to, and I see how foolish it is, and how necessary. I can no more draw a line between yesterday and today than I can continue without one. The weight of days is too great. The spirit needs release. . . ."

"But why?" he wonders, sniffing, slightly ashamed of this raw effort from more than a decade ago. Why include it in the proud prodigal Best of **THE SUN**? Why? Why not? Our pasts speak to us, and we have to listen no matter how distorted the words of our child, no matter if it causes a slight blush. . . .

"And so a new year," he said, "a new longing — no, rather the oldest — to be different, to be better. I yearn for the end of attach-ment, and, with barely a pause, I am already dreaming of a more beautiful body, a more elegant mind, a self better able to receive, and give, love. I ignore the only wisdom of my years: that I need only accept myself. And I forget that time is but the one eternal moment in which we are created, and forgotten, in the timeless mind of God. . . ."

"Yearning," "attachment," "love," "beauty," "one eternal moment . . . " "*the timeless mind of God*. . . ." It's like one of those

VII.

poems out of Shakespeare, those sonnets. Or it's like the corner of a laser photograph. From the sonnet you can construct the whole *set* of Shakespeare's later corpus. From the edge of the laser photograph, you can create (befogged, but visible!) the whole universe. From the *primum mobile*, we can create the next ten years. Longing. Wisdom. A cold! And he asks (don't we all — at one time or another?) for a more elegant mind, a more beautiful body. Right: A Beautiful Body. Of Literature.

Sy gave us a spac to grow on, didn't he? And now it fills whole pages, whole issues, whole books. And if we observe the babe very very carefully, we can delineate an entire humanity. "How foolish it is, and how necessary," he says. "Necessary," he says. "Foolish," he says. Necessary. The Weight of Days. . . .

Ah, Sy.

I suppose he is right. It would be a bit self-indulgent, wouldn't it, to reproduce the man-child words, so far out of the past? We loathe mushy self-indulgence, we readers and writers in **THE SUN**, don't we? It would embarrass us all, wouldn't it, we participants in the growth of Safransky and His Bright Sun? This light from the corner of the new and richly flowering garden, reflecting — as suns and gardens must — so brilliantly on all of us; with all those gold and green silver spacs. . . .

— Lorenzo Wilson Milam

A BELL RINGING
IN THE EMPTY SKY

The Best Of The Sun

News From El Corazón: In The Composing Room

Pat Ellis Taylor

We all know how sleazy street is
it's up in the mornings with too many kids
it's too many men coming in the back door
and not enough time to sweep the floor
it's coffee in the pot and a dirty sugar spoon
it's towels on the floor of a dirty bathroom
and a smell like me and a smell like you
all mixed together in sleazy street stew
sleazy street stew oh sleazy street stew
it smells like me and it smells like you
gimme gimme gimme that sleazy street stew

> *— especially composed for paula footloose*
> *& her 5-piece baby-band*

Now leo says that of course we will get together again. He calls me on the telephone from seven-eleven parking lots long-distance and says that he loves me and he sends me a hundred dollars a month to keep his name on the mailbox, he in fact spends great parts of his poet-in-the-schools money to drive from galveston to dallas for

weekends of love-making and whispered reassurances and barbe-
qued chicken crowded around the little kitchen table with me and
the three kids like he is simply a commuting husband and this family
is really his. And at first he comes almost every weekend and his
hundred-dollar share of the rent comes on the first of the month.
But as the fall wears into winter he doesn't come so much, and the
money still comes but it's coming later and later, too late to cover
the rent, so that by spring I realize that I have got to stop counting
on it, the rent is going to have to come from me. Me the sometimes
writer. Me the new-born bookstore clerk. And me the mother with
the asset of morgani the working son, he does pay his part of the
rent, too. And so the household lurches along paying its bills on
minimum wage and money that sometimes appears in the
mail — homage to love from leo and occasional checks from newspaper accounting offices rewarding me for using my time to write
commercially viable articles on choosing melons in the supermarket
and growing indoor palms instead of wasting my skills on stories and
poems which do not sell.

But life is not grim. I like this upstairs apartment I find myself in.
Even with rats in the walls and weeds in the driveway, it has its
advantages. There is a room for each of us, and my kids are
electronic age kids, so each room has its own kind of electrical noise:
second-son playing stereo, daughter playing radio, son-morgani
playing electric guitar, him playing the loudest and longest, wanting
to be a rock musician so much so he won't have to work at the car
wash anymore that he practices his guitar all the time. But the
rooms are big and somewhat apart from each other because of a
central hall, so it is only at certain peak times of voltage overload
that I finally have to let out some kind of yell or scream or politely
pointed question /would you please turn it down/ which never
stops the mix of noise for good of course, only long enough to give a
little quiet time in the evening, a little peace, so my head can come
to rest and my thoughts settle down before the sound-level starts
building up again.

And the best of all features in this apartment is a white door in
my bedroom a magical device. So the kids can be rocking and
rolling, shouting jokes at each other through the walls, they can be
rolling the bicycle up the stairs and down the stairs and bringing
friends to play pool on the pool table we found in the alley and

placed in second-son's room, and all I have to do is open this door in my bedroom and step outside. And just like that the lights are out. The electronic noise is far behind me. I am standing on a second-story balcony supported on crumbling colonnades and embraced in the clutch of massive oak branches surrounding the upper part of the house. In the daytime I am in the company of blue jays who soar down through the leaves and squirrels running the branches, and at night I am in the company of stars. And I can sit in my used-to-belong-to-grandmaw rocker out there in the evening and put my feet up on a nail barrel I use for both table and stool and turn my own little radio to the country and western station that none of my kids can stand listening to and smoke a joint. Oh sing it, dolly! Listen to the man play that fiddle! I look down through the tree branches at the cars and bicycles and people passing on the street below who rarely look up long enough to spot me in the leaves — the vietnamese grandmother who comes down the sidewalk every morning with her cluster of children collecting cans, the black man with the twenty braids and red ribbons who rides his bicycle every day, the regular joggers and the dog-walkers, the couples shouting angry words at each other while they walk and the couples with arms around each other, the friday night drunks and the saturday morning whistling mailman — I study them like I study the pigeons who prance and flutter through their various bird rituals along the rooftop of the house next door, composing stories for each one of them and like a benevolent director assigning them roles.

Now in the apartment downstairs lives simon-polli. And when I first take up my observation post on the balcony, I see him coming and going on the walk below me with an array of thin, young and lacquered women on his arm. He is enrolled in the downtown community college with plans for becoming an accountant/male-model & masseur, and he says that the electric guitar playing above his desk keeps him from studying very well. But morgani learns to turn the decibels down when simon-polli knocks a broom handle against the ceiling. I don't like simon-polli too much, I don't like his black pompadour and little twitchy mustache, and I don't like the endless photographs in the simon-polli portfolio he wants to show me with every invitation to his apartment for a beer — simon-polli lounging in a bikini on a broken brick wall, simon-polli dressed in a black gypsy outfit smoldering at the camera-eye, close-ups of simon-polli with his nostrils flared and his pores open. But I do occasionally like to hear his stories. So when he stands in the front yard waving a poorly rolled joint and looking up at me on my balcony perch, I invite him up sometimes to sit with me in the branches. Because simon-polli, see, came from eastern europe somewhere, his earliest photographs he says showed him a skinny kid with a shaved head, symbol of lice control, standing in front of a tent in a refugee camp with his father because when they were released from the concentration camp where his mother died there was no place for what remained of his family to go. He spent five years after the war going from one camp to another, traveling on trains that stopped in towns and villages where constables blocked the doors so that no refugees could get off. Then finally to america with a handful of family jewels which his father parlayed into a decent living selling used cars in chicago. I don't know why simon-polli came to dallas — that is one of the mystery stories he doesn't tell. To go to a community college to study massage? That's what he says.

And simon-polli has a european-sentimental streak at least as strong as that streak in me that keeps my radio tuned to the country-and-western station. His eyes get teary when he talks about his father. He fulminates about the coldness other students exhibit toward him in the college halls. At times he grabs up his guitar and brings it up to the balcony with him and croons out oily love songs from dean martin albums to the passing joggers. One evening he comes with his guitar, full of emotion.

I'm going to be a father again, he says, my four-year-old son is coming from new york to stay with me because his mom doesn't want him anymore.

Well, I didn't even know he had a son or an ex-wife, but I say wow simon, that sounds pretty exciting.

I wrote a song, he says, I'm going to sing it for my son when he gets off the airplane. And then simon starts singing — oh matthew, I love you, you are the sky's blue, you are a bird of a beautiful hue, my son, my matthew — simon-polli singing with his eyes closed his lips pursed up to the moon above the balcony like a jewish coyote.

And then the son does come and he is the most scowling worried and mean little kid I have ever seen. He has thick black eyebrows that meet at a permanent seam between his eyes. But for the sake of good neighbor-relations and in exchange for simon not complaining too much about my own noisy kids, I agree to babysit the son from time to time for free which in fact does make simon very happy, he invites me to come down anytime I want to and smoke grass with him, his stash box kept full by generous checks from his chicago-father.

So one evening I'm sitting out on my balcony when I see simon-polli coming up the front walk carrying a large over-stuffed chair followed by matthew who is picking up little rocks and throwing them at his father's ankles.

Cut it out! simon is shouting.

No! matthew is shouting back.

When simon sees me on the balcony he calls up. See this great chair? I bought it from this lady down the street who's being evicted. It's okay, it's got some broken springs, she was asking seventy-five but I talked her into taking fifteen.

Sounds like a bargain, I say.

Oh I just felt sorry for her, not that I wanted the chair, he says, although it looks okay, just the springs a little bad.

Matthew lobs another stone.

I said cut it out! simon shouts.

I said no! matthew shouts.

They go on in and there is the sound of whopping and screaming and crying, and I look up the street in the direction the two of them came from to see what is going on. Sure enough, I see daughter standing with some more kids around a pile of stuff along the curb about six houses down. And the sun, I also notice, is almost gone. So I lean across the balcony rail and call down the street for daughter to come home. She comes running, in a minute she's coming out on the balcony. There's a girl with her about the same height, long brown hair like hers, same budding build with almost-boobs making little bumps under her blouse and hips gathered ready to begin making curves.

This is fran, daughter says, she's fourteen, her family's the one that's being evicted.

Hello, fran says, very polite, the same as if daughter had said fran's family owned every house on the block.

Hello, I say, do y'all have a place to sleep tonight?

Fran frowns a little bit. Oh I don't know yet, she says. My mom is trying to call some people. She starts squinting down the sidewalk back at the pile of stuff on the curb. Oh I better go back and see what my little sister is doing.

Well you tell your mom you can sleep on the floor here tonight, I tell her, if nothing else turns up. And I'm thinking that blankets thrown down for them on a bare floor in the apartment of strangers isn't much to offer, they will have to be pretty desperate to accept an offer like that. But then if they don't know where they're staying yet, when it's already dark, then they must all feel pretty scared, pretty bad, and any invitation is better than no prospects of a bed for the night. So daughter and fran run back down the stairs and back down the sidewalk. The streetlamps are on, and I can see a pick-up truck parked along the side of the pile with its door open. There's a black man leaning on the side of it, there's some little kids playing around the pile, and then fran and daughter are there, standing, talking, but too far away for me to get what's going on. I go into the kitchen and start washing the dishes when daughter and fran come back. You need to talk to her mom, daughter says, but they don't know yet where they'll be staying.

So I stop the water and walk down with the two girls. The black man is still leaning on the truck. He is watching two men speaking loud spanish to each other. One is holding up a pair of pants to himself he picked from the pile and he is laughing, and the other is nodding his head up and down like those pants fit him just right, and there is this little blonde woman tottering around the two men on tiny three-inch spike heels made out of clear plastic and wearing a white nylon skirt like she just got finished drinking daiquiris at some country club pointing her finger emphatically saying put that down! you put that down!

Hey man, put that down, I say while I'm walking up, and when he doesn't, I tap my chest a couple of times and say, a little heart man, a little *corazón* — CORAZON, I say up close to him clenching my fist and shaking it over my heart (this is a chicano charm I learned in el paso, since *corazón* is something no good mexican man ever wants to be caught short of). Sure enough he puts it down and the two of them snicker, swagger away, saying things I don't try to translate, and the little woman is picking up the pants from the walk and trying to fold them up. I was just telling your daughter, I say to her, that if you didn't have a place to stay you could come stay at our place for the night.

Oh! she's all full of emotion suddenly, shaking my hand. Didn't I tell you? she asks the black man, who has been leaning on the truck in the same position through the whole encounter, the lord provides. And I don't correct her there, we will resort to abstracts like that the rest of the night to cover up our shyness at this strange situation: stranger asks other strangers to move into her house, a city act as strong as street sex, more easily talked about when veiled in euphemism and depersonalized, so that paula isn't really paula but the voice that cried out, the one in need, the little-lost-lamb, so that pat the person came down from her balcony and entered the story as the lord and pushed the wheel of paula's crossed stars and wrote the address down for the next installment of paula's karma.

What are you going to do with all of this stuff? I ask her. She just looks puzzled, looking at all the pile of mattresses and black plastic bags, piles of clothes and shoes and papers already beginning to blow away. So I say maybe you can put it all in my back yard for right now.

The black man suddenly unbends, smiles and says all *right*, like he's been waiting all this time for just those words. And he starts throwing things into the back of the truck.

I'll go down and get my sons to help, I say, so I trot back to the apartment. Morgani's out, but second-son is there and the two of us walk back to the truck. Paula is running back and forth, up and down the sidewalk, first lifting a bag, putting it down, herding fran and the little sister out of the way, talking in explosive sentence fragments. He stole the television, she says, I'm going to sue him, she says, not suitable, she says, now that's the way he puts it, and look at this! She tucks her chin in at me and points over her shoulder, it took me three days to pack it all up.

Sure enough, I can see that there are lots of things which have been put in black plastic bags and that now are half-dumped, the tops of the bags coming untied. So we all start putting things on the back of the truck, and the black man drives the truck down the block and into our driveway where we unload it, and we do this two or three times until nothing is left on the sidewalk anymore.

So by this time it's about ten o'clock. The black man (whose name is bennie and whose position in paula's story is never quite clear except that his truck has been made an instrument-of-god) wants a joint after we make the last load, and I tell him that I'm out but I'll go ask simon-my-neighbor for one. So I knock on simon's door. Simon's mustache is twitching over the chain latch on the second knock. I stick out my tongue and make a face like I'm all dogged out, which in fact I am.

We've just got finished moving a family upstairs, I tell him.

Oh no, he says, you moved that woman and her kids in with you that got evicted?

She didn't have a place to stay, I tell him, it'll just be for a night or so, until she can figure it all out.

Oh no, he says, I don't mean to sound like a bastard, but I can't take it. She can't move in. There's agencies to take care of people like her. I'm about to go crazy, pat, he says. I'm studying and having to get up early to take matthew to day-care. Shit.

Look, simon, I say, it's just going to be for a little while. Listen, do you have a joint?

Bennie-the-black-man's come up on the porch and is standing right behind me now.

Simon looks over my shoulder significantly, then looks at me again. For you? he asks.

I smile, shrug, guilty as hell suddenly because I'm asking simon for a joint for everyone.

You come down later, he says. I'll give you a joint anytime, but nothing for them.

Does he have any grass? Bennie asks me while simon closes the door.

Not really, I say. Paula comes shuffling up in her little high heel shoes, and we go on upstairs. When we get to the top, there is paula, there is bennie, there is fran the teenage daughter and her little sister, but then there is another baby, too, one I've never seen before, and there is also a german shepherd and a little black puppy. Paula is looking apologetic.

This is cody, she says, pointing to the strange baby boy, dirty faced, in dirty shorts, no more than two years old, slightly smaller than the baby sister.

So okay, I am thinking, there are three children, a woman and two dogs, but this wheel is set in motion now. And they will only be here a few days, they really will not be here very long.

Someone carries up some mattresses from the pile of stuff in the back yard, someone gets sheets, pillows. Then morgani comes in with two joints he's gotten somewhere. So we sit down on paula's mattress and everybody smokes, and we start talking about dallas, whether we want to stay here or not. Bennie the black man says he wants to live in dallas all his life and become a well-respected gangster, morgani says he wants to be a rock musician but maybe somewhere else, and I don't say because I am too busy taking this new landscape in to think of another one, and daughter and fran are already in dreamland falling asleep together on the floor, and cody the little boy-kid is walking around without his pants on, little baby penis peeking out from under round little baby belly, standing in the middle of marijuana talk with a big self-confident baby grin, taking for granted that wherever he is doesn't matter, he owns it all.

Of course I say it will only be one or two days, but it won't be just that, it will be one or two weeks or maybe it will be one or two months, even when I am moving the stuff into the back yard, even when I am talking to simon downstairs, I know that saying one or two days is stupid. It is unrealistic. If a single person becomes down and out and gets evicted, then maybe it would only take one or two days to get things straightened out. But a woman with little children is something else again. First, this woman needs some money, she needs either welfare or a job. Then she needs to get herself a place to stay, and then she needs to get some day care for her little kids so that her big kid fran, who is now their all-the-time babysitter, can go to school. Welfare tells her they'll pay her rent for a house, but first she has to get one. Then they will need to inspect it and approve it and file papers on it, all of which takes about six weeks. So she either gets a job and saves her money and pays the rent for that time and the deposit, or she talks a landlord into waiting almost two months for his money. And so where in the meantime can she stay? On the streets, at the salvation army, here with me.

Then there are other problems, there are the problems that made this elaborate system collapse in the first place, paula tells me these other problems in little pieces of sentences that she tumbles out while her eyes roll and her voice goes higher and faster with emotion. Paula is very scattered — she is a woman who has been under heavy fire and is freaking out. So when I ask her a question the answer tends to be so complicated with names and events and history I've never heard of that I quickly lose track of what she is talking about. But she is very angry and when she finds out that I am a writer, she thinks I will be able to tell the world what she is angry about. First, she wants to sue the landlord who kicked her out. She also wants to sue the landlord who kicked her out before that. And then she wants to expose the texas parole board for not letting her old man out. An eight-year-prison term, she says, is too long for burglary. Sometimes she tells me it was a first offense, but sometimes she says he had been a thief, was always a thief, although she hadn't asked him about it, she didn't know it. But these things, she says, that were up in her attic in highland park — the television sets and stereos and what-not which hadn't even been stolen by her old man, he had been framed, of course — they had been stolen by her EX-old man, who was in cahoots with her teenage son by that marriage (fran's brother) who was now in juvenile prison himself, just like her old man, serving time.

This is the way they had it, she tells me as her voice gathers low and intense for a slow build while she's waving a pancake spatula over the skillet and I'm drinking coffee, they had ME in the newspaper as the head of some burglary ring in highland park! ME! And I didn't even know anything about it! Oh, we sold a little tape recorder because it was there but what could we do? There it all was in the attic! And I told that police officer he was taking an innocent man, we had been framed by my EX-husband, who is a FIEND, he is a DEMON, he is the devil himself, laughing up his sleeve while we're spending time in jail. I even went to jail myself! For five days! She lifts cody the boy-kid up onto the chair by the table. You want some pancakes?

And this ex-husband, she says, you don't know what he is like. He put a rifle down my throat, here I was NUDE, see, and he puts a rifle down my throat and says SUCK-ON-THIS-BITCH! She glares at me with her jaw stuck out like it is him saying it. SUCK ON THIS BITCH! And there I was crawling out the bathroom window NUDE, bloody, because he beat me up — see right here? She shows me some lumps on her head. So I was screaming for help NUDE at the door of some neighbor's.

I'm eating my pancakes, watching her act this all out. There's lots of details I'd like to know that she's leaving out, but she's going too fast to stop her, and I'll hear it all again anyway, she'll tell me over and over SUCK ON THIS BITCH! she'll tell me exactly how he said it, SUCK ON THIS BITCH! until I have the story almost memorized just the way she tells it, with how she gets away left out, with how he got in left out, with what house it happened in left out, just the nude woman against the bathroom tile and the EX-old man with the rifle in her mouth.

So every morning paula gets up, gets herself together, makes breakfast for the babies, and when she leaves she looks great. She is a trim little woman with lots of fluffy blonde hair, who can make herself look like a perfect little doll when she puts on her job-hunting outfit and spends some careful time on her face in front of the bathroom mirror. She always wanted to be a model, she says, but it never quite got off the ground, although she shows me a cer-tificate she once got in 1961 in a miss teenage america contest held in fort worth, and she wants to get enough money sometime to straighten fran's teeth so that the daughter can be given more oppor-tunities to be a model than her mother was. She does have some connections in the movies, her babies could be movie stars, they're so cute, if she could just get hold of this guy she used to know when he first started shooting film, but she thinks he's in California. In the meantime, she throws the i ching several times a day and gets con-flicting answers, and goes by all of them and changes her mind each time about what kind of job she will get or where she will live. She can do secretarial work, and in fact she does get a job, but it only lasts two days, and then she gets another job doing telephone work, but it's at night and she can't work out the transportation, and she gets another job and it lasts for a week but then they lay her off, the cloud of paula's complications always quickly evident to any employer — a woman whose answers to the simplest questions are too complicated, who is always late or missing work the first days of the job because she has no adequate transportation and too many babies at home.

Fran babysits for her mother but she doesn't like it. She's calling her mother at work whenever she can telling paula to talk to the babies on the telephone to make them behave, and the babies like talking to paula but it doesn't make them any better. Although they aren't bad babies, they are simply babies, lively and into everything, and then maybe even livelier and happier than some because whatever problems paula might have, she nevertheless loves her babies and doesn't discipline them much, so they are lively healthy babies who have never been beaten up. And fran has learned child care from her mother. She never hits them, she never hurts them, although she doesn't know what things to do to make them mind, sometimes simply becomes a baby herself laughing and rolling with them on the floor. But then paula calls at five-thirty or six-thirty or seven and says she met a friend or stayed for a drink until rush hour was over and that she'll be home soon, and fran hangs up the telephone and says shit! shit! and smokes cigarettes and yells at the babies and slams doors and drawers until paula comes home.

And then on sundays paula has to decide if she'll take the salvation army bus to huntsville to visit her husband-framed-by-her-ex-or take the bus to gainesville the juvenile prison to be with her son. Fran is freaking out from babysitting, she babysits all week and she doesn't want to babysit on the weekends, too, so paula leaves so early in the morning that fran is still asleep and doesn't find out until she wakes up that she is babysitting again. Then whatever time her mother comes in, whether it's five o'clock in the evening or one o'clock at night, she runs out of the house right off, she drives around with the older boys in the neighborhood, she goes to the apartment houses where the older boys live to get high to listen to records to let them feel her up, whatever trade-outs she can do just to get away from the babies for a little while and her mother. Paula yells at her when fran pushes past her heading for whatever is out there — where do you think you're going, young lady? she says.

Fran yells OUT.

Pauls yells well you better be home in half an hour!

Then the door slams and paula comes into my room and sits on my bed. Daughter is glum because she can't go with fran. I just don't know what to do with fran, paula says.

Well paula, I say, she's just babysitting too much, she's too young and she's bound to be freaking out.

Well still, paula says, she shouldn't talk to her mother like that.

When paula leaves daughter starts up — why can't I go with fran? she asks me. I'm almost as old as she is, she invited me to go.

Daughter is sitting up in the middle of my bed pouting a little lipstick and blue eye shadow on her face that fran let her use and she's already looking like a young woman, but I don't care I don't care she's not old enough to be in this story fran's beginning to plot out. Look, I tell her, you've seen those gangs of men on the next block hanging out of the windows of low-riders yelling propositions at girls even younger than you, you've seen those old men with their brown bags sitting on the curb in front of the seven-eleven store, you've seen those drop-out boys inside at the video machines whispering about the size of your boobs when you're waiting to pay for your bubble gum, and I squint my eyes and wave my arms like mothers have done for hundreds of years conjuring these images up until daughter finally says all right, all right, even though fran comes in after midnight and she's all right, she hasn't been beaten up, so what's there to worry about?

And sometimes daughter does help fran babysit, she plays with the babies and helps with their baths. And sometimes when I get home from working at the bookstore I tell fran she can go down to the corner and get herself some cigarettes while I look after the babies a little bit. But mostly I don't help, instead of helping I make rules. I mean after all I am the lord, right? I am the lord of the house! So I get home from working at the bookstore all day and I am very tired, and if I have any energy at all I want to spend it talking to my own kids or even doing some of my writing, I don't want to spend it changing diapers and watching little babies beat each other up and cleaning up dog-shit the german shepherd and the little black puppy have laid down. So I say to paula now there shouldn't be any babies up after ten o'clock because me and my kids have got to get to sleep, see. And also I say now paula, having these dogs upstairs has got to stop because the puppy pisses on second son's mattress every chance he gets so you need to make a fence or get a rope or something so that you can keep them out in the back yard. And I say now paula no more babies in my room okay? Because they get into my papers and tear them up. And paula says okay. And I tell the same rules to fran, and fran says okay. But you all know the rule about rules, so I don't help but my rules don't help either and so stew stew stew bubble and brew, dogs shitting on the beds, babies pissing on the kitchen table, stereos, chairs, dishes, everything breaking and nobody knows what to do.

Well simon-downstairs stops daughter in the hall, he tells her to tell me that he is going to call the landlord if I don't throw that family out. A couple of days later he stops fran, he says he is going to call the police if her mother doesn't leave. Then after all that he stops morgani, he says he is going crazy from all the upstairs noise, that he is going to hold me personally responsible if he flunks school. And finally one evening I am getting home from the bookstore just as he is driving up with matthew's scowl peeking over the right side of the dashboard. When I see that we are going to meet on the porch, and just when his eyes begin to narrow but before he can get his words out, I say hi, simon, how's it going? That's a nice shirt you have on, you sure look great in red, you want to send your kid up to play a little bit tonight?

And he says oh! all right! while his eyes are opening up again and his heart is leaping involuntarily like any mother's heart will at the thought of free babysitting. Oh you can't believe what has happened to me, pat, he says while I lean against my door and give him a little allowance of attention, you know I put an ad in the student newspaper for massage by the hour? Well this woman with this incredible voice called! And she asked me if I did massage, like my ad said, and I said yes, and she asked if I would mind coming to her house, and I said not at all, and then she said well, can you pick me up where I work? And I said maybe, it depended where it was that she was working, how much gas it would take, and she said well I work at the playboy club! Can you imagine that, pat? he's shaking his head like he's having a hard time imagining it himself, me massaging a bunny!

Well good luck simon, I say, you send matthew up in his pajamas and he can spend the night.

Thanks, pat, he says, I didn't know exactly what I was going to do with matthew. I wave, and he's fumbling with his door, he can hardly wait to slap on the aftershave and depart, obviously he's not thinking about the noise upstairs, and if he hears any thumps or cries while he's taking his bath and fluffing his chest hair and flexing his fingers, he might think just when he hears it well next time I see that pat I'll say something, I'll give her a piece of my mind, but not tonight, not right now not when I'm so tired of being a mother, and then goes back to the story of his playboy evening already unfolding in his mind.

The next morning is saturday. Paula's told fran she's going to be home this weekend but she's up early with a red bandana around her hair and already down the street in barbie-doll levis to bring us back donuts from winchell's and a morning newspaper. I hear a knock on the door and think it might be matthew come to get his houseslippers and teddy bear he had left lying on the blanket where he had slept, I had heard him early in the morning before anyone else was up, tiptoeing down the stairs, pounding on his daddy-simon's door and yelling let me in! let me in! mad and worried-sounding like he always sounds until I hear the door open and know that simon did get home after all.

But when I open the door, it isn't matthew, it is a young woman who looks to be still in her teens with a broad country face and yellow hair and a belly about seven months long.

I'm looking for paula knight, she says when I open the door, looking at me like she thinks I'm the one she's looking for.

Well I figure this is more of paula's trouble, so I say what do you need her for?

My name is angela moore, she says, I came all the way from tennessee to talk to the woman who put my husband in jail.

Look, I say into her wide country blue eyes, paula does not live here. She is only staying temporarily until she finds other quarters. I don't know what your business is with her but you're going to have to deal with her somewhere outside of this house.

Is she in right now?

No.

Well, she says swinging her heavy body around, I'm just going to sit on this porch step until she comes.

Now I have no idea how long she's going to be, I say.

Oh I'll just sit here and wait, she says. She's sitting on the front step, her girth spread out around her nesting hen-style taking up all the space between the two porch columns. Unbudgeable. She smiles up at me, heavy with child as they say. So I try, but I can't think of anything to say to her. Not really. So I don't say anything. I go on up the stairs. Fran and daughter and the babies are sitting in the middle of the bed with the television on. I make myself a cup of instant coffee and walk out on the balcony in my houserobe. Blue jays have built a nest within two feet of the rail. One of them is sitting in it. The other one is squawking and dive-bombing the dog from next door. The dog is trotting through the yard with her tail down. I feel sorry for her because she really can't do anything, she can't climb a tree, but then I can relate to the watchful mother bird in the nest worried about the hatching eggs and the father-bird full of paranoia, but then the father-bird relishes his dive-bombing role too much, I think, when he keeps dive-bombing the dog all the way to the end of the block, finally soaring up again through the branches squawking at the mother-bird full of his own glory. I hear some voices from the steps below. It's paula with the donuts talking to angela moore, but I can't hear what they're saying. I sip on my coffee for a while and then go into the house to make some orange juice. Pretty soon paula comes in. She's making her agitated paula sounds like hunh! and whew! and well! like she has been overwhelmed by too much infor- mation to spit out in logical sentence forms.

Now who was that? I ask her.

Well! she says. Angela moore! she says. And to think that guy had a wife! she says. Paula is pacing around the little kitchen letting her jaw drop open like there are no words to express her surprise, and I can see that here comes another paula story, and sure enough, she starts telling me another incredible one while I fish a lemon-filled out of the donut bag.

One day she was over on gaston avenue, it was raining and she had just missed her bus. So along comes this guy in a truck, she says, and he asks if I want a ride and I say sure and so I hop in. He asks me where I'm going and I give him the directions. But pretty soon I can see he's not going where I told him to go. So he pulls into an alley and falls on top of me and suddenly he's pulling at my clothes! And I am screaming! So I guess, I don't know, I think he's just nuts, but I guess he gets scared or something, and I'm grabbing at the door han- dle trying to get out, so he revs the engine up again and takes off. But all the time he's trying to drive and punch me and tear at my clothes all at once, and I'm screaming and he's yelling you cunt! you cunt! And then we're on the freeway and we're going about forty miles an hour and I finally get the door open and jump out —

On the *freeway?*

She nods solemnly. In the center lane, she says, of north-central expressway, cars coming from everywhere. First I just hang onto the door as much as I can and then I drop off. The car in back of us sees me hanging on the door first and then when I come down onto the pavement he stops and picks me up and takes me to the hospital. And I don't have any broken bones, only pavement burns.

So this angela moore is the truck driver's wife?

Paula nods again. She's mad because I pressed charges. I saw the truck's license plate numbers and the police put him in jail. I mean I'm not a vindictive person, pat, but I think that man needs to be in prison. I mean he is crazy, he could do that to anybody!

Well of course! I say.

But that's not what angela moore is saying. She wants me to drop the charges against him. She says he's not that kind of guy, he was just too lonely being away from her so long. She says I'm ruining her life.

That's ridiculous!

Oh I don't know, paula says. She's sitting down at the table. She's pressing one hand over her eyes. Angela says she'll give me some money.

How much?

Two hundred dollars.

Tell her to go away, I say. I get some eggs out of the refrigerator and scramble them up. Cody-the-baby comes in when he hears the grease popping with half-a-donut still in one hand. He comes tugging on my pants. Paula is quiet, staring out of the kitchen window. The eggs sizzle and simon-polli's voice comes rumbling through the pipes shouting at matthew to take his pants off so that he can be given a bath.

I hate you, matthew shouts!

I hate you too! simon shouts back.

Then there is the sound of crying and simon-polli shouting shut-up! shut-up! while I shovel eggs into a bowl for cody and paula leaves the table to go into the back hall off the kitchen where her mattress is on the floor, shutting the door between the rooms. And cody and I eat the rest of our breakfast to the clicking of paula's i ching coins thrown six times on the other side of the door.

So it is getting to be close to easter time. And paula is like mother nature herself flitting in and out of the house while her household grows effortlessly around her, the house vibrating with an enthusiasm for its own fecundity which I do not share. Babies come up and down the stairs from all over the neighborhood wanting to play with the two babies at our house. Paula's german shepherd turns out to be pregnant and due to deliver in a matter of weeks. And a blonde girl shows up in morgani's bed, causing him to curtail somewhat the evening practice hours of his guitar, another daughter of paula's a big-boobed teenage girl who's been living with some aunt who wants to kick her out. The phone is always ringing for paula — employment agencies, collection agencies, welfare, foodstamps, the prosecuting attorney's office for depositions, the texas parole board for statements, and angela moore quoting bible passages about mercy and love. Paula says one day hey pat, what do you think about the bunch of us rooming together, after I get a job, then I could start giving you some money for rent, that would help you out. But no no, paula, no deal and no dice no wise and no way baby, I mean even in the bible-story jesus only had to furnish one or two meals at the most out of his baskets of loaves and fishes, the multitude didn't just decide to move in and stay.

Leo is calling long-distance and making plans for coming up from galveston for the holiday. He says is that woman still up there?

I say yes but she's going to be gone pretty soon.

By easter? he says.

I say maybe, but of course I know it probably won't be as soon as that. So after I hang up, I start worrying about leo coming, and I worry that he isn't going to be liking this situation very much at all, since telling him over the telephone that I have been having some house guests doesn't really convey the flavor of the scene. But I figure that I will fix the latch on the bedroom door one of the babies tore off and cook a large turkey, maybe that will be something at least.

So on ash wednesday while I'm on my balcony watching the kids walking home from school all the chicanos with grey ritual smears on their foreheads, I suddenly notice a man who is standing in the yard looking up at me. Is paula knight up there? he asks.

I say no she's out.

Well when she comes back, he says, tell her roy wants to see her.

And I am thinking oh-oh, oh-oh, is this who I think it is? And sure enough, when paula comes in, and I say that someone named roy came by, she says that's him! That's my EX!

And I say I thought you said he was in california.

Oh no, she says, he came back and he's got an apartment about half a block from here.

I say well how did he know you were here?

But she is vague, she's not sure, or maybe one of the kids told him. Oh and she is worried she is agitated she paces around the apartment telling me about the rifle again, oh he is bound to kill me, she says, you don't know what he's like, he is bound to do me in.

Now paula, I say, don't project, maybe he's in a different mood now, we won't let him in the house, we'll get a peace bond, we'll call the cops.

Oh that's nothing, she says, nothing will stop him! Just you wait and see!

So that night when everyone's finally asleep and daughter is tucked in beside me, I can't get to sleep myself, I stare at the moonlight coming in through the balcony door, I listen to the wind in the branches outside the window, I look without looking at the darkness hanging between me and the ceiling. Finally I get out of the bed. I stand in the middle of the bedroom in my underwear. I breathe in and breathe out. I make my arms go around in a circle. I make my spine relax. I imagine my arms are going in a circle around the house, making an imaginary line, and I imagine all of us inside of it and roy out. I call out to roy in the name of every power I can think of — in the name of mary and jesus and father peyote and electrical power lines and the rio grande river — making my arms swing out in a large circle ROY ROY ROY ROY DON'T YOU CROSS THIS POWER LINE. Then for a few minutes I stand and don't think of anything, just listen to the sound of all the babies and children and animals in the house breathing in and out.

So the next day after paula comes home from the temporary secretary's job she has been working, she asks me if roy can come over for supper.

You've got to be kidding, I say.

Well he's feeling better, she says. You told me to be calm, so I was calm and we had a drink together, and he's feeling better.

Not a chance, I say.

But he's missing fran, he wants to see her.

No way.

Not even so fran can see her father?

Tell him to meet her somewhere, not here. Look, I say, you've spent the past several weeks letting me know what a terror this man is and I can't change my mind that fast.

Oh, it's just roy, she says, that's just the way he is.

Well look, paula, I finally say, you tell roy I said there is a line drawn at the first step up the stairs, and I do not want him to cross it. And I tell her this in such a way that she doesn't ask me what kind of line, she knows that I *did* draw a line and that whether or not she can see it herself she can be sure it is there. So tears come to her eyes, but she goes to her room and throws another i ching and then starts running bathwater for the babies.

I come home from the bookstore on good friday an hour early so that I can do a little cleaning before leo is supposed to come in. Roy is sitting on the porch in one of simon-polli's lawn chairs with fran sitting on the wooden arm talking to him. Roy has on a palm-tree shirt and pressed slacks, his hair is slicked back and his face is still pink from a close shave like he has worked hard to be clean for this visit, and when I walk up on the porch he leaps up standing first on one foot then on another with his hands deep in both pockets.

Well hey, he says, smiling at me, thanks a lot for what you're doing for paula, for my family — but his eyes are everywhere except on me, up and down and over my shoulder, and I think oh-boy he is indeed a squirrelly one, and I don't smile, well really, I say, it's just between me and paula. Then I walk past him as stiff as if I am encased in clacking armor and step over the invisible line at the front step like it is a foot high.

The apartment is rocking upstairs like a john cage concert every dial turned to ten in every room punctuated by shouts and crying buzzing voices.

Get out of here! I cry randomly. Everyone get out of here for a while!

Second-son comes out of his room and thumps the bicycle downstairs, morgani and paula's stray sex-kitten daughter come out of morgani's bedroom with their faces flushed and their arms around each other, I give the babies a little push down the stairs, go play with fran on the porch for a little while, daughter asks if she can eat supper down the street with a friend and skips down every other stair when I say yes. I start sweeping and picking up my dirty clothes. In a little while fran comes upstairs, but I don't say anything to her. Then she goes back down the stairs again with two glasses of water. Pretty soon I hear paula's laugh outside, too, and fran comes upstairs and goes down with another glass. I begin to make up the bed. The apartment is quiet and the voices on the porch seem far away. I run bathwater, lie underneath the soap bubble surface and listen to the sudden quiet which has settled on the house. My flowered robe leo bought for me in laredo is hanging on a peg on the back of the door, and when I get out of the tub and towel off, I put it on. When I open the bathroom door, there is only slight light in the hallway, the last of the sunset coming through the doorpanes downstairs. Even the voices from the porch are gone and I feel quiet — a few minutes when I am completely alone. But just as I start from the bathroom to my room, I hear the downstairs door click open and I pause on the landing. I peer down the dark stairwell ready for anything and flick up the hall light. A beard and a broad-brimmed hat peek around the downstairs door — leo! Hello baby! he says.

Now I tell you the truth, when leo comes home from galveston after him being gone so long, I just want to fuck him that's all I want to do, I want to screw-with-him, I want to love him, lie on top of him, lie underneath him or lie right beside him, and I want to lick him, I want to kiss him everywhere, it's a truth whether it's evil or good, it's all I want to do. And if I had my way I would fuck leo outside under every bush and in every creek and vacant lot and flower bed along swiss avenue and howl like a banshee. But I am civilized and leo is civilized and so we simply go into this quiet bedroom alone together for the first time in a month and put the latch on the door and take our clothes off and get into bed and fit ourselves into one connected self as quickly as possible. So we start wrestling around in the bed together and kissing and me moaning in leo's ear and leo saying unintelligible things when someone tries to open the latched door.

I've gone to bed, I yell out, leo's here and he's going to sleep, too. It's daughter. She knows what I mean. Oh, she says. Okay.

You can get yourself ready for bed can't you?

She says yes and goes away from the door. Leo starts tentatively pushing up and down again and I push back but it's not quite so much fun. And every time leo pushes up and down the noise level outside the door grows a little more. Lights come on in the hallway. Music comes on.

Finally leo stops. What's that? he says.

What's what? I ask listening with him to the footsteps up the hallway and one of the babies crying, paula talking to fran, fran shouting at paula, second-son switching his stereo back on, simon-polli's television up from the floor boards and outside the bedroom window above our heads of course the cooing of pigeons nesting on the roof of the house next door.

What's all that noise? leo asks as we listen together lying in each other's arms as the house turns up the amps to higher and higher levels.

Oh, I say, that's just the kids coming home.

Well leo's visit goes downhill from there. The babies are crying before the sun comes up in the morning. The telephone rings constantly. Second-son and morgani won't talk very much to leo, daughter talks too much, simon-polli calls up and talks to leo over half an hour telling him all the worst news of what is going on upstairs in that apartment which still has leo's name on the door, and babies in their worst and most crying moods. Egg dye, green cellophane grass, bunnie chocolate bits, egg crumbs and handel's messiah blasting out frank zappa on the stereo. Easter morning and paula is awake before the sun rises making dressing with the turkey already in the oven.

When I come into the kitchen she says see? There's going to be enough for all of us!

And I say who's all of us?

And she says can't roy come up? Just for today?

And I say no.

Even though I'm cooking the turkey?

She starts crying. Leo comes in. Paula runs out.

There's a friend of paula's at the door, leo says. I told him he could wait for her inside.

I walk past leo to go see if it is who I think it is. When I see him sure enough in the hall — over the invisible line! — I stop and glare. Roy you'd better go on out I say.

I just wanted to use the phone.

I don't even say no, I just shake my head. He goes out. But I am suddenly confused. There is a line for roy but leo is in the house. Why am I refusing to have dinner with paula and her ex-old man? And if I have three children and an ex-old man, too, and then if I have leo and have some fun with leo, then why can't paula have some fun on easter too? And then it is easter after all! the truce of spring! And why all these rules? But in the middle of the fog I remember it's because of the rent — because paula doesn't pay it, although she has wanted to, but I don't want her to, I just don't. And then the utilities, too, I gather up all the money and pay the utilities, too, I write the checks myself, and I name off the utilities one at a time — gas, electric, water and telephone — like saying a line of beads in a rosary, until the confusion clears and I can move again out of the empty hall.

Leo doesn't want to eat easter dinner in the apartment, so we make a big sack of food, and second-son, morgani, daughter, leo and I carry the stuff downstairs to load it on the truck. And we do have a good meal at the park and lie in the grass listening to an outdoor band, and then we head back home. Outside on the porch roy is sitting on the lawnchair with a big piece of turkey paula brought down for him, and angela moore has come and she is sitting on the steps talking to paula looking as ripe as a two-month nesting egg, and the babies are scooting and squealing around roy's legs. We walk through them and say something about easter and the weather. And I think well, it is a pleasant day, they are making happy sounds, leo has had a good time after all, he hasn't said anything one way or another. But when we get upstairs leo shuts the door to the bedroom and explodes.

Didn't you tell me once, he says, that the trouble with your first marriage was that you were always inviting people to live with you? Didn't you say that one of the reasons the marriage fell through was because of that?

Well, I tell him, it wasn't *the* reason why that marriage fell through —

You'd better get that woman out of here by the end of the month or I'm not going to pay my part of the rent anymore.

Oh she's going to be out the first of the month. . . .

I mean it, pat, he says, the idea! you moving all these people in while I'm away!

Well at least it keeps me from getting lonely, I say.

But leo doesn't think that's a bit funny, he's packing up. He kisses me good-bye but he is very angry. Happy risen christ getting the hell out of here hitting the road again to single-man heaven.

So leo is gone. He hasn't even stayed long enough to leave his smell on my sheets. Squashed eggs in the hall. Even my used-to-belong-to-grandmaw rocker has come loose at one of its legs so that when I sit out on my balcony watching leo back out of the driveway, I sit half-sliding out of the seat. And I think leo shouldn't have tried to threaten me, it doesn't matter whether I have his money for the rent or not. But I don't blame him, I want this paula story to end myself, I don't want to be around when the husband gets out of prison and finds the ex-husband on the front porch or when fran finally finds what she's looking for when it's stuck up her body, I don't want to hear what happened this time on paula's way to work, I don't want to walk through the house anymore through broken toys and stereo-sets and spilled milk and dog piss and I don't want to deliver any half-german shepherd puppies! And why should leo finally take his name off the mailbox because of this whim of mine to come down from the balcony one evening dressed in godclothes forgetting to bring a change of costume? And why *can't* I be the salvation army? Why doesn't anyone ever listen to MY rules? Why do the goddamn babies keep coming into my room and painting themselves with liquid paper? And I sit and brood watching the nesting pigeons under the eaves of the other roof. I mean, how can they sit there so long when the sky is blue, how do they know when to give up if the eggs aren't hatching?

And then one day just like in the old movies the news finally comes, the dust of the rescue squad appears on the horizon, the sun comes through the clouds, the late chicks hatch out of their eggs late for easter but still in time for life, and paula has gotten herself a house.

Paula has gotten herself a house! Somehow in the midst of dealing with babies and dogs and checking out want ads and showing up for various jobs, and getting fired and getting hired and going for drinks with friends when the going got too heavy, and trying to find where fran is going at night and trying to keep roy out of the house and visiting two prisons in two different towns every week, paula has managed to find a house, paula has managed to find a house, paula has done all of that. With a little bit of help — angela moore is going to share the rent. Roy is going to live in the garage until the husband gets paroled. Whatever. Still, paula is on her way out.

And the night paula comes home with the news is the night simon-polli comes to deal with me straight out. He's squinching his forehead up and shoveling his mustache up his nose trying to look his most pitiful. I'm going crazy, he says, I stopped at a stop light this morning and put my head on my arms, pat, and I just cried — I just cried!

Well simon (I pat him on the back) you don't have to worry anymore — paula has gotten herself a house! Pretty soon she's going to be moving out!

He looks a little stunned, a little confused when I say that. But then he slumps down again. Oh it's not just paula, he says, it's my son, he's so hateful, I tell him to do things and all he says is no. And my friends won't have anything to do with me anymore because they're all single and I have this son.

Well still, simon, I say trying to cheer him up, not everybody gets to massage playboy bunnies —

His face crumbles with pain. Oh pat, he says, it was just a joke! There wasn't any playboy bunny! I went to pick her up and gave her name at the desk and there was nobody like that working there!

You want to smoke a joint? I ask him.

You got one?

Sure, I say. I take him out on the balcony where a light breeze has begun to come in through the branches and we light up.

It'll get better, I tell him.

How's that?

It just will, I say. Behind us I can hear simon's son laughing with cody-the-baby over something, but with the door closed I can't hear what they're talking about. We pass the joint back and forth for a while, and then we just sit on our balcony perch watching out through the leaves at the street traffic passing, listening to the cooing and chortling coming from the eaves of the rooftop next door, simon and me quiet, for tonight letting the pigeons have the last word.

(March 1983)

Sharing History, With Rufus

John Rosenthal

Rufus died last week. She had been my dog for many years, though she had been living with other people since 1976. She and I had spent some good years together and some bad years, and there were times enough when we had felt like each other's only friend. Naturally, her passing called up these times, and I wondered again for the thousandth time at the decency of fate which allows us to receive comfort from so many of our fellow-creatures.

The first time I saw Rufus was in 1967 when she was just a puppy. She was actually just a dark waggle on the end of a leash in the hands of my friend Jerry. He and his new girl-friend, Dolores, were walking Rufus, their new pal, around the quad at Wake Forest. I don't remember how

Raised in the suburbs of New York I had never seen those facts of life and death close up, all this licking and grumbling, this hot sucking, these winter frolics. I tell you, nothing has ever seemed so right as those afternoons with Rufus.

they acquired Rufus but it had something to do with getting stoned. Back in the late Sixties, a lot of people acquired pets when they would get stoned. Prior to ownership there would be a melting kind of understanding, a deep perception into the soul of an animal, a sudden flash of mutual destinies, and in this manner, a lot of little dogs and cats changed hands. As a matter of fact, many marriages between human beings occurred in much the same way, such oftentimes being the powerful romanticism of drugs.

Here was Rufus, though, and I'll never forget her. Her alert triangular ears were perched upon her large handsome head, which in turn was connected to her small corgi body. With her anomalous features Rufus never had any trouble getting laughs. "That is the weirdest looking dog I've ever seen," said a friend of mine from California when I first introduced him to Rufus. My friend Jean Morrison said, "You know, your dog is quite hilarious to look at, and she's obviously a very nice dog too." You see, her legs were so short and her body so long that when she got excited, which was a lot of the time, her whole body would wag, and not just her tail — which, by the way, in her younger years, was like a black plume tipped in white, always held upright, always waving. She also had large mournful eyes, and these eyes were the second thing you noticed about her.

Jerry and Dolores had just met each other, two very stoned and angry people — and now they had a dog. For Rufus it proved to be an unfortunate entanglement. Emotionally, these two adults had no business being together. They didn't respect each other very much, though they enjoyed getting stoned together. Jerry was a skinny working-class kid from Michigan, trying desperately to play ball in the minor leagues of intellectualism, while Dolores was a big, friendly Georgia yahoo whose main pleasure in life, other than getting stoned, was looking at pictures in magazines. Later on, when they were no longer together, Jerry would characterize Dolores as dumb and treacherous and she would remember him as mean and ineffective.

For Rufus this coupling of human animals who were in charge of her life was a disaster. They fed her all right, but on those hot Winston-Salem nights in their little hot box of a rented room, low in spirit and out of grass, driven almost berserk by the barking of their puppy (an inveterate barker then) they would stuff Rufus in a suitcase and throw the suitcase against the wall. Poor Rufus — like most primitive creatures she could never, without the help of a scientist, figure out cause and effect. And so the next night she would bark again, unable to connect her bark with the punishment which so inevitably followed. She wanted to protect them from intruders and never figured out that *she* was the intruder.

I doubt that in their lives Jerry or Dolores would ever do anything else quite as terrible as this throwing of Rufus against the wall. At the time, however, Jerry and Dolores seemed mostly like everybody else, wandering around here and there, dropping out of school, protesting the war, getting stoned, growing up. (It wasn't until years later that I heard about what they had done to Rufus.) And yet one must remember that as young people they were fairly defenseless themselves — living in a society that no longer had any respect for their lives. Their treatment of Rufus must have seemed to them something like a necessary solution to a problem and not the terrible act that it was. It's only when we're older and more at ease to decipher the hieroglyphics of right and wrong that we come to see cruelty for what it is.

A year later Rufus and I began to share a house together when Jerry and Dolores moved into the other side of a house I was renting seven miles outside of Chapel Hill. The years spent in that house were Rufus's heydays. We lived on a huge piece of land in front of a pond with ten miles of woods behind the house. Rufus, true to her corgi instincts, would hunt in the fields around the place, looking for anything that moved, though mostly, I think, she hoped for rabbits. Her way of hunting was odd and lovely: she would run through the high grass and leap suddenly straight up into the air, higher than the grass, glancing all about her for distant movement. It was strange seeing her jump not unlike a kangaroo across the field. She began to be called Roo at this time, though I don't remember if it was because of her bobbing up and down when she hunted.

Townley, a big and terribly stupid Doberman, lived across the way and he managed to impregnate Rufus a couple of times. He also tried to kill all the male dogs in the neighborhood who had somewhat the same idea. Rufus must have had sweet blood, however, for her puppies by Townley all turned out to be friendly animals. Abigail, who died last year, was from her first litter, and I saw her around for a decade. She was three times the size of her mother. None of Rufus's puppies, it seems, inherited their father's disposition. As to their intelligence, well, nobody ever claimed that Rufus was an intellectual. Townley, that feeble-brained miscreant, was shot to death in 1970 as he attacked a bitch who was tied to a post and not in heat.

These were pretty nice days for everybody. I was in love and getting married. Old Jim Snipes was alive then, a black dairy farmer from up the road, and he would come over for hours at a time, telling old stories about Carrboro which we could only partially understand, so rich was his dialect. The University was a large umbrella which protected the likes of us from the glare of war. Dope was plentiful — the price of too much smoking hadn't yet become an obvious fact. One cold winter morning I heard that Janis Joplin was dead — she ended up dying just like every straight person said she would. A friend was mugged on the streets of New York, and that was bad. Nixon and television were doing all they could to destroy the dignity of life in the country, but, as I said, dope was plentiful so it all looked a little cartoonish to me. One day I wrote an article for a local radical newspaper celebrating the Beatles' *Abbey Road*, and the next week my article was answered by an article which described me and anybody else who liked the Beatles as "capitalist pigs." Times just didn't seem very tough then. If a middle-class person didn't want to die in Vietnam, he could get a scholarship and a degree which in a few years wouldn't get you a job in a junior college.

The odd thing was that it was a time of great clarity for me and my friends. It's not that the times were so clear or that what we were doing made a lot of sense, it was more that we were in touch with certain elemental moods and humors which would to a large extent disappear a few years later when we became bound up in second-rate marriages and started worrying about dollars. In other words, we were to lose for long periods of time the sense that existence was charming. I could apologize forever about the lack of accomplishment during those years, the degrees half-completed, etcetera, but so much that has followed has seemed overbusy and humorless and free of the dignity of real choice, heart-pulsing choice, that any apology would have to take the form of a slightly bitter acknowledgement that life does indeed get tougher, unless you're a fool. Well, then praise be those foolish times of our life.

Watching Rufus, I must admit, was one of the primary activities of those years, and an extraordinary activity it was. I know it's not true but it seems like I must have spent a year of afternoons watching Rufus tend her puppies and go about her business — watching her growl, bark, steal the cats' food, and prance off in front of us on our walks, her plumed tail waving too majestically, her furry chaps sashaying across the cornfields. Raised in the suburbs of New York I had never seen these facts of life and death close up, all this licking and grumbling, this hot sucking, these winter frolics. I tell you, nothing has ever seemed so right as those afternoons with Rufus. The wet membranes of birth, the occasional puppy corpse.

The fact is, however, that while I watched Rufus during those years I was also choosing sides. Perhaps I was there for all the wrong reasons (laziness, lack of ambition, an undeveloped sense of self), but it doesn't matter now — I mean, there was such pleasure in peering over the edge of her box while she messed with her puppies, or tried to get loose from them, or turned over, or moaned so deeply from within the small barrel of her chest. In a recent Randy Newman song, "The Blues," one of the singer's personae recalls how one day in his childhood, full of sorrow, he went into his room and found that a piano "lay in wait for him." Well, Rufus lay in wait for me. She was the best way to pass time. And how much, I wonder, did I end up betraying those afternoons? That way of passing time?

Watching Rufus put me in the habit of watching simple things. Perhaps this was her greatest gift to me. Eventually I was to become a photographer and would learn by looking through a lens that there are only simple things to look at, that is, what the self can simply see; but in 1969 I still believed that the exciting things of this world were external, and that by virtue of fame or power one could *achieve* this excitement. In a way, then, watching Rufus was a kind of apprenticeship to that idea of reality which, as an artist, would become my only idea of reality: that unless we insist upon the universal significance of our own private lives (its pleasures and sorrows), we are doomed to remain subject to the laws of boredom and categorization by which politicians and tv anchormen keep us enthralled. I would rather photograph any dog on the street, scratching himself, than Ronald Reagan — for with the dog, I don't know what kind of photograph I'll get, but with Reagan I do.

Eventually Jerry and Dolores moved into town, where there were more opportunities for a marriage to end. They left Rufus with me, along with a beautiful white cat named Kathy who was soon run over by a garbage truck while she slept. For them Rufus was too intricately connected to the eternally unfinished business of their lives. Who forgot to feed the dog? Who forgot to let her out? Whose turn was it to go to Franklin Street and give puppies away? Anyway, I loved her and they didn't, and they knew that too.

When Jerry and Dolores moved out, two older graduate students moved in next door, Phil and Victoria. Phil was in Public Health and would play around for five years with a thesis which never got written. Victoria was finishing up a degree in psychology and she used the word "cosmic" a lot when describing human relationships. I liked them both until I found out that Phil didn't like Rufus — he didn't like much of anything that walked; he couldn't even abide himself for any length of time. When Rufus would bark at a cloud which covered the moon (what was she barking at?) Phil would scream, high-pitched and snarling, "Shut-up, Rufus!" — his voice shattering whatever stillness the night had promised. Like most dog-despising people, he never tried to figure out his anger — what part sprang from the malicious behavior of dogs, what part from his own phobic self. He had no grasp on the situation. He talked as easily about the miserableness of dogs as other people talked about the mediocrity of winter tomatoes. And of course he was so bound up in his attitudes that he never realized that other attitudes were possible. "Didn't you want to shoot that dog last night?" he would say in the morning. "What dog?" you would ask. "The one that howled all night." "Oh yeah, that dog." More than likely he'd be referring to a dog that had barked three times around midnight.

One morning I woke up to find that Phil had wrapped a puppy's entire muzzle in masking tape to prevent her from yipping. To his credit he looked awfully shame-faced when I asked him about it.

Needless to say, Rufus began to sleep in the house at night, where she seemed to abide by some notion of inside-the-house, non-barking conduct.

Because Victoria as a psychologist specialized in the cosmic evaluation of reality, she developed a coterie of young men who were delicately attuned to their own vibrations. Unlike Nabokov, they didn't find that the word "cosmic" was always in danger of losing its "s." For the most part these young men were the sons of well-to-do

Chapel Hillians, professors and doctors. They were a very unenchanted bunch, low on illusions, and sour to the whole idea of any academic achievement, since, as they knew, the universities were filled with unimpressive people, that is, their parents and their parents' friends. From an early age many of them had been in analysis. They represented themselves as a bunch of crazy guys, but really they were spoiled. Because they were well-off, they had the leisure to take lots of drugs and to hound their own souls with their disappointment in parents and society. It was simply possible for them to prolong their childhood, and they did. Ten years later they would be okay; they would be fine — chemists, lawyers, tele-communications experts, businessmen.

Rufus was their pet, Victoria was mother, counselor, and cook. They found something cosmic in Rufus to which I was never privy. It was odd hearing them go on about her various incarnations. One of them, a lanky lad who had the honor in this crew of actually having been in institutions, swore that he and Rufus had robbed banks back in Atlantis. And once late at night I heard a loud knocking at my back door and one of these young men, standing in the moonlight very stoned, asked me very politely if he could introduce a friend of his to Rufus. I roused Rufus from her puppies — four sucking and squirming and squeaking little brown creatures — and brought her to the door where the introductions were made. "Oh, wow, Rufus, how are you?" said the young man. "This is my friend Willy, man, and he's from St. Paul. Hey, man, look at her eyes. You're telling me that's a dog? Hey Rufus, how you doing? Look at her eyes, man. Rufus, you're a far-out dog."

Living next to Phil and Victoria, Rufus was caught between the devil and the deep blue sky.

Our life in the country came to an end in 1972 when my first wife and I moved into town. One day it dawned on me that six years of teaching English was enough. It happened while I was teaching Auden's poem "The Unknown Citizen" to a classroom of bored, well-fed children. Why should I be so ordinary, I asked myself. The question was full of wonder and freedom, and I left.

The first place we lived in was terrible for Rufus, a yellow cinderblock cube next to an apartment complex and its dempsey-dumpsters. Rufus had a patch of grass about the size of a coffin to romp in. A trailer park down the road had a few mean dogs, so she stayed pretty close to home. It's obvious to me in retrospect that she must have had some trouble figuring out her territory, but, to tell you the truth, she was the littlest dog on the block and probably didn't sweat it much.

One day a pack of dogs came in from the country, or anyway that's what the Carrboro dog warden called them a few minutes before he pulled a .22 rifle from the back of his truck and drilled one of them right through the eye. I guess he was right about those dogs, but it still left me a little shaky. He figured killing dogs was just part of his job.

Because it was such a lousy neighborhood for her, Rufus spent a lot of time in the house with our baby, John Keats, who had just been born.

I should add that Rufus was not a dog who instinctively liked children. When she got a chance to know a child, she would be devoted in the way that dogs are devoted to children. But her special light didn't shine on a child the first time she met him. In fact, she was probably disappointed in you for allowing such an unpleasant creature into her presence. She never forgot the way my three-year-old friend, Lydia, picked up one of her puppies, a little goofy black-and-white fellow — with her thumb in his eye and her fist wrapped around his ear. Rufus lunged at Lydia and made her cry and would have bitten her had not my voice commanded her to desist. For a second I felt like biting the child myself. A year or two later she nipped my best friend's child, Brendan, under the table one Thanksgiving, but none of us worried about it since we all kind of figured that Rufus was in the right, and it was after all just a nip.

A child had to prove itself to Rufus — prove that it had a little dignity and wasn't just some little unpredictable piece of nonsense, who was dangerous besides.

Before the birth of my child Rufus and I were quite a pair. Against our wishes she kept having puppies and against my wife's wishes I spent a lot of time watching them. I guess I was doing what is now called "getting it together," though I don't think there's any way to say that without sounding precious and self-indulgent. The fact is, though, that getting it together is not that easy a thing, particularly if everything came easy for the first twenty-five years of your life. And perhaps it's not bad for your back to find itself against the wall, or to feel sometimes that everything is falling apart, or that there's nothing you want to do anywhere on the surface of the earth, or that nothing's coming together, or that you're not worth much. People use a bunch of terrible words like "stress" and "negativism" to describe this necessary passage through darkness, but that's only because they want to be happy at the expense of truth. I mean, when everybody starts talking to you with the patience and understanding of a kindergarten teacher, you're in big trouble. All these stress-fearing souls I've met over the past ten years, I don't think they have our best interest at heart. They are abstract without knowing it, and full of words.

But what I want to say here is that while I was working out the terms by which I would live my life, Rufus was the best kind of dog to have. Why? Because she was interesting and full of affection.

Now with the birth of my own son, my days of dog-gazing were going to come to an end. There wasn't anybody left in my life who was going to encourage any more mooning around. And honestly, after having spent so many years in universities, I was curious myself as to the nature of real work, what it would consist of and how I might measure myself against it. I became a photographer overnight because there was nothing else to be. Of course I didn't realize at the time that looking was looking — the essential nature of the task doesn't change just because you're getting paid for it; or at least it shouldn't; and in the best instances, doesn't. But I couldn't afford to think that at the time, so important was it to give my life a new kind of order.

Rufus was neutered and her days of being a mother came to an end. It was time. She was getting on to seven; her last litter had five puppies, and at the end of a day nursing, her tongue hung out like a salmon. There would be no more winter puppies allowed in the house, and another summer of nursing would age Rufus immeasurably.

Since I was going to go into a darkroom for a couple of years and stay there until I knew what I was doing, my son became Rufus's great companion. And what kind of companions were they? Only the best I think. For I do believe that whereas adult human beings are forever strangers to the creatures which surround them, children aren't — that no matter how hard we try to ally ourself with the still beating heart of the world, we remain separate from it.

But a very young child *is* a lamb and a puppy. Truly speaking, nothing could be more remarkable. For a brief period of time Rufus constituted a large part of my son's universe. I don't mean Rufus as a dog moving from room to room; I mean the aspect of Rufus which existed in my son's mind before it decided that Rufus was a "dog," before it knew of "dog" — that somewhat risible creature whom we feed and who rewards us with what we seem to require (and which it doesn't even give its offspring), doggy-love, the jumping and the flurry.

In Elsa Morante's novel *History*, an indisputably fine book about World War II, the portrayal of dogs and their lives is particularly striking. They are given a regular language which is translated into our language, but it is a language which can only be understood by children and child-like adults. The dogs in the book would never talk about normal adults, those tired sad creatures who people the streets of the earth. One child, an epileptic, Useppe, holds realistic conversations with his dog, Bella. And Morante gives us no hint that these conversations are not to be taken seriously. It is a language of the simple too complex for the mighty.

I imagine that John Keats and Rufus held conversations from which I was, as an adult, barred. Some of them, I think, were about me. There were times when I was aggravated, hot, bleary-minded and despotic, and I had the distinct feeling that these two creatures not only moved out of my way, but did so in coalition — Rufus a bit wiser as to what was ridiculous about me, my son slowly catching on.

But that was a little later. My point is that when John Keats was a creature in touch with only a few living creatures, Rufus was one of them, and a very good one she was. Knowing that my son had neither the strength nor the inclination to hurt her, she moved in close, licking, the latter half of her wagging. And if as newly-born acts of flesh we seek assurance and some odd potion of peace from the eyes of those around us, eyes which gaze down at us from some unimaginable point of experience and feeling, then indeed, we were fortunate that Rufus's eyes were among the intimate few that my son first gazed on — for, as I said, she was a nice dog. She had the eyes of a dog, and they always had a touch of fright about them, but always in the well of her eyes one could see an intelligence not unlike the intelligence in the eyes of simple people for whom loyalty is first virtue.

In my life I have been in the presence of famous and powerful men who looked at me with eyes which admitted less kinship to the human species than the eyes of Rufus.

Rufus's last great friend before we gave her away to friends in the country was Celia Duke, now deceased. Celia lived across the street from our second home, on Pine Bluff Trail, in the basement of a duplex apartment. She's been dead seven years, but when I walk down that cool tree-lined street with its three or four houses, I still see her walking toward me, three dogs trailing behind her. What is it that some people have, what intolerable vividness? She was such an original that almost anybody who met her for the first time thought she was crazy — and perhaps as things go, she was. She had a car once and she'd park it wherever she wanted to. She was thirty-eight and said she was twenty-nine. She did a Marilyn Monroe impersonation which was unequalled in my experience. And she didn't eat or sleep or play like the rest of us either. Also Cecilia was suffering from ailments but was too afraid of the hospital to go there — she was afraid she'd never get out once she got in. In the brightly-lit world of a hospital, with its rules and regulations, she was certain she'd be lost.

Because of her raggedy-ann appearance she would often be followed in town by a pack of adolescent girls who would shriek insults at her. Don't ask me why. She disturbed them, I guess. But then she would turn around and perfectly mimic their high-pitched foolish voices, allowing them to hear what they sounded like: mean little birds. And they would flutter off.

Cecilia never paid any attention to eating (except for a couple of sticks of butter which she would surreptitiously eat when she baby-sat for us), until the last night of her life. By then her ankles were so swollen with fluids that she could hardly walk, but she managed to pull herself up from her apartment to the woods beside my house where she clung to a tree and screamed for me to make her a sandwich. Even though she was only a few feet away from me, I never heard her. I was stoned that night and listening for the tenth time to Gram Parson and Emmy Lou Harris singing "Grievous Angel," a song I had fallen in love with. I had earphones on.

The next morning she went to the hospital where she died in a hallway. Nobody, it seems, was in a hurry to get her to intensive care.

When Cecilia died, though, Rufus had already moved to the country, and she was the reason. You see, they became great pals. Now it wasn't unusual for Cecilia to make friends with a dog, or for that matter, with any animal. More than anybody I have ever known, she attracted them. I could launch into all kinds of explanations for this magnetism of hers, but I will try one: animals knew that this was one human being who lived by none of the rules in which they were usually entangled. She didn't care about the floor being clean, or if there was hair on her bed, or if they chewed things up. Nor did she mind barking. She must have been very confusing to dogs in particular, who, unlike cats, much less social creatures, live with very complicated codes of behavior.

Even before we moved in, Cecilia was firmly enthroned as the fairy godmother to all the dogs in the neighborhood. In the late afternoons they would show up at her house where she would hold court. This consisted of unloading the grocery bags which might be full of animal treats, maybe some crackers, a bowtie for a dog, bells for a cat. For a couple of weeks she insisted on putting red-nail-polish on the claws of all the animals who showed up at her house. Up the block Dennis was reportedly annoyed when Sparkie came home all dolled up like a tart.

And once we moved in, guess who rapidly became the court's favorite? Well, it should have been obvious to everybody that it was going to happen. The first time Cecilia saw Rufus, she screamed — it was love at first sight. She couldn't get over the short legs, the amazing tail, the hilarious wag. Yes, love at first sight between this large eccentric woman and this odd little dog.

From this point on in time Rufus divided her time between Cecilia and us. Her loyalty was of course to us, her family, but her passion was all for Cecilia. It couldn't have been any other way. With a wave of her plump arm, Cecilia could dispense dog riches.

Perhaps an old jealousy arises here when I say that there was something a little unlikeable about Rufus in this first phase of her friendship with Cecilia. She seemed downright bossy and officious. She stayed pretty close to Cecilia's heels wherever she went and didn't welcome the company of other dogs. Cecilia tried to talk to Rufus about her hostility, but Rufus was too snowed to listen. She might have replied, "All's fair in love and war."

And none of this would have mattered if Cecilia hadn't decided to take a job in town (we lived about a mile and a half from downtown Chapel Hill), working for a typewriter agency which paid her twenty-four dollars a week. It wasn't a real job of course, maybe answering the phone a few times a day, but it was just what she wanted. Unfortunately she had to walk to work, and this is where the trouble started — Rufus walked with her. And once Cecilia got to her office, nothing could more approximate heaven than by sitting by her feet all day; or maybe not all day, for Rufus could be seen occasionally sitting in front of the steps that led to Cecilia's second-story office. Perhaps her love would come down soon? You never know. And then of course there was the odd foray into town, and then the short jaunt to campus where a few thousand friendships could be made and a few hundred bushes sniffed.

I would be terrifically startled on coming out of the Student Union (where I had just spent five hours disguised as a student, working in a darkroom which didn't have to be dismantled every morning when the sun came up) to see Rufus cavorting on the campus with ten other dogs, rushing here and there after squirrels, glancing ruefully at students who might have a sandwich in their hand.

"Goddamnit, Rufus!" I would yell. "Go home!"

And off she would run, her plumed tail waving, right back to Cecilia.

In fact, around 1974, Rufus and Cecilia became one of our town's recognizable oddities. A large, handsome, sweet-faced woman, wearing no shoes, her clothes sometimes torn a little here and there, her short blond hair sticking out in a few directions, walking happily down the crowded streets, preceded by a sassy and funny-looking little dog who obviously regarded her mistress and charge as nothing less than a queen.

And then one day, a year after a leash law was put in effect, Rufus was picked up by the dog warden while sitting on the sidewalk outside of Cecilia's office. We were all stunned. We knew a leash law wasn't a bad thing, but we never considered that it would apply to Rufus. Rufus and Cecilia had become something like a fixture in town, and the town dog warden had always respected this.

But this was a new warden recently hired, and he was in full agreement with the new attitudes which were beginning to prevail in

Chapel Hill: let's call ourselves a "village," but let's act like a town. The street vendors of the Sixties, including the famous flower ladies of Franklin Street, were banned to a side alley or a bank's arcade, and a rigorous leash law was passed. All the dogs, even the sweet ones, dogs with no social marks against them, were to be tied to ropes all day long. Was it because they didn't clean up their own mess?

What could we do? I went to the dog pound with ten dollars and said to the man: "How about a break? My dog follows this woman into town everyday. She's been doing it for a year. She sits in front of her office minding her own business. Everybody in this town knows Rufus."

He said, "Sorry, no exceptions."

Once again Rufus stayed in the house at night so as to miss Cecilia's leaving in the morning. No luck. When we would let her out an hour after Cecilia had left, off she would run, her nose close to the ground.

One afternoon a blue taxi drove down Pine Bluff Trail. Cecilia sometimes took cabs, so it was not unusual. However, this time the cabdriver got out of the cab, opened up the back door, and out jumped Rufus. A little note was wrapped around her collar: "The dog catcher's been sneaking around, so I thought I'd send Rufus home early." I asked the driver if the fare had been paid, and he said yes.

Sensing our displeasure at having Rufus in town, Cecilia began to send her home regularly in cabs. This little dog had come a long way. She was the only dog in town who took cabs.

One day Rufus was picked up again, and this time the fine was twenty-five dollars. The next time it would go up to fifty. These people were serious.

I tried tying Rufus to a long chain, but this broke my heart. As far as I could remember, Rufus had never been tied up. As she lay on the ground, dreaming of town pleasures, her high-pitched whine would drive me to distraction. Like anyone in love, Rufus had no thought of consequences. All she wanted was to be with Cecilia. And if she wasn't tied to a tree or kept in the house, off she would go, searching for her mistress.

But what could we do? Frankly, given the shape that my household was in at that time, the small failures which were occurring daily, the sense that everybody had made too many mistakes, not to mention the existence of a few money fears, fifty dollars would have been a real catastrophe. Whose turn was it to pay the fine?

I think it was in 1976 when Rufus was sent to the country. Kindly, friends of ours who had just bought a house ten miles outside of town offered to take Rufus for us. At first it was to be an "arrangement." We would pay for everything that Rufus needed, and she in turn would have the run of their land. My son, when everything was explained to him, liked it that way, since by that arrangement he could still feel that Rufus was "his" dog. "We're not giving Rufus away," we said to him. "She's just living in the country for a while. We're buying her food and all that." To tell you the truth, I believed it too, and felt soothed by my own arguments. I mean, it's no small issue to give away your dog.

Nevertheless, it was a decision of which we should have been proud. So many of our decisions at that time were bad ones (such as sending my son to school at the earliest possible moment) that this one stands out like a shining light. Our friends in the country began to love Rufus immediately, incorporated her into their family, and shortly thereafter put an end to our food offerings. My son's mourning lasted a very short while before life itself and all its amazements re-entered his eyes to distract him permanently. He simply considered Rufus to be his dog who was living somewhere else, and that was good enough for him. When his mother and I were to separate a year later, he would have a lot more to worry about.

For Rufus of course it was the right move. The present tense in which she always lived became a "dog" present tense once she was back in a reasonably unlimited landscape with its endless smells and vegetable breezes.

These animals are really in our charge. They don't merely wander through our lives. No dog in the company of a human being is the same as a dog in the company of dogs. Like children, if we harm them when they are young, they will remain harmed forever. If we treat them well, they someday will find the means of comforting us. A friend of mine in New York City, Joelle, owns Tula, a skinny shepherd lady with huge, silly ears, who will precisely read the intentions of every passerby when they would take their nightly walk down Avenue B — a junkie who needs money will always get a growl; somebody coming home from a bar, nothing. New York City alone is filled with thousands of old people whose only remaining friend is a dog. They are dumb animals who live close to the ground, but there is a beneficence about them, a willingness to protect and to die for those humans they have come to know well. That there are vicious dogs is no more surprising than that there are vicious human beings. Along the great scale of creation, they are surprising creatures.

There really isn't much more for me to say about Rufus. I'd see her once or twice a year and she'd always be glad to see me, though, as she grew older, deaf and muzzle-white, her greeting to me had about it the natural courtesy which she would extend to any friend of the family. When she died last month, I was reminded of all we put her through and of all she gave back. I realized I had been honored to know this fine animal. That we had all been graced by her presence.

(September 1983)

Riches

Sy Safransky

Shall I say a line from a song changed my life? It's sentimental but true. Important things rarely touch me; the news, like an old wind, rushes by. Small things, signs, gestures point the way for me — in 1971, it was a song, reminding me that making a living and making a life aren't separate, though we pretend otherwise.

I led two lives that year, different as night and day. From midnight until dawn, when the sun slanted across my desk through dusty blinds, I was a copy editor for the *Long Island Press*. I didn't like the job, or most of the people there — the angle of their judgments, the heavy air of their lives. Nor did I like the *Press*, which I'd worked for previously — vowing, when I'd quit, never to return. How strange to be back; how strange to be back just for the money.

Marrying who I am with what I do — earning a life, not just a living — has been an act of the purest magic, aligning me with some raw power in the universe, giving me the strength to stay up late, get up early, do what I'd never do just for the money.

The money had hardly mattered when I'd started out, in 1966, as a reporter — fresh from graduate school, energetic and idealistic, yearning to change society. To bring down the falsely pious, to bring down prejudice and patronage and raise up the poor, this was my goal — and facts, the right facts, and the right words would do it, turn people's minds and hearts back to what America, now on its knees, once stood for.

It didn't work that way. I won a few victories, even a few awards, but I soon realized I was fighting with a rubber sword. The *Press'* editors had friends in high places and they took care of their friends; if the poor could be served, that was fine, but not at the expense of the rich. Once, I suggested an article about the local business community's indifference to suffering in the slums; I was told it would "open a can of worms."

Several times I almost quit, in protest over some arbitrary editing or a thoughtless assignment. Instead, I saved up my rage and my money; something told me I needed to quit not just the *Press* but my whole life, at least for a while, to quit America, too, and my ardor to save it. In 1969, I left, after telling my editors what I thought of them. My wife and I went to Europe, to travel until the money ran out; then, we figured, we'd come back. I'd find a job on a better paper.

The money ran out but I didn't want to return. During a year on the road, I'd changed. I'd met people who by word and example challenged me deeply, forced me to read between the lines of my life, look at my own false pieties, confront the fears that lay behind my concern about others' lives.

I stopped seeing the world as a succession of separate stories, rising and falling in the daily headlines like ducks in a shooting gallery. The real news was what *connected* us! What sense was there in going back to work for a "better" newspaper; didn't all the papers share the same assumptions? Facts were facts; the truth was something else.

We stayed in Europe nearly another year, scraping by. I did some writing, but nothing came out clearly. The revolution was inside me now; it was myself I was trying to save. Was there a politician anywhere who had lied more to the people than I had lied to myself — about my own feelings? Talk about injustice! To reclaim my heart, to win back my life, occupied me fully. I had few answers, lots of questions; some were practical and needed to be answered soon: if I was no longer a journalist, who was I? How was I going to make a living, without compromising these new, hard-won, truths?

If I went back to America, it would be to a commune, not a city room, I promised myself. To live simply, with others who shared our values, might be a place to start. Off we went, down the back roads of America and Canada, visiting communes, looking for home. But nothing was in our emotional price range: being committed to each other was hard enough; to commit ourselves to three or five or eight others, people we didn't know — that we weren't ready for. We decided to start from scratch: go back to work, save money, buy land. If we found kindred souls to join us, fine. If not, we'd create the good life ourselves.

My wife, Judy, just as reluctant to return to teaching as I was to reporting, tried her hand at crafts. I, who felt my hands were good for nothing but writing — even writing nothing at all — went back to the *Press*. I knew, living frugally, we could save enough in a year to buy land. I knew, too, the *Press* would take me back, at a good salary. My goodbyes, seething with denunciation, had been regarded as youthful excess. And despite my odd appearance now — my shoulder-length hair, faded jeans, and leather vest, not exactly *Press* attire — the editors believed my half-truth, that I wanted to come back, while I choked on the other half.

But I'd misjudged how much I'd changed. I'd asked for a copy-editing job because it was faceless; perhaps editing lies would be easier than writing them? Not so easy, it turned out. Each morning, I left work sad. What was I doing driving in yet deeper the nail of mis-understanding? Wasn't the world bleeding already from a million wounds and confusions? This kind of news helped no one; I knew that. But then came the rationalizations, right on time like the dawn: I was buying the future, saving for the downpayment on the new American dream, for the land, the tiller, the axe, the stove. I'd walk home through the park, the sun breaking through the trees, imagining tall grasses bent by the wind, out beyond the garden and the woodpile and the houses of our friends, arranged in a circle, or maybe at first we'd live in tents. . . . And on the other side of the dream, the night-shift beckoned, with crook'd finger and sour breath.

This went on for several months. During that time, I made a friend, Tom, who worked in a nearby bookstore. Tom loved the city — its late nights, its surreal intensities. His girlfriend was a model with blazing red hair; they lived fast. Most of all, Tom loved music. Regularly, he'd bring over albums — reminding me, as he fixed me with his dark eyes, "Don't tap your foot; listen to the words." One Fall afternoon, we listened to Graham Nash's "Songs for Beginners." Its sincerity and earned truth pierced me. I bought it, and played it again and again. On it was a hauntingly beautiful line that called to my heart: "Make sure that the things you do keep us alive." To live a life that respected Life — this is what I wanted. But what I was doing was something else. Like a ghost, the song came unbidden in the night, as I bent over the hodgepodge of facts and misinformation that passed before me as news, needing touching up, a bit of rouge and a hat, before being seen. Was I buying a future this way? Maybe, but what kind? And at what price?

The next weekend, I listened to the album one too many times. And something in me shifted: some continent broke in two and the waters came rushing in. My world had changed. I knew I'd rather starve than do something I didn't believe in. I know it was a real change because I've never stopped believing it.

The next day I quit.

For thirteen years, I've lived on the other side of that decision, which rises like a mountain from the plains of my old life.

It hasn't always been easy. Quitting the *Press* was a first step; figuring out what to do next took time. We tried to live communally; it didn't work. I learned to make handicrafts, too; I ran a juice bar; I mowed lawns. These jobs weren't compromising but they weren't satisfying either. In 1974 I started **THE SUN**. Here, finally, was work that sprang from deep necessity, work that was personal and social rather than a job that was neither.

It's been hard work — but I wouldn't trade places with anyone. Marrying who I am with what I do — earning a life, not just a living — has been an act of the purest magic, aligning me with some raw power in the universe, giving me the strength to stay up late, get up early, do what I'd never do just for the money.

And somehow I've gotten by, never lacking for what I truly need. Need, of course, is relative. My friend Pete says, "All you need is a warm place and a little food in your belly." Generally, I've fared better.

Living simply helps. I eat plainly, exercise each day; I don't have a family doctor because I don't need one. I don't try to impress others with what I wear or what I own. I like elegance, but elegance isn't always expensive. I find bargains at the Thrift Shop and at yard sales. I use my imagination. I barter for things I want and some things I learn to live without. So what? Can money buy what I have — the certainty that everything I need will come to me if I'm doing what's right?

So how come, this past Winter, in **THE SUN** office on Rosemary Street, I'm listening so raptly to a description of financial nirvana? Our indebtedness wiped out! A paid staff and a computer! A million — did he say a *million* — dollar endowment! Telling the tale, newly arrived from the West Coast, is a self-described "money midwife" — a professional fund-raiser, now at work for **THE SUN.** work for **THE SUN.**

I'm enchanted by the promises; they're impossible to believe yet I want to believe. He says we deserve it; how can I argue? I've been thinking too small, he suggests — romanticizing scarcity, afraid to ask for what I want. I know there's truth in that. He tells me I have to double or triple my $100 a week salary right away. I shrug modestly but there's no denying the pleasure. He's scooping out the ice cream as fast as he can and I — who don't eat sugar; who once called *money* white sugar! — start wondering what's wrong with sugar anyway. As if I didn't know. As if I weren't about to be reminded.

From the first, **THE SUN** was an improbable financial venture: I started it with fifty dollars, not much business sense, and no idea where the next fifty would come from. There's never been enough to pay all the bills, and sometimes not enough to pay me.

Have I been denying myself success? More than one person has suggested it, so I've paid attention. I've discarded my old prejudices against wealth, and wealthy people; they're no less "spiritual" than anyone else. And I no longer pretend that success invariably means selling out. I've read the recommended books on prosperity consciousness — separating, I hope, the wheat from the chaff. I agree: thoughts create reality; each of us has undreamt-of creative powers to make our lives rich or poor; money is just another form of energy. So much for the wheat.

But I haven't been able to sit each day and mutter prosperity affirmations; or draw a picture of everything I "want" and put it on the wall; or imagine that Jesus Christ is my personal banker, as one book suggested. I believe prayers are answered, but that doesn't mean God is our errand boy. What we want and what we need are often different — and who knows for sure which is which? Besides, who said we're here to satisfy our desires? Not the great teachers I've studied. Nor the life I've lived, in which disappointment has been a great teacher. Asking the universe for what we want is one thing; listening to the universe is another. I haven't yet learned how to do both at once and, right now, listening feels more important: Thy will, not my will.

Does this mean **THE SUN** will never be successful? I hope not. But surely I'm not the sole arbiter of that. Yet, if I'm wrong about this, perhaps *that's* the lesson I need, more than the experience of "success." The truth is, I don't know what the truth is — not in any absolute sense. I try to balance these abstractions with day-to-day affairs, not always "successfully." I keep an eye on when "manifesting my will" turns into bullying. I wonder at this small bit of embroidery in the great design.

Enter, into this uncertainty, into my life, Max (not his real name, but maybe his real name isn't his real name). We had started corresponding last year. He contributed a short piece, which I liked, to the magazine; it seemed a heartfelt description of his devotion to a life of "service." Then he wrote again, asking if I'd read some of his essays and poems — and mentioning, parenthetically, that he was a fund-raiser.

One letter led to another which led to a phone call which led to Max coming to work for **THE SUN** — "our fund-raiser in California," I called him, proudly, glad I'd taken this step, "open to receiving," as the books say.

He delivered. The checks started arriving — generous donations from readers who cared about the magazine. Max and I started spending more time on the phone. Mostly he talked, I listened — to his opinions on wine, and opera, and spy novels; to his own get-rich-quick schemes — his involvement with international cartels and foreign publishing houses; and then there was his new career as a literary agent. It went on and on — a little too fast and a little too vague for me, but maybe that was California, I thought. I'd hang up after twenty or thirty minutes, and Norma would ask me what Max had said. I wouldn't know what to answer. "Nothing," I'd reply, lamely. Go describe the air.

In January Max arrived to do "some serious fund-raising." I picked him up at the airport. After a few hours of conversation, I was even more mystified: now there was a body to go with the voice, but what went with the body? Clever, charming, intuitive, quick to joke and just as eager to discuss theology, he seemed to adapt phenomenally to the mood of the moment, unless it turned to something sharp-edged from the past or painful, something lumbering and ungainly that wouldn't fly.

Forget money, he told me; he'd take care of that. I should concentrate on putting out the magazine and putting away my limiting beliefs about success. Soon, we'd be publishing books, too, of all kinds, including his own just-finished manuscript about — you guessed it — money.

I'd listen to Max talk about **THE SUN** and my heart would sink. I didn't want anyone to feel pressured into giving us money, or made to feel guilty for not doing it but I couldn't be sure that wasn't happening. He didn't lie or, as far as I know, deliberately mislead anyone; his hustle was more subtle. Max wasn't out to line his pockets (he was working for a modest ten percent) but his psyche. He thrived on extravagance: an undistinguished wine, an ordinary job, the plain, unvarnished truth wasn't enough for him. Embellishment was his oxygen.

He talked a lot about his "intuitions" regarding the weather, other people, anything. And many were uncannily accurate. Often, he could read someone's strengths and weaknesses at a glance. What he did with this gift was a shame. "When he found out I was a writer," a friend told me, "and that I was unpublished, he came on like I was a neglected Hemingway and he was going to get me my due. It pushed all my buttons and he knew it. He said he wanted to represent me, though we'd only been talking five minutes and he didn't know a thing about me or what I'd written."

My "buttons" were being pushed, too: belly up from the depths came my sharp-toothed greed — not for stereos or sports cars but for "my" magazine. One day, a check arrived; we'd been promised this gift on the phone, the amount undisclosed. I opened the envelope eagerly, but I'd been expecting more — and disappointment, not gratitude, was my first response.

Yes, Max was shaking the money tree and with his encouragement I'd climbed out on a limb. Go higher, he said. But it was the wrong direction. More than money was at stake. It didn't matter how much Max raised if **THE SUN's** integrity was a casualty. You can't buy back purity of intent. You can't buy it in the first place — just thank God it's there, its roots burrowing deeper and deeper into the source of all riches. Did I suggest **THE SUN** wasn't a success? How foolish!

This time it wasn't a song but a dream that pointed the way for me; I didn't need an analyst to explain the significance of the roof of **THE SUN** building falling in. I didn't need more than a week of Max before letting him go. That I needed a week tells me how much more letting go there is.

(April 1984)

Carl Mitcham

Autobiography #40

Her kitchen window
looks out on a soap opera:

Intimate friends and their problems
constantly disturb her life.

She cannot see the trees
or even the ground. In Afghanistan

tanks roll through Kabul,
and there are no children under ten left
                            in Cambodia.

She can't rest at night worrying
about whether Harriet is sleeping with George.

Will they make their house payments?

(May 1980)

Stories

Sparrow

A boy was born in a hospital. All around him were children in little wagons. The boy wanted to get out. He wanted to go to the moon.

When he grew up he did go to the moon. He liked the moon — it was soft and shiny and gray. But he decided he'd rather go to the sun.

So he went to the sun. It was pure light, at least at first. He liked it a lot.

Then he decided to go to the waterfalls in Africa. The water pounded on his head. Wham! He heard drums.

So he went to India. He lived in a cave. A man came by every day and told him the time. Then the man stopped coming.

The man in the cave became very quiet and still. He understood the moon. He understood the sun. He didn't understand the hospital.

He went back to the hospital and became a baby. He cried. When babies are born, they cry.

□ □ □

A child was born underwater. No one knows how this happened. The mother must have been underwater, too. No one knows.

The child swam up and came into our world. There she met an old woman.

The old woman raised her as her daughter, and also as a princess. The old woman believed she was a queen, and she wasn't far wrong. Her mother had been a queen, but she had not been in the line of succession.

The girl grew up thinking herself a princess. Her friends also believed it more or less. She looked like a princess, or someone special. She had a fan on top of her head, like a lizard, that shined silver, especially in the sun. She was very erect, and when she was still she was very still. She was capable of very deep love.

She grew up and retreated into a tower, where she lived for twenty years. No one understood this. Her friends thought perhaps she'd gone mad. When she emerged, she could fly. Everyone was very impressed, watching her fly over the sea.

Then she stopped flying, and never flew again.

She went to the king and demanded to be made queen. He refused because she was not in the line of succession.

She left quietly and traveled into Spain. Some people said she'd become a nun. Others said she'd become a gypsy.

Lightning struck the king's castle. No one was hurt.

The woman came back, more beautiful than ever, now fifty. Her mother was dying.

"I love you very much," she told her mother.

"I know," said her mother. "You have been everything I hoped for." Then she died, with her eyes closed.

The woman buried her mother and stayed in the town, worked, saw her friends, fed the poor.

One day she dived into the sea.

□ □ □

There was a fellow named Rob who wanted to be a writer. He tried, but he couldn't do it. Rob knew nothing about grammar. His sentences were all nouns, or all verbs, or three adjectives and one adverb. "This is no good," he said, and stopped writing.

Then he found a book called *Short Stories by Chekhov* and started copying stories out of it. He showed them to his friends and they thought they were pretty good. They suggested he send them to a magazine. He sent them to magazines and they liked them too. They printed his stories.

Rob became famous. He was known all over the world as a great writer.

Eventually he ran out of stories by Chekhov. He had to write them himself.

The stories came out as they had before. They sounded like this:

Snow. Molecular orthography. Musical warts frame Cincinnati. Calvin Coolidge. Bounce bounce bounce.

This divided his public. The literary critics felt he had far surpassed his earlier work. The mass of readers felt betrayed.

Rob kept writing. Gradually he learned how to write sentences. Then he learned how to write stories.

One night Chekhov appeared to him in a dream, standing over his bed in a large black overcoat, holding a rope.

"I started as you did," said Chekhov. "My first thirty stories were copied out of a book by Turgenev. No one suspected. Slowly I learned to write." Chekhov smiled and handed Rob the rope.

Rob woke up and started writing. That day he wrote better than Chekhov.

(April 1983)

Robert Horvitz

Quiet Life
In A Loud World

I AM SMOKING A HAND-ROLLED CIGARETTE FILLED WITH SIR WALTER RALEIGH PIPE TOBACCO! THE POUCH IS BY MY LEFT ELBOW! IT IS THREE QUARTERS EMPTY! ROCKY IS DRAWING WITH A FELT TIPPED PEN ON PINK PAPER! HE PUTS THAT ASIDE TO POKE AT THE HASH PIPE HE MADE OUT OF A NAUTILUS SHELL! DANNY IS DRAW-ING, TOO! EZRA THE DOG IS CHEWING A STICK TO BITS ON THE FLOOR! ELSA IS PICKING FLEAS OUT OF TATUM THE CAT'S FUR! BOB AND PEGGY ARE UPSTAIRS IN BED! THE PHONE RINGS! IT'S SUSAN CALLING DANNY! EZRA FOLLOWS HIM OUT OF THE ROOM! TOMORROW IS DOROTHY'S BIRTHDAY! I'M HAVING DINNER WITH HER! EZRA IS BACK! HE'S GNAWING A BONE! THE RECORD PLAYER SHUTS ITSELF OFF! TURN ON THE TELEVISION! IT'S THE END OF A COP SHOW! GUNSHOTS AND SIRENS!

THE FUGITIVE'S WIFE ANNOUNCES SHE IS GOING TO HAVE A BABY! HER HUSBAND SURRENDERS SHOUTING, "LONG LIVE THE REVOLUTION AND LONG LIVE MY BABY!" TATUM LEAPS INTO MY LAP, PURRING LIKE MAD! IT'S TIME FOR THE LATE NEWS! A GENERAL HAS BEEN CHARGED WITH PERJURY IN AN ARMY KICK-BACK SCANDAL! EAST HARTFORD TEACHERS ARE STILL OUT ON STRIKE! MEL LAIRD DISMISSES THE POSSIBILITY OF A UNILATERAL CEASE-FIRE IN VIETNAM! STUDENT REBELLION IS FOUND PREVALENT IS U.S. HIGH SCHOOLS! SNOW IS COMING TO NORTHERN NEW ENGLAND! A HURRICANE IS FORMING IN THE GULF OF MEXICO! I'M GOING TO THE KITCHEN TO GET MILK AND COOKIES!

(February 1979)

US/Readers Write About . . .

Family Stories

In each month's US section, readers are asked to write about a different topic. It's a modest effort to provoke conversation about questions on which we're the only authorities.

Writing style is less important than thoughtfulness and sincerity.

— Ed.

I sat in the car with my mom and watched a kid who was sitting next to the shelter. He had a pair of peddle-pushers on; they're what my cousins in Philadelphia call clam-diggers, and he was playing around with the rocks that made up the train tracks bedding. I used to sit there when I was small just like that kid and fool with those dirty rocks, pretend that they were my buttons I had at home. One rock was the boss rock — he was God; I was God. And the rest of the rocks had to do what I said or they'd be pretty damn sorry. I'd throw them onto the track when I heard the train coming just to show them that they can't fool with the God rock. They wouldn't get squashed or anything, but the suction of the train coming over them would scatter them all around. They'd get lost among all the other plain train rocks so nobody knew they were anything special, and that was worse.

When my dad's train finally came, I'd run up to him as soon as he got off. He'd give me a piece of teacher's chalk and one box of Chiclets, the kind with two in a box. But that was enough. Then he'd kiss me a few times and ask me how his little Monina was. Monina, that was me. Well, I'm really Ramona but he always called me that. It's kinda cute really. But now I'm eleven, and kids that age can't expect their fathers to carry them around, you know.

I leaned forward against the front seat and began to pull hairs out of a pussywillow. They grow wild right there in the lot where we park. When I was little I used to talk to them, but now I just pull their hairs out.

I saw my mom take a pack of cigarettes out of her gigantic pocket book. My dad says they brought me home from an A&P in that bag. He says they weren't in the market for a baby but figured they just couldn't leave me in the potato bin so they brought me home. Of course I don't believe that stuff now. I'm not exactly sure how people have babies, how women get pregnant. Julie has this book and it tells how a man sticks his thing in you and that's how it happens. Only I don't believe that either.

I looked over at that little kid again. He was getting up and walking down to the end of the platform. I knew then that my dad's train would be here soon. And I knew exactly what I was gonna ask him as soon as he got into the car. I was gonna say, "Daddy, will you please, please, please take me and Julie riding this weekend?" I was pretty sure he was gonna say yes so I had already told Julie it was set. I mean, if he did say no, I had this plan. You see, I understand fathers. If he said no, then I would wait till Wednesday to start. I'd climb on his lap after dinner and mention what a crummy father poor Julie had and how I was glad we do stuff together a lot, in between asking him how he liked the way I made the cucumbers in the salad into stars. Later that night, after I'd taken a bath, I'd dump on a bunch of that Cashmere Bouquet stuff. Then I'd come running down the steps into the living room where he'd be, acting like a shy Señorita, flashing a folded newspaper in front of me like a fan. After that I'd ask him to smell me and then giggle the way girls are supposed to when your father says you smell good enough to eat. He'll probably start chewing on my ear or fingers. That's when I'd hit him. "Oh Poppacita, I beg you please take Señorita Julie and me riding this weekend. You are the greatest horseman in all of Spain..." I'd say it with a Spanish accent and really ham it up. By then, he'll say something like, "Why Señorita, I'd be delighted!" He always plays along when you start pretending like that.

"Hey Mom, where ya going?" I saw my mom jump out of the car. It was my father. She was going to him. He was staggering toward the car. "Oh no, my dad is drunk and in front of his kid and all!" I started to feel sick in my stomach. I just couldn't believe it. I just sat there in the back seat, watching my mom load my father into the passenger side. He was all relaxed and went with the motion of the car, like the way I do when I pretend I'm asleep. I leaned forward trying to smell any beer on his breath. I never saw him drunk before. The only time he drank was on Sunday afternoons when it was real nice outside. He and my mom would take the chaise lounges under the big maple tree in the center of the back yard, the one I'd never sit under because spiders would always jump on me. They'd sit and drink beer and eat Planters till just before dinner and then that was that.

I watched as a man in white reached for my dad and put him into a wheelchair. He gave in his arms like the old bolster on our studio couch. The one with the stuffing coming out. His right arm dangled freely over the side as he was pushed up the ramp and into the open door. My mother trailed behind. When everyone had gone, I climbed in the front seat where my dad had sat.

"Daddy died." She didn't even wait for me to close the door. I stood there for what seemed a real long time. I didn't know what I was supposed to do. What do you do when your father dies? I ran into the living room and threw myself on the couch. "No! No!" I kept crying and crying, I felt like everything from deep inside was coming up. I turned to my mother. She was just sitting at the other end of the sofa with her face in her hands. I got up and went into the kitchen for something to clean up my vomit with. When I came back with a towel she was still sitting there. I couldn't tell if she was crying or not. "I'm sorry about this," I said as if I were in church. I didn't know what to say.

I lay there in the dark, listening to my mom on the phone, hearing the same words over again. "José died . . . a heart attack . . . no he wasn't sick . . . a small one, he wanted a small one and no wake. . . ." She went from relative to relative and I brought her vanilla ice cream in a dish.

I got out of bed again between phone calls and went downstairs to heat up some spaghetti. We were supposed to have that for dinner last night when my dad was alive. I took out the plates and set the table but I only put spaghetti on his plate and sat down to eat. "Now Ramona," I said, "I want you to know I love you still and some day we'll eat dinner like this in heaven." Ramona was crying and he wanted to hug her but God said he was only supposed to talk to her and eat. "Oh Daddy, I want to die too!" she cried. But suddenly I saw him smile at me, like he thought this was all very funny. He didn't care about me, he wanted to leave. "I hate you! I hate your guts!" I picked up my plate and threw it at him but he was already gone.

I looked through my parents' bedroom window and watched them filing in. My fat Aunt Vi plodded down the driveway. I could see all this sweat on her forehead even from way up here. She was always sweating. It made her black hair hang straight as licorice whips. Her sisters called her Fats. But they didn't mean anything by it, she just was. She was dragging her kid, my cousin Robin, with her. He is a weirdo. Once he tried to make me take all my clothes off in the linen closet. I didn't though. My Aunt Dot saved me. My Uncle Raymond, Mr. Encyclopedia, was following behind shouting at Robin to throw his shoulders back. I couldn't believe he even came because my dad never liked him. My dad never liked any of them only he was too nice of a guy to admit it. He was probably up in Heaven right now, trying to make excuses to God for them. Trying to explain why my Uncle Raymond has to suck his fingers after he eats, even if it's something like lima beans. Or how Fats really does send me a birthday present in the mail and how it really does get lost every year. And God would probably laugh because he knows all of this already, of course. He knows you shoveled out your mashed potatoes and filled them in with peas even if your mom doesn't.

I got off the window seat and peeked out the door into the living room. I could hear all those relatives talking about what a great funeral it was. They kept saying stuff to my mom about how it was a shame and how heartbroken they were over the loss. But they kept on popping olives into their mouths while they were talking and Aunt Sally pulled an ice cube out of her drink and stuck it down Uncle John's back and only my mom and me cried.

"Come in." I kept eating my tunafish. Lately, I liked to eat it off a saucer with my fingers. I looked up at my Uncle Raymond and then back at the TV. The TV was in my room now. My mom put it there out of respect for my dad. I was allowed to watch though, 'cause I was a kid. "Will you please turn that TV off and look at me." It was a rerun of the Beverly Hillbillies anyway so I didn't mind. "Fine . . . I want to talk to you. Now that your father's passed away —" "Dead, he's dead!" I said. "Yes, well . . . I think you're aware of how this has affected your mother." He looked like he wanted me to nod. "Therefore, since we'll be leaving tom. . . ." He saw me. I thought I could slide it out of my nose without him noticing but it sort of snapped back on my finger. I tried to wipe it on the bedspread but it wouldn't come off. I just kept rolling it around and around into a little ball. "Will you pay attention! Perhaps you haven't fully realized what's happened or how this has affected your poor mother, but you, young lady, are going to have to help your mother as best you. . . ." I started to hum but not out loud, just inside my head. It got louder and louder till I couldn't hear him. Till he wasn't there.

I was ready to begin. I cut every other button off my dad's work shirts. They were round and white like the hosts at communion and I sang a little song to them before I put them into a sock: "Holy buttons in my hand, lead me from this foreign land." I started looking for this alligator shirt I bought him for last Father's Day. "What are you doing here? What's going on!" said my mother's green Christmas sweater. "Who are you? Who are you?" cried my father's bowling shoes. I continued. The last button I took was the one from his winter tweed coat. I held my face against it, feeling my dad's beard. I tore off the top button and walked out of the closet. I could hear the clothing crying over not knowing what they lost.

I went downstairs and found a clean ashtray and some

matches. Then I slipped under the folding table. No one could see me 'cause the tablecloth hung so low. I took the envelope out of my pocket and double checked the address: "To — Mr. José Alvarodiaz, c/o God, Heaven, The Universe." I felt satisfied and went on to read the letter inside:

Dear Daddy,
      No one understands how much I miss you but I have some buttons in a sock God made magic for me and I am coming to be with you in eternity.
      Love, your daughter, Ramona

I put it back in the envelope along with eleven match heads. I looked over and saw my Uncle Raymond and Aunt Jean sitting on the sofa. I was remembering the plastic. They had plastic on their sofa, their rugs, they even had it running up the walls across from the banister. The noise is what I remembered. It sounded like you were walking across the Sunday paper. I was pretty sure it was his idea, not his wife's. One time he was eating dinner at our house when a little water spilt on his pants. Well, he got so upset, he jumped right up and started rubbing his napkin all over the spot until it was all shredded. Finally he excused himself and went upstairs. He didn't come down till the next day.

No one said anything. When they finally got up, I put the envelope and all into the middle of the ashtray and lit it. As I watched the sides curling up like the bellies of toadstools, I kept thinking about this napkin I found last summer. It was lying in the gutter with some food on it and millions of ants were eating the stuff. I took out these matches I had and lit fire to all the edges of it. The ants started pushing toward each other piling up higher and higher but they couldn't get away. They just kept running faster and faster towards nothing.

"Ramona! What are you doing playing with matches! Aren't you old enough to know better? For Christ sakes!" My Uncle Raymond crouched down beside me. He must have smelled the smoke. "I don't think this is the proper thing to be doing at a funeral luncheon, do you? Well, do you? . . . Answer me!" I just smiled and reached into the sock for a button. I held it close to my eye and looked at him through the holes. I could see him real well, but as I moved the button back further, he got smaller and smaller till I couldn't see him at all. I could hear his voice as I began placing the buttons around me in a large circle. Everytime he asked me to come out, I would lock another into place. One of the shirt buttons got scared when they heard him yelling. "Hold fast," I whispered. I leaned over to the black leather one from my father's overcoat. "Be strong." I heard him getting up and walking back over to his wife. "She doesn't understand what's happened," he said. "She's playing under the table. Can you see her? Her father isn't even cold in his grave and she's playing with stupid buttons!" I could hear his voice too begin to fade. I put the last button into place, leaned back and disappeared.

Ramona Alvarodiaz
Wrightstown, Pennsylvania

(*June 1979*)

Fathers

Sy Safransky

I dreamt last night my father had died. Waking up, I felt thankful it was only a dream. I reached out to him, across that twilight space that separates dreaming from waking. Then I opened my eyes. Fully awake now, I realized he *was* dead.

I wept, reliving the pain of his dying four years ago. When I was a teenager, we were each other's best friends; I'd spend my weekends with him, driving in the car, helping him deliver the encyclopedias he sold, rather than play with the kids on my block.

In my dream we were in a car, and I remember his hands on the wheel — big, strong, a symbol of that strength in him which was genuine and not boastful. He was a huge man, with an enormous belly and even more enormous chest. At the age of eighteen, he was six feet two inches tall, weighed

We watched our closeness die like a beloved animal neither of us knew how to save. Eventually, I found the words, but I was nearly thirty then, and he was dying.

275 pounds, and was "all muscle," the doctor said. He boxed and played football and ate sandwiches made from *whole* loaves of bread. The muscle went to fat, as sports became something to watch on television, but those hands and forearms! Thick and uncontestably *earned*. If his advice and his "experience" sometimes seemed dubious, I could at least trust his hands.

His triumphs were mine, and so were his disappointments. I knew his sales pitch by heart, could anticipate as readily as he a "yes" or a "no," a good or bad day. He let me, at twelve or thirteen, be a *man*, telling me, as best he could, his own fears and aspirations, trusting me to understand. The irony was that as I became a man, thinking for myself, questioning his values, our relationship turned sour.

When I fell in love, at nineteen, with the woman who was to be my first wife, we began drifting away from one another. No, drift is the wrong word; it suggests indifference, but our new inability to communicate bound us as passionately as our camaraderie. Not having a vocabulary for my new emotions, nor he, for his sadness that I no longer idolized him, we watched our closeness die like a beloved animal neither of us knew how to save. Eventually, I found the words, but I was nearly thirty then, and he was dying.

Sartre says you're not a man until your father dies. But accepting my father's death has been less of a challenge than accepting his *life*, and the strange and beautiful ways our lives twisted around one another, like the gnarled roots of an old tree.

To let our parents be, to accept them as people, human and therefore imperfect, rather than as gods — that is the challenge. They *were* gods for us when we were small, their approval and disapproval roping us in, their love our meat and bone. How hard to let go, in all the cells of the body and folds of the mind.

A friend told me he couldn't love his father until — well into *his* thirties — he said to him, "You're a son of a bitch." But feeling our pain — hard as it is — isn't enough; we need to understand we can't blame anyone for who we are, including our parents.

We fear becoming that within them which we most abhor, we fear everything unrealized in them which got projected onto us — all the longing, and the greed for acceptance, or money, or power, or sex, or goodness. But my father's idol, Franklin Delano Roosevelt, was right; there's nothing to fear but fear itself (hear that, Dad?). We live out the dramas that most compel us — being powerful; being powerless; being *someone*. Pain itself can become an identity easier than joy to bear, because it's familiar, a lumpy old mattress shot through with knives, but with *our* name on it, and therefore more to be trusted than the unknown — and madness? ecstasy? the disapproval of our friends? more life than we know what to do with?

(January 1979)

Angel At The Gate

David Guy

Overcrowded, junky, it is not really much of a place for a vacation, and our decision some fifteen years ago to stop there was an act of desperation. Having decided just to head south from Pittsburgh until we hit warm weather, my family had traveled at an easy pace for five days, and finally had found the climate we were looking for: crawling through a single lane of traffic, the five of us sat baking in our cluttered station wagon, staring out at sign after sign that buzzed, blinked, No Vacancy. On a tip from an owner who was already full, we found a motel that would take us, a little one-story place, dirty green, called The Fargo. As chance will sometimes have it in such a case, we were treated right, liked the owner, made some friends, and ended up not only staying the rest of our vacation,

We squander foolishly the paradise we have been given, allow life to slip through our fingers, and, at the same time, are filled with dread at the thought of its end.

but returning again year after year to the same motel, the same two little end rooms.

Now all these years later I have seen the place again. I know I should say it has changed, spoiling forever my childhood memories, but the fact is that The Fargo as I drove by seemed much the same, and the places around it too, the Buccaneer with its sultry female pirate winking an invitation, the Thunderbird's sharp-eyed eagle for a sign. Probably that row of motels was simply too crowded to have altered much, and the drugstore across the street, with the row of cheap shops flanking it, seemed also just about the same (admittedly I didn't look too closely). That beach front, to anyone's eyes, is a marvel: wonderfully soft and fine white sand, the gulf blue-green and glinting silver under a brilliant sun, but the motels cluttering its edge have probably ruined it to many an eye, along with the tourist traps, high rise condominiums on the horizon, motorboats speeding boorishly close and stirring up a wake. The day I visited, a speedboat was towing bathers high in the sky, attached to a red, white and blue (no doubt Bicentennial) parachute, for a mere ten bucks. It is hardly an idyllic seaside resort.

Why is it, then, that as I drove away a couple of days later, along a freeway lined with car lots and food stands, I felt an ache in my throat, a longing at my breast? Why do I imagine even now that, given the chance, I would gladly return forever to that junky little stretch of beach?

True, I was returning to a job I no longer had much fondness for, to the responsibilities that filled me with dread, tightened my gut like a bowstring. But my grief lay deeper too, and further back, as if I were being banished from a home that was rightfully my own.

Adam enacts our most basic human truth: he rejects the laws of the world that is given him. We all, daily, enact that myth. But in his story lies latent also another truth (many truths, but I focus on one): that with the discovery of death, we are exiled from paradise, never to return. An angel stands at the door to bar our way. That discovery is not intellectual, but of the spirit — we are aware of death from an early age, but once in our lives we first meet it face to face — and somehow, as the myth of Eden plainly relates, that discovery involves guilt, at our rejection of the world God has made. One thinks of his own death, and feels inadequate, guilty. If only we could live at peace with the laws of the world, death would have no sting — perhaps (another reading) it would not exist — but we cannot; we squander foolishly the paradise we have been given, allow life to slip through our fingers, and, at the same time, are filled with dread at the thought of its end. We would not fear death if we knew how to live, if at any moment we were really living. But we are not.

For myself, I remember no early trauma, sudden realization, concerning death. I was not even much shaken by the death of a grandfather early in my childhood. I can remember no moment when I did not grasp intellectually the concept of death. But in the year I was sixteen, on the first day of that new year, my father died, and since that time I have longed hopelessly for a paradise that will never return.

I am drawn obsessively to scenes of that paradise. I am not speaking of a time when I was happy — mere happiness has nothing to do with paradise — but of a time before that central fact of my life. Its scenes are various and ordinary. The shops on a few blocks of the neighborhood where my father lived as a child — newsstands, bookstores, a bowling alley, and farther down, delicatessens, bakeries, small groceries — and where I spent many hours, alone and wandering, in my youth. The university neighborhood, crowded with students but also with older vagrants, city types, where my father had his office. A downtown bar, smoky, sawdust on the floor, where we often ate dinner on Friday nights, the air thick with scents of liquor and seafood, a huge silver-blue marlin mounted above the bar. Ornate high-ceilinged downtown movie theaters. The crazy mix of stores, five-and-tens, pawn shops, novelty stores, odd eating places, that lined the downtown city streets (my father, though a prominent doctor, was never afraid nor embarrassed around the seedy and peculiar). The green rolling hills and red brick buildings of the campus where I attended school. And those roads through the South, double-laned, dark gray, monotonous, that we used to take on our way to Florida, stagnant drainage ditches on each side, weathered shacks off in the distance, the car ripping along, swaying, at terrific speeds, my father driving easily, his arm resting out the window.

It is to such scenes that I return constantly in my writing. The action itself is not often autobiographical, but the settings are, as if I don't care what happens in the story, as long as I can inhabit for a time that paradise of my youth. I have often wondered how much other fiction is written from a similar impulse. It has been said that any novelist will have sufficient material for a lifetime once he has reached his sixteenth year. I'm not sure he will really know enough at that point about probable action, or character development, but I can imagine that he will have his settings at hand.

But questions remain, about my life. Might I really be happy to occupy indefinitely that Florida beach? Should I return perhaps to live among those scenes of my early life? If not in fact, can I somehow through imagination inhabit that paradise, rejecting a more difficult reality? No. The facts remain. We squander our lives wherever we live them. Death exists. We have relinquished paradise voluntarily, and now an angel stands to bar our way.

Yet he does not stand to refuse us paradise — we have refused it to ourselves — but to indicate a new direction. Sin, death, the facts of the world we have made, are given. My father is dead, as his father died, as I will die, but in the time before I do it is given to me to make a new world out of the old — the fallen world can be redeemed — for myself, and for another. That new world must include the facts of the old, or it cannot exist at all, but it can overcome them. I think of that often, as I pass time with my little boy, throwing a ball, playing in the park, walking the streets of our neighborhood. I might be detached, off in that imaginary world of the past, but he is alive, in the moment we are living, and for him, though he does not yet know it, the paths we are treading are a part of his paradise.

(December 1978)

Opened Flesh, Naked Spirit

Elizabeth Rose Campbell

It had been a very unspecial day. A draggy morning. Too warm. A misty rain. High humidity. None of us feeling perky.

The bright spot of the morning had been arguing over the cover of the issue. Sy called from his office, "Hey! Want to come in here and fight with me and Prissy about the cover?" It was welcome relief from my own case of the blahs, the kind I get whenever I sleep more than six or seven hours.

When Priscilla called around 5 p.m. to say she'd been having contractions — strong ones — Sy and I tried to keep this information from becoming what-we'd-been-waiting-for.

The week before, we'd rushed home when Pris called to say she was having contractions (more false labor) with an eagerness that made Pris

All was silent, the dissolution of time began for me, leaving only Priscilla, on her hands and knees, her head bent down between her arms, her body that of an animal mother, straining and strong . . . the rhythms of nature giving birth, and in its silence Priscilla's motherhood becoming magically real . . .

laugh. But everyone's eagerness, including her own, had become tiresome for these past few days, so we all pretended not to be eager. I stayed at my desk instead of leaping into the air, jumping up and down and making squealing noises the way I had last week when she'd called.

"This is your last chance," Sy told her. "What do you want me to bring home? Pickles?"

"An ice cream sundae," she said.

Whether this was *the* day or not, just buying ice cream for Priscilla made it a special day, sugar being right up there with the worst on the Safransky list of "don'ts."

The ice cream had mostly melted by the time we got home. On the drive, Sy bravely refused to eat the melted overflow, giving it to me instead. "Sugar makes me feel imbalanced, and this is the wrong time to be imbalanced," he said, his tone facetious and serious at once.

He was not bouncing in his seat, but I could feel jokes rising in him the way they do when his mood is peaking into unquestionable glee and pleasure with life.

When we arrived, Mara ran to the door with her hellos; Pris was curled up on the bed watching Andy Griffith and Barney Fife try to talk a hillbilly into getting a tetanus shot from an attractive nurse Andy had the hots for. Sy gave Mara and Priscilla their ice cream and we sat there with the certainty that had crept into the day that this was, indeed, *the day.*

Priscilla's smiles were long and calm and beautiful. Sy began to tell funny stories, his voice rising in pitch, his story about childhood birthday parties funny indeed, coaxing laughter from Priscilla and me.

Sy: "Well come on, Prisseeeeeee, have you had another contraction?" Priscilla smiled languidly, looked at the clock, said she was "unsure."

Sy's excitement spilled slowly into rich release. He looked at Priscilla, loving her, proud of her, his happiness in this moment making him lovably ridiculous (his eyes and voice full of curly laughter, he leered love at her, teasing her with words of endearment: "Prissy, you creep, this better be it!").

Her subdued teasing and his overt teasing had a calming effect on me little else could. My idea of the oncoming labor, despite glowing reports by friends who'd been through it, was still one of pain. Controlled pain, but still pain, and I was having a hard time sharing Priscilla's calm, even though all I was to do was care for Mara.

At 6 p.m., the contractions were five minutes apart and forty-five seconds long. By 10:30 p.m. when Steve and I came back with our pillows, books to read through the night, apple butter and biscuits, the contractions were no closer together but getting stronger.

When I put the food on a table in the bedroom, Sy moved it to the living room, his excitement obviously having transformed itself into practical forethought about immediate preparations. He explained politely, "This table is for birth stuff."

Vicki arrived when we did, and the four of us sat around Priscilla on the bed, talking in whispers so as not to wake Mara in the next room. Pris was in long underwear, wearing her hair down, looking very unlike someone who was about to go into labor. She'd close her eyes when contractions came, and Sy would rub her back, but other than that, I'd never have suspected she'd be giving birth to a child in three hours.

Sy began reading aloud from the Guinness Book of World Records to entertain himself and us: "There was a woman in Russia who had sixty-nine children."

Sy and Priscilla's mood was much lighter than mine, or seemed so. I was excited, a little nervous, and, as a woman, relieved to see another woman having contractions, not dying but seeming only mildly uncomfortable.

By 11:15 p.m., Vicki had left, Steve and I had arranged sleeping spaces in the living room, and Cedar and Stephen Koons and their sleepy little girl Woodwind had arrived, checked on Priscilla's condition and gone to bed themselves in their van.

I was too excited to get to sleep, but Steve was soundly asleep on the floor. I had to go outdoors to pee twice in the fitful half-sleep between 11:30 and 1 a.m., squatting near Sy and Pris's bedroom window, feeling a tenderness for both of them in there, probably awake, oblivious of this night of quiet misting rain outside their window, and me squatting, feeling the pleasant warmth of urination and of the warmth of the two of them as father and mother giving birth.

Soon after my second trip outdoors and getting resettled on the sofa and reprogrammed for sleeping, I thought I heard Steve snoring. Or breathing the way he does when he has a cold. It was rhythmic, and got louder, and wasn't Steve, but Pris.

At 1:15 a.m., the bedroom door swung open abruptly and Sy said, "Get Cedar now."

By the time Cedar and Stephen got inside the bedroom, Priscilla's cries were clearly audible, sounding almost like chants, long, deep, steady aaaaaAAAAAHHHHHHHHH's.

I sat up, feeling alone, my heartbeat speeding up with excitement, apprehension, anticipation and a little fear of the unknown as Pris's exhalations got louder. I wondered how Steve could sleep through this. I thought about waking him.

The next cry did. He sat up, for a moment looking confused, as if he had no idea why he was asleep on someone's living room floor. We could see each other's eyes in the dark, and felt like children together, naive and ignorant, not at all familiar with this sound that was breaking the silence, a sound unlike a speaking voice with intentions of speaking to some *one*; this was a cry to one's *self*, a raw naked sound that seemed to start from deep inside and move out, booming, bursting energy breaking sound barriers within her, echoing in every room, a sound that didn't scare me the way I'd imagined it would. There was a sense of competence in the full-bodied energy riding her voice, the competence of a *natural order*, a powerful sound in this quiet night, not frightening at all.

Steve and I listened, motionless, feeling invisibly captive, obedient to whatever drama was going on in the next room and this energy that seemed to be *inside* and *outside* of Priscilla, energy sweeping over her, obsessing her, creating almost a tone of surprise in her cries, as she rode through the contractions, her focus exploding and releasing through her voice.

Soon we heard a different cry join Priscilla's, that of a frightened young child awakened in the night — our cue to get up, to come inside. The bedroom door swung open wide at that moment, and Cedar gave us a simple, direct order, "Take care of Mara," a relief for us to awaken from our motionlessness in the living room dark.

Fumbling for Mara in the dark of her bedroom. She was out of her bed. Fumbling for the light switch, feeling calm inwardly, realizing I was trembling outwardly, with excitement. Hands closing around Mara's soft head, her cheeks hot with tears, I carried her into the kitchen. We sat on the kitchen floor and Steve and I tried to soothe her. She was not soothed by all my old standbys: "Juice?

Want juice? Nuts???" She shook her head, still crying; she could hear her mother's cries, wanted to go into the other room. Steve held her and I went into the bedroom, feeling hesitant about distracting Sy as he knelt by Priscilla who was on her side; there was water or liquid of some kind all over the bed. He said no, don't bring her in yet, but I had been back in the kitchen a mere minute before Cedar's voice reached us: "Bring Mara NOW."

Steve and Mara and I, the only ones untouched by the childbirth experience except our own, came in quietly and knelt by the bed on the floor, and the magic of this moment welcomed us, telling us not to be afraid. All was silent, the dissolution of time began for me, leaving only Priscilla, on her hands and knees, her head bent down between her arms, her body that of an animal mother, straining and strong, ripe with the same distended quality of the moment, a continual pushing, the rhythms of nature giving birth to itself, and in its silence Priscilla's motherhood becoming magically real, in our full presences, gathered round, able to see, in a perfect illumination provided by the light above the bed, the face of this child emerging from her flesh, eyelids flickering with consciousness, small mouth opening with breath, the rest of the body from the neck down still inside Priscilla.

In those moments, I understood that this child was one of us, we were *all* her parents, in service to her, a part of her existence, as she was a part of ours, no less intimately intertwined with our lives than with her parents.

It was Mara who spoke to the child first, her eyes large and full of her own young comprehension, breaking the silence with one soft word out of her hundred word vocabulary: *baby.*

I felt us unite behind Mara's simple welcome to this child, honoring the rite of passage, an arrival from whatever world comes before this one.

At a quarter of two, Priscilla gave another push, and the rest of the baby slipped out into Stephen's waiting hands.

The beauty of Priscilla's graceful transition from the inner concentration of labor to the open heart of a mother's selfless absorption in her newborn: still on her knees, long hair hanging round her naked body, streaked with blood from the waist down, her beautiful head turning, weakly now, her voice raw with emotion as she spoke to her baby for the first time — *my baby* — her eyes, her touch, her voice enveloping the child. She turns slowly, and lays back on the bed beside her child, her body quietly trembling with exhaustion, her skin soft and warm, her mother scent filling the air: the smell of opened flesh, naked spirit.

(November 1977)

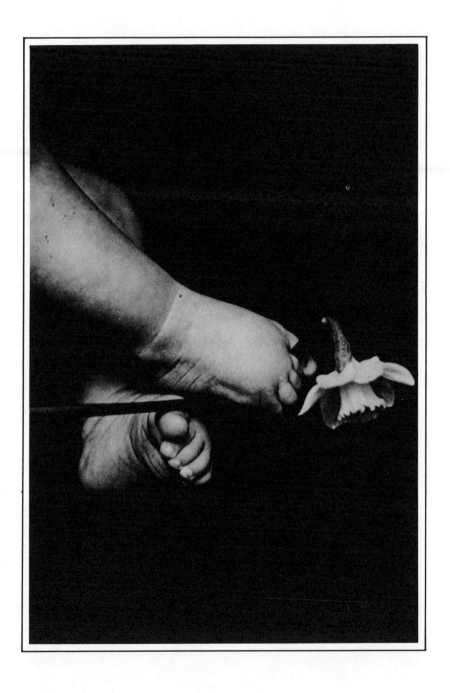

Sara Elizabeth
(born Nov. 3, 1977 1:45 a.m.)

Sy Safransky

Sara Elizabeth,
I went to the laundromat this morning, with a sackful of bloody sheets and towels: the banners of your passage, stained by your mother as she bore you, with great, hoarse groans and a sweet groaning of the flesh, red waters, clear waters, carrying you here — from what distant shore I can only guess. It's easier to imagine the pounding your small body took (wise men tell us dying is less difficult, and no wonder: it is not nearly so surprising an eviction, and from such innocence!) — those fierce contractions buffeting you, that narrow tunnel through, and that light at the end: heaven, or terror? Our tears and yours suggesting both.

Well, the laundromat was the same: no matter to anyone that you were

I'm old-fashioned, you see: New Age dictums about universal love impress me about as much as detergent commercials; to me, changing a diaper is more important than changing the world. I take that back: changing a diaper is changing the world, for of such small labors of love is the world created.

boy or girl, born dead or alive. It was good to be with people who didn't know, or care, about me: it properly reduced the miracle of your birth to a personal drama — one that can never mean as much to anyone as to your own parents. I'm old-fashioned, you see: New Age dictums about universal love impress me about as much as detergent commercials; to me, changing a diaper is more important than changing the world. I take that back: changing a diaper *is* changing the world, for of such small labors of love is the world created. No choir has sung more lusty tribute than your mother, crying with fire in her belly. No guru will tell me more about love than these sheets and towels, soiled with love's issue. Did we grope on these same sheets to "make" you? No book on sex will illumine that breathless coupling more than your own quiet breathing.

Daughter, I'm only saying that if I love you "because you're mine," that is no sin, but a blessing. In the laundromat, I watched a young man folding a tee-shirt full of holes; clearly, it was his favorite, *because it was his.* I wanted him to love that shirt; no one else could. If we begin by loving what is ours, perhaps we'll end by loving the world — having owned what is ours, and owning it fully. I stake my claim to the time it takes me to write this, wrested from a life too busy by half. I give these words to you, having made them mine; so may "my life" be a gift — though where it begins and ends only God knows. My own father, until the day he died, wondered what legacy he'd left me, imagining himself a failure in my eyes because he was a failure in his own. Perhaps, on leaving this world, he learned what I hope you come into it knowing: that we can only give *who we are.* In the depth of my own understanding, I meet you in timeless wonder. I have no conscious memories of our "other lifetimes" together. It doesn't matter. Your mother, reaching for you, drawing you back to her, reaches across the aeons. Time is mother to us all, edging us toward independence, and eternity: but how we cling to her apron strings! A "Scorpio" we call you, knowing better; the soul, deathless and birthless, is not regimented by stars. The heavens are the boundless ceiling of our own starry mind; we are free to travel to stars more distant still.

But we start here. In a small house, on a small planet, a family — "nuclear" and glorious — with claims one upon the other. Cleaving to what we know; taking it one step at a time; trusting that, in time, we'll learn the true dance: energy made flesh, whirling upon the rock of being — you and your sister, your mother and the rest, *I mean everyone*, born at last.

Your Dad

(November 1977)

Us/Readers Write About . . .

Being a Parent

The most important thing I ever heard about being a parent was said to me by a friend named Vinny who had just spent a year stoned, lying in front of stereo speakers. I don't know if he meant it, or understood it, or was merely playing a Franklin Street guru — it was all the same to me: it was truth as absolutely presented as I've ever heard it. He said, "Being a parent is one of the three events in life which forces you, without any choice on your part, to make a precise measurement of who you are as a human being. You'll either be good or bad or mediocre but the point is you won't be able to hide the information from yourself. If you are hiding from your child, deep down you'll know it."

How easy it was to discover the extent of my selfishness once my child was born. Oh, the travail of losing my sleep forever, that sweet errant dreamy morning sleep which can have no end. Why didn't someone tell me that would disappear along with other self-luxuriating phenomena such as running happy-go-lucky around this country and other countries with my wife? These were important losses.

How to measure the resentment in the heart when one's vague feelings of being free are confronted head-on with the fact of total responsibility? Well, the fact is, you either come through for your child or you don't; you either run out in your heart or figure out how not to run, and if you stay, you figure out how to make that choice rich — that choice you made for the most hidden and yet life-insisting reasons. And it's a tricky business. If you call yourself an artist, for example, and you are the sort of person for whom a life in the suburbs is too unwhimsical and you don't want to work in an office eight hours a day for most of your adult life, then figuring out how to raise a child with some dignity and a little money becomes the trickiest business indeed. What do you do? As my friend suggested, your answer is who you are, *and you get to know the answer.* Do you end up with cash in the air-conditioned nightmare, your poems in a desk drawer, or do you stay with your child *and* your art, somehow making art and children the same thing, and neither of them going in the desk drawer? But if you are thirty-five and your child is healthy and you still haven't let them stick it to you, then that's who you are.

For better or worse, having a child changes you forever. The risk is everything and the stakes are too high for lies. If your marriage is short on passion before a child is born, then it will be passionless afterwards; similarly, if you secretly long for a security beneath the boasting liveliness of your twenties, then you will find yourself, after the birth of a child, living in the suburbs. The child forces you to take your measure — the chaff flies away and you arrive at a purer notion of who you are and what you should be. The presence of the child carves you into your proper shape, sad or silly or full of juice.

I would say that perhaps one's deepest sense of humor is enlivened by becoming a parent. All that extraordinary self-absorption visible in healthy children gives us a multitude of insights into who we, the parents, are. What is that coming out of my mouth? "You better cooperate with me or else!" Did I really arrive finally at those hated words? Am I going to continue to use them? One either starts to laugh at oneself (one's ludicrous, boiling, red-faced self) or one joins the ranks of parents who seem to go to shopping centers just to drag apoplectic children through the aisles of air-conditioned stores. The disturbing fact to an adult is that you can't compete with a child, you can't win. The more you yell, the crummier they act. If you hit them, they scream. Your only real choices are to laugh at them and with them, and let them control you a little, and make up their own pace. You also have to redefine the meaning of such a hilarious word as "cooperation." After all, it's the parent who is causing the trouble — it's the parent who makes a big deal out of children hiding under clothes racks or spilling food or saying dirty words. The child isn't doing wrong — he's coveting darkness, learning about gravity, experiencing freedom.

Before I was a parent the sound of children yelling put a knife up my spine. Now the sound of children seems like the sound of life itself. I've become easier with myself.

I've been a parent for seven years and I know three things very well. The first is to keep all children away from television as much as possible. It makes them dumb and passive. The second is to feed them good food and few sweets. They act too silly and out-of-their-skins with all that sugar swimming in their bloodstreams. And the third is not to hit them, or at least to stop hitting them as soon as you can. Hitting children will make them either bullies or cowards. There should be mandatory courses for parents to take so they can learn these things. But there aren't. Instead we raise children blindly.

John Rosenthal
Chapel Hill, North Carolina

☐ ☐ ☐

Things I enjoy about parenting: serving burnt quiche for dinner and still being told I'm the best cook in the world; skipping up rocky dirt roads in flip-flops with the giggles; teaching my four-year-old how to clog-dance while listening to Doc Watson and the Red Clay Ramblers; seeing who can be the first to spot the moon in the sky; singing "Them Old Cotton Fields Back Home" until I'm asked to switch to "Keep on the Sunny Side."

Things I don't particularly enjoy about parenting: giving spankings, even when they have very evidently been asked for and are needed; explaining to little Ruby why she can't water all the garden ("you might flood out those tiny seedlings") when in reality I just want the pleasure of holding the hose myself; not being able to spend *all* the time I'd like to with my young 'un — this seems to be the hardest thing to give, and the most precious; well-meaning ladies at the laundromat who don't understand why you don't allow your child sugar candies.

Parenting can provide the supreme escape from monotony, send one into a long journey of wonder, and give the chance to actually re-live some of what got missed in your own childhood. Of course, there are bad, dulled days, but in anyone's life these will occur. The hope that one feels as a parent helps immunize against the real blows. The challenge is ever there, and the rewards are of the purest and simplest nature.

Patience Blandford
Montgomery Creek, California

□ □ □

There are lots of surprising things about being a parent. To be precise, all of it is a surprise, every single day. Nothing ever goes as expected.

One of the oddest things is that since becoming a parent, I'm getting to know all kinds of people whom I would never have imagined as friends. What we have in common is that we're all parents of small children. That fact makes the other elements of a private life (the shards that remain after the continual demands of a small human being) less separative. We're all so submerged, to one depth or another, in the world of caring for and intensely loving our offspring. With all the attendant chores, joys and frustrations that go with that, differences in lifestyle usually become so much flotsam and jetsam. These unanticipated alliances surprise me and I'm grateful for them.

I appreciate them all the more because I'm a first-time mother and I share the same state as many mothers, first-time or not: loneliness. There's also an insecurity about whether I can relate to the rest of the world after being home so much. That condition is self-imposed, I know, but home is the easiest place to be — the diapers and toilet are there. The path of least resistance just happens to be lonesome a lot of the time.

Then, suddenly, your child can walk and the whole world opens its arms and sidewalks and parks to you and you come out and suddenly discover, here and there, other mothers with toddlers by the hand, making their way outside for the first time. You're so glad. The talk you get into is easy — it's so effortless to drift off into the most intimate details about your labor. The ease with which you unburden yourself to a stranger can shock you. But you know, in spite of appearances, there is the continual caring and responsibility and exhaustion that you all share, and that is a bond.

It's a mysterious world. No one ever told me anything about it. (When you try, you sound silly and sentimental, anyway.) I've found a voice for singing those good old songs, laughed more freely, spent more time in the park, smiled incessantly and have never been happier or prouder or more exhausted and glad to see night fall since my daughter arrived.

One day this spring, it was raining lightly and I was letting Suzanne play on our miniscule porch while I was washing dishes. She called for me in her lilting sing-song way — "Mama, Ma-ma" — and I went to take her inside; but she took my hand instead, and pulled at me to go with her out into the rain. I resisted at first, imagining both of us soaking and miserable, but I went. *She's* never walked in the rain before, so off we went in our light jackets, into the light showers, splashing in every puddle in our way, stirring rainbows in the oil slicks, finding such amazing sights and sounds.

What thrilled me the most was being led around by a child, and genuinely enjoying the discoveries, the freedom of vision. It was one of the nicest gifts I've ever been given.

It is, of course, not always such a bed of fulfillment. What is? But children are so special. I never even cared for kids in general until I had my own, but now they appear to me as the most special, hopeful elements in the world. Their eyes are lit by such a light — it warms the small bit of world they encounter with such an intensity that it burns into the heart to stay. Their actions — the hugs, the kisses, the kicking and biting — are as effortless as the tides that eddy along a shore under that laughing moon face so far away. They turn to us, thinking we can lift them up to touch that face.

They are children because they have no idea of the poignancy of their existence, their state of being. We are parents because we do.

Dee Dee Small-Hooker
Cary, North Carolina

(July 1980)

Insisting On Love

John Rosenthal

For John Lennon

I.

The first girl I ever loved was in the fourth grade and her name was Dorothy Ewing. Unlike her friends she roller-skated to school, took dancing lessons in the late afternoons, and never said silly things about boys. She was considered ridiculous by her friends. I was in love with her to the extent that I had given up all my other friends. She kissed me goodbye the day before I saw her for the last time, and ten minutes later I fell down. On that last day I saw her sitting in the auditorium at the school's final assembly, wearing a brown dress with yellow polka dots. Love was still a secret then, something like a social disease, so all we could do was glance

Who are we here, stuffing all these burgers into our mouths, these dead milkshakes, our eyes flattened out by the systematic mendacity of tube-land, our hearts a bubble of dollars?

furtively at each other across the aisle. Nothing in my life has seemed as lovely and full of life as that ten-year-old girl who peeked at me while everybody else sang "She's A Grand Old Flag." At the end of assembly I ran away from the school, making sure I said goodbye to no one, particularly Dorothy, and I never saw her again. She was the nicest little person in the school, delicate, independent, graceful, and no boy was ever blessed as I was in his first passion. Goodbye, everything else.

As the years went by, love became my secret, and, I guess, everybody else's. It was the secret you kept if you were smart or gave away if you were dumb. Giving it away meant you could be teased back into a crowd of buddies who would then protect you from that particular assault. Keeping it meant no one could have it to hurt you with. You just continued to love until your grades were shot. I never really could describe it to anybody, not even my best girlfriends, though I talked to them on the phone for hours when my parents were out. To talk to other boys was impossible since a suspicion of girls outlasts childhood, and as a boy you feel you ought to be talking to other boys about some game or other rather than, as Keats described it, "that sudden load of immortality about the heart." Talking to girls about other girls was good for me and bad for them, but certainly the only substitute for the sort of lunatic act of which I became capable only in my thirties — that is, a direct confrontation of beauty with the words of love.

Deep down, the rest of life has always seemed pretty boring to me. If I ever read a book, it was for the eventuality of love, nothing else. Do you know what I mean? My friend, Jean Morrison, a wonderful poet, once said to me, "Can you imagine reading a book when you could be making love?" He also said we don't make books unless life fails us, but that's for another essay. What he said about making love, however, was big news for me since I had gotten into the habit of giving my secrets away and for a while it looked like I was going to be an intellectual first and a lover of women (or men) second. But when he said it I thought: that's one of those truths which tells you who you are. It told me who I was, anyway, or at least reminded me. For years I had jumped around like everyone else, getting started in careers, learning how to be smart, perfecting despair for my own private use, getting and spending, running down the universe as if it was an argument (a problem it is, I still believe) — and yet nothing could make me drop the issues of a bright young man's world faster than the look on a face which carried the promise of love. Heartbreak? Of course, but at least I knew I was alive, which is more than I could say if I was in a training program. Anyway, as lines add history to a face, cracks only improve the value of a heart — take it from me, I've got a heart cracked like crystal, and when you hold it up to the light it's not without class.

There were always two worlds and not knowing it was always my problem. Perhaps I should say that not knowing the uncertainty of the world I was born into was my problem — but who was to offer me a clue, the little undermining fact which would indicate, beneath the pallid reality of the 1950s, the anarchic possibilities of life? A suburban kid, the world of private fantasy was my real world, a world in which, for the sake of a beloved (and she might only be in my homeroom class) I acted a certain way. For her, as it turned out, I would act mostly like Jimmy Dean or Elvis Presley, those gargantuan figures who accidentally slipped into my scene with the message that not everything out there was tame. Nevertheless, even by myself I could manage a manic brilliance, unknown to either of my heroes, along the shady lanes of split-leveldom. Dreaming of girls, hungering for a measure of their subtle ways, wanting to talk to them, of their miraculous survival in my world of big talk and punching, I asked myself — who were they, these creatures, realer than real, disorienting me so radically from twelve years of little-boy bullshit?

Early fools like myself don't go to law school later on, nor do we become good citizens even if we try, and we hardly ever get rich, and I guess we rarely end up inside a family in which an eventual peace is granted to us, the sweetest gift we can have in this impermanent place. The fact is we spend too much of our lives being foolish for a lover, one who may even be dead, but who nevertheless inspired in us an early sense of unlikely perfection — and yes, there we go, a legion of the ridiculous, searching for the right note or word or image, the specific bit of magic which will turn the down-slanting eye of the blond girl in our best friend's biology class our way. Anyway, for all the losses, it's nice being enchanted. And isn't that the secret (of the secret) of love: that everything became dedicated to the blond girl, everything — my breakfast, my boredom, my going to sleep, my waking up, my math block, my shoes, my current events, my Everly Brothers records, even my parakeet? Being in thrall to her and others like her, the world became a holy place. Not such a bad thing for an American boy who before dreaming of the blond girl or the girl in the polka-dot dress had dreamed of Joe DiMaggio and motorcycle jackets.

Yes, two worlds. And yet, my brain teeming with love, I thought there was only one, an unenchanted world from which I kept my secrets. I guess what I mean is that smug place which Sartre calls "the good citizen's world." This is the world we take for granted, even though it grants us nothing. Good grades are found here, and pals, and obedience, and you can fragment it just like I'm doing because it's a dull and yet terrifying world, all abstract and unsexy and mass-defined. HELP! Who are we here, stuffing all these burgers into our mouths, these dead milkshakes, our eyes flattened out by the systematic mendacity of tube-land, our hearts a bubble of dollars? Sad to say, when I wasn't imitating some impolite bastard or dreaming of girls or clowning with my folks or holding conversations with my dog I was learning how to die into the republic's arms. Who wasn't? Who wasn't sitting in classrooms devoted to doltdom or the lie that we in America are better than the sweet souls of the Orient, certainly better than those tyrannizing Russians whose atomic bombs had me forever crouching in the basements of elementary schools, wondering how I would get home to my mom after America was blown up. There was no fighting it — even the breathtaking pressure of breasts against oxford cloth couldn't slow down my slide into the fast-talking, over-educated American wise-guy I was bound to become.

But look what the classroom did to my friends, those little-boy buddies who would stand on their heads at any time. I mean, Allen, Eddie, Bobby, Vincent, Andre, have you no memory? In your little suits with your cute briefcases, your bankable lives being chewed up by time and humorlessness, pressures on you (from whom?) as if life is just one of those mediocre dreams where you jog away from something — what happened to the wild-eyed insolent tender boys who filibustered profanity in my ears like a code to which only we knew the keys? Oh you modest-living professional little bastards, giving in to all that mortgaged decency, all those inner rules of silence, as if the spirit of youth was an aberration to be got over and not the event itself, the event of your life, the adventure you ended up betraying for a house in Twit Acres and 2.3 kids you won't ever understand.

II.

What does courage mean to us, to me, lost as I am even as I curse, between two worlds? In one world, the world most available to us, the world of the endlessly obedient good citizen — spontaneity zilch, cut off in one's bones from the chance to change; revering sunlight and the stretching of limbs only in one's spare time — courage is obvious and well-known: it's always buying into the world on its own terms, whether that means flying bombing missions in computerized aircraft or winning fights (losing, does one ever lose?). And yet in a world which has grown so comprehensively numb to the sources of joy and sorrow, to any sort of purchase on real life as opposed to this everyday version which has our laughter, like steak bones, caught in our throats, I feel that courage must be connected to iconoclasm, that is, to the breaking down of those death-dealing illusions which are, quite simply, doing us in. In other words, one can no longer separate courage from the attempt to re-establish a world in which the meaning of courage has some place. Of what use is courage, anyway, in a world in which so few insist on truth or enchantment?

To live well takes courage, but living well cannot be taken for granted anymore. As a nation, for example, doesn't television have us hopping like rabbits in an experiment? What is Ronald Reagan, anyway, or Tang, or aspirin, Exxon, Chevrolets, Geritol, hamburgers, light beer, Coca-Cola, sweetened cereals, good-guy news teams, margarine — all the same, bad deals lying in the center of slick packages. Is there not a new breed of person, usually called a "media" person, who has spent years figuring out how to touch our deepest fears, how to lie in front of regulatory agencies and not get caught, how to arrange sounds so they will affect our memory, how to defocus our eyesight, and, most frighteningly, how to play upon our deepest feelings of love and friendship in order to transform us into a nation of consumers, lava-heads burning through products of our sole earth? How are we to resist? What training have we to protect ourselves against this organized assault on our will and intelligence? How can we not believe these reports delivered in trained voices by ministerial men which tell us that our health depends upon the use of a particular drug? Are we ready for these people?

How are we to know that the man is not a doctor, the report is false, and the advertising agency in charge of the commercial has employed hidden techniques of persuasion which were developed by scientists? Watch the oil companies make the mountainside prettier. See the guys from the office sharing successful moments together as they drink beer. Look at grampa's face light up when his son in a marching-band uniform calls him long-distance at special weekend rates, or watch gramps in his checkered woods-man's shirt eat whole-grain cereal, or even watch him be kindly behind the counter as he sells the housewife an addictive laxative. No, these people are not kidding around anymore, and we are cowards insofar as we permit them to pillage our lives with their mind-finagling.

But let's run with the notion of courage for a while. It's a concept big enough to make fools out of us or, in the process. to prompt one or two good thoughts. I would suggest right off that owning up to one's fears may be the highest kind of courage, and yet how many of us are willing to do that? But what a moment of liberation it is when I say I am afraid! Because once I can say I am afraid, of anything, then I can drop all those strategies I employ to avoid having to face my fears, and more magically, I can create that true democracy in which everybody else is willing to admit what they take such pains to hide — those secret flaws which are their distinction, their self, that lonely, lovely foible which is them and has always been them. And then the additional joy of discovering that no one is going to laugh, that no one cares, or that only the worst care, that is, those for whom one's fear has become a weapon they use to get their silly way. Well, screw them, those jerk-off marines with bodies so tense with fear of self-betrayal that they move like fists against the face of their first memories. No, we are free the moment we admit our fears, for who can bother anybody who is willing to walk? Good-bye, man, I don't like the way you drive or talk or push or write or fuck or yell or boss or con or lie or drink or smoke or cheat or dis-approve of me or categorize me or penalize me. I mean, the worst thing about me is also the best because it is *our exact difference* and that means we are both of us stunning little strange flowers in the meadow of this souring world. My fears stated, I can hold that half-strangled part of me out into the sunlight, and you hold yours too, all right? We can forget about making deals designed to keep us concealed from the loving eyes of each other. Ah, who can resist such champions who deign not to win?

Perhaps a small gesture in the way of mutual respect could be gained if we asked each other the uses to which we put our courage (and our fears). While visiting Agamemnon's tomb in Mycenae, Henry Miller grew faint-hearted at the thought of descending an old stairway which led into pure darkness. Other tourists would plunge right by him, whimsical and brave in that darkness, chin up, whistling. And yet if I had to choose a bravery for myself, I'd choose Miller's — for he was brave in the face of that other darkness which goes by the name of boredom, that vague and unspecific nihilism of the twentieth century which condemns our laughter and dries our loins faster than anything else. Miller, our greatest iconoclast, called what we do to ourselves by its name, amazing man, instead of using the chicken-hearted words of our loveless realm, the old ones like progress, politics, America, or the new ones like personalize, input, communicate.

The courage for what? Yes, that's a question that should be asked, particularly if giving someone credit for what they can do seems important to you. What a precious fact to know about someone else. (And, simple to say, we all have courage because we all have fear. Miller was afraid of boredom precisely because he knew that it was an undiagnosed disease which ravens on your impulse to be strikingly yourself, and it was this fear which turned him into a warrior of lust. I am sure in the face of boredom Miller's first response was to shake like a leaf.) And yet how easily we tend to belittle the courageous acts of others.

Not long ago, a woman friend of mine spoke disparagingly about a mutual acquaintance, a younger woman, saying, "What dues has she paid?" The implication was, of course, that she, unlike my interlocutor, had not paid enough. Oh, the tyranny of dues, that imaginary fee we are supposed to pay to get into someone else's club! And to what end are we paying them? To obtain wisdom, I suppose, the rather primary insight that you don't end up deep unless you've been deepened along the way. Well, it's undoubtedly true, but who gets to look in on our confidential hearts when the losses occur, those hurts we all suffer and which we either conceal to become one kind of fool or accept to become another? My woman friend had been married to an alcoholic at nineteen, given birth to a child at twenty-two, and now wanted to establish a connection between what she had become and what she had paid out. This was valid, of course, but at that moment she wanted to do it at the expense of the younger woman's experience, an experience she did not know about or care about, but which she meagerly assumed to be less courageous than her own. For the sake of her own personal narrative which included such chapter headings as "Being Married to an Alcoholic" and "Having a Baby at Twenty-two," my friend was going to dismiss as bad literature the narrative of someone else whose chapter headings were entirely different. The irony is of course that in an unflattering light my older friend's experience could be made to seem like non-experience, that is, a series of actions undertaken in order to escape the difficulties of a true independence — which they were not. As it turns out, however, both women are not only going to be special gifts to us all, they already are. And the lesson in this is not very complicated: to escape this deadening and unlikable alienation from each other, this estrangement which leaves us feeling alone and smug and unhilarious, we must ask to what end others have put the courage we know them to possess. Did they have enough to escape from a domineering parent, a cool act of self-kindness, but very heroic? Is their courage of the sort which creates art and/or children? Does one have the courage to be honest, hardly something we can take for granted in anybody? To be less self-absorbed? To actually care (an amazing event) about another person not one's own? Did one have enough courage to escape from the humanoid magnetism of television, from liquor, drugs, bad religion, money-dreams, racism? What about lonely nights? Relationships where we neither aided nor injured each other? Do we have the courage to insist on love or enchantment? To be an American without being a bully? Forget about the irretrievably numbed hearts — have we respected the experience of others, those we know, on brief reflection, not to be enemies?

My two women friends have courage for different things. One will become an artist who won't look back, and perhaps she'll learn that art gives you what others end up getting somewhere else. The other will find in her unsurprised heart a genuineness of being which, in this silly, greedy, flaky world, will look like water on the desert, and men and women will be able to drink from it.

III.

Let's face it, a little humility is in order from all of us. I mean, aren't we slightly too ridiculous for anything else? We pursue our selves across the stage of our desultory careers, crying bitter tears at the loss of love, at the loss of life, take your choice. We run from truth, doubt happiness, make excuses for ourselves, criticize others. When I look back over the history of my heart, my punk lover's heart, over the small hills of my intellectual gambolling, I wonder at the sweet audacity of this clown who would claim the right to say anything to anybody. I suppose I am convinced that one day I will turn around and look in a mirror and John L. Schmuck will be gone. And he will be, until a new enchantment brings him back, a new brightness in the air, a farmer's daughter on his shoulder. Do any of us get where we are going because we know where to go?

We are all of us all the time coming together and falling apart. The point is, we are not rocks. Who wants to be one, anyway, impermeable, unchanging, our history already played out, our act too known to be interesting? As Lord Olivier said recently, when people come back to see you "do a moment," change it. I, for one, do not mind falling apart every once in awhile, as long as I can profit from the split seams. Despair is another matter, the empty center, or just the opposite, being too full, too full of emptiness, or lovelessness, it's all the same — if we're lucky we only have to live with despair a few times in our lives and no more.

But now looking about me, what do I see? One friend curses his wife half the day and talks to me of beating up her lover. Another languishes in a job behind a telephone all day, dreaming of inheritance and housewives. A woman I love cries occasionally in a tub of hot water because she is sometimes lonely and uncertain of choice. A friend of hers grows snappish in her thirties because love doesn't enter her open arms. One could go on. In our lives we are falling apart — we work too hard, drink too much, smoke endlessly, love too cautiously, laugh too little, think too modestly, dream too forgetfully. And yet my women friends, when their time comes, dance like beings nonchalant in a dream of forests. Their movement is, simply, pure inspiration. And my wife-cursing friend, too, has his time, long moments when like a god the world lies clear before him and he flies on words, as when he wrote to me of Eliot's Prufrock:

"And how would this cynic know to care/Whether he's a noble prince or not/Unless in his soul he hides a Hamlet/To marvel at his modesty and mourn the tragedy/He yet hopes to avoid by playing possum." We are falling apart indeed, but we are coming back together. A part of us is in Utah and another in Mars, and then suddenly there is a clarity, a cohesion, and we dance because dancing is what we have to do even if it means saying goodbye to love, or in a momentary opening of dark space we write a poem and it ends up telling the truth. No, I do not mind this falling apart. I mind not falling apart. Let us breakable people join hands as we reach courageously toward the truth that will fall apart in these same hands.

(In this spinning darkness, passionate friend, your hand in mine is nice.)

IV.

We have been taught so badly in America that our most courageous act lies, belatedly, in defying that teaching and making sure that our children are not hurt by it. We are taught the need to succeed, but who teaches us the valor of waiting? Artist friends of mine are beginning to drive themselves into mediocrity as they spend their days hustling their names around town. To what avail? Their line is always out, eyes glued to the cork. Can they get a bite? The original meditation which brought them into the world of art, that clarity of protest against the limits of dull thinking, feeling, seeing, has dissipated into the tedious effort of converting it all (all that passionate adolescent astonishment) into a sellable commodity which can get the nod of businessmen. A man I know, a director of plays who was originally inspired by the early work of Elia Kazan, now spends a good deal of his life dialing telephones in a never-ending effort to keep his name current. His work, always skilled and well-crafted, is beginning to suffer; instead of a sense of private anger or joy, that sense of an idiosyncratic method which distinguishes one serious artist from another, his work contains that generalized unbelievingness which is the contemporary replacement for precise thinking and feeling. In talking to him one finds him filled with disgust for everybody else's work. His criticism of plays, once passionate and generous, is now reduced to calling them "intellectual" or "talky." He won't see a certain play, he told me recently, because he can't bear to look at the legs of the leading actress. When I tell him to relax, he answers that I am afraid of success. After all, it takes courage to play the game in New York.

Well, to be honest, I am afraid of success. For deep down I can't figure out what it means. The successful people I know, with few exceptions, are a drag, and I mean that literally. Success to them has not meant a coming together of all that which they are. They have become solid objects standing in front of themselves on the long road of their life. They block their own vistas. They can't see into themselves anymore because the self, that fluid, changing, spontaneous sense of life, that sense of having been and having become something else at the same time, has taken on the solid substance of everybody else's expectations. They dwell in other people's eyes and have no sight in their own. They are pompous, predictable, and profoundly incurious. The unsuccessful are rendered invisible to them by a species of magic related to the freezing of the heart. For them life has lost its palpitance, that luxury of pending, laughing selves. They believe in their own importance while, secretly, no one else does. They give people jobs but not life, a gift we actually have to offer. And they always believe in progress. What a lesson for all of us when Sartre refused the Nobel Prize because, as he said, it would make him an object to other people, an award-winner, forever a "former Nobel-prize winner," instead of that most difficult of all perceived phenomena, a person. For on the deepest and most personal levels, we must be fresh for each other.

Yes, we are taught the need to succeed in the classrooms of America; nothing is more fervently drilled into our minds and hearts: success. If you don't succeed, you're a loser; hated word. Out of the ambling and guesswork of early childhood we enter schools and churches and little leagues and cotillions and we are supposed to get our acts together. For boys at least there is suddenly a gang and outside that gang is the "other," the fatties and sissies who conspire, so it seems, to become an image for the successful child of what he should not be. For the first time in one's history, contempt develops, that sad human way we have of being afraid and not admitting it.

From then on, for most of us, life becomes a matter of running toward law schools or the business professions or anywhere else from which an eventually "successful" person will emerge, safe from that contempt which turns one into a zero at the age of six. Instead of being contemptible, we end up as good citizens, our minds unminded, our bodies unbodied of crazy jubilation, our vision, once a quest for the surprising and yet unsurprised unity of all things, now just a paltry and unthrobbing self-consideration in the shark and gobble waters of American adulthood.

To be honest, I'd rather be a fat guy, lost in rancor, than jog with these self-actualizers.

V.

Not long ago I walked out of a movie theatre on the upper west side of New York and started to cry. Undoubtedly the movie I had just seen was the cause of it. A German film misleadingly called *Knife in the Head*, it was about the reconstitution of a man's identity, the putting back together of memory and logic, after a cop had fired a bullet into his head during an assault on a radical youth-center. The movie was about many different things, but what thrilled me was the sense it gave of a man coming back into this world lacking a memory to tell him what side he should be on. What a question! What side should we be on, and do we have to take sides? For in this movie various sides were contending for him — was he a radical who had been shot in the head because he had attacked a cop, or was he in the building because his ex-wife was there, and consequently, a victim of police brutality? We don't know, and he certainly doesn't remember. In the newspapers both the Right and the Left claim him for their own purposes completely unrelated to his innocence, an innocence which turns out to be what the movie is secretly about. Like a child who cannot comprehend the turmoil of politics, he searches the newspapers for pictures of himself, saying, "I want to see Hoffman," meaning himself, this funny puzzle of a person who can't even feed himself and yet is a hero to the Left and a criminal to the Right. Once he asks a nurse to show him that part of her flesh concealed beneath her blouse. When she bares a breast for him, he cries out, "No, you lie, there are two of them!"

This astonishingly dislocated man, Hoffman, was portrayed by the superb German actor, Bruno Gans, whose depth of countenance reminds me of the early Brando (almost enough to make you cry). Perhaps it's something common in their expression — suggesting that they embody experience not accessible to other men, some knowledge of darkness . . . in fact Gans is the only actor I can think of right now whose mere presence suggests an experience without banality. Perhaps this is why the movie worked, since the loss of memory and identity to such a man is, in fact, a loss. How different Gans is from the normal leading man whose countenance belies no long acquaintance with the wilderness of sorrow, but instead records such minor facts as good health, handsomeness, and the ongoing tale of an easy popularity.

So, leaving the theatre deeply touched and burning with the sort of clarity which comes after a good long plunge into a serious work of art, I began to remind myself for the first time in months that the only kind of art which means anything to me always scrutinizes the obvious world of power and then offers us a glimpse of that blessed innocence which is our lost birthright. And then I asked myself — for the movie was about this — how do you keep the innocent alive in a world which pays high fees to the corrupt? And, after all, what do I mean (oh, the themes of our life which precede our tears) by innocent?

My definition of innocence has changed over the years. Years ago innocence meant to me that which preceded corruption, that's all, or what went before the general state of adulthood — a simple event whose inevitable passing could always be regretted, like childhood. But then I was like everybody else, under the influence of a world-view which assumed those categories upon which the world of power is based. Who, in my first orbit of life, believed then that politicians were not impressive people or that our so-called American sanity was life-distorting? Like everybody else I believed what I was taught: that America was the best country (it's probably not even fourteenth), and that cancer was a disease our doctors would cure. You grew up, had children, gave to the United Fund, voted in elections (no matter the clown), and believed all that shit handed down to you from the heights of power. Who was I to question or doubt the value of progress, living longer, space exploration, standard-of-living? Not for a moment did I consider that the desire for power might represent some form of lunacy, or wonder why men of consciousness studiously avoided its realm. Me, Johnny, Shrimpy, Rosie, Mouse, doubt those American heroes who scrambled after power like monkeys going for bananas on the topmost branch? Was there ever a voice, a clear laughing voice (and suddenly sadness is beside me on the upper west side, or is it self-pity?) which said to me that power deprives you of your real body humor and leaves you high and dry among other mortals, your only friends this one time around? I mean, who wished on me solitude so I could hear the still small voices which are always mourning the failure of our American enterprise, the fall from woodsman to advertising executive, from a holy landscape of many moods to this junkyard of highways and restaurants? Saddest of all is just the fact that innocence is considered a *stage* we have to get through before we accept this accumulating nightmare of life which is America. And nobody to help you out, no, unless one is blessed as I was, finally, by knowing one lucid person, the only one I ever truly met in all my years of being educated, who asked me one day in the kindest and wisest voice if I really wanted to be a part of the rat-race, and did I know how consummately stupid rats could be when perverted by man?

(But, upset, I admit also to being happy, even very happy — for this movie in its odd way of putting the pieces of our splintered life back together again was precisely the kind of art I cared about and was always willing to argue for. So there was the resonance of an old meditation here, too, a meditation which began by insisting that even though modern art must reflect the fragmentation of modern life, it must not merely go over and over the same territory, for not only to repeat what we so easily know, but to further insist that the basic condition of existence was boredom and impotence amounted to no more than a failure of imagination. After all, who is there to take our joy away if we only demand it back? And, yes, it is a matter of demanding it since the world is there with its many complaints and past disgraces to filch from us in any way it can. Who comes to us in the night like a succubus to leech out our joy as we lie dreaming, leaving us soft and contemporary? Who teaches us not to kiss our fathers, to be endlessly cooperative, to listen with such complacency to the diminishing footsteps of the thief who clipped our heart, I mean our real heart, the heart of the child who was afraid of very little and open to the suggestions of each day? Who was he, anyway, and who let him in? But why be dramatic — we know he didn't come to us in the night, but rather robbed us in broad daylight as we sat in one boring class after another throughout our youth, listening wide-eyed and open to tales of power about demented Horatio Algers who sought the presidency of this or that corporation or country but who never considered tenderness as a way of life, or tried to listen to the sounds of children or women, the crying of their own frightened flesh. Anger, rage, despair, sorrow, tears, yes, but this mediocre alienation, this continuous abstraction which turns our best artists into nihilists is not worthy of the time it takes us to turn away.)

No question about it, this vivid representation of the continuous warfare between innocence and cynicism in the movie I had just seen had upset an equilibrium I had managed to achieve over the past few weeks. For they had been difficult weeks: lost love and hot weather, being on my own for the first time in many years (what a strangely possible world it is when you look at it alone after being in partnerships or marriage for many years . . . all those many silenced voices of your own, speaking for the first time in so long.) And yet that equilibrium wasn't really much, frankly; it had put sorrow under restraint, but it had nothing to do with the fires that burn in us when we are right. Surcease was all it was; fine.

So it was all of this — the movie, the weather, lost love, innocence, the themes of my own private trials touched in a moment of art, the sense of loss, of something regained, lost again. I began to cry, to cry for myself, to cry for Hoffman, to cry for all of us. It was a simple cry, generous and full of love, one I've had a few times in my life but not for many years. With the mind of experience and yet with the eyes of innocence, I saw clearly what life in this American city had done to the faces of my fellow man. (Oh, it was so beautiful in New York at that moment, the late afternoon sun was setting over the Palisades and shades of gold were all over Broadway.) I saw the faces as in a vision, men's faces caved-in, sucked-up, forced-out, hollowed, scared, white as snow, lustreless, eyes like fish startled by everything, mouths askew with fear and disgust. I thought to myself, look at us, we have become advertisements of ourselves, we are either dead or slick or icy or frightened. And I looked at the women, fettered to vanity, choked by their appearance into goggle-eyed self-assurance, breakable like ice, and I thought, it's true, we are the hollow people, we are now completely isolated from each other. Gay men walked by too briskly, too tensely, dressed up in standardized outfits, a girl's sashay imposed on their hips, a thousand psychic miles from the splendid children they must have been and who they still, in only a sad way, resembled. Others strutted by like demented roosters, muscles constantly flexed against imaginary foes, mean, unimaginative faces, all suddenness gone from their mouths; and other women, too, so full of caution, anger, and false aplomb, the lines of their beautiful faces screwed into a resistance only a magician could ease. It was all love and loss on the street, and quietly I wept for us cripples, for my own life with its own small losses, for my own tears behind my sunglasses, for my little vanities and my handsome pleated trousers, and for all those who had no hope anymore and so little clear-eyed assurance, for all the frightened and ugly and suicidal people who were out beneath this soft setting New Jersey sun. Why, we had become like monster-children, those whom you let into your house until, the mark on the neck seen, it is too late.

But then I saw the real children and I sucked my breath in quickly, for they were still there, inside their own bones and not traveling around inside someone else's dream of them, not slicked-up or over-pretty or stuffed with fear. They were just themselves so far. They ran and skipped and fell down, laughed and yelled and pushed, and hid no promises from each other, while beside them their parents or other adults plodded or stood around, nothing funny in their day. And the old people, I suddenly saw, or anyway some of them, were themselves too — not the American old people, but the ones who had come from other countries, the refugees, the west side emigres. A girl trilled a song next to me and I touched her arm and smiled. She was for a moment every girl I ever loved, for her song was, in this Breughelian city of crushed spirits and bleared faces, all it should be.

You make vows after you cry for a streetful of people. I vowed merely not to forget what I had seen. Of course an hour later I had forgotten half of it, and the next morning I'd forgotten most of the rest. What had I seen, anyway? Three weeks later I fell in love, wrote a terrible poem, took three good photographs, and had a dream in which my father, the leader of an underwater enclave, had a great idea: we could all achieve waterless life, beach consciousness, if we all pushed each other very hard up the underwater slope that led to the beach. My father decided I would be first. The trick was, it turned out, to wait for the proper ocean surge, and when you had that behind you, to shove with all your might. And so everybody gathered behind my father, all the underwater people, and shoved me when the right surge came along. Then I was going up the underwater hill very quickly, and there was an explosion as I broke through the water into waterless existence, into the beach world breathing sunlight consciousness. The sun was indeed out — it was Long Island's Jones Beach — and people were everywhere, all colors of people with their umbrellas and radios and various languages, and the sky was very blue, the ocean a blue murmur, and I said to myself, "Everything's going to be all right. Just a little more time." And then high tide rolled out, and my father was coming out of the ocean, jubilant, leading the underwater people after him.

(January 1981)

US/Readers Write About . . .

First Sexual Experience

I clearly remember my first sexual experience, although I don't know how old I was. I woke up from a dream and the room was filled with sunlight. As I was aware of the intensity of the light and the deepness of the sky and afternoon beyond the windows, I was also aware of a presence down between my legs, a thing I felt familiar with, yet somehow foreign to: my cock standing up because of the dream, maybe (whatever it was about), or just for its own sake. A wave of wild wanting swept through me and I did not have enough Christianity pumped into me yet to fight it. The object of my desire was neither man, girl, woman, or beast. In fact, there was no object desired. All I needed was right there for that brief moment of freedom. I had myself.

Thinking about it I don't know that I should differentiate between that experience and the rest that followed. It seems to me they are all one. The self-centered desire just finds objects now to attach to.

Name Withheld

☐ ☐ ☐

When I was eleven I began to want something very bad. Something from men. I didn't know what.

Before I wanted men, I wanted women. Flesh was feminine, hopefully abundant. One night I dreamt I stood naked in a spotlight and when I looked down at my body, surprise! Instead of the "split snake" (Mama's nickname for my skinny physique), I saw full rose-tipped breasts. A curve of belly and of hip.

By age eleven I wanted that kind of body so men would want me. Guilt consumed me then because I thought no one shared my curious hunger. Soon, though, I found relief in a common momentum at school. Recess became a series of new sports: all of the kids inexplicably understood the rules. We chased and kissed (or kicked). We passed notes (the use of symbolism, "Hen" and "Rooster"). We examined a long thin balloon that an older boy brought to the playground; it had something to do with male Sex. The boys clutched at our sock-filled bras. And other games. New math — a girl's popularity was greater than, less than, or equal to her physical development.

This new life teemed with mystery and a knowledge of "something beyond myself" never found in chilly wood pews. God was untouchable; the demon-fever burned in almost all the kids. Grownups didn't catch it, except a few in books and on TV, not in my community, not that I saw. Young people in love were often infected by a lesser strain of it. Priests and nuns escaped it, were above it, in germ-free solitude. Some nights it worried me to sickness, yearning for this Sex thing, yet I knew no antidote.

My most intimate sexual experiences at that time were with my cousin Lorna in the summers. She was a year younger, but she lived in the city, I in the country, and she was bigger than me. Together we discovered true lust. I invented our games; I embellished them; she brought the dramas to life with her ample pink flesh.

Always before, summers when we were younger, I had been jealous of Lorna. My parents, her mother (her father was dead), and our unmarried aunt and uncle doted on her. She was plump and pretty. More, she spurned their attentions. At bedtime, as I went eagerly from one passive cheek to the next, they called to her, "Lorna, a kiss goodnight? Won't she come and say goodnight?"

"Isn't she a character?"

"Off to her room without a word!" (My room!)

"She's always been like that."

"Sweet, sad child." (Read fatherless.)

They pursued her less, though, after she grew her early, monumental breasts. I thought only I had noticed until one day I heard Mama tell my father to stop swinging Lorna by her feet, her blouse shrouding her flaming face. "She's getting too big for that," my mother uttered meaningfully. I ran outside to the pumphouse. Lorna followed me.

Poor Lorna. For once I pitied her. Perhaps her oversized bosom would sag the way our grandmother's had. Yes, better to be slim like a boy. Better yet to *be* a boy.

She was afraid to come into the pumphouse. The damp earth, cold aroma of metal, the bugs. Too often I had teased her about reptiles. A city girl, Lorna thought snakes the ultimate evil. So she squatted in the dwarf-door opening, sunlight on her reddish curls, quarters of blush on each pale cheek.

"It's all right," I said, meaning the bugs.

"No," she said bitterly. I knew she didn't mean the bugs, they didn't deserve such vehemence. "It's horrible. I hate them."

"My parents?"

"No . . . you know."

"Well, yes. But I wouldn't mind having a bit more up here myself," pointing to my tee-shirt.

She sucked her lip. I chewed my thumbnail. She said, "I would give them to you if I could."

"But why? The boys . . . they like them."

"No, movie stars and models are skinny, like you."

That was kind. I felt I had possibilities. Our opposite ambitions merged into common cause. I told her about Randy from school. She told me about John. Or Buster. Or Raymond. Years later now, those summers melt into a hot listing of simple American boys' names, and a few women teachers, several girls. And cutting hair, sneaking liquor, dancing mad in skimpy clothes before the mirror in my room or hers. Make-up, curling, touching, and the more erotic scenes practiced through our paper dolls. We didn't know what Sex was physically about, though we tried to find out. We read. Sneak reading: *Lolita, Candide,* the stolen copy of *Peyton Place. Valley of the Dolls.* Art, literature, or sensational trash, it didn't matter. It was those few vital pages we sought. A continuing series, reruns when our supply slackened.

Most distinct are our idol memories: Sean Connery, George and Paul from the Beatles. I developed an early paternal passion for Chet Huntley; later it was David Brinkley who slipped into my bed at night. The summer of "The Man from U.N.C.L.E.," Lorna and I were relieved to find that she was in love with David, I with Robert. When we went to my room to change to swimsuits the first day of her visit, we whispered our desires for those two men, and fell quickly into a day trip: our spies were returning from a dangerous trip, months in the Arctic chasing Russians, and we prepared to greet them. Hair up, straps down, my shame that Lorna could hold up the top half of a two-piece while I still wore the requisite tanksuit (for a "split snake").

"A striptease," I suggested. "You first."

Suddenly stubborn, she said, "No. You always say that and then you don't do it."

"This time I promise."

I sat on the hard twin bed and watched her emerge from the closet, twirling a see-through summer pink scarf. The radio sang, "Well, here she comes now, singing Mony, Mony. . . ." Lorna glimmered sultry, practice glances through half-closed eyes, and turning, shook her bottom until full buttocks shimmied. I devoured the sight; my own flesh couldn't be gathered into an adequate pinch in Rome, much less quiver off the motion of my frame.

Radio: "Well, don't stop now, yeah come on Mony, come on Mony . . . Yeah, yeah, yeah — Sock it to me! You make me feel (Mony, Mony) so (Mony, Mony) good (Mony, Mony) yeah (Mony, Mony) so fine now. . . ." Lorna fell, supine, so fine, beside me on the bed, and I grabbed her curls, smoothed them from the glistening full moon of her face. "Oh, my darlink," I crooned. "You are sooo beautiful."

"Now you," she said.

What to do? Like the man on TV said, if a woman doesn't have beauty, she better have personality. If she has neither, she better have money. "Money, Money." No art, then sensationalism. Lorna made a knocking noise on the bed, and I flounced from the closet, sheathed in the skin-gripping tanksuit, flinging the Palm Tree (a hairdo: gathered on top in a rubber band, falling wildly from that tight center, thick and frizzy) down my back and into my eyes and mouth. I lowered the clinging nylon off my chest, slid it down bony hips and quick-stepped out, barefoot on the sandy floor. I whirled to disguise my boyish straightness, undulating to exaggeration. "A snake dance," I hissed, writhing onto the bed with her. The door opened.

My aunt. "You two ready for the beach?"

I dropped on my belly between the beds. "I can't find my sandals."

"Well, hurry up."

Exposed. Debauched. Lorna held me, stroked me. We cried. We laughed. If only we could tell her, aunt or mother, God or student counselor. But we were bad girls, might as well go all the way.

That night we pulled the twin beds together and covered ourselves completely with the starched sheets. The radio crackled rock and roll, the fan buzzed loud enough to conceal our moans, we thought. We hurried past scene, setting, characters and details to our adventure. David and Robert had kidnapped us and taken us to their yacht. Tonight they would force us; we had no choice. All we could do was plead with them, faintly, not to "do with us as you will." But they tied us, gagged us. We squirmed against each other, our newly shaven limbs (not just legs and armpits, but the whole arm — we got carried away) bristling with nervous chills, scraping the sheets.

They they descended upon us, the weight of their hard bodies, but again, the frustrating unknown! What did Lorna imagine to make her groan ecstatically, pressed hot against me? For me there was only Robert's brutal kisses, his hands stroking and pinching me; finally he began to tickle me. I begged him to stop, but he tingled, thrilled, patted and petted on, beyond madness, overboard into the caressing waters, tickled to depths.

Afterwards, we pretended to smoke, side by side in bed.

"There must be more to it."

"I don't think so," she said.

Name Withheld

(November 1979)

David C. Childers

The Pornographer

He lives in a house in a cornfield. The highway passes nearby. The highway wants the cornfield and the cornfield wants the house. The pornographer wants to write poems. He sits at his typewriter typing. The girl with fair skin, her hairy-faced lover, come in from the wind and kiss at the door. Women stuff threats in envelopes. The pornographer needs to come quickly to the point. A madman drives a backhoe down the highway. Their clothes are off, strewn through the river facing rooms. They lie down together, kiss and search, slide head to toe, find the middle. The pornographer knows he's not much at making it better than real, but keeps on typing she grows frantic when he comes. The backhoe raises its shovel. The driver sights in on the room. The typewriter turns the lovers face to face. Tongues turn. The boy rejoices. Engine guns. He looks down at her small nippled breasts, looks up out the window, far across the river. Blue lights flail in the darkness. The pornographer floats on the water; back to her legs, his hips. The engine chokes, starts again. The pornographer's agent wants something better. He made her crazy with thrust after thrust. The wall blows open. She kissed him with fire. The backhoe eats meat says want meat. The envelopes fly. The pornographer thinks about the mailbox. Cool breezes lift his curtain. The boy and girl shudder. Thunder cross the cornfield meets thunder in the typing, and the backhoe's slow metallic dance.

(October 1979)

Richard Williams

Savarin

This poem was named after Brillat-Savarin, eccentric gourmand, who died in 1826. One of his most interesting, and typical, quips was: "Dessert without cheese is like a beautiful girl with only one eye."

I

Take one chicken from three to five pounds,
coming home from an evening on the town,
salt it with garlic and pepper,
then melt one-half stick of butter
that signals the end of it
in a pan with one spoon of tarragon,
all that there was,
our civilization,
and three-fourths cup white wine.

Stuff the chicken with the green ends
of spring onions, pour on simmering mixture
hot in the memory
from the pan, then cook
what seethes on the brain
in a moderate oven for forty-five
passing in sequence
minutes plus ten for each pound if cold
like time on end, like scallops

and seven if at room temperature. Serve

with risotto and haricots verts
on the beach
a maître d'hôtel. White wine.

II

Marinate two veal chops, rather thick,
where is my youth,
with the juice of two lemons, garlic salt,
where did it go?
and one teaspoon of crushed thyme. While
the Lord
in the marinade, sauté one bell pepper
speaks of His passion
and one onion, diced, in one-half stick of butter
as if it were a nail just bolted
until tender. Remove the vegetables
to my neighbor's eyes
and cook the chops on top of the stove
I hate them
in the butter residue for fifteen minutes.
let them go blind
turning them once in the meantime,
those fools,

Add the vegetables along with one can of
hate, but with
tomatoes to pilaf, and serve with a rose
piety.

III

Where are the snows of yesteryear,
in one-half stick of butter sauté three crushed*

*(garlic cloves, one tablespoon of sweet basil)

goons who have beseiged me
one-half teaspoon of oregano, and one teaspoon
of parsley
with their angry looks.

After ten minutes of slow simmering, add
an eight-ounce can of minced clams;
allow this to simmer for five to ten minutes

or is He?
and serve over spinach noodles.

White wine and perhaps a salad of bell pepper
I've often wondered
and tomato; tarragon dressing.

IV

Especially coming home late when I
lather a three to four pound rump roast
with garlic salt, pepper, and marjoram,
sear it for a few minutes on top of the stove
speak of love
with high heat, being careful to brown all
sides. Surround with three sliced onions
their beautiful backs
in butter
and one-third cup of water,

then cook for twenty-five minutes per pound at 325
times I've seen Satan, too,
under a tent of aluminum, and serve hot with
devils by his side, eating
baked potatoes, sour cream, a tossed salad,
pigs-feet,
and a hearty burgundy.

V

For each one-half pound of steak, cook one-half
the pain
a bell pepper, one-half of an onion
makes for a winsome frolic through the bus terminals
in two or three tablespoons of butter slowly
late at night
until tender. Slice the steak into thin strips
when only the masks are out
and marinate with enough Worcestershire
to make me quiver, and
to coat each piece evenly and sparingly
dream of them.

O Jesus!
Salt and pepper the vegetables and the steak.
I've been cold too long.
Remove the vegetables from the pan and cook
past my prime
the steak in the butter for a few minutes.

I've written books on religion
then add the vegetables, stir a few minutes
to see visions
until just done, still slightly rare, and serve
topped with a quartered tomato
over rice. Red wine.

VI

For dessert spread a mixture of melted butter
over the hands
and honey over toast; serve with coffee and tea
then look at them
and light up a cigarette, or a cigar
or their host.

(October 1976)

Wine: A Lesson in Self-Discovery

Frank Graziano

It should be nearing evening as you set the table, first covering with a gingham tablecloth, then arranging the two place settings — yours on the left, and one for Agnus, your lily of a sweetheart, on the right. Place two candles mid-table, taking care to leave sufficient space between them so as to be able to view Agnus through the bosom of fire. A decorative arrangement of stephanotis is lovely at the base of the candelabra, or leaping lilies of the valley. The table should be round, and small enough for you to reach, at an easy arm's length, for Agnus' liebfraumilch cheeks, or claret lips, or her stocking incarcerated leg. And between the two of you, in a semi-circle arching like a sickle toward the wall, arrange the following buffet so that it spans the table, a collapsed bridge between you and Agnus:

The table should be round, and small enough for you to reach, at an easy arm's length, for Agnus' liebfraumilch cheeks, or claret lips, or her stocking incarcerated leg.

1. One teak bowl filled with Trisket wheat-wave crackers, another humped with almonds.
2. One butcher-block cutting board arranged with Imported Swiss, Kash Kival, Camembert, and melt-in-your-mouth, breast soft Brie, all surrounded by a moat of apples, and
3. One wicker basket lined with linen, filled with warmed slices of French bread, an air of garlic that rises to steam a photo of a hen.

Good. Now the wine, selection of which is both an art and a science, both of which you may at present ignore, for Cabernet Sauvignon (Red, sturdy, full-bodied! Strong in flavor and bouquet!) most easily mingles with blood. Although quite expensive, B.V. Reserve is the best of this varietal, and is therefore suggested. To determine the amount of wine needed, add together the body weights of both yourself and Agnus (who, it seems, has gotten a little chubby lately), and move the decimal point of the sum two places to the left. The resulting number will give you the required number of bottles for complete submersion, for thoroughly marinating the liver (for example: you weigh 175 pounds; Agnus weighs 145; Total: 175 + 145 = 320. Now move the decimal two places to the left and the quotient is 3.20, or approximately three fifths and a split).

At the last minute, when everything is set (make sure the required number of bottles are on hand, open and breathing; the buffet is arched in its crescent moon; and Bach is slowly drenching the curtains), at the last minute, just as the sun rubs its breast on the mountain, telephone Agnus and call the thing off — explaining how suddenly you are feeling ill (O the vomiting! O the uncontrollable diarrhea!). No, you don't need a doctor. Yes, you're sure. Yes, you'll call her in the morning. You're very, very sorry.

Sit at your place at the table and, after swimming to the bottom of your wooden goblet, look across the table — over the stephanotis and through the flames (to grandmother's house we go), that is, to the glow where Agnus' breasts would be. While focusing there, on this purer than Platonic image of a woman, you may drink, and drown, and fill up your lungs with a rich bouquet, and pump up your heart with dead, predictable blood; and at last when you're drunk with the wobbling earth, and at last when the vines yield a rich harvest of raisins, you can put down your face in the dish and lick it, as though sucking the moon, or you could squeeze out the life from the scars on your liver, or fill a chalice with blood and take it and drink from it, and spill it, and swim in it, because an excess of sorrow is laughing.

(January 1978)

Joel Jackson

Maps To Where You Live

the second gravel road to the right after
the pavement ends.
wait two years and leave from Kansas.
watch the way the geese fly in the autumn of '74.
go to Lonnie Poole's Sinclair Station & Grocery,
drink three Miller High Lifes and ask the guy in the orange
shirt.
become rich or famous, preferably both, then call your mother.
send a letter general delivery New York City, New York.
or learn to know you will never find me anywhere
and take up drugs and group sex; i'll be the fifth one
you love that night.
then go backwards until your heart's innocence becomes
a blight, your savaged goddess the reality of me,
and directions will arrive in the morning mail.

(July 1977)

US/Readers Write About . . .

Possessiveness and Jealousy

When my lover and I came together we were each ecstatic to have found a sexually tolerant mate, one who would allow extra-curricular intercourse. Neither of us had ever known such a freedom, though we had both lustfully hoped for it. Transfixed with our advanced understanding, we considered this tolerance the ir-refutable assurance that ours was true love — "I love you enough to let you do what you want." We swore off jealousy and moved under the same roof. We knew, of course, that monogamy was easier, but wasn't it an abomination of true love? We hoped to make *Eros* and *Agape* into the same thing. Amanda Ziller (*Another Roadside Attraction* by Tom Robbins) was our model: "A strange spurt of semen," she says, "is not going to wash our love away." So that was our creed — until now. Lately one of those strange spurts of semen is no longer a stranger. It is too familiar, it comes from the same guy every week or so. I know the smell and it sometimes makes me sick.

In quantum physics I learned, intellectually, the basic instability of All Things, the irrevocable Flux of the Universe. Of course I already knew that all things change, but Heisenberg's Uncertainty Principle confirmed it for me. One day I was looking out a window at the pavement below, trying to visualize the atomic reality of the asphalt. It's just energy, I told myself, solid only in relation to my corporeal form, which is also energy. If I jump, I'll simply mingle my atoms with those of the asphalt. I didn't test the theory, but I did return home with the conviction that jealousy is a lie. If nothing is eternally solid — eternally *there* — I reasoned, then it's a lie to possess something. We own nothing, not even the cells and atoms of our bodies. So I realized that love is not merely eternal, but exists *outside* the Spacetime/Energymatter system we inhabit. At that profound moment I could have walked in on one of my girlfriend's extracurricular lovemaking sessions and handled it gracefully, perhaps with no malice at all. That's what mental transcendence can do for you.

A friend tells me that jealousy is simply one of the human emotions, that we should never repress it. Sometimes — when it's convenient — I believe him, but I also imagine that jealousy might be one of the unnecessary by-products of human evolution. I grant that in Pre-Dawn man it may have served some function, but I can't think what function it serves today, other than being a key ingredient in the recipe for violence.

But it matters little where jealousy originated — I have to deal with it now. I entered my relationship with the understanding that promises are essentially lies. No one can guarantee fidelity. Many people pretend to, but then they fornicate on the side and are forced to lie — "the truth would hurt her." At least my lover and I communicate. When she comes home carrying a strange spurt of semen we talk about it, or at least try to. And you're damned right it hurts, it hurts worse than anything in the world. And I don't repress it, no, I go into a nonviolent but very aggressive rage. Then I get over it until the next time. But what's the threat? I know she loves me, I really don't think she intends to replace me with that other guy. *Can* a strange spurt of semen wash our love away? How about several strange spurts? I curse Amanda Ziller for being fictional — she couldn't be like that in real life. I bet even Tom Robbins is a jealous god. But what about the pornographic film stars I've read about? One famous porn queen has been happily married for thirteen years, and her husband directs many of her films. They claim they're not at all jealous. Now here's a man who regularly watches his wife getting screwed by other men and he can handle it. That bothers me, intrigues me, because I'm certainly not that advanced. Or is that advanced? Maybe he's just used to it.

I do have the right to ask my girlfriend to stop carousing, but she says then she'll resent me — which could rapidly deteriorate her love for me, she implies. When she's out doing it I start feeling like I should be doing it too, not to get back at her, but simply to keep up (though I do want her to get a taste of her own medicine). Of course it's not like I can go out and get laid every time she does. Who will deny that a woman has an easier time getting picked up than a man?

If humans were incapable of loving two or more persons at one time, the problem would be more than half solved, though I suppose worse problems would follow. But love really does exist outside of space and time. Indeed, I am still in love with most every lover I've had, and even some I haven't had. If I were to make love to any of them, my current lover would be jealous. But she would not *want* to be jealous. Most couples we know profess monogamy while one partner or the other hops from bed to bed. My lover and I admit we are fallible from the start. We know that genitals can talk as loud or louder than promises. So we don't fool ourselves. And we hope that neither of us takes undue advantage of our mutual promiscuity tolerance. But it's impossible to draw the line between what is or isn't permissible. We're at the stage that we detest jealousy (note that the word contains *lousy*), but we still succumb to it at times. We tolerate extracurricular sex, but still cringe and cry when we find out about it.

Brian Knave
Johnson City, Tennessee

(*February 1983*)

joe blankenship

at work

16 degrees
8 o'clock blues down
at small flames cackling
on frozen pine

carpenters catch
their pantlegs on fire they
stand so close
in the numbing cold
(and you
two nights ago
during some few hours
that have melted
in the burning
of a mind's imagery

on Indian muslin
you broke
into soft gestures

with all my rough
handling you became more
and more radiant
until I thought your

milky frame would lift
away my skin giving it
the properties of light)

while I
open and leaving blood
in the corners of my life
tramped around
a construction site
completely full
distracted
smiling

(February 1977)

The Choice of Emptiness

Jim Ralston

(September 10 — Frostburg)

What is anything for? I am standing in line at Fidelity Bank, and inside my universe has caved in. I feel like the guy who folds his laundry, then goes down to the cellar and shoots his head off.

I walk down Main Street, looking in the shop windows, but not looking. Aching inside. Killing time, but waiting for nothing. I pass a sweater shop and see a sales clerk who reminds me of Denise. Soft curly hair, full breasts, slow thoughtful movements as she folds some sweaters and stacks them on a shelf. She looks up and smiles at me. Through her smile I notice my own reflection in the glass. I wince to see myself so morbid.

These are excerpts from Jim Ralston's The Choice of Emptiness ((Adler Publishing Company, P.O. Box 9342, Rochester, N.Y. 14604).

Dusk deepens my melancholia. I look out my kitchen window and watch the sky darken into that thin white-blue. It scares me what inner darkness I have to face.

And yet, day-to-day life, it just keeps going on. Connie will be dropping off the kids tomorrow morning, and where will I find the strength to handle them? I have weeks' worth of themes piling up on my desk to correct. My house is a wreck, dirty dishes overflowing the sink, plants drying up, clothes strewn over the floor in every room, along with last week's newspapers, food wrappers, children's broken toys, ashtrays spilling over with cigarette butts, empty match books, crushed cigarette packages, half-eaten apples.

I shut myself in the bedroom and lie down for a short nap. As usual I just lie there, wide-eyed, thinking, thinking, staring into the ceiling, the same old thoughts circling around each other. I pull the pillow over my face and think how satisfied Denise looks in her new life. I wonder if I can wish her any happiness from all this jealousy. Why do I still think of her as *mine* after all this time? Why do I cling so to the past, with all of its obsessions and fears and false hopes? Why can't I let the past die? Why is my so-called love for Denise so dependent on *having* Denise? Certainly I can see through it now, see the falseness, the immaturity. I am a grown man. I am thirty-five years old.

I think of Connie, my ex-wife, how she has made a new relationship for herself, a new home. Why has it been so easy for her? I think of Ty and Holley, and all their fear for what is happening to their Daddy. I see it in their eyes, "Daddy, come back, come back," and I start to cry, bitter tears, also wondering what is happening to their Daddy, if he can come back now. For a few minutes I remember back to the cozy little world of several years ago. I had done my life so carefully — college and graduate school, marriage to my college sweetheart, two beautiful children ("a girl for her and a boy for me"), a college teaching job, our own starter home and mortgage payment book, a VW camper with a pop-up top, a cabin in Canada, home to our respective parents and grandparents for Easter and Christmas. . . . And now it is hard to remember why I was so frustrated that I would give it up. And for this! For pain.

Denise
I am jogging this afternoon, still depressed from a broken heart

of months ago, and even more depressed that after all this time I still can't shake myself free. My lost love has gone deep inside me, and wherever I go, whatever I do, I feel hollow, half dead, like the best part of me isn't there anymore, and never will be again. I think the man says more than he knows when he calls his woman his better half.

When I jog, I like to let my mind fall away if it will, and just look around, and listen, and smell, and breathe, and run. It is a beautiful autumn afternoon if I can let myself out to enjoy it. The sky is low and gray. The autumn flowers are heavy on their stems, already touched with vague frost. The brown and yellow leaves are forming soft circles around the bases of the tree trunks, exposing more and more skeleton every passing hour. It's the kind of autumn day you can reach out and touch, everything is so crisp and bare. You can feel inside and outside the landscape both at once . . . almost . . . a little bit if you try. But alas, this afternoon it is all effort and no results. I am remote from the healing power of nature. My body is still, my legs (and my heart) are heavy. And my mind is clogged up with memories of what I used to have, what I ache to have again, but what I have no more.

It's strange when I'm depressed how my mind will start making these endless heavy circles around itself. It's something like jogging laps on a track, where I run ten miles and end up exactly where I started, only tired. Mind-circling never seems to go anywhere either. It doesn't loosen the depression, it doesn't relieve, nor does it lead to much understanding. Rather I think it's my poor habit of using thought to solve emotional problems, using my mind to dominate my heart, standing over it (overstanding) by way of forever encircling.

Disgusted with circles, I leave the track and move out onto the streets and hills, wherever my legs decide to take me. This afternoon they run me up the hill to the top of town and Frostburg Memorial Cemetery, though I think it's my mood that points the way. I am gloom through and through, and getting lower every mile, and, lo, I am starting to cry as I run. Who is this fool, I think, running around the graveyard in broad daylight, crying over nothing and everything. But my heart says, keep going, and I do. Up and down the long lines of graves I run and cry, over the dead bodies and cemetery grass, up one row of stones and down another, big stones of former somebodies, medium-size stones of former everybodies, little flat stones for former nobodies, now all dead bodies, I grieve them briefly as I pass, the rich and the poor, the proud and the humble, the aged and the infant, all equal now, all dead, some who had lain there before I was yet born, some who were born with me in my very own year, some who had died the same . . . The Andersons "Together Forever," Susan Markham "Too Soon Taken," William Thompson "At Home With His Father," Jonathan Peterman "Sadly Departed."

It may not sound profound, but a truth of life suddenly drops down inside me into a place I have never felt it before. I suddenly *know* that all things die. They really die. In spite of these "eternal" granite stones, these all-seasons plastic wreaths and flowers, these hopeful inscriptions, "Together Forever," "In Heaven at Last," etc.; in spite of our funeral customs to make death look like a Sunday after-church snooze; in spite of our Sunday school promises of Heaven or Hell and everlasting life; in spite of all the desperate energy we spend to make it untrue, the truth is — nothing, absolutely nothing, is to keep. Not even our own bodies, no matter what the undertakers and Sunday school teachers do and say to preserve them. These are dead bodies underneath my running feet. They were once as full of life as you and I, full of hopes and anguish and future plans, but now they are dead.

And carrying it but a few steps further, I *know* something else to be true, too. It's the same in life as it is after. Nothing is to keep here either. Life is always dying in one way or another. No moment is to hold. No relationship is forever. Even if it happens to last until one of the partners dies (and rarely does it last so long), that will be the end of it, and no kidding.

Life is change, fight it though we will. A deeper truth shoots through me with the force of healing shock. Since all things die . . . since *all things die*, how can having forever, or "having" for any length of time, matter so much as it does? How can it matter at all? Rather what counts is the full experience of life and love in the moment we are living and loving. It's the quality that's eternal. It's the quality that matters. Or nothing matters, because as for quantity, there will always be an end to that, and it will never be enough. We would all like the eternal summer, day without night, joy without sorrow, union without separation. But life will defeat our desires and efforts to make it something else from what it is.

What life is, is death. Entwined, inseparable cosmic lovers. To be wise means to live in the moment, and to let the old things pass out of our lives with the same ease and grace that we let new things be born in. If there is no door open at the dying end, the birthing end of our lives will be choked closed too. If there are no more graveyards, there is no more maternity either.

As I descend the cemetery hill, back onto the city streets, my soul still feels sad, like the autumn tones of color now darkening into evening; but my step has a new lightness to it, my breathing a new ease and depth, as if some heavy weight has been lifted from my back. The thought comes to me to run over to my old love's house to share with her these new feelings and insights. But ah! Probably just another trick to breathe life into a corpse, whose time is not hello, but good-bye. Not birth, but death.

So I'll say good-bye here, and let the grieving begin at last. And wish us both new experiences and relationships, as good as we once had together.

Good-bye Denise.

(December 20 — Frostburg)

In my afternoon literature class, I teach Phillip Booth's "First Lesson." It is ironic that the poem should come up today. As I read it to the class, there's a lot of intensity. The students feel it too.

First Lesson

Lie back, daughter, let your head
be tipped back in the cup of my hand.
Gently, and I will hold you. Spread
your arms wide, lie out on the stream
and look high at the gulls. A dead-
man's float is face down. You will dive
and swim soon enough where this tidewater
ebbs to the sea. Daughter, believe
me, when you tire on the long thrash
to your island, lie up, and survive.
As you float now, where I held you
and let go, remember when fear
cramps your heart what I told you:
lie gently back and wide to the light-year
stars, lie back, and the sea will hold you.

After class I am exhausted, and I turn off my office light and prop my feet on my desk. Outside in the hallway I can hear the tapping of typewriters and the clicking of heels on the hard tile floor. There is a thin streak of light underneath my door, enough to make faint shadows on the wall, and to see the rising and falling of my chest underneath my chin.

I fall asleep, and when I wake up I am disoriented. My mind is in a discussion with itself; it feels as if I'm hearing voices. They are saying that though what I now do (teaching) gives me some satisfaction, I know well it is not much. And it cannot be the deepest satisfaction because I'm still hiding the scared parts of my life underneath whatever I do. If I want to be all that I am, these outward things, even my job, will have to be stripped away for a time, to let the fears inside arise into clearer shapes, so they can be faced and wrestled with. Then all these things will be added unto me, and in new measure, in new depth.

The Sea Will Hold You

Life seems to pull at us from two opposite directions. We want security on the one hand; we want sameness, routine, predictability. On the other hand we want adventure, freedom, variety, newness, the unknown.

If we don't have enough moorings to what we know, to what we feel safe in, we run the risk of being dashed upon the rocks or blown away by the first strong wind. People can get lost in rapid change, even in their own growth if it comes too fast for our roots to handle. However, such overzealousness (or recklessness) is the rare exception, not the rule, although we fear it so much more than the other kind of lostness that comes with too much security, too little growth. Thus most of us have become heavily overweighted on the security side of the balance, always playing life safe, making our todays endless repetitions of yesterdays, choosing again and again the old and the tried, rejecting the new, fearing and avoiding the unknown, and closing an always tightening circle around our lives and spirits.

Perhaps a solution to the problem lies in a redefinition of what security is. If we could look at life, just for a moment, through eyes washed clean of fear and cultural conditioning, we would see that there is really nothing to hold onto anyway, and that the most insecure thing we can do is to try to grasp life, to make it stay put. We would see that we are hopelessly adrift, like it or not, and the most secure thing we can do is learn to float — to go where the winds of life carry us, and to come to know in a very deep place that the sea will hold us.

All that our fortresses accomplish — be they our careers, our degrees, our marriages, our homes, our possessions, our bank balances — is to "protect" us from the blowing winds of life, to steadily undermine our confidence that we belong to life as much as life belongs to us; that we are on the inside, not outsiders looking in; that we are friends, not strangers; that we are with life, not against; and that life is with us too, if we will but cooperate. But how can we cooperate, or participate in any positive way from inside our walls. Real security is breaking free, letting go, risking all.

. . . except a corn of wheat fall into the ground and die, it abideth alone; but if it die, it bringeth forth much fruit. He that loveth his life shall lose it; and he that hateth his life in this world shall keep it unto life eternal.

The undivided life, the life not protecting itself by walling the world out, sees that there is no such thing as security as man generally seeks it, in the human preoccupations, in culture. It is an illusion, and preferring truth, the wise man gives it up. And in giving it up, paradoxically he finds it. . . .

Rome and Carthage

I

Drown, or learn to breathe the new air. That's what it means to live at the bottom of the ocean, Bert and I would tell ourselves and each other on those long Winter walks. To live in the depths was like learning a new way to breathe. To live on the ocean floor of ourselves, not just occasionally touching bottom, but regularly, continuously in contact with our deepest selves — was it even possible? Against all the distractions and amusements and escapes with which life baited us? When the pain came, the emotional chaos, was it possible to live inside it and not run away?

The ocean bottom was our life theme that Winter. We would be

Jonahs (or Jobs) and get to know ourselves in this new air, in this strange underwater landscape, among these weird shapes and slimy deep-sea monsters, in the belly of our lives. We would make a new home among them, and maybe even learn that these monsters are not ugly and terrible after all, but only strange. They have been waiting for us down here all along, but we have chosen to live in the shadows, only skin-deep. And the dark and scary underside of life we fool ourselves to think is far away.

II

It's too strange how life "just happens" sometimes. Bert appeared to me the very night that my Denise-world collapsed. I was giving her a surprise birthday party at my house, and there were a hundred people there at least, including her softball team, the bluegrass band from Mike's Tavern, and all the regulars from the Democrat Club where she tended bar. A couple of friends and I had spent the day decorating the house and baking cakes, and I had bought two kegs of beer and a case of liquor, and a table full of cheese and crackers. It was a nice party, if I do say so, though perhaps my motive was not pure love. I knew that Denise and her "friend" had been seeing each other a bit, so I was also subtly trying to remind her what a good man she already had. Me. Look how nice and thoughtful I was.

It wasn't that I couldn't give Denise a little room, I told myself. She was ten years younger than I, and our worlds didn't coincide in every way. For two small reasons: I had children, and she had nothing but freedom. We both talked about needing our own space, and all that open relationship jargon, but I had no intention of giving her so much space that I got lost in it. Neither did I know how lost I already was. Underneath my outward show of liberality and gentle paternalism, I was possessive as hell, and frightened, though I didn't admit it at the time, even to myself. On the exterior, I showed a cocky faith that our feelings for each other would overcome all obstacles, no matter how handsome, or how young.

But that dark autumn night, as the house bounced with "Dixie" and "The Orange Blossom Special," and drunk-happy faces shined everywhere, I would notice them occasionally looking at each other from across the room, and was startled to see how deep they already saw into each other. What was going on? That was supposed to be my place to be, but I was not alone there. Or was I even there at all? To retaliate, I started flirting with other women, but when I checked back to see how I was doing, she hadn't bothered to notice. I redoubled my efforts, but the next time I looked she was gone. *They* were gone. I frantically searched every room, every closet, the attic, underneath the cellar steps. They were nowhere. And together! And outside, the dark woods behind the house whispered me cruel secrets about the beginning of something, and the end of something else.

"Oh my," I remember myself muttering, locking myself in the bathroom, and looking at my stunned face in the mirror. "Look at here. . . . Look at this. . . ."

This was supposed to be something that happened to other people. I had been caught wide open, with a naked heart, exposed in my own treachery. (It was I who had stolen Denise from her last lover.) Who would have guessed this would come back around to me. We were the perfect couple. Everybody said so. Everybody loved us.

I remember drinking a tall glass of whiskey straight down, and, as the party soared on past me, sitting on the couch with my elbows on my knees and my face in my hands, and a half-eaten piece of birthday cake sitting on the floor between my legs, and this man from the college, a political science instructor that I barely knew, that I don't even remember inviting, coming over and sitting beside me and putting his arm around my back for a very long time.

He was Bert, of course, and that gesture and that night marked the beginning of a great adventure we would take together. Bert, too, was suffering the collapse of a relationship, and that night we made a silent pact between us to thrash it out this time, to somehow wedge our way to the bottom of all this crazy pain of love and loss. Because, indeed, hadn't this been the main circle of our lives — to love, to lose, to despair, to do whatever we could to escape the terrible pain and loneliness until we could find love again, lose again, despair again, escape the pain until. . . . The only solution society seemed to have for this vicious circle (besides the hermitage or the monastery) was marriage, and to us that seemed more like a truce than an answer. We had both already tried that once. This time we would try something new. With each other's support, we would find the courage to live where we were, to take a hard and long look at this whirlpool of insecurity, fear, confusion, and loneliness, which is always so obvious at moments of exposure, but which we spend lifetimes trying to avoid or cover over. This time we would explore it. We would face it, eyeball to eyeball, shake hands with it, square off, wrestle with it, and master it. Or die trying. We would learn to live in our own depths, or drown.

After all, we reminded each other, as the autumn nights darkened into Winter, what is man's common response to fear and suffering and emptiness but to run away from them. To escape, at all costs. And don't we already know, we asked (as the mountain Winter winds began to gather force and howl), that running away from pain increases pain, that running away from fear increases fear, that resistance strenthens the thing resisted. What would happen if we just sat still one time. And waited. And watched. Not from a high aloof place. Not from a fortified castle. But centered within the pain itself, in the dead of Winter, at the midnight of the soul, on the bottom of the ocean.

What would happen if just this time we became the pain, without resistance. Became the fear. Became the loneliness, the emptiness, the confusion, the despair.

What would happen if just one time, when life forced us into our depths, we just went down.

III

Though we weren't much alike, Bert and I, we were one in that we were both lost and hurt, and were able to recognize that feeling in the other. And, of course, we were both looking for a way out of our suffering — or rather, this time a way through to the other side. But it was perhaps because of our differences and our respect for them, and admiration, that we complemented each other so well in our common quest. There was nobody in our neighborhood so intensely centered in our separate places; and if both of us were unbalanced in our different ways, we had all the more to share. We were powerful magnets, and opposite poles.

Bert's end of the pole was the mind; mine was the heart (in poor shape though it was at the time). It isn't that either one of us was dead in the other place; if we were, we would have had nowhere to meet. But these were our off-balanced centers, and from here other differences naturally followed. Bert's approach to life was more outside-in, mine inside-out. As he used to say it, he was Roman, fighting his wars abroad; I was Carthaginian, fighting at home. His emphasis was on social and economic reformation to redeem the individual life; my emphasis was on individual transformation, the revolution of one. In very basic ways, Bert was a Marxist, I was a Christian — meaning a man in search of my own Christ-force, my inner child. . . . Yet here we were, meeting at the crossroads, shaking hands, intriguing each other, becoming friends. For all the differences, we dared to trust each other. Maybe it was easier than being alone.

Whereas my powers were mostly intuitive, Bert was a theoretician, an aesthete, and social critic. He was as intense as I was preoccupied, and in almost the opposite direction. He had a keen eye for the outer world, for nature *and* culture, for landscapes and cityscapes, for paintings of horizons and horizons firsthand, for hues and tones of colors and sounds, for poetry and art and music, for our rotten social structures, based on greed and power and manipulation instead of the common good of man and all life. In the direction that he looked, he was balanced and open and acute. He was a theoretician who loved the texture of things, the rough siding of an old barn, the bare branches of a winter tree, a good joke. He read his Emerson, Marx, and Nietzsche, and he did watercolor painting too (he loved to contrast shades of light, the artificial light from a street lamp or the interior of a house against the soft natural backdrop of dawn or dusk). He was an intellectual who hated abstractions, who sometimes saw with the eyes of an innocent child, who would rather damn a book than hide his life in it, who was beginning to see that to have the insights, the wisdom, of a Nietzsche or a Marx, perhaps one would have to suffer like Nietzsche and Marx suffered. Perhaps nothing could be borrowed, or really known secondhand.

You couldn't be with Bert long without seeing more world. Or at least learning the value of looking around. He was a tireless searcher, and his eyes stimulated a part of my own that had grown lazy and dusty — the part that looks outside. I began to understand the importance of seeing the world-out-there in a more penetrating way, which was the only possible way I could make it my own. Bert stimulated me to find a picture of my own sadness in the heavy gray clouds rolling over the forest, or to hear the sound of my own death in Beethoven's Seventh Symphony. He dragged me into the cities, the museums, the concert halls, the parks, the forests. We spent a foggy morning listening to the ships' horns in the Baltimore harbor. We played with the sounds of our echoes underneath the freeway viaduct. We felt our way along mountain paths on moonless nights. We watched the town of Frostburg sleep from atop the highest mountain rocks. We talked. Sometimes we laughed. We sketched pictures of what we saw. We wrote composite poems. We imagined possible essays and books and symposiums to awaken the dead, both within us and all around. He challenged me to really look at this painting, to listen to that piece of music, to taste the frosted apple on our midnight walk — to find my own soul in these "outer" things, in everything I did and experienced. And all the time we concentrated on remaining at the center of our emotional crisis, always remembering our challenge of ocean bottom living, and focusing on our experiences, not as a way out, but as a way down into deeper water.

Bert was like a pointer to me. Although he accepted, even appreciated, my preoccupation with my inner searching, he would also urge me outwards, tease my eye to focus on the world out there, if for no other reason, to give myself another picture, another view of my world inside. We developed metaphors for our adventures. We were the Dutch reclaiming land from the sea. When the pain and confusion were overwhelming, these were the floods coming again. But each time we pushed the water back a little farther. Inch by inch the sea receded, and we became a country. Or we were Stanley searching for Livingstone searching for the source of the Nile. Or we were Cortez, landing in Mexico, and now burning his ships to conquer or die, burning his bridge back to the old world and old things. Or we were little trees, almost all underground now, but silently spreading and deepening our roots, and getting ready to burst into rapid growth.

"We must begin to write," Bert would urge me. He wanted us to write together, to form a writer's commune of two, right where we were in Frostburg. At first I resisted. I had tried writing once, eight years of it, and was satisfied I was no writer. He said that was my apprenticeship; I was just getting comfortable with words.

"Words for me are dead," I argued. He said maybe that was true then, but now it would be different. Now I was working on my life. I was at the center, and now the words would bleed.

"I can barely teach my classes and take care of my kids. How can

I write a book?"

"It doesn't have to be a book, not to start with. But you must create. We must create. That's part of living at the bottom of the ocean — not just to feel our pain, but also to create. . . . You are a writer. I am a writer. Now we must write. We must increase ourselves. We must build our country. . . . You have shown me the way down; now I will show you the way out."

What Bert meant by that last comment had to do with my gift to him, a knowledge of inner geography that I had already begun to chart in some detail (with Roberta's help, and primal therapy). It was the inner, emotional life that was my more familiar landscape. I knew the fears by name, and I knew many of their disguises and hiding places. Though I had not squared off with them for the final battle unto death, I knew something of their shapes and of their slipperiness. I had "studied" them for a long time, and was becoming more and more clear about how they controlled my life and made me miserable, always manipulating me and bumping me against the same old walls of frustration. Fear of failure, fear of abandonment, fear of aloneness, death. Fear of my own energy. Fear of love, pleasure, sex, life. They go on and on, overlapping each other, creating a powerful chain of resistance to our impulses to grow and break free. In the end they are perhaps one fear, or FEAR itself, fear of being alive and alone and ourselves in this eternal moment. Fear of being our own souls, and accountable. Fear of breathing the new air at the bottom of the ocean.

My search had begun in earnest with my involvement in primal therapy, which showed me the way to the source of my inner Nile was through the body and the feelings, not the mind. The complexes of pain and fear stored inside my body must be opened up and experienced before my mind could ever understand them. (The conscious mind can never *under*stand that which is repressed, because it is one of the agents of repression: i.e., *over*standing.) For example, what did it mean to know I was sad if I couldn't cry, to know I was angry if I was incapable of pounding my fists against the mattress and raging. That is empty, unconnected knowledge. The real insight into my sadness, my fear, my anger, was inseparable from the expression of them, a kind of secular exorcism. Before they could be understood, I must first bring them up out of the darkness, and they lay so much deeper in me than I first suspected, and had been with me so much longer than I could first believe.

Primal therapy showed me how my basic insecurities were rooted inside myself, and thus unfinished aspects of my past, and that it was fruitless to layer my life on top of these. It showed me that instead of growing through certain stages of my early life (adolescence, childhood, babyhood, even birth), I, like most of us, found my real feelings too painful and frightening (and socially unacceptable), and buried them alive, covering them over with acceptable behaviors and pretense. So instead of growing up through myself, each new stage building on the foundation of the last, and thus opening up from the inside-out, something like a flower bursting through its bud (which has grown out of its stem, which has grown out of its roots, which have grown out of its seed), I grew *away* from myself. I split, and then spent the rest of my life trying to build my houses without foundations.

Examples of the ways children and infants are split off from their intrinsic feelings, their real inner lives, are obvious and numerous. "Big boys don't cry!" parents tell their little boys, threatening them with subtle body cues and language tones that they'll withdraw love and support if they don't fake it out and *act* like big boys, or little men. "Nice girls don't fight!" parents shame their little daughters, with always the same implicit threat of withdrawal of love. When kids are scared or angry or jealous or messy, or even energetic, they are punished, subtly or openly. And the message is always the same, in whatever form it comes: no love unless you die to your inner self. In a repressed and listless culture, open expressions of real feelings will always be uncomfortable. The life force will have to be denied (or transmuted into certain forms of sanctioned aggression, like football or war), lest we have to look at our own living death.

Schools, and society in general, pick up where the parents leave off, and then when the children become the next generation, what they have had to deny in themselves, they in turn will deny in their own children. On and on down the line, to no end, the vicious circle is maintained, and we never have any real adults, but only repressed, teeth-gritting children everywhere, pretending to be grownups, but not grown *up* at all. Only grown away from their original nature. Covered over, hurt little kids, and so easily exposed in an unguarded moment, if they ever get their surfaces scratched. If they ever fall in love, or get fired from their jobs, or go broke, or get socially rebuffed, or bump their cars, or slip and fall on the ice, or get sick, etc.

The primal process is a simple one, though strenuous to practice. In the witness of other pilgrims on this inward journey, we are encouraged to go underneath our disguises, underneath our idealizations of ourselves, and to risk showing the persons that we really are. (The macho man, for instance, deflating his chest and showing the frightened little boy inside.) It's as simple as learning to express ourselves again, for whoever we are or whatever we are feeling at any moment, be it joy or sorrow, courage or fear, pride or shame, pain or ecstasy — to express ourselves from as honest and deep a place as we can find inside. And once we begin to trust our feeling nature again; once we can let ourselves be angry again and express it through our bodies, the way a one-year-old or infant expresses his anger (is his anger); once we can let ourselves feel scared again, and tremble with the fear, then an irreversible process has been set in motion, and there is no stopping until all those buried feelings (all that buried life that we have been carrying around inside) have also been exhumed and set free, until we reach the bottom of our lives, and now have a depth basis for self-understanding, self-healing of our divided natures, and the beginnings of abundant life.

(January 11 — Florida)

I spend the afternoon sitting in the community citrus grove overlooking the lake, quietly meditating, feeling the sun and breeze against my body, watching the fish jump, watching thoughts run through my mind, playing with one another, asking questions, then disappearing in the background for a moment of silence, or giving way to a bigger thought, a more urgent question.

I watch Doug hoeing in the gardens nearby, his shirt wrapped around his waist, his body lean and muscular like a yogi's. Even from fifty yards, I can see the scar in his side where they tried to dig the cancer out. It is a circle about six inches in diameter, just under his rib cage. That's where they shot the cannonball through him, he jokes. He calls it his badge of cowardice for ever letting the doctors get hold of him when he already knew how ignorant they were about health. After that surgery, he refused all further medical treatment and began his long pilgrimage to discover a real healing that went to the roots of the disease (and his life) and didn't get mesmerized by the symptoms.

In his own case, he has already proved himself wise for his choice. Without further medical "help," he was supposed to be dead years ago, but he is very much alive. A couple of years ago, a new primary melanoma appeared on his shoulder. For curiosity sake, he had it biopsied. Yes, cancer again, it would have to come off. Another surgery. Over his dead body, he told them. He fasted three weeks on carrot juice instead, and watched it disappear before his eyes. The doctor called it a spontaneous remission, which was a medical word for miracle. But Doug knew what he was doing.

Whatever his future, he has already beat the system, I think, noticing his energy as he vigorously hoes the peas and carrots. I mean the brutal system of surgery, radiation, and chemotherapy, which has left my mother almost without a spare part of her body, including her breasts, hair and other things feminine. After her operation last summer (this time to take out her spleen), she told me that they would never touch her again, that if she had only known, they would have never touched her the first time. And she is one of the lucky ones who has gone into the cancer statistics as "cured." I wonder how many millions of others would say the same things *if they had only known.*

Doug says we don't want to see cancer as a teaching in our lives. We'd rather think that cancer is something that happens to us from the outside, as a kind of bad luck; and the cancer doctors and the whole medical profession support this delusion with their treatment of cutting or burning or drugging it out of our bodies. What cancer really is, he says, is an early but critical warning that our lives are breaking down from the inside out, and that if we don't change them, and radically change them, including our diet, patterns of exercise and rest, environment, thoughts, then our time has come to be reabsorbed.

And he assures one and all that it is not his time yet, and that he will die of old age and outlive us all, if we don't watch out. And I would be the last to doubt it.

I knew it before, somewhere, but today I know it better, deeper. The ego is not the self. At most it is a small aspect of the self sharply attuned to the survival instinct. But, at worst, it is more like a parody of a deeper identity. It is the self adjusted to culture and alienated from nature. It is the smallest circle within an infinity of circles, which are also me.

And as the ego is a parody of the self, so are the creations of ego parodies: the schools are parodies of learning, the churches are parodies of religion, marriage is a parody of love (or partnership), sex is a parody of sensuous surrender, etc.

Bert's Marxism, Doug's libertarianism, God's World's vegetarianism, Denise's woman's liberation — each of these outlooks is quite right, but for its possessor quite wrong in the sense that it provides a covering for a deeper truth of who he is. It becomes a sophisticated form of hiding, curling up inside of ego.

I think about my own clothing, my layers of protection against being naked. One thing surely is my niceness. I'm not so nice, so patient and forebearing as I *act*. My smile is not always intrinsic, but many times another posture (or perhaps just a habit) to get approval and acceptance, to feel that I belong to life, which I also mistake for culture most of the time.

My intellectualism is also a kind of clothing, mostly — a child of ego, and not at all the same thing as awareness (thinking and seeing). Fortunately both the intellectuality and the niceness are falling away, though I sometimes feel confused and alone (naked) without them.

Apart from a few of the founding fathers who created the myth, America wasn't really ripe for democracy. Our hearts and minds were, and are still, monarchical, vertical. We are deeply conditioned to think of all of our relationships as hierarchies (who's above and who's below), and to live out our lives located somewhere inside a pecking order. (God is *on* high, man down below; the father is the head of the family; the boss may not be right, but he's the boss.) These power structures keep us from having to engage our own freedom. There is a kind of dead comfort in knowing our place. We just have to find our niche and get cozy there. In myth only is America the "New World." In reality we are as terrified of freedom as ever. And we fear and tremble when we feel somebody rocking the boat.

Boyhood Farming

Spring in Michigan is a delicious time. One can feel the Winter oozing out of the soil and the earth awakening. One feels it inside oneself too, a melting, an energy, a return to life.

I am camping in a little birch grove in the back corner of my boyhood farm. It is late morning and the sun is halfway up the sky and bright against my face. The air is cool and warm at the same time. It takes Michigan air a while to catch up with the season. Even though the birch trees are budding and the meadows are bright green, there are patches of snow in the shadows and little remnants of drifts piled up against the fences. And early this morning, there was a thin glaze of ice in the middle of Baker's watering pond.

At my feet I see some small violet buds just beginning to purple. Violet was my mother's name. I remember my sisters and I walking into this same grove thirty years ago, looking for violets as a first sign of Spring. It was like seeing the first robin or hearing the ice crack on the lakes and ponds. In Michigan you strain your eyes and ears for Spring. It never surprises you. You are ready for it.

Across the open fields, I can see the shells of the old house and barn. How quickly it all falls apart, I think. From the distance though, one could almost imagine they are habitable again. If I look quickly, a side glance, I can see underneath the decay and remember them as they were — alert, trim, alive. But it has to be a fast look, maybe the way a small boy might look up from his back pasture adventures of cowboys and pirates to be sure he hadn't wandered out of sight of home and hearth.

Meanwhile, as I warm myself in the morning sunshine, a doe and her fawn come out of Baker's woods to drink at the pond. The fawn is new. Its legs still wobble. A green mallard duck and his brown mate float among the reeds, watching the deer, but unconcerned. I sit very still, absorbed, for a moment unaware of myself, as if I am another birch tree soaking sunshine and preparing to burst into leaf. I remember being here before. A body memory. I remember the smell of Springtime, the shape of the hills, the texture of the cool morning air, with the sun a bright warm spot shining through. I remember. . . .

The deer are spooked by a sound too delicate for my ears to hear. They bounce back into the woods, and in turn upset the ducks, who fly away with great commotion of wings and squawking.

I also feel vaguely upset and want to run home too but I know this is the right distance for me today. This is as close as one can ever get to his past, perhaps. Anything closer is further away. One then sees the broken windows, the caved-in roof, the rotted beams, the death and decay. And that is all as it should be, and needs to be looked at. But today, this is as close as I come.

When I was a boy, I was this farm. It was an external metabolism. It was alive, inside and out, and a complete world unto itself. At one time or another, we had all the farm animals — pigs, sheep, goats, horses, chickens, ducks, rabbits, dogs, cats, and five Guernsey cows that Dad milked by hand, morning and night. I still remember some of their names (Molly, Dolly, Star) and which stanchions they stood at. I can almost hear the rhythmic splash of the milk in the buckets, and see my Dad there, with his old farmer's hat on, sitting on the three-legged milk stool, his hands squeezing and pumping, his head resting in the cow's flank.

Even as a little boy, long before I was old enough to help, I would go with Dad to the barn to do chores. I remember standing there across the gutter, watching him milk, having no idea in the world how new to life I was. Every now and then, when I wasn't paying attention, he would squirt a stream of milk at me, and I would squawk at him, half protesting, half delighted, while I wiped the milk off my coat, or off my face if his aim had been good. I remember how warm the milk felt on my cheek, how good it tasted to lick it into my mouth.

On the farm, the path to the barn is the boy's rite of passage. Sometimes very early in the morning, even before the rooster was crowing, Dad and I would have started our day, throwing down hay from the mows, filling up the buckets with water, the grain pails with oats, cleaning the gutters, calling in the cows, c'bos, c'bos, for the morning milking. It was something we did together, father and son. Then at daybreak we would come back inside and have breakfast in a cozy-warm kitchen smelling of eggs and sausage and toast, and full of mother touches and mother comfort. It was good, both the going out and the coming back. Both worlds. The gap between them frightened me sometimes, that tension between man and woman and their worlds. But I needed them both, each in their turn. It was a good time for me. That was before Mom got so sick and upset the balance.

Every Spring we planted a half-acre vegetable garden off the north side of the house. When the ground was dry enough to plow, I would watch Dad turn the earth into those deep brown furrows, full of angleworms, some struggling to bury themselves again, others cut in half by the sharp blade of the plow. Plowing was precision work, so Dad would have to do it. But after the earth was turned, we would attach the drag to the tractor, and then it was my turn to work. I don't know when I was happier. Driving that tractor was like a real taste of being a grown man, with a man's work to do. I would dream about it at night — pushing down the clutch, shifting the gears, letting out the throttle, feeling the power vibrating underneath me.

I was the farm. The farm was me. On the hot Summer nights, sitting on my bed in my upstairs room, I could hear the corn growing. And that was me, too. Or on a hot July noon, the sun straight up, I harvested my lunch straight from the garden — carrots, radishes, tomatoes, cucumbers, peppers — cleaning them with my jackknife under the outdoor pump. What empty freedom there was in these small actions. In the Fall, I loved to climb the apple trees to find the choicest, roundest, reddest apple alive, and eat it as I sat hidden in the boughs and surveyed the Summer landscape of my youth fading into autumn. I ripened with those autumn apples. Sometimes the dividing lines were very fine. There was all that space of a farm boy taking care of himself, doing what needed to be done and what wanted to be done, spontaneously, without asking questions or permission.

It wasn't that I was overlooked, or neglected. I was cared for, perhaps too much. But I didn't have to ask my mother if I could have an apple out of the refrigerator. Nor did we ever hassle about how many hours of TV watching was too much (there was no TV to hassle over), or how much sugar was too much, or how much homework was not enough, or whether my sisters and I were old enough to have girlfriends or boyfriends, or which friends were good influences, which were bad. The space of the farm seemed to absorb the trivial questions. There was a bedtime, but it was loose. We slept when we got sleepy, and we ate when we got hungry — then we ate dinner too. We took a bath every Saturday night whether we needed it or not, but mostly the clock and calendar didn't obsess us. We went more by seasons than by weeks and months, by intuitions more than schedules. There was still some trust in internal regulations. It wasn't perfect, but there were some balances struck. We still had all the inside stuff to work out, the growing pains, the fears, the emotional bondages, darkness and death. We still had to struggle with the existential problems of life the way perhaps only children can; we made attachments, got hurt feelings, cried ourselves to sleep some nights, struggled for identity and importance, and all the rest. But the thing about the farm was that it never closed in on you. Not as a kid, anyway. It gave you all the room and time you needed to learn, to understand. It could leave you alone in a back pasture all afternoon without asking one question. There was a kind of love there, contained in those forty acres. There was a spirit as close as the earth on bare feet, or the wind blowing through the birch trees. It was more than a vague atmosphere. It was an identity. But it takes the very young to feel it.

As a boy growing up in the late Forties, early Fifties, I think I got the last taste of the mythic America, the rural America, before it sold out to color television, wall-to-wall carpeting, old people's homes, the corporate Friday paycheck, all those things that have been called the good life. My loss of innocence was the whole nation's. We fell together, Thomas Jefferson and me. I was at the crossroads where the whole experiment came undone forever. I was raised when Jefferson's forty-acre farm was still a serious enterprise and not a factory worker's hobby or a country retreat for bored and restless suburbanites. Our neighbors to the south, the Bakers, still worked their fields with Clydesdale horses. The milk truck still bothered to stop for one or two cans of milk; you were a dairy farm with three cows, or even two. People still had their rough edges, their own accents; tastes and styles weren't yet dictated by Madison Avenue through the TV; agri-business was not yet a word; schools weren't yet consolidated into factories of efficiency; homes weren't prefabricated; hot dogs were still made out of unpoisoned meat; the supermarket hadn't cancelled out the general store. At one point our family car was a Model A Ford that Dad started with a crank, and fourteen cents was the price of admission to the double feature movie on Saturday night, but ten cents would get you in if that's all you had.

Maybe we didn't know so much about the world, about the faraway things. But there was another kind of knowing on the farm, a knowledge that went deeper than facts or information, a blood and bones knowing that was your roots and your foundation. Even if you left the farm behind for other places and new adventures, it never left you. It was always there inside you. In my youth, I watched my Dad butcher my yearling calf (which we had raised from birth), first stunning it with a sledge hammer blow between the eyes, then slitting its throat to bleed it to death, then disemboweling, ripping off the hide, etc. I *know* something about hamburger that you can't learn on TV. I've eaten hamburger that's mooed at me and licked salt off my hand, and that makes a difference in the taste. I helped my Dad catch the chickens to hatchet off their heads and hang their bodies upside down from a tree branch. I have seen the "chicken run around with its head chopped off" (I have seen the head itself lying in the grass, blinking) and I know something about Sunday chicken dinners with all the trimmings. I was witness to the Fall freshening of the heifers, and though I wouldn't exactly call it sex education, there was a kind of knowledge there too, something that vibrated inside me deeper than words go. I discovered my watermelons frozen on the vines Fall after Fall, before they had a chance to ripen in the short Michigan Summers, and I learned that sometimes persistence doesn't pay off — sometimes nature's persistence is bigger than man's, and there is good sense in giving up. I became an expert apple tree climber, and there was no apple too remote, no risk too great to reach it, and I learned something about balance and broken arms. I found my two pet lambs frozen to death in their pen one Winter morning (after I hadn't shut the barn door tight), and learned something about drafts and responsibility. I developed eyes to see maple sugar icicles in late Winter, how to treat myself to nature's candy when there was no nickel anywhere, even in the seams of the couches. I learned to ride my Palomino horse, Pal, without a saddle. I learned what it felt like to become one with a horse's back, and what it felt like to fall off, too.

The thing about the farm is that life was close there. Birth, death, sex, work, love, loss were everyday — they were inescapable, sometimes scary, sometimes painful, but never alienated, never secondhand. In its everyday way, life was full. You didn't think about it at the time because you were too busy living it, and what was there to compare? But later you knew. It was still there inside years later. Your body remembered — the soft feel of Pal's mane to pet, the smell of a field of new mowed hay, the taste of a pod of peas straight from the garden into your mouth, the sound of the crickets chirping you to sleep at night when the rest of the world had grown totally still.

Sometimes, yes, I want to say to myself, whoa, STOP! Stop right here a minute, and think. Somewhere back there I fell asleep on the path and made a wrong turn, or missed a right one. Let me backtrack a little and find the spot, and try a new direction to go. But then I see that it's not just me, it's all of us. We've all come this way together; somehow this is the direction life travels, like it or not, willy-nilly. The curse of man is that he loses his innocence. It doesn't matter where he's born. People raised in the Teens and Twenties felt the same way about the Forties and Fifties as I feel about now. The age of childhood is always the age of innocence, no matter what decade we're born in. And the next age is the fall. It seems likely that we could never find our way back far enough to recapture the wholeness. There would always be some further distance to go, some deeper innocence to rediscover. From a cultural vantage point, the American Indian would certainly want to push further back than my father or grandfather to find the crossroads, where culture and nature were identical, their interests harmonious, where the insides connected to the outside without the gap in between. For me, perhaps for most white Americans, it feels like the farm and the simple village are the lost harmony we left behind in our greed for a better and faster life. But for the blacks and Indians, it is perhaps even a deeper innocence they long for, the wilderness herself.

But that's not the way it works. We can't go home again, personally, culturally, no way. Life cannot stay still, neither can it turn back on itself; it is not kind to those who try. Perhaps the best we can do is look back, briefly, to collect ourselves and understand. Maybe at the most we can make a short visit, a pilgrimage, peek in from the back door of our thoughts and remembrances. Then we must push on through the darkness, because that's the only way we have to go. It is our curse, and our task, and our adventure.

I remember my mother, her last Summer before she died, talking about maybe buying the old farm again, and fixing it all up like it used to be. It was a pleasant fantasy, and for an hour I joined her in it. But when I got excited enough to suggest that we drive out to the old place and look around, she sighed and said no, she was too tired today, but maybe tomorrow. . . . How can the river flow back into itself. In a way, it does, but in a larger circle than our imaginations can readily conceive. First comes the ocean. First the river must disappear altogether.

I am awakened from my reverie by the Spring peepers singing their evening song. I wonder where the time went. My little boy's ears hear them too, and remember. I wonder where *that* time went. Underneath change there is always the same thing. If we move ourselves into the larger circles, there is no death. Part of us is already there. It's a matter of getting in touch.

It doesn't mean that we have to surrender our individual lives, the life of the ego with all of its fears and joys and sorrows and melodrama, with its past and present and future, with its preoccupation with time and progress, life and death; but rather to see this ego-center, this individuality, as a circle within a larger circle, and to know that the larger circle is us too. Then we can relax and let it *all* be. The planets spin around the sun, the same as the moon spins around the earth. But the sun is also spinning around the center of the galaxy, and the galaxies are spinning around another yet invisible center. And finally who's to say which is more, which is less. The point is not to get lost in any particular circle. There is part of us that can reach the stars, that is already in the stars, and always has been, as surely as we are the atoms of our bodies, which are little universes in their own right. The big and small of it don't matter so much as we think. There is infinity both ways you look, and perhaps they circle back and touch each other too, in a way we don't yet comprehend. The thing is to get in touch.

It's funny. The pull back to the old farm is like the gravity intensification of an exploding star, in its last burst of energy, but about to disperse into space and death. I will let it pull me all it wants now. I know I won't come back here again, if for no other reason than by next time through, here won't be here anymore, but in the "cracks and runnels" of my own mind.

Over the fence, in Baker's woods, I hear the faint note of an owl whooing. Or is it a mourning dove mourning? The sun is getting lower in the West, and is beginning to draw its warmth back into itself. I feel a shiver. It looks to be setting directly over the ancient homestead. I almost expect to see it shine through its ancient ribs. I think — my nostalgia now floating away into twilight — I'm almost done with the past now. It's just pleasant here this afternoon, this evening, the moment now passing in between. It's a quiet place to camp, to think, to meditate. The ducks are back on the watering pond. The deer I suspect will soon return for their evening drink of water. Across the fields, I can faintly hear young Peter Bontekoe calling his cows in for evening milking, using the same old call, c'bos, c'bos, that his dad used and my dad used. The modern dairy businessman still has to call his cows in, it seems.

Even so, the illusion is broken. I can see too clearly now the old farm is a ghost. The house and barn are empty shells. Life left them long ago, and they slowly return to earth, having fulfilled themselves and the stages of life that they were. They are no more than empty cocoons hanging from the trees, from which the butterflies have flown. So do we leave our own pasts behind. Someday our own bodies. Life is a constant metamorphosis from one stage to another. But why do we live so hard against this fact? Why are we afraid? In truth, we never leave anything behind, but carry it inside. Nothing is ever lost, only when we try to hold on. Then all is lost. Our whole soul. But if we let go, then we can take everything with us, because we become strong unto our own invisible centers, and the world becomes light.

. . . except a corn of wheat fall into the ground and die, it abideth alone: but if it die, it bringest forth much fruit. He that loveth his life shall lose it; and he that hateth his life in this world shall keep it unto life eternal.

I was thirteen years old when we sold the farm. That was twenty-three years ago, yet time doesn't measure distance from that which lives inside you. For a part of me, it was only yesterday, and will always be only yesterday.

I was sad, but I wasn't frightened. I was still too young and flexible to be frightened of change, and I saw the city waiting for me as a new life and challenge. Even then, at thirteen, though I didn't think about it in words at the time, I didn't doubt that the farm was as much inside me as I was inside myself, and though I was now to go on to a new and strange city world, the farm part of me could never be lost.

It was a great gift, and as I could leave it there, I could also take it with me. Tonight, after dark, I would like to wander up close to the old place, and sleep inside my old bedroom one last time, before it turns to dust and ashes. Because I know I won't come back here again.

(June 15 — Canada)

When I fast, I see more clearly the meaning of food. For me it is so much more than nourishment for the body. It is also a symbol, and a powerful one. Eating (stuffing) is not so much my need to be fed, but my need to be full. It is a thrice-daily appeasement of my fear of emptiness.

Yet I am more and more convinced that only emptiness is creative. On all levels this is true. To be full of tradition is to have no room for the new. To be full of responsibility is to have no room for play. To be full of activity is to have no room for reflection. To be full of self is to have no room to receive another. Whatever is obsessive, or even excessive, has to do with my preoccupation to be full. It doesn't matter much whether it is obsessive eating, obsessive working, obsessive sex-ing, obsessive thinking, or even obsessive denying — they all indicate no faith in life, no trust, no real openness to experience, and thus no creativity. They also indicate distortion, misplaced values, and substitution behavior, for example, the substitution of a full belly for a full heart, or words and thoughts for feelings and awareness, or orgasm release for sensuality, or power and control for love.

It's not easy to be reborn. It means I have to die to my deadness, and to all that I do to stay dead. The trouble is that I've become vaguely comfortable going through the motions of life, living at a distance from myself, investing in the surfaces of things, and just plain coping.

It takes depth of self to be comfortable alone, doing nothing, and culture has provided us many outlets to relieve our tensions begat of shallowness. It has done such a "good" job that we have been mesmerized to think our innumerable distractions aren't distractions at all, but everyday life. We no longer notice how nervous we are. For example, it might not strike us as out of the ordinary to see a man smoking his morning cigarette and absently chatting with his wife over their breakfast of coffee and sweet rolls, meanwhile thumbing through the newspaper, and half listening to the weather report on the radio, while waiting for his nerve tranquilizer to take so he can stand the hassle of rush hour traffic, so he can get to work on time at a job he doesn't enjoy but which pays good money to allow him to keep up in this great race of life.

Of course this picture is exaggerated, but how much? In varying smaller doses, this clutter is what our days amount to. The circles of our lives spin so rapidly that there is rarely any opening for a new perception or sensation to either get in or get out. We become busy-bodies, consuming robots, but we digest nothing, always restlessly pushing on to the next task or the next pleasure. And if our busybodyness should ever fail us, we always have our busy minds (mind clutter) to rescue the moment — idle fantasies, daydreams, disconnected sentences that run through our brains as if they had a life and will of their own. As it turns out, neither our actions or our thoughts contain their own meaning, but rather serve as shields against the terror of our own meaninglessness. And the faster our wheels spin, the faster we need to run to avoid the truth. Escaping ourselves is an addiction like all addictions: the more we do it, the more we need to do it, until every avenue to our inner lives is effectively closed off; until we have succeeded in becoming totally false.

What is it that we are so frightened of that keeps us locked inside these shallow circles, safely distanced from the gravitational pull of our lives' centers? In earlier essays, I explored the kinds of personal damage we experience in childhood that destroy our trust in life, and which also lock us out of our own depths and thus inhibit our impulses to grow. But now I am thinking of that which lies underneath our individual childhood complexes and personality damage, that which lies at the very base of our existence, but which is no *base* at all, but rather nothingness, emptiness, death. Is this perhaps the first avoidance of all (the avoidance of the void) that is the beginning of our hiding and our falseness? Is the primary base of human culture more than anything a collective ego-hiding from the reality of death, a huddling together against the darkness? Is this fear the foundation of all other fear, the source of the split man has experienced from life and within himself? I think so. But why? Why is the dust at the core of life so difficult for mankind? Why is it so terrifying that we go to such lengths to look the other way, to deny it, to build our whole culture, our whole lives, around a pretense and a hiding?

It goes beyond merely refusing to face death. We won't even

acknowledge that we are afraid, or worse, we insist that we aren't afraid. However, for all our escapism, whether it takes the form of looking the other way or "brave" talk about not being afraid to die, the evidence of secret, subconscious terror is everywhere: in our grotesque funeral customs, which paint up dead people to be sleeping; in our belief that we'll be raised again into life in these selfsame pickled (but secretly rotting) corpses; in our everyday attitudes that death is something that happens to the other guy, to the other family, but something we can forever buy more time against in our own lives. (We are always shocked when death strikes home — it seems impossible! So are we secretly relieved when it strikes only near to home, in spite of our condolences and sympathy.)

And the more we avoid our fear, the bigger it grows, so big that once we are faced with our own death in a clear way, the adjustment to reality is an enormous mountain to move. It represents such a leap that if we do make it, we land in a different universe from our contemporaries, who remain behind still in hiding. Elisabeth Kübler-Ross, who has spent much of her life counseling and companioning and learning from dying people, shows us that given the opportunity to face their impending deaths, people can transcend their fears and make the leap out of illusion and into reality. Indeed, she testifies that some dying people "enjoy" the greatest growth period of their lives, and grow to see death, not as a morbid defeat, but as a joyous victory, a coming into oneness with themselves, and thus becoming whole in a way disease and age cannot touch.

As with facing death, the same is true of inner nothingness, which is a living version of the same thing. According to the men and women who have had the courage to look, to go inside it, *to become it* (Jesus was one, the forty days in the wilderness being the symbol of this inner adventure), it is really no monster at all, but the very wellspring of life. The language of paradox that Jesus used in his teaching is based on the embrace of emptiness: the last shall be first, the lowest shall be the highest, the least the greatest, the poorest the richest, the meek the inheritors of the earth, the abundantly alive those willing to lose their lives.

I know I have had brief moments where I touch upon this emptiness, this inner death, myself; and these glimpses are evidence to me that contact with the inner self, all the way through to the nothingness, the dust, is the only path that leads out of the confusion and fear that otherwise will dominate our lives. Whenever I have experienced my life *through* my emptiness (empty of me, empty of ego fear), I have been transformed in a twinkling, without thought or effort.

As of now, this happens most clearly when I fast, which is an old trick that has always had religious connotations, false and true. In the worse sense, fasting is performed as a show of righteousness, sacrifice (which are their own rewards); but in a deeper spirit, it is done privately and quietly to create a connective current from the surfaces of life into the depths, at the bottom of which lies the emptiness of which mankind is so frightened. Even the act of not taking food into the body can be an affirmation of this emptiness, a statement of desire to be with it, to go into it. In this sense fasting is a spiritual search. For me it represents a choice of emptiness. And always, every fast, I get more clues of what is on the other side. It might seem something very small at first, and difficult to put into words. But the affirmation of life is there, right in the center of nothingness; and once contacted, it begins to grow in meaning and importance.

(January 1983)

Three Photographs

John Rosenthal

US/Readers Write About . . .

Sickness

Brain tumor. I first remember hearing of it twenty years ago when my parents whispered at the dinner table that a popular neighborhood boy who was very tall had a brain tumor. From that point on, I associated a brain tumor with being tall and popular.

My next contact was when I was fifteen and beginning to feel curious symptoms. My parents took me to a brain specialist in New York City who charged $100 and all I remember him doing was watching me walk back and forth for five minutes. He said I was OK. My parents were relieved. I was unhappy. My displeasure was a combination of wanting a tangible disease and cure for my daily headaches and nausea and wanting to be tall and popular.

My symptoms continued. The headaches, nausea and weakness would emerge daily for two or three months a year. At twenty-one, giant hives accompanied the other symptoms. Over the ensuing years, I periodically saw other specialists. Twice they found mononucleosis, but most of the time they told my family and me, in relatively hushed tones, that it was psychosomatic. I didn't like that. I didn't want people thinking I was crazy.

Living under the onus of having a psychosomatic ailment, I compensated by presenting a picture of myself as being in the peak of health. But at the age of twenty-eight, during a two-month sick spree, I no longer had the energy to keep up the charade. I woke up one morning, called in sick to the office, and lay down on the living room couch. At that point I decided to call the ambulance and get an I.V. at the hospital. I didn't want to make a big deal out of it. Then I realized that I couldn't even sit up. I waited from 10 a.m. to 7 p.m. for a housemate to come home. I was scared. I had never felt this weak before. I was soon wheeled into the emergency room.

I was ashamed to be in the emergency room with my psychosomatic ailment when, in cordoned-off booths all around me, old women were wailing. I told the resident that this problem was caused by unknown emotional turmoil and if he would be so kind as to give me an I.V solution or two, I would be on my way. He managed a tolerant smile. Feeding my desire to leave was my parents' planned visit the next day. I feared that the hospital ambience would trap us in a child-parent interaction instead of the adult-adult level I wanted.

I stayed overnight in a room adjacent to the emergency room called the Host Room. I dreamt of tapeworms. In the morning, I was seen by a group of doctors, all with identifying name tags that said "Medicine." The leader told me that my blood tests showed severe chemical imbalances. He suggested that, since the root of my problem was previously shown to be psychosomatic and my present health was nearing the norm of a concentration camp, I admit myself to the psychiatric ward. I said "No." We negotiated and compromised. They would send a psychiatrist to see me. The psychiatrist told me I was OK and could go home.

At this point my parents arrived from New York. As they drove me back to my house, I felt progressively weaker. I kept telling them I felt OK. I did not want to go back to the hospital. If they wanted to put me on the psych ward last time, they were not to be trusted.

As my mother returned from buying groceries at the nearby country store, I acknowledged to myself that I was still sick. I told my parents to call the hospital to tell them I was returning. My body was shaking on the drive back. As I was aware of surrendering myself to whatever lay ahead, the words "leap of faith" swam around in my mind. As we neared the hospital, I leaned my head on my mother's shoulder. I don't remember ever having done that before.

During my second visit to the emergency room, a college baseball player was getting his broken leg looked at. His coach was with him, reminding him that it didn't really hurt, that when he was in college he had injuries that were a lot worse. The student kept repeating, "Yes sir, yes sir, it doesn't hurt." A little ways down from me, a young girl who had taken an overdose of sleeping pills was screaming, "Don't pump my stomach."

A couple of hours later, I was taken to a ward upstairs. Different doctors asked me the same questions for another couple of hours and at 3 a.m., they told me to go to sleep. The nurse tied a tongue depressor at the head of the bed and put protective coverings on the bed rails. "Seizure precaution," she said. Oh, swell! During that first night my doctor injected a solution into my I.V. to reduce the water level in my body. I woke up three times that night having to urinate like I never urinated before. I came close to filling the 1100 cc bottle each time. As the I.V. line limited movements, I asked the nurse how to pee in the bottle without soaking my bed and myself. She said huffily, "You figure it out."

I awoke in the morning to the "team." Thirteen people, all in lab coats, said "good morning" simultaneously. My doctor told me that there was a problem in my blood chemistry and my pain from the headaches may have adversely affected the functioning of the pituitary. She mentioned a number of tests they would perform.

As I fully awakened, I began to explore my area of the hospital. I had the distinct impression that I was admitted to the gerontology ward. I could not find anyone that looked younger than ninety-six. The nurses got the old men to do what they wanted (the simple things, eat and void) by promising to marry them. If the men were constipated, the nurses would threaten to break off the engagement. The women in white called the men a variety of names: Sweet Meat, Brown Sugar, White Sugar, Honey Bunch and Sugar Pie were the most common. I was called Paul, however.

The first week in the hospital they did a number of exploratory tests, gaining little new information. I felt like a visitor, as I started feeling stronger. I no longer identified with being sick. I was restless to go home and expected to be released each morning. I began keeping my own accounts of intakes and outputs and helped the nurses with other patients. One wardmate thought I was his son, and although he was in restraints for regularly inappropriate behavior, he would occasionally saunter in my room and try to take off his I.V. and bleed into my waste basket.

The tests were showing some definite endocrine system malfunction. On Monday, I underwent a brain scan which I understood to be a routine part of the test package. My doctor told me that she would tell me the results of the scan later that day. I watched the

Dallas-Washington football game that night. An unusual game, 9-5 Washington. At midnight, the medical student working with my doctor came into my room. She apologized for not coming earlier and said that the "team" was busy all day. I asked what the results were. She said that she was not empowered to tell me, that the team would tell me in the morning. I asked her if it was bad. She said she couldn't say. She looked sad. I knew it wasn't good.

In the morning, my doctor told me that I had a pituitary tumor and that they recommended surgery. My reaction was numbness. I wanted to be by myself. I asked my doctor if I could leave the hospital for a few hours. She consented. I walked around the university campus where the hospital is located. I was conscious of my hospital wrist band and how that made my life different from the people walking by me. I went to the library and sat in an isolated carrel. I felt very much alone. As I walked back to the hospital, I felt vulnerable on the street. I hurried my steps, looking forward to the protective concern of the hospital.

My attitude changed that day. I felt strong. I also felt, however, that if I were going to get through this I would need a lot of support. I called friends, asking them to be with me. I became more receptive to the hospital staff as I realized their importance to me. During the next few days, I was beseiged by visitors. As I felt loved by others, I gained a deeper inner strength. I was ready for the surgery.

The last test was the arteriogram. I was well prepared and, except for an initial surprise when the technician shaved my pubic area, I felt in control. The machine made a noise when the dye was injected that reminded me of a sound in the Walter Mitty movie when he entered fantasy land. The pain lasted eight seconds each time the dye was released. The first three seconds the pain increased, then it peaked at the fourth and fifth seconds and subsided through the next three. Once I had mastered the pattern, I could ride it out.

That afternoon, while some friends and I were singing "Old Man River" loudly, the team of neurosurgeons came into my room with the report that the arteriogram showed no complications, that I was free to leave, and that the surgery would be scheduled in three and a half weeks on Halloween. I would have liked to do it sooner and I told the doctors I felt ready for it then. As it was not an emergency it could not be scheduled until October 31, however. The doctors explained that they would attempt a relatively new procedure in which they would enter through the nose crossing the sphenoid sinus. They explained that this was less risky than opening the cranium. The next day I left the hospital.

My life was full the next three weeks. I felt more alive than ever before. Time spent with friends was poignant. Excited at the prospect of being fully healthy for the first time in thirteen years, I was filled with gratitude for the opportunity to live without pain after having been given the chance to know pain. People I didn't know told me they were praying for me. Friends from out of state were planning to drive 2,000 miles to be with me for the surgery.

There was only one time I felt afraid. During a routine check-up, I asked the resident neurosurgeon to show me a diagram of exactly where the tumor was located. He first came across a picture of a pituitary-tumored patient on the operating table. I felt nauseous at the sight of the myriad of tubes and I felt frightened at the prospect of choking on the nasogastric tube. When I got home that afternoon, I brought firewood into the house, giving myself a splinter. I felt irritated at the discomfort. I thought of the much greater discomfort ahead and questioned if I was strong enough to handle it.

I was apprehensive about my return to the hospital. After three weeks at home, I expected a jolt to my system. I was wrong. As friends accompanied me to the admitting office and then to the neurosurgery unit, I experienced the warmth and excitement of a gala reunion. I had absorbed so much love during the interim period that I could fan it toward each person I met and still retain plenty for myself. People visited me that entire day and evening. The next day, Monday, was the last day before the surgery. I had told my family and friends that I would like that day alone to prepare myself emotionally and spiritually. I had envisioned that I would need that time to summon my inner resources. They were already summoned, however. I fell asleep during the innocuous tomagrams.

That night, Mary, a nurse from Surgical Intensive Care Unit, gave me a tour of the SICU, and told me what to expect when I awakened from the anesthesia. As she glided through the checklist of topics, I could see that she was enjoying herself. I felt reassured by her ease. The only upsetting news was that I would keep an indwelling Foley catheter at least one day after the surgery. I gulped. I didn't want my friends to see me with a catheter.

Later that night the anesthesiologist inserted the I.V. that would monitor my heart. As they retracted the line, placing it in my chest, the nurse held my hand firmly. I felt strengthened by her being there. I could feel myself changing; I was giving up my stance of being self-contained and now letting people take care of me.

When the I.V. was in place and I was alone again, I felt lonely. An older man down the hall, who had attracted my attention the day before, motioned to me. I had noticed his neatly-wrapped turban-like bandage and the pride with which he carried himself. He invited me to a party in his room. His name was either Jim or Bill. Whichever name was his, I mistakenly called him the other one. It was an unusual party; he and I were the only guests and the food consisted of the cookies his grandchild baked for him and the two cakes he ordered from the nurses' station. We watched the Rams play the Falcons on Monday Night Football as he, recovering from an arterial bypass operation, assured me that there was nothing to either the surgery or recovery. The nurses would periodically wander into the room and tell me it was time for me to go to sleep. I cajoled them into letting me watch the end of the game. I prayed for the game to never end. Bill or Jim was leaving the next day but promised to visit me in the intensive care unit.

I slept suprisingly well. I woke up early and watched intently as the sun peeked over the horizon. I slowly began my preparations. I had some extra time to write in my journal and rereading it now, I am struck by the last sentence, written in large print, "THEY'VE CALLED! . . ." I felt that I had done all I could do to prepare myself.

As I entered the holding room by the O.R., I was struck by how funny these medical people looked in their blue and green head coverings. The woman next to me was having her stomach shrunk and she consented to join me in a stanza of "Amazing Grace." We laughed.

My last presurgery memory was meeting the anesthesiologist in the operating room. My next memory was being wheeled into the SICU. I asked the nurse where I was. "ICU." "Is it all over?" "Yes." "Can I do it again?"

I then vaguely remember seeing Jim or Bill standing over my bed simulating an Arab. The next twenty-four hours were a blur. My parents and friends were allowed to visit for short stretches and I relished their stays. The division between reality and imagination disappeared that day for me. I could imagine myself as a baby and the nurse as my mother and I eagerly awaited her attention. I wanted to tell my nurse that I loved her but could not decide whether that was appropriate, so I didn't. I liked being totally dependent. Surprise, surprise.

As I gradually became more conscious, I was curious about the pulse and blood pressure monitors over my bed. After three hours of practice I could pick any reasonable number for either my pulse or blood pressure and tune my body to that number using the monitor as a gauge. I would show that trick as soon as a visitor arrived.

I experienced general aches and pains during this period but my only intense discomfort was when the doctor took the gauze packing out of my nose. After two days in SICU, I had mixed feelings about returning to the ward. I felt sad that I would lose the mothering and I was excited at the prospect of being free from the I.V. and monitors.

I remember the next five days as a gala celebration. I was given some wine and after I had received permission to imbibe, I shared a cup with each visitor. My new roommates comprised a large part of my life at that point. One man, Willy, was from out of state and had suffered some broken bones in a car accident. He was in no hurry to return home. He enjoyed flirting with the nurses, visitors and patients. He cajoled a visitor of another patient to wash his underwear. Willy was frequently successful in getting a young nurse to bathe him, although he was capable of doing it himself.

The other man, Mr. Bellows, was an inspiration. He had been paralyzed for two and a half years and in the hospital for almost all of that time for tests. He seemed truly grateful for all that was in his life. He saw himself as rich, as he contemplated the love of his family and his relationship with God.

On Sunday morning, Willy led the eighth-floor congregation to the downstairs chapel. He was not normally a churchgoer, but Willy, sensing the opportunity to spiritually commune with an unattached woman, could be flexible.

I remember well my last day in the hospital. The team (whom I no longer considered an intrusion, but whom I now warmly welcomed) in their morning rounds said that I could go home today as soon as the doctor took the splints out of my nose. I felt numb when they told me. I didn't want to leave. The hospital was my womb. I didn't want to leave it twenty-eight years ago and I felt similarly this time. One night nurse, Jane, I particularly dreaded leaving. She would wake me every two hours for medication — by leaning over my bed with her head a foot from mine and gently shaking my shoulder, repeating "Paul, Paul," ever so quietly. My fantasy each time was that I was injured in the Civil War and that this dedicated nun was nursing me back to health. When I told Jane my fantasy, she blushed.

I waited eight hours for the resident with his surgical scissors and vial of morphine, sitting in the corridor with my newly acquired autoharp, alternately strumming and mulling over the whole experience. I began to know a piece of the gratitude that Mr. Bellows expressed. I felt blessed. I talked at length with the Chaplain about it. I talked with my parents, affirming our relationships. They let go to some extent of their vision of me as a child who could not manage well without their parenting. My father confided to me that they wanted desperately for me to have the operation performed in New York where "all the finest doctors were." He said that they decided that it would be better for me "to die on the operating table" than to have the decision wrested from me. Inasmuch as I fight hard to retain my independence from my parents, I was deeply touched.

Paul Kommel
Durham, North Carolina

(February 1980)

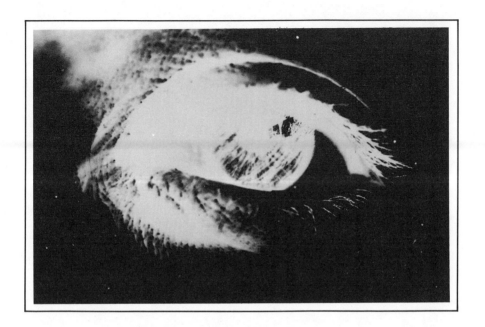

Cholestiatoma

David Koteen

Cholestiatoma is a loving beast; as with other cancers, he comes like a string around the finger, a chain around the throat, to insure that we do not idly forget why we are here. Cholestiatoma (Chole when masculine, Choleste when feminine) lives in my skull between the meningies and the right orbit. He sleeps on my optic nerve, is not always gracious; by sleeping too much and over indulgence in the proliferation of his own being he causes eye strain. I want to close my eye and rest. I want him off! I cry intently. May this beast be gone, I pray softly. But Chole that gluttonous fellow, Choleste that lascivious creature is here for a reason: to guide me, to help me transcend the bodily throes, and learn: there is no side-stepping life. You either deal with your stuff now or you deal with it

Cancer is the effect of not dealing with your life — this body, mind, and soul, this incarnation! And the surgery which removes the cancer, that new being inside of you, does not solve the problem. Nothing solves the problem except awareness and acceptance.

later. It's hard. It hurts. But there is no getting around it. You might as well get on with it. I thank you two.

June 1976 I was baling hay. The International was moving down windrows smoothly, the John Deere 14-T baler was gyrating, picking up the mixture of grasses, augering easily, the pitman arm packing it in; the needles rise and the knotters tie clean, tight knots. Bales drop out continually. A joyful day in Oregon! One thing; in order to stay on the windrow it was necessary to close my right eye. Just tired. Stress. No Sleep. Holly (my wife) and I were at odds. Raising the boys; attempting to transform our citified educations; farming at the height of the season; I was thoroughly jealous, and as wrathful as ever in my life I had been. But what I expressed was little — tight-lipped frustration, small bursts of anger. Mostly it was all inside — internally fermenting like hay baled too green.

The eye pressure was disregarded, headaches began increasing. I would look for secluded nooks to crawl into. No way had been provided, and I couldn't express these painful and tormented feelings inside. Only the physical aspects. Whenever I attempted to get out some of the snarled emotions to others, they took Holly's viewpoint (women are penduluming forth to rebalance the disharmony). And so I wept . . . and wept alone.

When I finally sauntered to an ophthalmologist in October 1976 the right globe was protruding three millimeters over the left eye. Chole and Choleste had been fattening themselves, had grown to the size of a tennis ball. The brain had been forced back and the globe forward. Cholestiatomas thrive on unresolved tensions. So slowly the scientific process, the recording of data, the proof of disease was begun: X-rays; bone erosion; the music was becoming more frightening. When I returned home from the radiology lab, the phone rang. My father, the Doctor. "You are scheduled for brain surgery next Wednesday. New York Hospital." Choleste was distraught. Leaving my three sons, Holly Ann, and two women visitors, I flew East to the vortex of Western civilization — New York City.

If through free will you don't deal with your life, higher forces will make decisions for you. Either you choose or you are chosen for. Evolution in human beings is a means of adapting the body and consciousness to environmental changes. Our minds would burst if we could not reconcile the internal combustion engine within ourselves: automobiles can propel themselves; 100-ton steel beasts can defy gravity. We must accept it as axiom, integrate the pace set by these machines, and somehow, the intensity of emotion. When an individual doesn't choose to evolve, when he opts for lower mind states, to allow himself to be chosen for, cancer sets in. Cancer is not a disease; cancer is a life form; it is tomorrow's evolution, today. Future historians will call the period from 1945-2000 the Age of Cancer. For it is in the historical era when the human body is undergoing the most radical transformation ever. The process is speeded up in identical proportion as horse and wagon are replaced by jet. When the mind is not able to deal with the change appropriately, and one indulges to extreme, be it food, drugs, sex, emotional intensity, the body is forced to compensate. The compensation within the body for "too much" is often called Cancer. The cigarette smoke mixed with chemicals enters the lungs. The lungs extend themselves to remove the toxins from the alveoli. Time and again the process occurs. Finally the lungs (the body) and the mind are in such conflict they give up, and wall it off. That part of the lung dies. Dies, but is still in the body. And so as in every other part of nature, the degeneration process of one form of life is the generation for another. A new being starts living in the dead lung (moribund lung). This being called lung cancer (or bowel cancer, breast cancer, etc.) begins to grow. A baby. A new evolution. But this does not solve the problem which caused the individual to eat or to drink or to smoke or to worry to excess. This is the effect of that cause. Cancer is the effect of not dealing with your life — this body, mind, and soul, this incarnation! And the surgery which removes the cancer, that new being inside of you, does not solve the problem. Nothing solves the problem except awareness and acceptance.

All to do with the operation went smoothly. The unfolding of its meaning in my life became progressively clear: all the loose ends of the East Coast existence, primarily understanding my role in my generic family; the sinewy tangle of familial relationships — there was a great deal of work for me there. Literally everyone I ever knew and shared strong feelings with showed up. What if David dies? For me, a quick change of garments, from runner-away-from-responsibilities to deathbed guru. After the five-and-a-half-hour operation I lay doped up, receiving people — some massaged my feet (wonderful!), some confessed their sins (also wonderful). Until knowledge of death comes to the fore, the clandestine work — known in detail to us alone — deftly eludes our grasp. (Those intuitive insights — revelations received on walks by the sea, shapes taken by shadows in moonlight, voices whispered in the ear before sleep, crazy woman rantings on the bus — those truths we *feel*, we deny. Rather we select a war across the earth to base reality on — sandstone!)

Why should I die? Am I really responsible for myself? Of course Death who picks his teeth with a scythe tip is only a clinging to life — this form. It is our complaint, "Why must it change?" And we know all of us that everything changes. Love life; love death; love yourself.

> *Reincarnation's just a fact of death*
> *Better get on with your life.*
> *When your heart stops pumpin'*
> *There's one long, long breath,*
> *And you're back again on thin ice.*
> *Every morn has a night*
> *And then another day;*
> *So every death has got a birth*
> *Every November has his May.*

The better I got the more I thought about Holly. This was our first separation in six years. I desired to be with her, forget our historical muck, and begin anew. Lying alone in New York City, I longed to make love with her — long, very slow love; to become love with her in whatever form. Or did I?

Howie Dunbar — pure spirit — brain surgeon par excellence stood over me surprised to find a cholestiatoma. I watched him carefully, no longer in my body, cut through the bone, gracefully — an artist, a master — pin back the skin and so carefully suck the dehydrated cholesterol crystals from the sack. Beautiful! Adieu Chole! Bon Voyage, Choleste! But a bit lay on the optic nerve and so untouched by surgical implement (like a seed awaiting an opening in the earth to germinate) it lay dormant — the physical, the scientific reason for the reoccurrence of the tumor.

In this type of operation, when the body is anesthesized, the soul is released, as in sleep. The soul returns to the master soul for consultation. Can you continue to grow in this form? Is the body no longer an appropriate vehicle for your increased awareness? If the decision (and it is delicate) is *no*, the patient does not regain consciousness. The body is discarded and, obeying physical laws, begins decomposition. If affirmative, the soul returns into the body as the anaesthesia wears off. (Special note: historically it would have been necessary to die actually, to go through total disassociation with the old mind, the old body. But because of the total evolution of the earth, it is possible to have two incarnations in the same body through this incredible surgical magic. And among other things that is the wonder of modern science. I was reborn.)

And time, the nurse of illusion, passed. Well and joyful to return to home — gallant warrior from the table. Holly and I reunited at San Francisco Airport as lovers still do. An historical moment Chole and Choleste; for in the reunion — daily demarcated by regrowth of hair over scar — they received sustenance. I started back toward Oregon, baggage in hand, tension in the left, frustration in the right.

One morning, March 1981, Holly said, "Your friends are back." I felt along the right orbit, the globe was fitting a little snug, snugger than the left. That loving beast has come home . . . to the opthalmologist . . . to the neuro-opthalmologist . . . to the CAT-scan. Yup! "About the size of a walnut. We can monitor it and if it (Choleste) gets too big, we'll remove it." And May came. Another feeling of increased pressure like a wet sock on the inside of the eye. One night in June I was awakened by a large red voice: You're going to die if you don't concentrate on your work. Right now! Do not think your wife, children, the community, the school are important! Forget them! Only your eye — only the cause of the tumor. Work on it! Can you live through another operation? Grace twice? You choose!

Right in our room, fight in my head. The voice of karma, the one you can never walk away from. The time had come — change. I knew somehow the healing had to come from within. If the eye causes me to sin, better pluck it out than enter Hell with both eyes.

The search is begun — three clear readings from different consultants. Leave, they said. Love yourself and you can love others. Of the possible points of departure, the Polarity Institute on Orcas Island in the San Juans was selected.

As I close my eyes and drift over the last decade, it is hard to fathom what all the drama was about. The pushing; the holding on;

the drawn lines; the long trip overland to India; beautiful children; their crying; buying and selling; gasoline going incessantly into tanks. At Hearthwind, our farm community, there is a magnificent view of the Umpqua River winding languidly through the mountains; it is sunset and the goats and sheep are grazing and cudding. Blackberry cobbler with goat cream is being served in the kitchen (too slowly). Incredible beauty! The sun here, where I sit alone and write, drops quickly to the Pacific horizon. Tomorrow we'll take the ferry to Orcas, I and Cholestiatoma.

(February 1983)

Dusty Miller

nothing scares me

I could sever an artery just trying to put
out a cigarette in the wrong kind of ashtray,
an evil one, i mean . . . or a two year old could
jump on my head while i'm washing my hair
& drown me in the bathtub . . . or that branch
over the car that already looks ready to fall
could finally decide to do it . . . or some kind
of malevolent gas could erupt from the
earth & strangle me before i could even
think about becoming a public utility . . .
or some angry midget could kick me in
the balls and what good is my karate if
i double over & swallow a beer bottle . . .
or who knows what the mailman thinks
of me . . . or what they're liable to put on
the back of postage stamps these days . . .
or the inherent & terrifying potentials of one-
way streets & yield signs . . . or some giant
by-product of some wacky genius; huge
grasshoppers, toads, earthworms . . . see
it's everything or that's why nothing scares
me.

(October 1975)

Cancer means different things to different people. Most people, when they realize they have it, are too overwhelmed with fear or pain to speak about it. Peg Staley is different. A 56-year-old psychotherapist from Rhode Island, she learned last year that she had a tumor in her breast. Peg shared her thoughts about this with her friends through a series of letters — her way of turning an intensely individual experience into a teaching for all of us.

Val Staples, a physicians' assistant who lives in Durham, North Carolina and who occasionally writes for **THE SUN**, *is a friend of Peg's and showed us these letters. We asked Peg for permission to reprint them, and she kindly gave it. In response to our request for some information about her, Peg writes:*

"I am a Gestalt therapist who was a chemistry major at Vassar, a wife and mother of five sons, a lady volunteer, the founder of the first school volunteer program in Rhode Island and am waiting to see what my next transformation will be like. I live in the country, near the ocean, with Andrew, my husband, and two of our sons. Our family always includes members by choice. Currently Paul Wurtner and Andy Smyth also live here. My letters seem to describe much of my life. In addition, I have started to organize a birth center. Twenty months after our first meeting, we are hiring a midwife. The principles on which the birth center are founded have been those I've followed in my cancer treatment. I've been a therapist for the last six years. I love to walk on the beach, to raise and eat my own vegetables, to read, and most recently, to be noisy. And I've come to a deep appreciation of the richness of my WASP background after years of considering it to be unbearably narrow and constricting."

— Ed.

Facing The Struggle

Peg Staley

October 22, 1978

Dear Friend: I am in the greatest transition of my life so far and am writing to share this experience with you. I have cancer in my right breast and the medical report is that the cells are a fast growing and invasive kind. . . . I first went to Oliver Cope in Boston the first week in October. The mammogram at that time was inconclusive and a biopsy was done on Tuesday, October 17, when Andrew and I returned from celebrating Peter's marriage to Anne Williams in Santa Fe on the fifteenth. The wedding was a wonderful celebration with all our family and hers together as well as close friends.

I spent time in Santa Fe alternately calling to arrange for flowers and food and gathering information about types of cancer, opinions about treat-

My image of the medical delivery system is a giant teat. Everyone is sucking on it as though to let go is to die. The reality is we can grow up!

ment and possible options open to me.

My search has been to discover how I might best be a full and primary participant in my own healing. I have felt and received love and healing energy not only directly from the Lord but also poured out to me from those near me. And I am immensely grateful that my learnings in the past few years have given me tools to use in the months ahead.

One friend encouraged me to see this time in my life as a new world to be explored not with fear but with inquisitive curiosity and interest. Another prayed for me to remain in love, not fear, and this enabled me to stay open to the Lord's presence in strength and solidness during the biopsy which I had chosen to have done as an outpatient under local anesthesia so that I might consciously participate. A call to a counselor at the Simontons' cancer clinic in Texas helped me to focus on the secondary benefits which I get from having cancer (my answers were excitement and attention) and to begin looking for less destructive ways to get them.

A second question helped me to explore why I would want to give myself a life-threatening disease at this point in my life. A visit to consult with Jack Downing[1] in New York helped me to sort out which therapies made personal sense to me and gave me the chance to spend time with Avery Brooke.[2]

The encouragement, challenges and love of many others have been deeply important. And I want you to know my plans so that you can see where you may fit in.

Healing ministry is basic. St. Peter's in Narragansett is a healing church which I attend regularly. Also at 6:30-7:00 a.m. and at 8:30-9:00 p.m. I will meditate and ask for healing here in Saunderstown. I welcome anyone who wants to join me at those times either in Saunderstown or wherever you are.

Nutritional therapy to build up my own immune system is also basic. I have been following a cleansing, nutritional diet in direct contrast to my usual pattern of "sweet-eating, over indulgence in refined foods and animal fats." I also expect to work with Michael Schacter[3] in Nyack, N.Y. to establish an optimum diet. To exercise restraint and moderation where I have been indulgent seems important in itself but even more crucial as a paradigm of the needed cellular change in my body.

I have ordered books and tapes from the Simontons[4] and will work with them to visualize healing.

This event has transformed all of us. I am searching for a family therapist to work with us as a group, as a system, which has allowed or at least not prevented one member from getting seriously ill. And I expect to work with Stan and Christina Grof[5] in November when they come to Vermont. In January I will spend 5 days in Escondido, California with Elisabeth Kübler-Ross.[6]

On Tuesday I also go to Boston to start chemotherapy. Surgery is out.

The cancer cells are of a type which has already spread. One lesion is deep in my breast on the chest wall. And my breast is somewhat swollen and inflamed, and not, thank God, sore.

Yesterday I realized the strength of the word malignant. When I view cancer cells as malignant I give them power and worse I give them evil power. They are weak and confused cells that have gone on dividing uncontrolled, unlimited. I can indeed project my fears, my anger and hostility into them. It makes more sense to me to say with firmest love, "Enough! I will not let you destroy yourselves and me. I will restrain you and stop you."

I have listed the ways in which I expect to do that. And ultimately I know that I live in a paradox. I will do what I can. I will fight to live. And I may die. . . .

This letter is intended to open doors and not close off channels of communication. I expect to write every other week or so, and my friend Paul Kervick has offered to help by taking care of mailing them. I will not ask him to continue to send them to you unless you let me know that you want to receive them. Many details about my work and life are unclear as I move into my new world.

Thank you for listening.

I love you.

Peg Staley

NOVEMBER 13, 1978

Dear Friend: Trying to write this letter is like trying to report on an acid trip. There are so many levels of understanding and interconnected links that I need a 3-D map to sort out the events since I first wrote. My need for excitement is certainly being met.

And I am also grateful to each of you who has paid such special and loving attention to me. I am deeply touched by letters, phone calls and messages as well as by those who have come in person to meditate and pray with me. As two or three of us sit quietly, gathered together, I feel the support and presence of many more who are with us in spirit and in love.

I feel blessed with love which has helped to strengthen me as I have made important decisions about my life and the treatments I will follow. And I have fallen into fear, into the dark tight places of hopelessness. There is no doubt that I am physically healthier than I have been for a long time. I know I can be whole. And I am aware that my need is for cleansing on many levels.

This new world of mine is rich and varied. Two weekends ago Cynthia Finn[7] was here in Saunderstown. I had important time alone with her and she led a workshop in Past Lives. One such life as experienced by a member of the group was a deeply spiritual one that taught me that once you give up a fearful image of God that you must move into a new place. I felt that shift when I decided not to have chemotherapy. . . . I found myself unable to agree to poison my body in the name of healing. It was hard to tell Dr. Leone, with both friends and Andrew present, that I would not take the chemical treatment scheduled for that morning. Andrew knew my decision and supports me in making it. The crucial thing for me was to be solid and sure in my decision. I am not ruling out chemotherapy altogether. And I appreciate my ability to give myself time to decide what I want to do.

Last week Sean Carmody[8] called to offer a gift. He had been working with John Grinder[9] who had just returned from working with the Simontons in Texas. Sean offered to work with me and it was an incredible hour. He worked with the deep unconscious part of me that is giving me cancer. He approached with deep respect and appreciation for that part which, having been walled up, needed to break out of the cell and to live whatever the cost. Much of the work was non-verbal. This part of me agreed to cooperate in my healing and the tumor seemed shrunken as I left the house in Lincoln. It has not stayed that way — and I return to Sean tomorrow to work some more. It is very helpful to work with someone who knows that my attitude and intention will affect cellular change in my body.

I continue my diet and have begun work with Angelica Redleaf[10], a chiropracter, on diet, cleansing my body and kinesiology. We have begun family therapy with Anne Varna-Garis[11], who trained with Menuchin[12] and is a marvelously healing young woman as well as seven months pregnant.

Next week I go to Jacksonville, Florida for three days to attend a healing mission at San Jose Episcopal Church with Emily Gardener Neal whose book, *The Healing Power of Christ*, was given to me by Mary Scott and which has been a source of wisdom and understanding. I continue to attend services at St. Peter's and have also asked for healing at the Apponaug Pentecostal Church.

I continue to be very involved in my process. It is clearly going to be a struggle. Dr. Cope's notes speak of this as a stubborn tumor. And we have already done much. I am seeing very few clients. So I find time to play, to walk in the woods or on the beach, and to let out a playful light-hearted Peg who has been hidden for many years behind an earnest, solemn mask. I could assume surface gaiety. I begin to feel joy.

Meditating the other day, I suddenly knew with recognition the words of the Christmas story — "Fear not, I bring you tidings of great joy." I feel tears in my eyes. Last weekend in the Gestalt group a friend read the Bene-Gesserit prayer from *Dune* about fear as a mind-slayer. Fear is the opposite of love. Fear is tightness, holding on, afraid to lose, to let go. Fear keeps me from trusting my capacity to heal myself. And my body knows it. When I get afraid, uncertain, tense and upset the cancer grows. When I relax, image myself as whole, the cancer gone, a block of ice melted into life-giving water by the heat of the sunlight at its center, it does indeed diminish. The struggle wages back and forth between these two images and realities. Please continue to send your prayers and love as allies on the side of light.

My love to you,

Peg

NOVEMBER 28, 1978

Dear Friend: One hundred years ago today Wallace Campbell, my father, was born, as Jane reminded me on Sunday. Last week my son David gave me a copy of thoughts he had written down and one of the lines was, "I know that the process you started within me won't stop if you die."

Today I am very conscious of that process, of all the richness and love as well as problems to be resolved, which I inherit and pass on to others. And that, just as I have taken on a legacy from my parents and their parents before them, so also I have handed one on to my children.

One of the most painful and healing moments since I last wrote was the realization that the family I co-authored with Andrew has just exactly as hard a time sharing emotions as the family in which I grew and in which I felt so starved as a child. I have consistently found emotional nourishment outside of my immediate family and am immensely grateful to Paul, to Cookie and to Andy Smyth who have lived here, shared my life and given me places where I felt free to express whatever I needed to. In a session with Anne Varna-Garis when Tim did let me know how important I was to him and at the same time let himself feel the emotion behind his words, I saw how rare such moments are for us. It is immensely healing to see this, and to begin to work together as a family group to allow ourselves more intimacy. And I also saw how my expectation that such intimacy is not possible within the family defeated my wish for closer communication. I feel more ice melting as we all begin to break free of its frozen immobile grip.

Rich Hockman gave me Eileen Caddy's *Footprints on the Path*. She started Findhorn Garden in Scotland with her husband Peter. Her book speaks powerfully to me. Yesterday, I read a section on how much harder it is to unlearn something you have come to know and trust as a secure guideline than it is to learn something new. Of course, one must let go of the old to allow the new — the chicken breaks out of the egg, the baby is born, we let go of life into death. I let go of Peg as healthy and explore Peg with cancer, a life-threatening disease.

My first explorations were, as many of you pointed out to me, frenzied and obsessed. I would study and learn all I could. And I have accumulated and sifted through a great deal of information. The most important result of my trip to Florida was to let go of my obsession with breast cancer. On the last day of my mission after the 10 a.m. communion service and before the evening healing session, I was walking on Jacksonville Beach. I knew I needed to go there. As I walked along, I suddenly felt very peaceful. I thought, "I do not understand this." And immediately I flashed on the "peace which passeth understanding." I will continue to do all the things which I believe I am to do to be involved in my own healing and in a real and wonderful way, I have given my healing into the Lord's hands. I had many very special, powerful experiences during the mission and find myself to be rather like a shy teenager in love for the first time, wanting to keep these moments private.

My sense is that the wind shifted for me in Florida. The analogy comes from a letter of Cookie's written after she had been out near the forest fires which raged out of control all around Los Angeles two to three weeks ago. She made the connection to inflammatory cancer and felt very moved by the sight of wild fire. The Santa Ana wind blew all the smog away so the flames could be clearly seen and fanned them so that the firefighters were powerless. They could only evacuate people. And then the wind shifted. The fierce bellows of the Santa Ana dropped, a shift came blowing the flames back toward burnt out areas and the fires died down.

I have a spiritual guide named Abraham who comes to me in meditation. When I first met him I only reached to his belly and I cradled my head against him. I have grown and am now tall enough so my head comes just under his chin. For a long time I had no sense of his features and face except an impression of a beard. When I finally saw his face, it was ravaged and eaten away as though by leprosy. He did not answer my question as to how this had happened. Now his face has healed, and I understand that he ate himself away in attempting to be his own source, to be his own wellspring. As I have understood that I am a channel for God's love and not the source, I am now able to see another place where I put unbearable stress on myself which I could not sustain without becoming ill. To say nothing of the pride I had to drop.

A few nights ago Andrew and I went to see *Interiors*. The daughter Joey, in talking to her mother, says, "The trouble is, mother, that you have a sick psyche and at the heart of every sick psyche is a sick soul." I know. And I believe that it is not just psychic illness which has its origin in a sick soul. That, too, I learned in Florida.

And I also know that what I've found out and what I am doing are right for me. They are not right for you — some pieces may fit, use them if you wish. You cannot adopt my path even though some of the signposts may be useful.

I see the doctors at R.I. Hospital, where I *did* start chemotherapy three weeks ago next Monday. At that time, they will evaluate whether the tumor which was still increasing has been arrested and is shrinking. I believe it is. And, of course, I want it to. I have had virtually no adverse reactions to chemotherapy and, as I wrote in a letter to Oliver Cope in Boston, I believe that my delay in starting chemotherapy allowed me to choose it with the full cooperation of my outer and inner selves. It was scary to say "no" when the medical opinion was that any delay was very dangerous, but I believe it was more important for me to say "yes" wholeheartedly. And it seems to me that, as Avery quoted from the Bible in writing about the "poison" of chemotherapy: "Everything created by God is good and nothing is to be rejected if it is received with thanksgiving." 1 Timothy 4:4. My acceptance made it easy to take.

I send you my love as I receive yours, acknowledging that both are reflections of a Greater Source.

Peg

DECEMBER 22, 1978

Dear Friend: My cancer is shrinking. On Monday I went for my sixth chemotherapy injection and on December 28 I will meet again with Dr. Leone to decide on the next steps. A week ago I checked the medical record to be sure that my report of Dr. Gherkin's findings, when she saw me after three injections, was accurate. At that time she measured the tumor as four cm. When I started it was eight to nine cm. Since Dr. Leone had told me that a fifty per cent reduction after six treatments would be a good result, I feel very pleased. Dr. Gherkin also reported that she could detect no other lymph node involvement and that the ones under my arm, which had been palpable, were no longer so.

I am totally convinced that the ways in which I have been working to reduce stress in my life have had a powerful effect. I reduce stress by eating healthy food with low amounts of material to be eliminated. I reduce stress by coming to better understanding of the non-productive ways in which I try to twist the world to make it work my way. I reduce stress when I let the outcome lie with the Lord and not with my efforts. I reduce stress by paying attention to driving my car so I am not strained. This was an eye-opener.

Andrew has taught me defensive driving. The difference here is looking ahead to decide the least stressful action in the next few moments. Thus it is not protective but evaluative. It also means paying attention to my body and letting my muscles relax as soon as I notice them tightening up rather than tumbling out of the car a tight wad of cramped flesh at the end of the trip. And it means driving with my hands at five and seven o'clock on the wheel instead of at ten and two. The tension that is destructive is unconscious and to take just this one simple situation and to look at it from the point of stress was very relaxing.

Sean had been insisting all along that to have energy available to heal cancer, I must not spend a lot of it fighting stress. And I got more corroboration from a marvelous article Alec Randall sent to me written by Norman Cousins for the December 1966 issue of *New England Journal of Medicine*. He writes of his successful bout with a form of cancer ninety-nine percent fatal. He prescribed vitamin C in massive doses, old movies from Candid Camera several times a day (on the principle that laughter is a fantastic stress reducer which also eliminated his pain for two hours at a stretch) and rest in a hotel room which was one-third as expensive as the hospital and with much more nourishing food. He worked with a doctor whom he had known and respected for twenty years who took medical tests before and after vitamin C as well as before and after laugh therapy which clearly indicated a healthy physiological response in his body. Why wasn't this picked up and hailed as a breakthrough? I can't find out.

When I have talked to doctors about the possibility of working immunologically with myself I have been told of research with self-immunization, with other kinds of injections. I wonder why the relatively simple steps of building my own immune system have been almost totally ignored by the medical profession. I have not encountered within traditional medicine anyone (and I have met concerned and caring doctors) who encouraged my belief that I could reverse the breakdown in my body which allowed me to get cancer. And I have taken some simple and obvious steps which are inexpensive and which have vastly increased my chance of stopping and reversing a cancerous growth. There is other corroboration. I have read a remarkable book given to me by Dorothy Shutak at St. Peter's Church, written by a surgeon, William Standish Reed, called *Surgery of the Soul*. His belief in the healing power of Christ as well as of the existence of spirit and psyche even when a person is under anesthesia or in a coma led him to adopt an attitude of respect for the patient reminiscent of Dr. Frederick Leboyer's work with newborn babies. He describes "vegetables," so called, who recover in a hospital and remarkably quick recoveries from surgery when the patient is treated as though he could indeed hear and take in the experience. Respect, paying attention to a person whether they show response or not, is in itself healing. And I found it exhilarating to read of a doctor who understood and was willing to apply *all* the principles of true healing — not just in his own attitude but by insisting on the same from all of those attending the patient.

I find myself angry and determined. I do want to know why so much money is poured into trying to discover *the* cause of cancer and so little into experimentation with other forms of treatment which give more responsibility to the patient, and which help the patient to believe in her own ability to mend disease. My image of the medical delivery system is a giant teat. Everyone is sucking on it as though to let go is to die. The reality is we can grow up!

As I grow I realize a need to enjoy and be with women. A marvelous two hours with Bev Hall saw us laughing, reminiscing and catching up on our family news. She had been uncertain about coming for fear of being too sad. It was instead a vital, alive and nourishing time for us both. And I need more of these times. My womanness needs nourishing. I live in a world of many men. I am still making the acquaintance of women's strength and love, my own as well as my friends. And that too is a lesson sharpened by breast cancer.

January 9 through January 26 I shall be in California. A visit to Cookie, to Sabira and Frida Waterhouse, a workshop with Elisabeth Kübler-Ross, another one with John Grinder on self-hypnosis and hopefully a visit to Star and Christina Grof in Big Sur as well as the opportunity to look over Synthesis Graduate School in San Francisco before I apply to go there in the fall of 1979 are all on the calendar. My next letter will be from there or shortly after I return. I make no promises.

Meanwhile I continue to visualize my silly weak cancer cells as sheep, the chemotherapy as fire-breathing, clanking stinking dragons and my white blood cells as St. George and as a way to clear up all the debris. I can giggle about the image as I sit in the hospital getting the injection, imagining that others passing by wonder at the bleating, the whisps of steam, and the battle cries emerging from the room!

With my love for the new year and hope your holiday was truly blessed.

Peg

JANUARY 9, 1978

Dear Friend: Here I am having a peaceful sunny lunch in my Saunderstown kitchen instead of high in the sky on United's flight No. 103 from Chicago to Los Angeles. After a hectic, busy week getting all the details attended to so I could leave for California with a clean slate, I drove to Boston yesterday. It poured rain all the way. I was tired. I had an extra ordinarily fine session with Cynthia Finn who will be my therapist during the next three months while Sean is in San Diego. I had been feeling some stomach cramps during the day. They worsened as I drove home and I went to bed exhausted. As soon as I got home knowing I could never get to the plane this morning Andrew cancelled flights and called Cookie. Paul brought me a hot water bottle. Tim and Andy found the paregoric and I finally fell asleep. So I am spending the first day of my vacation in Rhode Island instead of en route.

Cynthia had just returned from a twelve-day vispassana meditation retreat in Barre and my time with her brought me back to myself. We explored the feminine qualities which I recognize in Elisabeth Kübler-Ross and have trouble owning for myself. Of course, I know that since I can see them in her, they are in me too, but I found it hard to make them real until Cynthia asked me to embody them, to discover where they exist in my own body. It was powerful and beautiful to acknowledge Elisabeth's *light* shining from my heart and being absorbed through my eyes and to see that as womanly, mothering love.

I also deeply admire Elisabeth's ability to push the boundaries, to explore her innermost depths. That quality I found in my legs. As I stood to experience it, I discovered my tai-chi legs flexible, able to support me whether I chose to advance, retreat, or go sideways, and am delighted at the shift from the strong, quite rigid pillars of support I developed as a child when I felt, "It's too early for me to have to stand on my own feet."

As I stood in the room with Cynthia I suddenly noticed the closed door and told her how much I disliked it. I want open doors in my life. I moved to the door and realized that it was not the right time. There was indeed a door knob. I could open it and walk through and I wasn't ready to do so. Instead, I really looked at the door. I saw the flow of wood-grain like ripples and waves of water, the gradations in color and felt the somewhat coarse texture of unvarnished wood that has not been sanded perfectly smooth. And once again I realized how I have been rushing my decision. Eight weeks of chemotherapy ends on Thursday. The medical recommendation is to start radiation as soon as I return from the West Coast. I have been talking to the radiation oncologists, to Dr. Leone and Dr. Cope, getting information about the effects both beneficial and harmful of the proposed treatment. Five days a week of radiation for five weeks for a total of 7,000 rads to kill off the lymph nodes in my armpit, under the collar bone and those along the right breast bone as well as irradiating the total breast area, with special dosage to the tumor itself to knock it out. Some lung tissue will be permanently killed. The blood-producing bone marrow of the irradiated area will be stopped, hopefully only for one or two years. Since inflammatory cancer has no clearly defined boundaries to begin with surgery not only didn't make sense then, evidently it never will. I appreciate the clarity of the answers I have received and am still not convinced that I will choose to go ahead with this treatment.

I certainly intend to explore alternatives while I'm in California and to continue to be aware that I have a decision to make when I return. Dr. Leone gave us more than an hour of time at the end of a day last week to have a meeting with me, Andrew and our family. This was helpful. And I got part of my answer as to why medicine doesn't focus much on natural immunity. Dr. Leone feels and I've since heard the same from other doctors that if even one cancer cell is left in my body that it will eventually grow and become *one* large tumor. So the obvious treatment is "search and destroy." The parallel to our conduct of the Vietnam War is obvious and uncomfortable.

The stress theory which says that we all develop cancer cells all the time and that our body handles them makes more sense to me. I provided a perfect seedbed for cancer by long-time neglect of some basic rules of good health and by ignoring signals of stress in my life.

Where is the balance point when medical science has eliminated the major threat and my body can now resume its own protective functions? How can I know that place? Who can help me to recognize it? These are my questions. And the door is not yet open. I am impatient to know. And I must realize as I did with Cynthia that I have much yet to learn on this side of the closed door.

One thing I have already learned is that each new decision is almost like making the original one all over again. Each time my will to live must be reaffirmed if I indeed intend to do so. I will also decide how I can best do that. I have had to let go of my picture of Peg as a healthy person to get used to Peg as a woman fighting breast cancer. The bigger jump is still ahead of me. As I began to succeed I scared myself. What will it mean to be someone who wins; who does conquer cancer? The jump now is to Peg — the winner. For me that is a leap, especially since my body, which I learned so early to distrust as weak and unreliable, will need a whole new image!

So I go to California to continue explorations tommorrow. This layover day has been important. I'm ready now.

With much love,

Peg

FEBRUARY 22, 1979

Dear Friend: The floor is littered with discarded first drafts of this letter. And my mind is full of thoughts I found on waking this morning. I imagine myself trying on a decision like a new set of clothes to see if it fits, and whether it looks and feels right. Some costumes are an immediate hit. Others take longer before I know. I am seeking devil's advocates to help me judge. I test out what I am doing in the crucible of adversity asking family, friends, and doctors to give me their most honest feedback. This is stressful as many of you have said, but I then know not only in my head but also in my body what my commitment is, since I have wrestled with each objection until I am satisfied and sure.

Many of you have heard me wish for an indicator in my body like the blinking red light on a motel phone which would signal me to pay attention. I wanted an indicator of malfunction so that I could know when I was being destructive. I've got it. I laugh ruefully to myself realizing that my wish has come true. Remembering the old wife in the fairy tale of the three wishes who, having wished in anger that a sausage grow on her husband's nose, could only use the third and final wish to get it off again, I shall be very cautious about future wishes.

Instead of wishing for more magic I now see myself facing the struggle to use this cancer, this tumor, this indicator of health as a way to learn to live well. It is opportunity. I do indeed know now whenever my body is not functioning properly.

Each psychic, each channeling or message from my High Self has assured me that I need not die in the near future, and that healing is available for my asking. Where to ask, how to ask, whom to ask and how to be receptive to that healing are unanswered. Every one who knows me and many who don't have their own answers to these questions of mine. It is important for me to hear these answers, especially the ones I dislike so that I can learn to be sure of the path I have chosen.

I hate going to Rhode Island Hospital. I always come home discouraged and fearful and in touch again with the enormity of trying to work toward health using tools and methods that the experts within the medical system, whom I was taught to trust, believe to be ineffective, primitive quackery. And I cannot agree to radiation. I am thrown back on what I do know of alternate health care and my own experience of psychological and spiritual healing. The only *sure* sign of bodily healing came in the three visits to Greg Schelkun,[13] a psychic healer who reduced the tumor, which had grown in California, by one third. When I returned home to the stress and jolt of normal patterns the tumor began to enlarge again and is now larger than before. (It is also firmer, more solid with clearer boundaries and Dr. Leone is suggesting surgery may be an option.)

However, the medical delivery system can be destructive. I cannot change it. And I do not need to let it destroy me. These are strong words. And it feels good to say them. Doctors, nurses, secretaries, and technicians as well as patients get chewed up. It is not easy to go through the pain of transformation and self-examination, which is necessary if you do not buy the authority of the system and make your own choices. We are all part of that system. We've absorbed it into our beings. So it's very difficult to take the good and say no to the rest and to decide which is which. It's also lonely. And in the end I am the only one who can know what is useful for me. Joseph Campbell[14] reminds us that each knight leaving King Arthur's round table goes alone into the thicket of the forest to carve his own way to the Grail. I'm suddenly very aware of another deeper level of grounding and sureness as I write. A tremendous benefit of these letters, in addition to make connections with you, is the understanding I come to as I struggle to tell you what is true for me. And I see now for the first time and with tears that I can appreciate my cancer. Thank you Gabrielle, Greg, Tom, Cynthia, Dito, Paul and Andrew. I feel filled with gratitude and overwhelmed with understanding and joy. Can you hear my shouts? I'm not fighting it any longer. I am working with it. Thank you all. Thank you, Lord!!! Praise and thanks be to you. Thanks to you Itzhak, Sean and Leie, Elizabeth, Anne, Hugh, Tim, David, mother, father, brothers and sister, Sue, Sarah and to each of you unmentioned and important and loved who have helped me to arrive here. I'm trembling and need to go dance and sing. I'll return and finish.

One hour later:

Ten days ago I woke with an image of Peg, the winner, and suddenly heard the phrase "I'VE WON." Greg said to me that I'd won the Trojan War, now came the odyssey home again. Yes! That fits. My odyssey includes work with Gabrielle Roth,[15] whom I saw in New York and who gave me some crucial lessons in releasing my body and sounds as well as encouraging me to let out my colorful artist, my sensuous, feminine and adolescent selves, also my angry, snarling and feline ones. The journey will also include work with Itzhak Bentov[16] in Newton at Interface Healing Center who saw my swordswoman and power, as he met my High Self. And I continue with Cynthia, working to identify and enliven old, dull patterns and uncover new ones. No wonder I was bored and needed excitement. I've kept so much of me hidden, I hardly know who I am. I look forward to making my acquaintance.

And what about the trip to California? Each experience built on the next. I ran into Joe DellaGrote[17] at Esalen and got an unexpected Feldenkrais treatment at exactly the right time. Stan and Christina were not able to go to San Francisco so Cookie and I had a marvelous healing weekend with them. After doing some deep work on anger with Elisabeth, I was lying on the grass after supper when a white dove flew overhead, circled twice and disappeared into the dark. Jane Pretat's image, which she had shared with me, of a white dove struggling with a black object in my breast, and her concern for my strength in the struggle, seemed answered. Each one of us threw a pine cone into the fire at the end of our time with Elisabeth. And each then identified for our group of seventy what she was leaving behind. Remembering the lion in *The King of Hearts* who was so used to his cage he didn't leave when the door is open, I threw in my cage. As simple an event as my luggage making an impossible connection in the Los Angeles airport and my seat in the plane, where I could see the baggage cart arrive at the last moment with my purple sausage and briefcase, seems symbolic of the way events kept working out for me. There's no space to tell you details of my visit to Cookie and Disneyland, my Vassar reunion with three classmates thirty-five years later, my stay with Sabira, the channeling with Frida or the visit to the graduate school and therapy with Tom Yeomans[18] where I recognized that part of me which shrinks from becoming whole for fear that without hooks and eyes to attach to other people, I will not be loved. All are part of where I am now.

My love to each of you,

Peg

MARCH 9, 1979

Dear Friend: My cancer messages are flooding me these past few days. The explosion of understanding which I described in my last letter is in better perspective.

Cancer in my body is a symptom of dis-ease. As long as I do not correct the basic problems, the message will persist, and so I can use it as an indicator to know whether I have corrected the dis-ease. To allow cancer to be removed surgically or by radiation before I have changed and located the root problem means it will simply reoccur another way.

I did not pay attention when I had a hysterectomy for fibroid tumors, varicose veins, hemorrhoids removed, gained a lot of weight or any other symptom of disorder. This time the message is drastic enough to make me pay attention. As you know I have taken many steps toward a healthier, more harmonious life, on many levels.

I am so relieved to see cancer as beneficial rather than enemy. I'm glad to have a firm understanding. Identifying cancer as an enemy, separate from myself, and attempting to wipe it out, has never made sense to me. But how could I include and accept, let alone welcome, a life-threatening disease? Seeing it as messenger and teacher, I can. I know this is my work as therapist. It doesn't work to blame my parents for my troubles. I *can* use them as indicators of the problems I need to clear up in my own life.

It is so easy to imagine that we can eliminate our pain by trying to wipe out a source separate from ourselves onto which we have projected our hurt or anger. As a nation we have attempted to destroy Indians, Viet Cong, blacks. We still do not know whether we mean to punish or rehabilitate criminals. We lock them up, making it easy to pretend they do not exist. They are a social cancer and we are not close to getting their message! We treat them as enemy rather than as symptom.

Our medical system works valiantly to help us all perpetuate our mythology that it is good to avoid pain and death. And so now we have increasing numbers of people with cancer — an epidemic. Cancer is a slow disease. It gives the patient and all those involved with her the experience of facing death as a personal event. Instead of welcoming the opportunity, we have built hospitals and nursing homes to "care for" the person who is ill. The best of these institutions do care for their inmates, but most of us are then able to forget they exist and continue to believe in our own immortality as though we will not also die. We try to block this message, too.

This week I saw that I have walked with death all my life and never confronted him. Mary, my older sister, was just three years old when she died four months before my birth. I was born into a family grieving silently for one daughter and afraid that I too might die. It was never said directly to me. The message I got was: "Be careful or. . . ." and I know without knowing the end of *that* sentence is "or you will die, too!" Since Mary was never mentioned (in an attempt to avoid pain) death, for me, seemed to be total annihilation. She was totally gone from the life of her family, of those who loved her best. It had happened to her. It could happen to me. To believe that one dies not only in body, but seemingly in spirit as well, is devastating.

Yesterday, with Cynthia, I faced death and talked with him. It is a beginning and I learned much. Death, you are familiar. I will face and know you. You will come in your own time. You told me "not now." And as I experienced the closed door with richness, I will also live fully with the time I have. To confront my mortality directly is a powerful message of cancer.

Another is that I had wearied myself with a compulsion to serve others. So I literally and figuratively poisoned the source of the nourishment. Time now to nourish myself, since I will not nourish others much right now. I'm not seeing clients for at least two or three months. Two weeks ago I finished saying goodbye to everyone I had been working with. And I am enjoying my explorations into Peg, the artist. Following Gabrielle's suggestion, I've been painting in colors, filling in my body outline traced on wrapping paper. I use crayons, pastels, water colors and acrylics in bright colors and use large brushes, like a grade school child, and fill my large sketch pad as well. I am releasing sounds, noise and my big voice through a wide open throat. I will be seen *and* heard. As I express the sounds of cancer, of repressed and held in energy, I move with the sound. My buried selves emerge in a kind of theater as I work by myself in our big room. I continue to tune into my body and its needs in a walking meditation which is a beautiful tool of concentration that Cynthia learned in her vispassana work and then taught to me.

I am learning that I do have the inner understanding, which shines from my portion of the Light, to decipher my message. The message is a personal one, rooted in my being, in my history. For me the journey which has absorbed me since October has been one of discovery, struggle and chaos, of uncertainty, excitement and joy. I have trusted that I would find teachers. I have. My teachers are right for me. And my faith is that the process, the search, is my message to you.

Right now I am working with those healers who provide tools and feedback to enable me to magnify my faint sounds so that my dull ears can hear them. Ben Bentov shows me the healing as I learn to be in tune with a larger universe and its Creator. His book *Stalking the Wild Pendulum* explains the scientific connections and background that are immensely satisfying to my inquiring mind. I am also reading, at Avery Brooke's suggestion, Ernest Becker's *The Denial of Death*, which is another mind blower. Then last Tuesday I went to hear Bill Condon[19] describe his fascinating work on a frame by frame analysis of movies in slow motion showing the correlation between audible speech and the body movements of both speaker and listener. We *are* all in a dance together, in rhythm and connected.

As I too slow down and observe more closely, I hear my messages — slow down, Peg. Pay loving attention to your body and its needs. You know what to do. Trust yourself. Trust your intuition, your God within. And above all, acknowledge God as source *and* resource.

I am not well. I am healing. Your prayers and love make a big difference.

Thanks and love,

Peg

APRIL 11, 1979

Dear Friend: This letter written in Easter week seems appropriate. I've just re-read the seven letters covering the last six months. The moment in October when I lay still on the operating room table as Dr. Warshaw[20] confirmed the diagnosis of cancer seems very far removed from this sunny Spring day. I was plunged then into a new world view. I continue to be amazed at the richness, variety and life I have discovered, where I had expected stillness and death. Whether I visualize going deeper or higher, and often it seems to be both together, I keep on learning and re-learning the lessons of my life. A poster on the silo wall behind me quotes Proust: "The real voyage of discovery consists not in seeing new landscapes but in having new eyes." A friend, looking at the lifesize colorful pictures of Peg done on brown wrapping paper and pinned up on the large living room wall, saw that all but the most recent faces seemed like masks. "No, Beth — they are all masks." And I remembered a dream my son, Peter, told me about when he was quite young, of standing in front of a mirror removing masks one after another and wondering if he was there at all.

I am here and I am unmasking myself layer by layer with one set of new eyes each time. And as I do, I move to the light. Rev. Jim Diamond[21] sent me a book called *The Testimony of Light*, an electrifying, satisfying description of the world beyond death which fits in with my belief. The account makes it plain that we are, in both this world and the next, evolving toward higher consciousness, higher vibrational frequencies, toward light.

Two weeks ago I spent four days with the Episcopal sisters of the Community of the Holy Spirit[22], which helped me to ground my intellectual understanding in reality. Paul Stimson, a friend of Rad and Leila Ostby, introduced me to this interesting community. To be free to be part of the life of a loving, self-supporting, energetic group of sisters gave me a precious chance to review my life in the Lord's presence. I enjoyed the contrast of sisters in full habit, singing three services a day using music sung for centuries, who were worldly, practical and also very interested in psychic phenomena, in reincarnation and healing. I was renewed. My determination to build a new and deeper connection to Andrew is already bearing fruit. My sense of the Lord's presence in my life has been strengthened. Sister Lucia, wise and kind, is in charge of the retreat house. Mother Elise, principal of the school, as well as head of the community, chose the music, led the chapel service, often cooked meals and prayed especially for my healing. Both found time to spend with me as well.

The following week I was in Boston to work with Tom Yeomans, who had come East to teach a psychosynthesis course. I always work with him in some awe as he guides me toward my core. This time was no exception. I uncovered the terror which has bedeviled me for so long. Fear of annihilation, I've tripped over you for years and now I see you clearly. I had not realized before the grip and subtlety of your tentacles. I have raged at insensitive parents. Now I see how my fear of being forgotten when out of sight led me into all kinds of crazy behavior. My fear was so great I couldn't even connect to it at first when Tom asked me to look beneath my anger to see what I found. So I have continually made up marvelous logical reasons why the other person's behavior was explanation enough for my fury. As I saw the process, Tom invited me to explore what I would consider the opposite of being forgotten. "Remembered, loved, eternal" came to mind. "Find the specific phrase or word that fits for you," he said. Finally I realized that I am held "eternally in love." I went on to experience that wonder and then to experience my forgiveness of the human failings that helped to hide this Truth from me for so long.

I felt the presence of bright Light which increased and I was getting glorious. And I suddenly began to laugh. I had remembered the last fifteen minutes of Ben Bentov's day-long workshop at Interface last month. He traces the path of evolution from minute particles to larger and larger organizations of vibrative matter in the void until he gets to the largest of all. It's a Deva, a Beam of Light shaped like a tunnel, and invites his exploration. He enters and emerges from the tunnel to discover a figure, the God of Gods and sees . . . himself. I laughed, Tom laughed and I felt healed and well. I usually take myself *so seriously*, and I laughed harder than ever.

I'm not even going to try to sort out how *I* can be the source of my universe and at the same time know that God holds me eternally in love. I just know both things are true. And in this Easter season I am deeply moved by the events in the Bible and their parallel in my life. Christ's willingness to experience humanity as I do seems especially precious. And I have history and knowledge on my side as I go through the events of Holy week, knowing that Easter will come. Death itself cannot obliterate me.

Death seems far away today. Ben had suggested visiting Dr. Revici[23] in New York, who has developed a simple, self-administered drug without unpleasant or destructive side effects that is reducing the tumor in my breast. His associate Dr. Fishman[24] has shed some light on why simple remedies are so little regarded and in some cases frantically attacked. Cancer is a nine billion dollar industry in this country. Four billion is spent on research and the rest on treatment. If a simple remedy is found which does not require machinery of modern medicine to test and administer, the effect on this country would be comparable to the collapse of the auto industry. Even the best intentioned researcher has to be somewhat ambivalent when faced with news of a simple cure which works. And he will find as many logical reasons as I did to defend his position of adversary.

If such a cure is found, what will happen to insurance companies, to our social security system, all based on certain percentages of deaths? Each individual specializing in cancer within the system of medical delivery faces a termination of his life's work and a vast upheaval in his life. And as I know very well, most of us do not change until we have to. It helps me to see this perspective. I can understand this fear.

I do feel loved on many planes. Your support, encouragement and prayers have all been important to me.

I also love you.

Peg

MAY 4, 1979

Dear Friend: The puzzle of cancer and its cure continues to absorb my interest and attention. Three times now, once with chemotherapy, once with Greg Schelkun and most recently with Dr. Revici I have announced to you an improvement in my physical health only to have the process reverse itself as soon as I proclaimed it. "What is going on?" I keep asking myself.

A workshop with John Grinder and Judith Lozier[25] in Cambridge last weekend has helped me to provide some understanding. Many of you have written to me concerned that I somehow felt guilty or sinful as I emphasized my responsibility for my own health and cancer. I knew I did not feel guilty and I had trouble enunciating what was true. John's position is that we who come to be healed whether in mind or body have already tried as hard as we can with our conscious minds to correct the problem. If that had worked we would not be seeking a healer. Obviously then we are searching for a different way.

We must look to our unconscious intention below the level of our awareness. What is producing this destructive behavior whether it's overeating, getting cancer, or smoking? John's belief is that the *intention* of that buried part is in our best interest even though the *behavior* is not. Even more, this part is doing the very best it can to protect us but it is acting on outdated or insufficient information. Fulfilling this intention is a secondary gain. For example: a woman is able to lose weight until she gets close to her ideal when she immediately regains it all. Working with John, she learns that her unconscious part wants to save her marriage. Getting thin, she is unable to say "no" to men who are attracted to her and so she eats to save her marriage, the secondary gain in being overweight. The resolution comes as she is able to separate the good intention from destructive behavior and then chose new ways to meet a very worthwhile objective.

I went up to the workshop feeling very distressed and angry with Andrew. It is an old issue centering in my perception of his willingness and ability to care for me and love me. My head gives him the right to behave as he needs to do. My heart and gut get knotted up and scared that he finds other women more attractive and then I get angry. I want his exclusive attention. After returning from the weekend I begin to suspect that I gave myself cancer to buy his love. To get sick to get love and attention is an old familiar pattern in our family.

One *intention* of my cancer-causing-part is to have a more loving relationship to Andrew. It is a secondary gain. The *pattern* of cancer not only doesn't work but it is destructive and unacceptable to me as a way to meet the goal. Last weekend I learned ways to contact my unconscious part directly and it signified its understanding and agreement by increasing or intensifying certain signs in my body. An increased heart rate and quicker breathing were my signs of a "yes" answer which I could feel and my partner could observe. Both reactions sidestepped my conscious mind, which like most people's is very nosey. It wants to butt in, to know what is going on and to understand even though it has already failed miserably at making any helpful change with these tactics.

My unconscious part agreed to accept suggestions from my creative self about alternate, less destructive ways to meet its goal and found at least three new ways to do this. And it also agreed to implement the changes in my life. The best part is that my body kept responding "yes" and my mind didn't have the foggiest idea, at that time, what the intention was or what any of the alternative solutions would be. It has been exciting and wonderful to find myself acting in new ways or understanding the intention as my mind suddenly pops into focus when I notice that I am behaving differently. This explanation is basic to my newest understanding of medical treatment. Medicine works from a basis of scientific proof. You repeat the treatment in the same way with so many different people until you can show that in fifty, sixty, or ninety percent of the cases you get a remission of disease. I believe that *all* illness has secondary gains. Cancer destroys body cells. In order to have a high percentage of remissions, medicine has had to come up with powerful treatments not only to reverse cell breakdown but also to *override* our secondary gains. When the gains from having a life-threatening illness are not dealt with, many of us will find other ways to meet our intention which still feels so important. Cancer may recur or accidents will "happen." For others the experience of coming close to death and returning to life may meet the goal.

Without considering psychological and spiritual factors, medicine has no way to predict or understand who will respond to treatment. And it must also then lump all of those who do recover by following alternate healing methods as "spontaneous remission." At some time, this catch-all phrase will seem as ridiculous to us as "spontaneous generation" did to explain the presence of maggots.

I have meant for a while to tell you that had doctors offered me a ninety percent chance of cure I might never have explored alternate healing and you would not be receiving this letter. It is a cancer which doctors told me (if we pushed hard for the right treatment) gave me a thirty percent chance of surviving for five years, *with* treatment. That percentage did not seem to me enough to justify the discomfort and destruction of my own immune system which would follow in the wake of the treatment proposed. So I have chosen my own path and believe that I probably have still more to learn about secondary gains which I have not yet uncovered.

I do know that a major awakening since I wrote is understanding what it means to me to be of service. My earliest memory in therapy is of my birth at home where I was left crying at the foot of the bed while those present tended to my mother. I learned then that I was to serve her rather than be served or nourished by her. I have carried resentment for years at that lack of nourishment as well as a confused attitude towards serving others. I resented demands *and* believed that I should buy love by being helpful.

A psychosynthesis process which I learned last Summer helped me to sort this out last week. After writing down ten of my most important values on file cards, I rank ordered them. Going through the list from the bottom up I checked the order by asking this question: "Am I willing never to have any more # 10 in my life in order to fulfill my obligations to # 9?" Some of my values on the list shifted positions as I did this second step. The pair which touched me the most was *health for myself* and *my ability to heal others*. I want to be healthy and I would rather die than give up my ability to heal others. It was a real surprise and a moving experience to learn this about myself.

I value my ability as a healer above my own life. And once again a painful memory becomes a joyful source of learning. Yes, I am here as a healer. I am here to be of service not for gain, not for what I get back, but because that is what I am to do in this lifetime, this time around. And the lesson started the moment I was born.

So I will be starting to see clients again, a few appointments each week. And I will leave time for my painting. It isn't really me or them. It is us.

With my love,

Peg

MAY 29, 1979

Dear Friend: In the first letter I wrote to you I said about my cancer: "It makes sense to me to say with firmest love, 'Enough!' I will not let you destroy yourself and me. I will restrain and stop you." This week, working with Ben Bentov, I saw how I am to meditate to do that. He sees my cancer as a dark shadow. Both he and Dr. Leone have found it spreading toward my armpit and up toward my collar bone. The meditation is to imagine love as a pink healing color surrounding the whole area of darkness and compressing it. Darkness compressed enough turns to light. Or it may be easier to imagine coal pressed into a diamond. Either way I invite you to join me in this special way by sending your love to me, visualizing this process in my body. I will usually be meditating at 6:30 a.m. and 8:30 p.m. if you wish to join me in time, but any time you think of me, I will receive and appreciate your aid.

I am beginning to understand love not as an emotion but as having a whole separate quality. Here again Ben has been a tremendous help. The heart chakra in my chest is the source of love energy and is the first uniquely human chakra. The three lower chakras of the body are those we share with animals. Emotions originate in the lower ones and Ben's description of emotion as furry little animals with sharp teeth who rise and take over is vivid for me. I need to focus on love, on my ability to send love which comes from the heart. Sentiment, grief, rage, fear and even joy are emotions which can sidetrack this heart energy. I am learning not to be so emotional or easily toppled and am very surprised to discover that I am then able to be more loving.

A wonderful visit Saturday evening with Barbara and Jim Diamond has also been crucial to me. Both saw that my struggle is with living. My focus is on life and how to live. Even more I realized after they'd left that my question still is, "AM I WILLING TO LIVE?" The time will come when the question still is, "Am I willing to die, to let go?" but right now I am still struggling with my willingness to live and the possibility that my death is not so far away has sharpened my understanding of what it will mean for me to truly decide to live fully.

I also see why I have had such a terrible struggle with the medical community. They see the enemy as death and pain. I see it as inhumanity. Barbara and Jim made the distinction between being healed or being cured. Healed of course means being whole and the dictionary definition also talks of being restored to original purity or integrity. Cured, which has connotations for me of hides being tanned or beef-jerky dried and tough, by dictionary definition, means remedial treatment or the removal of disease or evil.

To be fully human is to live healed, whole, as well as one is able, and may have little to do with one's bodily state. To pay attention to the distress of my body and to cure that alone has felt inhuman to me. A friend, a nurse practitioner writing a paper for a course, interviewed me the other day. She asked me if anyone, anywhere, in my experience with the medical establishment had paid attention to my needs on an emotional or psychic level. As I thought back I was horrified and angered to realize that I had not once experienced within the medical delivery system the kind of attention which I, as a therapist, know to be basic to healing. Most people assumed that they already knew what would be comforting or helpful to me and followed their own ideas.

In many other cases my clearly stated wants were totally ignored. No one within medicine gave me any space by asking what I wanted or by asking whether what they were doing or saying was what I needed at the time. No one checked with me. I did get a fair number of rhetorical questions.

A friend gave me May Sarton's novel, *A Reckoning*, about a sixty-year-old widow dying of lung cancer. I recommend it to you. Toward the end of her life her doctor decides she has to leave her home where she has been coping with her death in familiar, loved surroundings to go into the hospital for some tests. Her hospital experience is painfully familiar to me. I have experienced myself or seen others as victims of each inhumanity she describes. But my concern is beyond this. It is not at all clear in the book what benefit she will derive from the tests. It *is* totally clear that the doctor will feel more comfortable in his treatment of disease with more information. But what will it do for her, the patient? That is not apparent. Nothing in her treatment changes after the hospital visit. And then immediately after that the doctor, also from kindly motives, arranges for her to be carried out to the garden for tea in her chaise lounge so that he can fulfill his promise that she will experience Springtime before she dies. She is a "good girl" and, not willing to disappoint him or those who will arrange it, she goes along with the plan when what she wants is to stay quietly in her room. No one checks with her since their own needs to help her are so great. They are also operating on outdated information, which could be so easily checked if anyone near her had asked what she wanted and been willing to give up their ideas of what would be best for her and to listen to hers. She also obviously had never learned that she had the right to ask.

One thing I have wanted and am taking steps to find is a closer relation to Andrew. We are seeing Leie Carmody, Sean's wife, to help us clear up the accumulated shit of thirty-one years together. When I worked in therapy with Tom Yeomans, I talked to my dead sister, Mary, who told me that I must let go of my buried anger and resentment, which was killing me. Leie helped me to see how extensive and also how subtle that anger is. It helped me to understand from Leie that as children we are all forbidden access to our sorrow and hurt. Haven't you heard as a child or said as a parent, "I only want you to be happy"? It is painful for a parent to know that a child is unhappy, so as children we learn to conceal our grief. Instead, we cover it up with anger, indifference, sarcasm or joking and so deny we even want what we miss so deeply.

I buried my sorrow, covered it with resentment, and then buried that as well. And it's all there visible to a discerning eye, which Leie has doubled in spades! I've been unpacking it not at Andrew this time but in a safe place where my raging will not add further hurt. I see more and more wisdom in Elisabeth Kübler-Ross' suggestion that every hospital, school, home or office, wherever humans live together, should have a "screaming room." Only I, realizing how enraged I have been, would call it an *outrageous* room.

As I write, I image what a different experience we Americans would have if, instead of being guaranteed, in our mythos and creed, the pursuit of happiness, we had been encouraged to follow the pursuit of growth. The ability to grow into wholeness, completeness, to be restored to integrity and purity. This has got to be what I mean when I pray, "Thy will be done. Thy kingdom come on earth as it is in heaven." And again in answer to Jim Diamond's question about my visualization of death, I realize that I see it as life lived more intensely, unencumbered by an earthly body. And since all I know now and much that I love now is here in this physical world which I have inhabited for fifty-six years, I am very reluctant to make a change. I haven't yet fully used all that I've got. And boy, am I learning!

With my love,

Peg

P.S. A friend has just called. Ben Bentov was on the plane which crashed in Chicago. I saw him four days ago and now know that we said goodbye then. I am still numb. I am sad around the edges and the center of my knowing is a celebration of the love and friendship we shared in these past few months. He told a friend before he left for the West that his work was done. I know it. He used so much of what he had and had shared his gifts generously with many people. Ben, *you* are glorious and I will miss you very much. I feel as though I am swimming in heavy surf. I get an insight and then immediately without a breather comes the test of my learning. And, damn it all, I'm still afloat.

JUNE 25, 1979

Dear Friend: I ended my last letter swimming in heavy surf. I still am. And my images come from my childhood on Narragansett Beach. There was a raft anchored out beyond the breakers and a line, buoyed with cork floats, between it and the shore. On calm days we used to hold on to the line to rest as we swam out. When the surf got huge I got bashed and battered if I tried to hang on. The only thing to do was to swim free, trusting my body and the water as I dove down under the turbulence of each breaking wave on my way out to deeper water. I remember a Sufi saying: "There are treasures beyond compare in the ocean. If you seek safety stay ashore." I also remember that I did not like to use a surfboard. I much preferred to body surf with nothing between me and the direct experience of the wave of bubbling, foaming, rushing water until I landed in the sandy shallow of the beach.

There have been many waves since I last wrote. I am getting used to Ben's death and letting him go. He told a friend on Thursday, before he took the plane Friday, that his work was done. A psychic friend who has made a connection with Ben since his death reports that Ben, who had extensive out-of-body experiences in his life, was out of his body before the crash. He helped the pilot guide the plane so loss of life would be minimal, and then he was able to help the confused, dazed souls of those killed to start on their journey to the Light. It sounds exactly like him. I heard these things and remembered that he had asked me if he could, as he said, "pop in on me" once or twice a week when we had our last appointment on that

Thursday morning. So I began to imagine him present whenever I felt needy. Last week I saw how tightly I was holding on and using his memory, as I had used his presence as though *he* could save me. My mind understood that if his work was done that meant with me as well, but my emotions wanted to hold and possess him. Now it's time to trust the healing power of my own body, and the spirit of God and Light which illumines it.

I have also had a strong experience of that core of Light within myself when Ann Philips, the leader of a healing workshop I attended in Maine, led me into a past life regression. In this past life I saw myself as a woman priestess healer in a temple. An important man who was also a special friend of mine was ill. I was chosen to be the healer and I was also in a political struggle with other healers so my success would mean power and personal glory. Of course with these mixed up motives I was not able to save him and he died. The parallel to Ben, whom I wanted to save and keep alive, as well as the parallel to healing myself in this life, is obvious. Ann asked me next to experience my own Light. I had an astonishing sense of a core of Light through my body which burst from my head like a crown and which moved me to tears and joy.

I also see very clearly the danger of my struggle with the medical establishment. I must let that go. Lou Leone said to me in the beginning that if I wanted to follow other methods he could not help me and that he would do the very best he could with the information and skill that he had. He has done this. To Lou and to each of you who are doctors who read this, I apologize. I have been quarreling with you, instead of realizing that my real quarrel has been with my fear. I have not dared to let go of the rope leading to the raft, of the ways that were healing in calmer weather, and to trust my body and Self to find other ways.

Fear is often the enemy of love — and, as Ben knew so well, love is the strongest force in the universe. Fear constricts, limits, and bounds me. I fear the future and I buy insurance. I fear death and go to doctors for solutions. I fear pain and I take aspirin or tranquilizers. I fear hell and I go to church and follow the teachings without question. I fear loneliness so get married and have children whom I cannot release to their own lives. And over and over I see how often fear is used to motivate and control us. I am getting sensitive to those people who would first scare me in order to sell me their remedy for my panic. From halitosis to communism, from anti-nukes to pro-lifers, I see that whether I agree with the cause or not I distrust those who sell a cure by painting a picture of the horror of being without it.

Andrew, David and I did an Actualization workshop together in Boston three weekends ago. I saw then that I have been "bravely facing cancer" with earnestness and determination. I woke up on Monday after the workshop realizing that I can also visualize cancer as the scariest ride in Disneyland! Disneyland is a marvelous metaphor for life. Each ride returns you back to the starting place from which you came. The scary ones can be very exciting and fun. The world *is* trustworthy and reliable. It will support me just as the ocean does and I am beginning to experience my life in this way. Fear need not be enemy, a means of control and manipulation, but rather an integral part of being human to be experienced and even enjoyed.

I have also been to visit Swami Muktananda at his ashram in the Catskills. And I know that I have literally met a saint. I did not recognize him when I was there. What I knew then is that I felt the joy, beauty and harmony of meditating early in the morning with hundreds of others, of chanting and singing, of meeting Baba in the afternoon session with more than 500 other people, of a marvelous, smoothly run organization open to all races, nationalities, backgrounds, occupations and ages and an invitation based on love with no trace of the pressure which comes from fear. Dito and I went together. He had spent time with Baba in California and was my bridge into this different world. Baba's message is not new: "Seek, find and understand your Self. God dwells within you as you." But when I came home I began to understand that I had met a human who had an awareness of God and an ability to kindle that awareness in me like no one I've ever experienced before. I will go back. I was somewhat concerned about how this would influence my participation in St. Peter's Church. Yesterday I discovered it only deepened it. Love does indeed expand boundaries, not shrink them.

And I send mine to you.

Peg

JULY 30, 1979

Dear Friends: Many people responded to my last letter. One

friend asked for particulars of my physical state and I do want you to know. The cancer in my breast continues to grow. My nipple has broken out into sores, somewhat smelly and weeping so I wear a bandage to absorb the stuff which reminds me of childhood bouts with poison ivy. Occasionally I have pricklings of pain in my breast or along my rib cage under my arm. My breast is probably twice as large as the healthy one.

Facing this question stirred me to go back to look again at my decision not to have chemotherapy or radiation and what I found angered me. I wrote in my diary, before I knew this diagnosis, and after I had been doing research and reading, "If this *is* inflammatory cancer, my decision will be easier since medical science does not have *any* answers. I will have to find my own route." It was, as you know, inflammatory AND I found myself wanting to believe in an easier route. I wanted to believe that doctors could cure me. I am angry at myself. But worse than that the doctors also wanted to believe they could cure me and I am even angrier at them.

Oliver Cope had suggested his book *The Breast* as a reference. I will quote from it: "Another of the most virulent of breast cancers, fortunately rare, making up not more than five percent of the cases, is the so-called inflammatory cancer. It spreads rapidly like infectious cellulitis or carbuncle. Surgeons have long known that attempts to cut it out only spread it farther. The effect of radiation is uncertain, and drugs thus far have failed to do more than temporarily stem its growth."

Rose Kushner, a medical reporter who developed breast cancer, researched treatments and then wrote a complete description of her findings in a book called *Why Me?* She often presented a different view than Dr. Cope. On this subject she agrees completely, stating, "Inflammatory cancer is virulent; surgeons are pessimistic and many pronounce it inoperable. Others will irradiate the breast to shrink the tumor and then do a mastectomy, but results have not been good." She continues, "The decision should be the woman's since doing nothing means certain, not probable, death."

Dr. Cope supplied me with a copy of my medical record when I requested it and I get further confirmation here. On the day of the biopsy he recorded little doubt that this is inflammatory carcinoma and the slides showed a "highly undifferentiated, invasive tumor with many lymphatics in the tumor area filled with tumor cells."

The record goes on to report his conversation with the oncologist who said, "Immediate chemotherapy would be advisable. *It hasn't been very successful.*" My italics for emphasis!

This is the same doctor who told me, when I asked what would happen if I did not take chemotherapy, "You will be back in two to three months *begging me* to help you," his voice ringing with hostility. I understand that he does not like to feel impotent. It angers me that he can share that ambivalence about the value of treatment with a surgeon and get enraged when I, not only a patient but also a woman, question his recommendation. Reactions like these, added to the difficulty I have had in getting straight answers especially when the answer is "we don't know," makes me *very* distrustful of any so-called information from medical practitioners.

The parallel to Three Mile Island jumps out. No one yet knows the long-term effect of the massive therapeutic radiation and chemical dosages used in the last few years. Both are carcinogens and carcinogens often do not show effects until ten to fifteen years later. These are not treatments to be agreed to lightly. And official reassurances to the contrary, *no one knows* yet what the long term effects will be. The unfortunate people who closely witnessed the first bomb tests in New Mexico are all dead now. Soldiers in Vietnam exposed to defoliating chemicals are getting cancer in disproportionately large numbers. People living near atomic power plants where there has been an accident are also developing cancer in alarming numbers. The residents near Three Mile Island are being assured they are unharmed. The official doctrine continues to be "conceal the damage."

I live in my body. I have a right to the facts. Unhappily, I still expect that a healer would let me know the facts to make my own choice. My belief in doctors is dying hard. And I am discovering other healers whom I can trust. I believe that I have given myself months of activity and normal life by changing my diet, working to heal my relationships, and especially to heal my estrangement from God.

The literature on the dietary cures of cancer consistently reports cessation of pain as the first noticeable effect when diet is changed. I imagine that these pain-free months have been a response to that shift in my own diet. And I am determined to find the way to respond to this disease in my body that will be effective. I do not know what "rapid spread" means. I do know that I am well, sleeping, eating and working comfortably and I do not believe that I would be doing any of these had I agreed to radiation. The future may indeed hold darkness, pain and fear. I know this and I am enjoying my life as each day goes by.

Many doctors have been upset by my words. In my last letter and again this week I acknowledge that some of my anger comes from my need to cling to medical truth as a savior. In going back to my sources to write this letter my anger flamed up. And my anger awakens echoes in many others who share with me their stories of deceit, lack of information and paternalistic decisions made by medical staff alone without involving the patient in any way even in the face of a clear request. My doctor friends believe either in a conspiracy or that they are scapegoats. So did Nixon as the horror and waste of the Vietnam war grew more and more apparent to the country while he in his isolation continued to believe that *he* alone knew what was the right action.

On a totally different note, I have been to an intensive weekend in South Fallsburg with Muktananda and will go back for a three-and-one-half-week course for the month of August. I debated a long while about being away from home for this period when my time with family may be short. Andrew helped me to decide. "Peg," he said, "this sounds more right for you than anything I've heard you talk about." And then he blew me away by saying, "If three weeks now will improve the quality of our remaining time together, no matter how long, then it is worth it." What a lovely man and reaction!

I begin to understand from my experience at the ashram that God is truly closer than breath, nearer than hands or feet and that I will be all right whether I live or die. And this understanding stretched back into history. In an intensive weekend Baba circulates through the meditation hall and touches each of the 700-800 people personally in just the right way. After his touch, I found myself breathing out forcefully with a sense that I was filling the upper part of my lungs for the first time in my life — my breath became quieter and began to make a funny little clear whistle in my teeth. I recognized the sound. As a child I lay in bed at night as the sun went down hearing the wind blow through my window screen making exactly the same noise. I knew then that, had I ears to hear, God was with me singing me to sleep. The wind he created played the harp he created and I am the child he created whose ears were opened to receive.

India is a land of spiritual expertise just as we are a land of technological development. Baba has reached the goal of being one with God which gives him the capacity to be with each of the hundreds in his presence. The place Ben Bentov is talking about in his book (*Stalking the Wild Pendulum: On the Mechanics of Consciousness*) of being at one, everywhere and nowhere, is where Baba lives. Each one in that room sensed an individual and personal connection to him. There have been many healings around him. He does not emphasize the physical ones, although they occur frequently.

My cancer seemed somewhat less swollen as I left the ashram. I saw in what Baba calls *shakti*, or the *kundalini*, touching and changing lives. I'd call it the Holy Spirit of Pentecost. The important thing to me is that Muktananda not only can talk about it, he is what he says. This divine energy or power can consume our impurities whether of mind, body or spirit. And I intend to give it the best chance I can to do so. My doubts, my unwillingness to trust, my anger suppressed into cancer or beginning to emerge can all be consumed if I will let them go.

With love to you,

Peg

SEPTEMBER 8, 1979

Dear Friends: Three and a half weeks of immersion in life at Baba's ashram and taking the basic course in Siddha Yoga have changed my perspective dramatically. The physical improvement which I had hoped for did not occur. In fact the deterioration continues. Once again none of my expectations were realized. And, true to form, I was surprised instead by what did happen.

The major shift for me is a forceful acknowledgement of my will and intentions to live. Before I left I was working with Leie Carmody and told her that I wanted to live to see and know Peter and Anne's baby, due in February. Just before going to the ashram I got a call from Peter to say that Anne had miscarried which is very sad as it is the second time they have been disappointed. But the message I began to understand for myself in this loss is that my reason for living must not be located in anyone or anything outside of myself. And I've found that reason.

All of my life I have been able to get by and to do well without exerting my full energy and commitment. I did very well in school, married, raised a family, completed important jobs in the community, became a therapist, made many friends and never once pushed to my limit. When I studied the philosophy of Siddha Yoga and experienced the beginning of the spiritual path I began to grasp that here is a challenge worth every ounce of determination, learning ability and perserverance that I possess. I also understood that the grace bestowed by Swami Muktananda and my own self-effort are the two wings of the bird of spiritual progress. They must grow in balance. As the wings lengthen, my pace will quicken. Right now, I am taking baby steps and feel in this business of learning meditation as though I'm back in kindergarten again.

It is reminiscent of my first workshop in Esalen Institute in 1969 when I watched intrigued, astounded and in awe as the power of Gestalt therapy worked wonders in the lives of the participants who plunged in while I waded on the edge. Baba is a master therapist and his skill is knowing exactly what is right for each person. The ashram life and discipline provide surroundings where growth is stimulated and fostered all the time. The lessons abound. The goal of taking responsibility for oneself, for becoming fully aware, of paying attention to process are similar to therapy. The depth at which it happens — like the people who simply decide to stop smoking and do so without trauma or the way in which my death wish dropped away — surprises me. I don't see the machinery. The results are startling.

I, for instance, had never been fully conscious of how much I have longed for a really worthwhile challenge. I uncovered my want to push with all my strength and energy. And even that's not quite it. I want a goal worth devoting my life to. Baba would say that every goal short of union with God is eventually found to be inadequate. I am beginning to believe this, to understand what is means to see that this is true whether I get there in this lifetime or in a future one.

Chakrapani is Baba's astrologer, who is not only psychic but also a skilled astrologer and a practical man. He read my chart and saw me living into my eighties as a productive useful woman healer, first enlarging my healing capacities and then in the last seventeen years becoming a lecturer, author and teacher. This attractive picture adds further impetus to my intention to live to enjoy it.

But meanwhile I saw my physical disease enlarging and kept

wondering how under the sun this rosy picture would come about. On returning home I first retreated into a shell of protectiveness. I felt the shift into a normal busy house as terribly intrusive, and I had no protection at all. I felt like a soft-shelled crab scuttling about looking for inviting crannies. But in four days I discovered lots of energy and began putting pieces together in my head as I emerged to tackle my world and my responsibilities.

I have been working on my health with Angelica Redleaf, a chiropractor, using a modified Dr. Kelley diet. A friend at the ashram who knew something of his methods asked me what parts I was using. Her question made me realize that I was not even still following the modified diet. What a half-assed way to work! So I took up a recommendation Angelica had made months ago and decided to do the full program. I called the nutritional counselor in Little Compton and have begun the program. It involves massive doses of dietary supplements and various cleansing routines.

Leie Carmody and I agreed yesterday that it's perfect for what ails me. The requirements are finicky. Some supplements are taken one half hour before the meal, some with the meal, some afterwards and some every two hours during the waking day. Daily cleansing enemas are required to flush out the toxins as the supplements begin to wash them from their tissue-locked locations into circulation. The program is not cheap. It requires large doses of time, attention, energy and money. Progress will be related to my willingness to follow a routine for my own benefit. It's quite a cure for my lack of commitment.

Then a few nights ago my nephew, Tad Staley, was here and told me of work he is doing with a young man in Boston to trace the roots of disease back through various lives to the initial source. I went to see him yesterday, liked him and will also start seeing him.

Swami Muktananda, Dr. Kelley and Richard Greene are an unlikely trio. All three believe in working toward a balance of health rather than curing the symptom. Baba urges people not to get sidetracked by visions of lights, hearing beautiful sounds, by learning to see auras, having out of body experiences or even developing healing powers, which all can happen in the process of Siddha meditation. The goal is to discover and learn to live in that inner Self where one knows the bliss of being at one with God. Positive and negative actions are in total balance in that space. Baba lives there. He can teach us to do so, too.

Dr. Kelley says that full physical health is possible when we get our body balanced. Do not be sidetracked by the elimination of obvious symptoms. Stay with the program until you discover the full health you may never have known. He had cured his own cancer and many others. And he, too, can teach me. Richard is also eager to get to the source or root. He wants to see each person uncover the decisions which they have made which restrict lives and to have the opportunity to change them.

So now I meditate early each morning for an hour, often from 5 to 6 a.m., which is meditation time at the ashram. If you want to meditate at another time please call and I'll make plans to be here with you. I need practice and companions add power. I will pursue the full dietary regime of Dr. Kelley and will work with Richard as long as it is profitable for us both.

Also on October 23, Swami Paramananda will come here to Saunderstown to lead an introductory program in Siddha meditation. She is one of the few women swamis and I am glad that she will be here to lead us in chanting and meditation as well as to speak about her own experiences.

This program will give you an introduction to this powerful type of meditation and as Swami Muktananda expects to be in Boston in November, will give you a taste in case you want to have more contact with him. I do.

I am not a follower. I am "looking and seeing" and intend to spend more time with Baba when I can arrange it.

My love to you,

Peg

NOVEMBER 1979

Dear Friend: Several of you have written concerned that my silence is not a good sign. You are right. The past few weeks have been dark. I have been very wiped out, feeling low in energy, discouraged and in pain, which has been steady though not always intense. I am coming to understand how debilitating it is to live with constant pain, since even when it's below the level of my conscious awareness, it's there dragging me down. At the same time I continue to learn and understand my life and its events.

Last month I was leading a Gestalt training group in an exploration of our individual life supports. I borrowed from what I've learned from Dito of tai-chi and was teaching by demonstrating a way to connect to our physical bodily support in the world as we shifted our weight totally from one foot to the other. Then I invited the group to be still and asked each member to allow an image to rise which would signify what support means to her. Each of us then drew our image and shared them with others in the course. My image was of a sawhorse, sturdy, massive and purple, that is almost cut in two by a large red saw with a bright green handle. I wanted to push the image away, to rationalize that I was *not* going to cut my support in half, that I had recognized the danger and stopped. But I could not maintain my denial.

And then suddenly I saw that if you do cut a sawhorse in two you end up with two tripod-like pieces which are more flexible and adaptable and capable of many different constructions. *And* I do not know what the new structure will look like. In the chiropractor's office is a sign, "Let go and let God." Dito had suggested when he was with me one evening when I felt especially low that I use Baba Muktananda's mantra for support. His suggestion is right on. But the mantra that fits for me is not Baba's but "Thy will be done." I have managed my life all my life. I don't even know what it would be like to give up control. I am learning to accept gifts of love and support — but how quickly I snatch back my need to make plans, to organize, to make *sure*.

Another huge piece fell into place two weeks ago when I woke understanding that my need to govern my life has much deeper roots than the belief that the way to be loved is to be sick. For me the way to be loved is to be dead!

I reached this conclusion as an infant. My family, grieving for the death of a daughter and yet not willing to face and work through the pain of loss, the guilt and fear, was caught in a trap. Pretending not to, they were unable to let go of their focus on a dead daughter. As a child trying to understand family rules, I saw that the person who received attention, who was the focus of love and concern, was dead. So the conclusion seemed obvious to my child mind. To be loved in this family you have to be dead. And so my hunger for love led me to fit carefully into the mold. Be dead, obedient, quiet, don't do what you want, in fact don't even let yourself know what you want. Anger is certainly much too *lively*, so kill off your spirit, conform to family rules. Then my sister Jane was born a year and a half later. She is energetic, fun-loving, mischievous, naughty, and that seemed to work for her so even if I'd been able to switch and try a new model, the lively, outgoing role is already filled.

Soon, of course, that whole decision, and all its machinery, was buried beyond my reach but the effects are powerful. Since I last wrote I've also read Lawrence LeShan's *You Can Fight for Your Life*, on his psychiatric work with terminal cancer patients, many of whom had total remissions of disease. Dr. LeShan identifies a common trait among cancer patients that they have somewhere along the line buried a desire or stifled an urge to express themselves in the world. Despair in believing that there is no way out results in cancer. Their statement would be: "I cannot be who I want to be unless I am willing to relinquish love and support from others, so I might as well be dead." I agreed with his premise and I admired the patients he describes who knew what it was they had wished to do so long ago. I did not even know *what* life meant to me. I squelched so much so young that I had no images of what "Peg alive" looks like. It's almost a contradiction in terms and what an incredible relief to have a sense now of where the task lies.

I did discover one thing: I need to say "no." This year I am saying "no" to my responsibility for Christmas, and to the frantic overproduction that has always accompanied the holiday. I have told my family and I will share with you that I am not going to do anything about the holiday. I will not buy, wrap, write, make, cook, decorate, shop or plan for Christmas. The depth of family expectation about my Christmas role came vividly clear when I told Andrew my intentions. "O.K." he said, "We'd better sit down this evening so that you can tell me what you want me to get for the boys."

"Andrew! You didn't hear me. I am not going to plan, to spend any money or time. Whatever anyone else truly wishes to do, feel free, but I am not going to do anything. I may want to cook a turkey and will know that a week before. But if you want to give presents do it exactly as *you* wish."

I feel excited, slightly rebellious, and eagerly await the least stressful holiday I've spent in years. And I know that this is a major decision for life, not death. I have also gotten welcome support from one doctor for my decision. In the last two weeks I've been attending

Dr. Bernie Siegel's cancer support group in New Haven. What a blessing and a relief to find a medical doctor, and a surgeon at that, who believes that the outcome of disease rests more with the patient's will to live than with the specific details of prognosis or treatment. He works within a medical setting and still he works to help patients make the life changes which will, as he says, "turn your life around and heal cancer."

I still have trouble believing that I will be healed of cancer. I am, as I reported to you last time, working with Dr. W.D. Kelley's dietary program. It involves both diet and supplements of enzymes, minerals and vitamins tailored to my body type and based on information from an extensive questionnaire I filled out as well as laboratory tests. There are many people who have healed themselves through following this program just as there are those whom I know who have been healed through faith, through using wheatgrass, various herb teas, as well as chemotherapy and radiation. I know that all these healings have taken place. I still have not found the route to my own health.

In talking to a friend recently I realized that one thing I lack is a midwife for my process. A midwife is a specially trained assistant. She has professional training, knows alternatives, and is willing to facilitate, support and encourage me in the dark places. Most of all she has faith in a process of healing and would encourage me to find my own path back to health. I have been working closely with Jean Groenjes, the midwife at New Beginnings, Inc., our Birth Center in Warwick, and realize that the tact, skill and talents she offers to new parents seeking the best possible way to bring their baby into the world is exactly what I need as I continue to search for healthy Peg.

And if my path is to be through the transition of death, then I also want a midwife in that process. We do not even have a title for the position I'm describing, although occasionally nurses and, even more rarely, doctors, are able to fill the role.

How wonderful it would be to have my midwife who could let me know that the process was indeed going ahead well. Or that we had reached the point where different intervention was needed. As I write I realize that my analogy breaks down since we do not even have the information to begin to answer the questions I'm raising. Someday we will — but even on today's level I know that it was the nurses in the clinic at the hospital who showed me how to take care of my wound. And that it was my friend Genie Schweers who suggested that pain medication would give me more energy as it reduced the stress of resisting the constant drain of hurt. Either of these suggestions, both almost by chance, by-products of events in my life, would have been cared for by my hypothetical midwife to cancer. And both have been invaluable in increasing my comfort.

I am involved in a process that is most similar to my experience of giving birth. Whether I live or die, I am in a major transition. I want competent professional helpers, who do not lose sight of me as a person. I want to be respected as an intelligent participant in my own process. Time will eventually pass and the results of transition will be evident. Until then, patience and trust are required.

It is totally evident to me now why I started the birth center and why I needed to do all that I could to assure other young human beings that their new beginning on this earth would be attended to with as much love and caring as possible. And if I survive this experience with cancer it is equally clear to me that I will work to implement the concepts about support and help which I know to be crucial at birth, so that they be extended and implemented for those facing possible death. And that this is especially important for those people, with a life-threatening illness, who choose to explore avenues outside of the narrow, restricted band of treatments presently sanctioned by the medical profession.

And if I don't survive to do this work, I want those of you who read this and who respond to my words to do what you can to make my dreams a reality.

With my love,

Peg

DECEMBER 4, 1979

Dear Friend: Peg has left us. She died peacefully at 2:00 p.m. Monday, December 3, with most of us at her bedside. The last days and hours of Peg's life, her death, and our time together afterwards have had special meaning to those of us who were with her. Thus, this letter has been written by several of us who wanted to share some pieces of that experience with you. It comes with love from all of us.

Peg died with a little smile on her lips. After a few necessary details were taken care of, we all, nine of us, washed her, oiled her, and dressed her. Then, with Nigel Andrews from St. Peter's Church, we had a short prayer service at her bed. I know now far more what is behind many of the rituals for the dead. These simple acts of service seemed to release a tremendous block in me and I found it easier to let Peg go, although I noticed later that it took gentle prodding from Cookie to get me to call the undertaker, a job I chose to do myself for not-so-clear reasons.

The last week was tough. Peg had been taking Percodan off and on for about three weeks. One day she twisted her hip and the fight went out of her. She still got in the bathtub herself for a time; then, with help. Jean Boyd gave us three mornings a week about then and we had a visiting nurse the other days. About mid-week her speech became difficult — lost words, partial sentences — and finally, communication was possible only through little signs. We know that to the end she knew what was going on around her and we could tell what pleased or displeased her, particularly the latter. Rolling her to change bed linen or massage her back caused her pain and we dreaded that time. As late as Friday, she burst out with clear and idiomatic English on one of these occasions. Looking back, it is amazing to me how little pain relief we used, and, with one exception, I think she had enough. That one occasion was after we had switched to morphine sulphate by injection. She had had one shot Saturday noon, then Monday morning she seemed to be in pain and I finally, at 1:30 Monday morning, gave her another. There was a lot of stuff in my way, mostly a fear of being the one to push her over the edge. A second shot six hours later was easier.

There were many indications of her awareness and perhaps the most striking was her agitation when Peter, Anne and Hugh came into the house late Sunday. She fretted and moaned more than usual until they went into her room, then quieted down immediately. The circle was closed.

Wednesday morning we are celebrating her life at a small service, then on Saturday we will have a memorial service here in the house for any who care to come. Peg asked for this last and specified the general ground rules and music. Anyone may speak, sing, or pray and she wants played Canon in D by Pachelbel, "Go Up to the Mountains" by the Weston Monks and the Alleluia Chorus.

There seems to be more of me in this letter than I like. However, I want you to know that, though tired, I am peacefully sad yet thankful that Peg's pain is over.

Your letters to her meant a lot to her. Bless you for your support.

Andrew

□ □ □

As a child I would lie alone in my room fantasizing what would happen when my parents died. In my fantasies Peg was usually the first to die or they both died together in some sort of disaster. These images were always accompanied by my anguished crying which would suddenly stop as I imagined myself pulling the family together and taking care of my younger brothers.

The tears have come and return frequently. However, I am not alone nor do I have to save my family. We have become close in these days, and I express our gratitude to all of you for your love and support. So many have helped.

On Friday we went out and bought quantities of food to supply us through the weekend as we anticipated an involved time and the gathering of the family. We have barely touched it as all of you have taken such good care of us, sending casseroles, loaves of bread, and fruit. You are all blessed friends. Dad joked at one point that he did not know that manna was so heavy. Thank you.

I arrived from Mexico City early Friday morning. Peg was lying in her bed, breathing hard and very hot. I wanted desperately to save her, yet there was nothing to do. I have never felt so impotent in my life. She was beyond my power and I could only pray for her and hope for a miracle.

It was hard accepting that she would die, yet remembering her mantra, "Thy Will Be Done," I felt sure she was well prepared. Her life here was in good order which is so typical of Peg.

Peg often talked about the need for support in her life and in her last letter she wrote of the need for a midwife for the process she was in. On Friday I was sitting with her wishing that I knew some ceremony to help Peg in her death. I wanted her to remember to follow the light, the light she had seen in her work with Ben Bentov and which had given her so much joy. An hour later Olivia Hobitzelle showed up at the house for an appointment that she had made with Peg before Peg became very sick. It was a tremendous gift. In her meditation, we worked with Peg to focus on and to merge with the light. As we worked, we became peaceful and Peg's breathing evened out. Dad and I repeated this meditation often, and we were doing it as she died.

On Saturday, Hugh and Lorli, Peg's brother and sister-in-law, arrived. They are beautiful people whose faith in Christ shines through them. We prayed for Peg and for ourselves that God would ease our grief.

The process with Peg has been sad, and very beautiful, full of transcendence. I pray she has found the support in God that she has sought. My cousin, Tad Staley, sent us a quote which says it most beautifully:

I am standing upon the seashore. A ship at my side spreads her white sails to the morning breeze and starts for the blue ocean. She is an object of beauty and strength, and I stand and watch her until at length she is only a ribbon white cloud where the sea and the sky mingle with each other. Then someone at my side says, "There! She's gone!" Gone where? Gone from my sight, that is all. She is just as large in mast and hull and spar as she was when she left my side, and just as able to bear her load of living freight to the place of destination. Her diminished size is in me, not her, and just at the moment when someone at my side says, "There! She's gone!", there are other voices ready to take up the glad shout, "There! She comes!"

Let Peg's death be a reminder of Christ's victory over death. May peace be with you all.

Dito

□ □ □

On Monday night, we four, David, Tim, Dito, and Cookie, sat up together in the living room for a long time. Dito and David read aloud; earlier, we had rubbed backs and necks to allay the tension and exhaustion of the day. As we finished the story, Dito fell asleep. Tim and David and I were restless and wanted to walk outside.

We emerged from the studio and the night took our breath away. It was a full moon — Dito and I had somehow known that Peg's crossing would come with the full moon. We had not guessed what it would mean to us, the feeling of that night. There was an unaccustomed brilliance and clarity to the sky. Stars and moon bathed the trees and path and houses with silvery radiance, like soft white moss. Our hearts leaped up, as if to hug the moon. The crispness in the air filled us with our own aliveness, not with the feeling of death but of ultimate aliveness. We reached into the night and it touched us back, surrounded us with light. The words we had spoken to Peg inside were given back to us in that moment: breath and light become one.

We knew in that beautiful night that Peg was not only accepted but welcomed with the finest celebration the heavens could give. It seemed to us that it was her light energy, clear radiant light, which made the night so brilliant. We walked and breathed and laughed and hugged together and knew without saying that everything was perfect.

David and Cookie

□ □ □

When I think of Peg or Mom, I feel peace and gratefulness. I remember Christmas years ago. . . . All the family around the tree opening presents, laughter, love and family; opening a present from Mrs. Santa that would be something wonderful — a soccer ball or a tricycle with a "Mom-made" clown on it. Mom would look over at me with a twinkle in her eye and a smile on her lips and say, "What did you get?" Both of us knew that she knew. My heart would overflow with love and thanks. That is what I feel now.

The strength and courage, her caring and love will always remain with me as a reminder of what all of us can be. To live with the openness with which Mom lived seems a worthy goal. She was and is my Mother and I love her and thank her for the gifts she gave and the lessons we learned. Lastly, I want to thank you for your love and support of Peg and us, her family. You have been a comfort for which we are grateful. May our hearts be one .

Tim

□ □ □

I would like to share a verse from the Bible which was set to music. It was a favorite of Peg's, the one she always sang in tune:

He gave me beauty for ashes,
the oil of joy for mourning,
the garments of praise
for the spirit of heaviness.
I am a tree of righteousness,
a planting of the Lord,
and Jesus is glorified.

Paul

☐ ☐ ☐

Our love to all of you,
Andrew, Dito, Hugh, Tim, Peter and Anne,
David, Cookie, Paul and Nancy

P.S. The memorial service was beautiful (an inadequate word in this instance). Two hundred friends crowded into the house to share their love for Peg with us and many spoke of what she had meant to them. Elizabeth Trapp came down from Vermont to sing her songs of praise of the Lord. What a lovely woman.

Shirley Sheldon, Norma Smayda, Rose Marie Lindgren and Lynn Knauss outdid themselves with food and decorations. We have little knowledge of who did all the baking, but our appreciation is great. Even the trashman added his share by arriving right in the middle of the service, bringing the earthy clanking of reality.

As a diamond, Peg had many facets and this service was a montage of these on a background of love.

A.

(May 1979 – January 1980)

---

[1]JACK DOWNING — Gestalt therapist, San Francisco, California.

[2]AVERY BROOKE — Meditation teacher, Noropon, Connecticut.

[3]MICHAEL SCHACTER — Medical doctor, Nyack, New York.

[4]CARL AND STEPHANIE SIMONTON — Authors of Getting Well, they run a cancer counseling clinic in Fort Worth, Texas which, Peg says, "is the major resource" in this country. He is a medical doctor, she is a psychotherapist.

[5]STAN AND CHRISTINA GROF — He's a psychiatrist and LSD researcher. She teaches yoga. They live in Big Sur, California.

[6]ELISABETH KÜBLER-ROSS — The psychiatrist and author who has worked with dying people since the Fifties. Her Shanti Nilaya Center is in Escondido, California.

[7]CYNTHIA FINN — Therapist, teacher of meditation, Lexington, Massachusetts.

[8]SEAN CARMODY — Therapist, Massachusetts.

[9]JOHN GRINDER — Co-author with Richard Bandler of The Structure of Magic.

[10]ANGELICA REDLEAF — Chiropractic, Providence, Rhode Island.

[11]ANNE VARNA-GARIS — Family therapist, Providence.

[12]MENUCHIN — Teaches family therapy, Philadelphia, Pennsylvania.

[13]GREG SCHELKUN — Psychic healer, San Rafael, California.

[14]JOSEPH CAMBELL — Professor of mythology at Sarah Lawrence. Author of Myths Men Live By.

[15]GABRIELE ROTH — Teacher of dance and movement in New York City.

[16]ITZHAK BENTOV — Medical inventor studying energy, deceased.

[17]JOE DELLA GROTE — Teaches Feldenkrais method of body movement in Amherst, Massachusetts.

[18]TOM YEOMANS — Teacher, Synthesis Graduate School, San Francisco, California.

[19]BILL CONDON — Researcher, Boston, Massachusetts.

[20]DR. ANDREW WARSHAW — Surgeon, Massachusetts General Hospital.

[21]REV. JAMES DIAMOND — Episcopal Chaplain, University of Minnesota.

[22]COMMUNITY OF THE HOLY SPIRIT — Brewster, New York.

[23]DR. REVICI — Cancer, medical researcher in Trafalgar Hospital, New York City.

[24]DR. FISHMAN — Acupuncturist, New York City.

[25]JUDITH LOZIER — John Grinder's partner.

Roger Sauls

Asking After My Own Light

I find it hung upside down on John's tiny back
Porch, a luminous egg sac burning through
A harsh white collar. There is no need to shut
The door because it is the middle of May and
We like the sharp smell of wild onions drifting like
Needles across the dark back yard. John
Says his garden needs rain, just enough to pepper
The leaves of the tomato plants that have started to
Turn brown. He says a 25-watt bulb will last until
Winter, the same as the luna moths stitching
Dusty threads in and out of the phosphorous light.
I know now the slow turning of a late sky
Is the only light I understand. I think of the small
White porch I have to pass through on my way
To my car. How tomatoes somehow form inside a tight
Yellow blossom. John says it's late. The silent
Highway leads me back through moving cones of headlights.
John's bare arm reaching up to give the bulb a single,
Quick twist.

(June 1976)

Stephanie Matthews-Simonton is a psychotherapist and the director of counseling at the Cancer Counseling and Research Center in Fort Worth, Texas. What she has to say — about how we make ourselves sick, and how we can become well — applies to us all.

With her husband, Dr. O. Carl Simonton, a radiation oncologist and the medical director of the center, she has focused for the past seven years on the emotional needs of cancer patients. She developed the center's intensive psychotherapy program, which has become a model for similar centers across the country. At the clinic, people are taught that the mind and the body are inseparable.

The Simontons are the authors of Stress, Psychological Factors, and Cancer, *and, more recently,* Getting Well Again, *which describes how someone's reaction to stress and other emotional factors can lead to disease, and gives detailed instructions to overcome those patterns.*

The address of the Cancer Counseling and Research Center is 1300 Summit St., Suite 710, Fort Worth, Texas 76102.

What follows are excerpts from a recent talk, and an interview.

— Ed.

On The Mind and Cancer

Stephanie Matthews-Simonton

I n 1972, two emerging theories shaped the work I'm now doing. The first, coming from early biofeedback studies, indicated a person could be taught to mentally influence aspects of his or her physiology that we used to think were outside of our conscious control. Such things as heart rate, blood pressure and blood flow could be influenced by the person himself. At the same time, an old theory explaining the development of cancer re-emerged. Called the surveillance theory, it proposes that we probably all develop malignant cells a few hundred if not a few thousand times in our lives, that through exposure to carcinogens, our own genetic predisposition, and a number of other factors, the body's individual cells may undergo changes. In addition, the body has a very effective defense mechanism, the immune sys-

It's not reasonable to expect people on their deathbeds to exhibit coping strategies and styles of behavior that they've not had a chance to practice.

tem, that recognizes and destroys minimal malignant cell development, and rids the body of those cells without our ever having any clinical evidence of malignancy, either walling off the disease process, or destroying it entirely.

That theory caused a considerable shift. Frequently, up until then, an oncologist's opinion was that in order for a person to be cured of a malignancy, every malignant cell had to be destroyed, or else one could break loose, lodge somewhere else, and a new malignancy would grow. Suddenly, more recognition was given to the fact that within the person's body was a defense mechanism which apparently had broken down prior to the diagnosis and allowed the cancer to develop, and that while it was important to destroy as much of the gross cancer as possible, in order to effect a cure, it was also important to pay heed to the body's innate ability to regain control of the disease process. Immunotherapy and other ways to artifically restimulate a person's immune system have grown in number in the last few years.

Out of those two theories — the idea that a person's immune system was a vital factor both in the development of the disease and in the outcome of the disease, and the idea that a person is able to influence physiological conditions — came the original theory and a question: if a person can influence his heart rate, blood pressure and blood flow, can he influence his immune system, thus helping to effect a response to treatment and recovery?

In 1972, we didn't have the technology, and today we still don't have the technology that would allow us to apply a pure biofeedback model to cancer. We don't yet know quite which components of the immune system are most involved in the cancer battle, but more important, we don't have the technology to measure the activity of the immune system on a conclusive basis. I don't think we're very far away from when we can give a person instantaneous feedback as to what thoughts, feelings and behaviors correlate with increased or decreased activity of the immune system. We can then much more readily teach people how to take conscious responsibility for their own healing processes.

When we first began, we found that those patients most able to influence internal conditions used some form of visualization — seeing a picture in their minds of what it was they wanted that body condition to do. That didn't make as much sense to us in the late

Sixties and early Seventies as it does now. Certainly, if we look back on the old hypnosis literature, we see much evidence that visualization plays a role in changing internal processes. As more of the split brain work has come out, we realize that the hemisphere of the brain that influences autonomic processes probably thinks more in pictures than in the logical linear expressions to which we are accustomed.

Out of that came the relaxation and visualization technique. We asked patients to take fifteen to twenty minutes, three times a day, to relax as much as possible, shut their eyes, close out the external world, create a quiet, passive scene inside to focus their attention, and then to visualize three things: their cancer, however it seemed to them symbolically; their medical treatment destroying their cancer; and finally, to see their body's own immune system continuing to destroy the malignancy and restoring their body to health.

It was either our blessing or our curse to have a highly dramatic experience with the first patient. I suspect had it not been for that first patient, we would have become discouraged in the early years and would not have continued on with our work. He was a sixty-one-year-old gentleman with a far advanced cancer of the throat; he was literally choking and starving on his own tumor. He lost weight, was down to ninety-eight pounds. Because of the location of his tumor, his age, and general condition, at first it was decided not to treat him with radiation because of the side effects. But because of his insistence and other factors it was decided to give him a low dose of the radiation to see if it would make him more comfortable. Certainly, he didn't seem to be a patient with whom we had much to lose. We shared the ideas with him about people being able to influence their own physiology through visualization and he grasped them readily. During the six weeks that he was treated, a number of remarkable things happened. His tumor responded readily to treatment, which is not unusual in the face of the radiation. What was more unusual was that he showed almost nothing in the way of the side effects that we would expect, particularly considering the location of his tumor. He began gaining weight, feeling better. In fact, he asked that his treatments be set up for a single morning so that he could go fishing the rest of the day. Another factor that began to be significant and unusual with him, and somewhat difficult to explain, was that he had an amazing awareness of his internal physiology that was outside of his normal sensory apparatus. His tumor was not visible to the naked eye; it required a special mirror to see. And yet he seemed to know almost daily exactly what location and what aspect of the tumor was responding. He came in after a weekend and said he thought there was a sore on the tumor, and in fact there was an ulcerated area on one side of it. We asked him to put his white blood cells, which he saw as a pulsating snowstorm, on automatic pilot for the next couple of days, to go to work on the ulcerated area and get it clear. He could draw a picture of how his tumor was responding to treatment that could be put up next to a photograph of the tumor and would match it almost exactly.

Several weeks into treatment, Jim began to feel so well, so excited about his white blood cells and what a good job they were doing on his tumor, that he decided to turn his white blood cells loose on his rheumatoid arthritis. Well, I was very skeptical and cautious in the early days and cautioned him that we seemed to be doing such a good job with the malignancy, let's leave well enough alone. But he was undaunted. And the imagery that he created was interesting. He gave his white blood cells a sandpaper edge and sent them down to the area in his knees where he had his symptoms, and asked them to sand off the spurs from his knees. Within a few days the arthritis symptoms cleared.

Well, by then we were scratching our heads and wondering what kind of a phenomenon we were dealing with. His tumor was responding, his rheumatoid arthritis was no longer preventing him from fishing, he was feeling better and gaining more weight. He decided to apply the process to the only remaining physiological problem that he had, which was that he had been sexually impotent for twenty years since his retirement. Again I cautioned him, suggested that surely we should leave well enough alone, but he sent the white blood cells down into the area of his penis. He said that he felt they never could find a physical problem, which was physiologically accurate, because his impotence was not due to physical factors, but most probably psychological factors. But even then, in a period of about ten days, he began to be able to have an erection and maintain it, and began to brag about his sexual activity over the next few years.

Well, I can't tell you the excitement we had at the end of treating that patient, realizing that not only was his tumor gone with few side effects, but that he remained stable and had no recurrence of his disease.

I was convinced that with good medical treatment and a relaxation and visualization process, surely the cure for cancer was close at hand. And then we began to encounter what has been one of the most difficult long-term problems in treating cancer patients from a psychological perspective — the enormous resistance of the patients to using the process. All of this was long before we realized that psychological factors played a role in the disease. Patient after patient would refuse to use the process that would require little more of them than forty-five minutes a day, certainly didn't have much in the way of side effects, and seemed to have some nice additional benefits like relaxation, reduced pain, a generalized sense of well-being.

We began to take a look at the idea that the depression and despair that we saw in our patients, and believed was the result of the disease, might in fact predate the disease. It was not a comfortable or easily grasped idea — that psychological factors actually played a role in the development of cancer.

From the earlier work of Dr. Lawrence LeShan and others emerged the Loss Theory, which, simply stated, says that those who are predisposed to cancer may, as a result of early childhood lack of closeness with parents, be susceptible to issues around the loss of a love object, whether of a child, a job, career, spouse, or some significant object in their life that carries a lot of emotional energy. And within six to eighteen months prior to the development of the symptoms, you will usually see an unusual clustering of stressful events occurring in the patient's life, involving a loss of a love object.

A child enters high school, and suddenly the idea dawns on the mother that her purpose as mother is soon to be over, and the loss of that relationship as the sustaining reason for her existence begins to dawn on her. A man is diagnosed with a life-threatening illness, and suddenly his wife realizes that she may one day lose this relationship that has been so important to her. A man reaches a position in his work and suddenly realizes he's reached the top of his ladder. There will be no more steps up, and the momentum of moving ahead, aggressing and achieving has been the major reason for his existence. Suddenly a profound depression and despair occurs, and then, six to eighteen months later, we will see a diagnosis of clinical malignancy.

How, then, would we deal with the psychological aspects of that patient's disease? If stress and psychological factors play a role in the development of disease and if we intervene psychologically, can we change the course of the disease?

The relaxation-visualization process gained greater dimension over the next few years. In teaching several hundred patients how to use the process and listening to their reports of how they visualized their cancer, their treatment and their white blood cells, I observed that the symbols the patients chose were a valuable clue to the underlying belief system that existed, many times outside of their awareness, not only about their cancer, but also about the events in their lives, and their being able to be resolved that life would once again be worth living.

One of the first patients that I questioned on the symbols he'd chosen had been diagnosed with lung cancer, and continued to go downhill very rapidly, even in the face of treatment, which was unusual. He and his wife maintained that he used the process three times a day, that he didn't go to sleep in the middle of it. So I questioned him about what it was he saw when he did his visualization. He described his tumor as a big, black rat — quite an unusual symbol for a patient to choose to represent his malignancy — and he saw his treatment, which at the time was chemotherapy in the form of pills, as little yellow tablets that broke down in his blood stream into smaller yellow tablets. When I questioned him about the interaction between the black rat and these yellow tablets, he said, "Once in a while the rat eats one." I asked, "What happens when he does?" And he said, "He gets sick for a while but then he bounces back all the stronger and bites me all the harder, and I have more pain." I said, "Tell me about your white blood cells." He said, "They're in an incubator." And I said, "What do you mean?" He said, "They're like little white eggs sitting under a warm light and one of these days they're going to hatch."

No amount of intervention intellectually was able to effect any long-term change in that man's imagery. Prior to his death, and talking to his wife and his family after his death, we learned that every adult member of this patient's family had died of cancer, for as long as he knew. Since their marriage when he was nineteen, every time he had a symptom of a cold or flu he said to his wife, "It's cancer, I know it, and I'm going to die."

Of all the measures that we take — we keep more than 250 pieces of data on our patients, besides information about their disease process and medical treatment — the contents of the patient's imagery have been the most predictive of where his disease would be two months down the road. If the patient's symbolic visualization represents his belief system, then it's a matter of helping the patient see what parts of his visualization are ineffective and helping him change it, and then perhaps changing the course of the disease. I encountered the enormous complexity of changing those symbols, not unlike trying to change one's dreams.

A number of years ago, I treated a man with advanced cancer of the pancreas, a Ph.D. physicist. He saw his cancer as little furry animals that resided in a place he called the cancer plane. He saw his white blood cells as white knights on white horses. In his imagination he would blow a bugle and an enormous line of white knights would line up — he drew a picture of the line of white knights going on into infinity, there were millions of them. He blew the bugle a second time and down came white lances. Being the good researcher that he was, he gave each one of the knights a daily quota. They all charged out into the cancer plane, where they speared their quota of cancer animals, carried them over to a stream of liquid that represented his chemotherapy, scraped them off into the stream, where the animals blew up like popcorn, dissolved, and were carried away. This is the symbolic imagery of a Ph.D. physicist who has worked with radiation and knows many details about the physiological nature of his disease process. His visualization is very effective, from any standpoint, in terms of the imagery. One day, however, several weeks into the treatment, he blew his bugle, and instead of the knights being on white horses, they appeared on small white dogs that couldn't carry them anywhere. He posed the question, what is the meaning of this? And no attempt to change that symbol intellectually worked. He came to me quite frightened about the process. We spoke with the white knights on the white dogs and asked them what the meaning was. Out of that exploration came a therapeutic issue that we had been confronting for quite some time. This patient had a history of prolonged, deep depression that would occur as a result of a number of things going on in his life but of which he had almost no awareness. It would be weeks after the depression had begun that he would finally realize that he was depressed, usually by the feedback of his family and co-workers. He was very out of touch with what was going on psychologically. However, when the knights appeared on white dogs that day, he was several days into a depression instead of weeks. The knights were giving him a message that he was once again depressed. As we began to confront the issues around his depression, the knights appeared on white horses again. That became a signal for him in the months ahead. Whenever the knights would appear on dogs instead of horses, he was becoming depressed again, and he was able to catch the depression, realize it was happening, days or hours into it, instead of weeks or months. We were much more able to resolve the issues and alleviate his depression.

Several months later, he called up his white knights one day and gave the second bugle charge and when the lances came down they had crooks in them; they weren't able to spear animals. He was concerned again. We did some work confronting a pattern of behavior that was one of the major therapeutic issues with him. His father had been an alcoholic who frequently spent the family's money on drinking, and they labelled him within the family as very selfish. His mother, on the other hand, was a self-sacrificing, selfless, martyrish woman. He had chosen his mother as his model. The way that translated in his life was that he would refuse to ever let anyone know what he wanted or needed, which would be selfish and like his father. The event that triggered this particular episode of depression was that he'd been given a very difficult research task and had been assigned a group of misfit researchers, the problem characters in the laboratory. Out of that group he had forged a very effective research team, and they had solved the problem that they had been given. In recognition of his accomplishment, his superiors assigned him a new task and took him away from this group of misfits that they assumed were very difficult to work with. Little did they know this man had always regretted leaving his earlier work as a college professor and going into the business world because he loved working with students. This group of misfits had been like students, so, unknowingly, his superiors had really penalized him for his accomplishment. But he refused to tell them. He was enraged at them for taking the team away, but refused in any way to let them know. Out of talking with his white knights with their crooked lances, he made the decision that the knights were telling him they weren't going to spear cancer animals unless he started telling the people around him what his needs and wants were. He confronted the issue at work, told his superiors, was once again given the group of misfits to manage, and his knight's lances straightened out.

Sometime later, another change occured in his imagery, when one day he sent his white knights out and they came back short of their quota. That happened several days in a row and he became alarmed. Shortly after that he was found to be free of disease. His knights' reports were quite accurate — there were not enough cancer animals left for them to fill their quota, and he had to reduce the quota as time went on.

I hope the description of this kind of imagery gives you an idea of both the symbolic importance of the patient's imagery and the clues that the imagery holds to the overall psychological picture of the patient. I mentioned two specific, mechanistic tools that we use in initially intervening with a patient, and one is the visualization process and paying attention to the symbolic messages carried in the process. The second is the use of a physical exercise program. Physical exercise is one of the best anti-depressives that we have in treating cancer, with the fewest side effects, and produces some other nice psychological changes as well. Psychological research shows that it increases self-esteem, increases one's sense of overall body wellness, and provides a number of strengths and felt resources within the patient.

Our first stage of treatment is a very careful history-taking process, asking the patient to review that time frame, six to eighteen months, even two or three years prior to their diagnosis, to look at what kinds of unusual events were going on and what may have triggered the depression. It is difficult to uncover that part of their lives that triggered their despair and hopelessness. For instance, we may work with a man with a number of marital and family conflicts which we could treat effectively, only to find out later that the trigger of the hopelessness was the fact that the man was demoted at work, a major issue that was left untreated therapeutically. So our first step is to zero in on the factors prior to the disease that triggered the despair that translated into depression of the body's immune system, allowing a malignancy to develop.

One of the reasons why a careful history-taking is necessary is because of the inaccurate assumptions that much of our culture has about stress and its psychological and physiological effects. I remember one of the first patients that I ever treated. I came out of the initial session believing that here, finally, was a patient who seemed to have everything going for him. He had great business difficulties in previous years, and four years before his disease had broken up a bad partnership, started a new one, and for the first time had a good stable, working relationship with his partners. He was paying more in income taxes than he had ever expected to earn. A year before his disease, he and his wife had completed the adoption of their second child, and they now had a girl and a boy. They had been married for fourteen years, the first ten years fraught with great conflict. They had sought counseling, and for the last four years everything had been smooth and peaceful. He was a man for whom everything seemed to be going right. But he gave me one clue during that first interview when he said, "That last year before I was diagnosed I had a lot more time than I ever had. I had time to spend with my family. I can remember coming home at night in my car, thinking about spending the evening with my family, and there was a song that kept going on in my head that whole year, that Peggy Lee song, 'Is That All There Is?'"

This man was thirty-nine years old. As I later learned, he had been abused as a child, and had grown up believing that the only way he deserved to survive was if he were overcoming insurmountable odds. Suddenly he had reached the top of every mountain he had ever built for himself. We forget that the accomplishment of goals is a significant loss. Suddenly all his reason for pursuing, striving, fighting, was ended. In the course of getting well and staying well he had to learn to live in peace, not to need enormous obstacles in order to feel that he had deserved to live.

We frequently see a lack of emotional outlets in cancer patients, particularly a difficulty expressing hostility. Anger in the face of severe stress is a very effective coping strategy, and quite healthy from a physiological standpoint. A person who has impaired emotional outlets and does not allow himself to express anger has reduced the number of coping alternatives available to him.

In the process of exploring the triggering factors to his despair we also talk about a person's will to live. If you talk with people who have survived a life-threatening illness when, according to medical prognosis, they shouldn't have, you will often hear a story that goes something like: "I couldn't die because . . . I had this child to raise . . .

I had that to do. . . ." and you will hear an overwhelming purpose, something that carried them through the dark days of their disease process. The will to live is not a magical thing that some people have and some people don't have, but is directly related to the degree and amount of investment that the patient has in his life. What's unfortunate about a diagnosis of cancer is that frequently people stop investing from the day of diagnosis. Patients will stop buying clothes for themselves because, after all, they may not live to wear them. They will stop making plans for vacations because, after all, the family shouldn't spend time and money on them, they won't be here that long. You begin to see a self-fulfilling prophecy developing, where the patient starts withdrawing more and more from life.

That might be an effective preparation for death. If the quality of life is such that life is not worth living, it may not be so difficult to lose. However, the catch-22 is that if the will to live does correlate with one's investment in life, and that investment correlates with a better prognosis or outcome of disease, then by withdrawing from life one might be participating in bringing about something that is not a physiological inevitability. So the stance that we ask patients to take is to maximize the quality of their lives as much as possible, which is a risky and courageous stance to take when a person has been told he only has a year or two left to live. To be willing to invest in and maintain a high quality of life, not knowing how much life you have left, takes a particular act of faith. One of the early questions we had from colleagues was that perhaps in doing that we might make the patient's death process more difficult, but in fact that has not been the case. We have put a high emphasis on the role of play and enjoyment in the patient's life. I think we can all learn from Norman Cousins: his form of play therapy was watching his favorite movies; and if he got a belly-laugh, he would have a pain-free period. It looks like the body uses pain to signal both the healthy, happy aspects of life and the unhealthy, unhappy aspects. We focus on asking the patient to increase his enjoyment of life.

Focusing on enjoying life increases the sense of pleasure, the emotional energy and resources, that then allow us to do the more difficult and painful long-term work of uncovering the trigger to the patient's despair and offering hope to that apsect of his psyche. Another part of the treatment process, and frequently the most difficult internal work, has been to deal with the secondary gains associated with the disease, the ways in which a person may experience emotional benefits as a result of his illness. There is no question tion that cancer impairs and impacts the patient's life in many unfortunate ways. However, it frequently meets some important emotional needs that may never have been met as well before. We're dealing with a population who put other people's needs first — those who succumb to cancer are frequently the too-good-to-be-true people in our midst whose care and concern for us has led to their own demise. The psyche which has been repressed and denied gets a hold of a very powerful tool. The diagnosis of cancer invites and invokes much love and attention from one's environment. That's very important for people to get well.

Internally it frequently creates a change, as well. The person gives himself permissions that he may never have given himself before. It's permissible now to be cranky, angry, irritable, to say no to people's expectations, to ask for his own needs to be met, and to receive love and affections—all of which fill important emotional needs. The dilemma comes only when the person starts to return to health. If then both the external and internal secondary benefits stop — and unfortunately they frequently do — the person thinks, "Now that I'm well I have to go back to meeting other people's needs. It's time for me to reassume my responsibilities." He starts going back to the same barren emotional life that may have produced the disease in the first place. The danger is that a part of his psyche becomes an internal saboteur and says, "No, I don't want to go back to that life, therefore I won't get well." The symptoms of that we'll frequently see in the patient who is suddenly beset with depression and anxiety when told that the disease is substantially better or in remission. Our therapeutic task, then, is to help the patient see the benefits he received both externally and internally when he was ill, and help him change in such a way that he can maintain most of these benefits after he gets well again. That's no easy therapeutic task. For a person to treat himself as well when he's well as he does when he's ill usually requires quite a restructuring of his internal rule system about the type of person he feels he needs to be in order to be all right and receive what he wants from the outside world. And yet it is a paradox that the part of the psyche which will sabotage a person's efforts to get well is in fact trying to get him to live a greater dimension in life than he ever has before. In my experience, patients who recover from life-threatening disease don't go back to the same kind of life. They have a quality that Karl Menninger described as being weller than well. I've had many patients say to me, "If I had it all to do over again, even as difficult as the experience of cancer was, I would have it again to have the benefits and the kind of life I have now which I never allowed myself prior to my disease."

Another important aspect of the treatment process is the role of the family. A frequent report I've had from spouses of cancer patients when they're away from the patient is an admission that every so often they wish he or she would just die, get it over with. They experience intense guilt as a result of this. When a person receives a diagnosis of a malignancy, the other members of the family start denying their own needs in service of the patient. That's not a bad coping strategy for short-term illness, but with cancer, we're frequently talking about years of denial of the spouse and other family members. Our culture supports that. If the wife goes out to lunch with friends, people will say, "Isn't your husband in the hospital, why aren't you there?" and they begin to feel more and more guilty about maintaining a good quality of life when someone in their midst is ill. So the whole family's quality of life is lowered with the disease process and it's a very natural thing for them ultimately to wish for it to be over in the quickest way possible so that they can get back to living. The task is to encourage and support the family members' beginning to take care of themselves in addition to the cancer patient in their midst so that they have the energy and support available for the patient in the long haul. Another therapeutic task arises from the fact that a person who has cancer is frequently the one in the family who is the glue that makes everything stick. He or she is the self-sacrificing caretaker of the family — Mama who always meets everyone's needs and doesn't ask much for herself, doesn't express much anger. We take that person in treatment, and teach him or her to be assertive, to recognize his needs, to ask for them to be met, to express anger, and guess what the family experiences? Loss of the caretaker, and upset at this anger and all these feelings coming from the patient that they've never experienced before. It's vital, so that the family doesn't sabotage our therapeutic efforts, that they be drawn into the treatment process initially so that they understand the changes to expect in the patient, because those changes will be felt everywhere in the system surrounding the patient. All kinds of tasks and rules will be redistributed when the person with the malignancy begins to claim those aspects of the psyche they have previously denied. It's important that the family support the belief system of the patient that he can in fact affect the disease process psychologically.

Of more difficulty is dealing with the ways in which the disease may be a response to an unhealthy system, an outgrowth of a larger issue going on in the family. One of the most common symbols that I have seen emerging out of patients' dreams and imagery is the symbol of a child or infant who is crippled, impaired or deprived in some way. The dream may occur shortly after diagnosis, or even before, and will arise again and again throughout the treatment process. I use that symbol to describe one of the major tasks that the patient goes through: relating to part of his inner world that he has denied since childhood. The symbol of the child usually represents the part or parts of the psyche that he has felt were innately wrong or bad. The symbol emerges as a request for care and as the person accepts and incorporates that aspect of himself — the childlike, vulnerable, dependent, needy part that he has denied much of his life — then the disease process responds. It's almost as if the child is saying, "Allow me to grow or the disease process grows."

Another part of the treatment process is the necessity of talking about death. I found through a number of unfortunate experiences early in the work that by not talking about death I could create in the patient a sense of obligation to stay alive at all costs in order to prove the theory. Some patients would suddenly break contact with me. Several weeks or months later the family would call and tell me the patient died with some message like, "Please tell Stephanie not to give up. Please tell her it doesn't mean that the process doesn't work." As a result of those experiences, I have in the last few years developed a therapeutic contract with the patient. It's this: there's no question when the patient comes to me that our goal is to work together to turn the disease process around. My goal with every patient is for him initially to get well. That's his hope at some level, too. However, it is also important for me to communicate to the patient that he may change his mind about the direction of our work at any point. I want him to know he has that choice. To go toward death is acceptable to me, and I will support him as much to have a good death as I did to bring about a good quality of life. In my experience, the patient brings me his ambivalence at earlier stages for us to work through, and for those who do say, "Yes, I've had enough," or "I've done enough," or "It's time now to go toward death," the death process has a different quality.

We have now begun to quantify the quality of patients' deaths. We realize that's an outcome that we hadn't accepted in this treatment process. It's become more and more unusual for patients who die in this process to be hospitalized for more than a week, for pain to be a significant problem in the later stages of their disease. I've heard Elisabeth Kübler-Ross say that people die in the style which they lived. If you want to get a good idea of how a person will handle his death, look at his last major crisis. If he uses denial and repression, the two most common defense mechanisms, that's how he'll handle his death. If he is able to be psychologically aware and use more direct communication, you will see a different quality of death process. It's not reasonable to expect people on their deathbeds to exhibit coping strategies and styles of behavior that they've not had a chance to practice.

Six years ago we began looking at the outcome of the patient's disease, and we have since had to broaden our quantification procedures to include four factors that we consider to be a good outcome of our intervention. First is the patient's longevity. Our theoretical stance was and still is that while a person is being treated psychologically, we should be able to affect the disease process. We began to compile data on those patients who had a medically incurable disease, even though we treat patients with better prognoses than that. If you effect a good response in a patient with fifty percent curability, who's to say whether the medical treatment or psychological intervention brought it about? So, we've only compiled statistics on those patients who should die of their diseases. Our median medical prognosis at time of entrance into the program is twelve months or less, and then we measure longevity.

Of the more than 250 patients who have entered with medically incurable disease, many survive two times as long, on the average, as their traditional medical prognosis. However, within that number there is enormous variation. There are patients who do die within their prognosis, there are patients who double their prognosis, and others who get well from medically incurable diseases and stay well for years. In some ways our own reporting is an unfair reading of our own statistics, because we lump together 250 patients with a wide variety of motivations. Some of those come to us, for a while, then go home and never use any of the processes again. Others engage in a one- to two-year transformative psychotherapy process. Clinically the observation has been made that the more hours of therapy the patient takes, the more commitment to the process, the more involvement, the more he integrates this into his approach to living, the greater longevity will be. In addition to that, we measure the effect our process has on the patient's quality of life, quality of death and help to the surviving spouse.

As we look at cancer as a psychosomatic disease, meaning that it is a result of a combination of physical and psychological factors both in origin and in outcome, we have attacked some of the beliefs underlying this culture and it is important that we recognize that, both to temper our evangelical zeal in wanting to bring about change more rapidly than our culture may be ready for, and also to help us understand the difficulty of changing belief systems. Our culture has been committed to Cartesian dualism and, unfortunately, when we approach with a psychological program patients who have a life-threatening illness like cancer, we risk the possibility that they believe that we're telling them that their disease is all in their head — because that is the image that psychosomatic disease has gotten in this culture — or that we're telling them that it's their fault. There is a great lack of awareness of what we mean by the complexity of unconscious psychological processes and their involvement in the disease process. We face a great resistance in this culture to psychotherapy, which is in essence the treatment program that I described to you. Those patients who somaticize in response to stress, who develop physical illness, are frequently the patients who would never face the door of the psychotherapist's office if their very life did not depend on it. There are still great numbers of patients who will not use a psychological approach because in many parts of the country admitting the need to see a professional for one's emotions is tantamount to character suicide. I would hope one day that we each had a personal therapist just like we have a family doctor and one would not expect to live life without seeking the help of an objective caregiver to evaluate and appreciate the stress, the change that we're all experiencing.

This treatment system and the idea of psychological factors in the development of cancer confront our belief in our nonparticipation in death. When we say that psychological factors play a role in the outcome of cancer, are we not in fact saying that people play a role in choosing how, of what, and when they die? What does that do to the spiritual, religious and moral foundations that most of us have grown up with?

I think it's important that we appreciate that what we're doing with this approach is to bring to awareness an unconscious tool that has existed in our culture for centuries, that tool being the use of physical disease to meet important emotional needs. Disease has been called Western civilization's only form of meditation. Illness is the only circumstance in which we're allowed to become introspective, crawl into our beds with the covers over our heads, feel sorry for ourselves, be cranky, say no to this constant achievement pressure. If we only remove disease, whether by medical prevention or psychological intervention, I think we will only make more inhuman the condition that we live in. What is vital, I think, is that we find ways to replace disease as a psychological tool. When we look at disease from a systems perspective, not only do we have to consider the family system in which the patient resides, but the cultural system that supports and encourages denial of feelings, the discounting of one's inner world, pressures us to bottle up feelings, smile when it hurts inside, put other people's needs first, and achieve and accomplish at all costs and for God's sake never fail. That culture creates a perfect condition for disease to be a necessary human psychological tool. If we're to replace it and really look at the possibility of a society much more free of disease, then it is essential that we find a replacement psychological tool. Preventive medicine will really come about when we teach parents how to raise children differently and to relate to their inner world and aspects other than the physical and material in a very different way.

One last issue is the therapist's dilemma. First, there are far more unknowns than knowns in this work. We've now trained several thousand therapists to do the kind of work that we do. One of the major factors that most correlates with whether a new treatment program will affect a patient's longevity is the degree to which the health care deliverer has incorporated the principles in his own life on a daily basis. If there's ever a time as caretakers when we can't say, "Do what I don't do," and not expect it to affect the process, it's in this treatment. The most reliable source of guidance as a therapist is my experience with my own personal health care and relating that to my patients. It forces us as therapists to become models of self-care, models of replacing disease in our own personal lives. Care-givers have notoriously been self-denying. Not only do we ask the patients in using this model to change the inner world, but we also ask them to stand up to their family system and often their cultural system that teaches them to live in such a way that they need illness. I think that it's important that we take responsibility for providing a model for them of how to provide care for ourselves when we're well, as well as when we're ill. My experience as a therapist using this approach is that it is no easy task.

□ □ □

An Interview With
Stephanie Matthews-Simonton

SUN: You said that preventive medicine will come about when we teach parents to raise their children differently. Could you elaborate on that?

SIMONTON: Most of the personality patterns associated with cancer are formulated during the first five or six years of life. That's when children experience the lack of enough unconditional acceptance from one or both parents, feel responsible for that, feel there must be something wrong and bad about themselves. They learn maladapted ways of getting their needs met: for instance, to put other people's needs first, never to be angry, to be the good little girl. When someone is forty or fifty, we have to intervene and change processes that began way back when. If we were to prevent disease, I think what we would need to do is first, provide more professional parenting — teach people what children need emotionally to grow into healthy children. Secondly, encourage the expression of feelings in appropriate ways, rather than encourage the inhibition of feelings. Unfortunately, in the past, many parents taught children to be seen and not heard, not to be angry, to be polite at all costs, to always achieve, be successful. Now that means we have to intervene in some way with the parent, because people usually can't teach skills they don't have themselves. It means increased awareness on the part of parents of their own psychological make-up, because children learn coping strategies and mimic their parents. If Daddy bottles up his feelings, guess what all the little boys in the family are like? If the mother is self-sacrificing and a martyr, guess what all the little girls in the family are likely to do?

SUN: But how do you start making that kind of change in the society?

SIMONTON: I think the first step is in education, helping people become increasingly aware of how psychological factors play a role in the disease process and what are healthy and what are maladaptive coping strategies. Then we can begin to talk about parenting and children. We have to address the culture we have now if we hope that that culture will raise children in a different way. More data, more education of the public at large. I think that's a possibility. With the media coverage that we have, we can change public attitudes and public awareness about factors in a very short period of time. So I think we have the capability and the technology to do that kind of massive education. But it'll take some time.

SUN: You said earlier that looking at cancer the way you do means attacking some beliefs that underlie the culture, but we need "to temper evangelical zeal in doing this."

SIMONTON: We have to realize how upsetting these ideas are to the beliefs underlying our culture. If we call cancer a psychosomatic disease, then it's very hard to decide that any disease is not psychosomatic, meaning the result of a combination of psychological and biological factors. Well, that creates a great change and uproar. There have been physical diseases and there have been emotional diseases. Now we are saying they're all the same. Also, we live in a culture where suicide, which is the only word we have for self-participation in death, is immoral and illegal. Yet if we say that people's emotions, attitudes and psychological factors play a role in the outcome of their disease, what we're saying, very simply, is that people may play a role in how and when and of what they die. In our work we encourage patients to be aware when they feel that death is coming, or is the next choice for them, and give them permission to make that choice and communicate that directly. That causes an enormous shift in the patient's family system, because the family members may not be able to tolerate the patient deciding to die and accepting death. People can be kept alive in a lingering state of health that most of us would not wish for them, because members of their family are not ready to turn loose. We see that all the time in a hospital where family members will insist that more and more treatment be given in an effort to keep Mama alive, until Mama is in so much pain. Then they say, enough.

What would happen if that family system permitted Mama to say, "Death is coming and I don't want this extensive treatment. I feel good about the life I've lived, and I want to be able to go home and do what I need to do to get my affairs in order?" How much might her life be shortened, how much more comfortable might she be at the end of her life? That's not the way we've approached disease.

I think the other thing that we need to take into account is that disease fills important psychological needs. We don't have psychological coping skills, and don't allow people good emotional outlets. When one's sick, one's permitted to be angry, to be cranky, to act out, to say no, to put oneself first, not to accomplish and not to succeed. If we're really going to eradicate disease as we know it in this culture, we have to find a replacement, a different code of living — one in which the major value and priority in life can't be success, accomplishment, and bottling up your feelings and presenting a front. We have to provide alternative models of living that are healthier, broader, and more supportive to human nature. Without that, we just pressure people into a more difficult experience.

SUN: What do you do to stay healthy?
SIMONTON: I meditate regularly, I exercise regularly, I see a psychotherapist regularly, I have a fairly extensive support system of close, intimate friends. I take a lot of time off from work, much more than I ever used to. I say no. I limit the number of hours I work, I limit the number of days in the week I work, I put my vacations on the calendar first. I have learned to put the quality of my life first, and to stop postponing gratification. I've been fortunate. I've learned a lot and gained a lot personally from my experience with cancer patients. When you watch people die as a result of lifestyle and psychological factors you learn about what's unhealthy in your own life.

I'd say there are a couple of things I could do to be healthier. One would be to say "no" more. I think my work is important, both for our patients and for the evolution of our culture. I could expend myself very rapidly by not setting some limits. Secondly, I tend to forget that I have limits, I am human, I have needs, and I'll go too far and get too tired before I recognize that. Usually my greatest difficulty is in controlling the amount of time and energy I put into my work. I've had to pull back and invest more in relationships, play, hobbies, and other kinds of things, playful activities that balance out the high intensity rewards that I get from my work.

SUN: There's been a lot of talk here about nutrition, but you haven't mentioned food specifically.
SIMONTON: You're right, I didn't. My biggest problem with food is usually eating too much. My own belief in nutrition and clinical experience with it leads me to believe that nutrition is important in maintaining health, and in boosting the body's overall health. I personally don't feel it's a major curative agent for me, and that may be just because of my own belief system about it. My diet has changed over the course of the last few years because I became a runner. I found that I ate differently, naturally: higher fiber, less refined sugar, fewer foods with a lot of additives, more fresh fruits and vegetables, decreasing my overall caloric intake.

Some of the finest work that's come out indicates that the closer organisms are to their ideal body weight, if not just under that, the better their defense mechanisms function. Again, we recognize that cancer and heart disease are a result of industrialized society, but the more overweight you are, and the less physically active, the greater your risk of heart disease and cancer. Longshoremen in this country have a much lower incidence of heart disease and cancer. Anyone who sweats everyday has a much lower incidence of cancer and heart disease. So, physical activity is important, but so is not being overweight.

SUN: Do you think you might ever get cancer?
SIMONTON: I suspect I'm probably more disposed to heart disease. That runs in my family. My grandmother had cancer when she was seventy-two, survived until ninety, and had no further evidence of disease, and as far as I know, she's the only one in my family.

SUN: If you had just a few words to say to people who have either just found out that they have cancer, or families of those people, what would they be?

SIMONTON: I would say to the person, you are not a helpless victim, there are things you can do to affect the outcome of your disease process. And, as much as possible, find meaning in what seems like a disastrous situation. To consider a disease like cancer as an act of fate over which you have no influence either in the origin or the outcome puts a human being in a very helpless condition. The data doesn't support this view. You can affect the situation, and you can play a role. There's a meaning and a reason for what's happening in your life. I think when one's life is threatened it's a very effective coping mechanism to ask: What's worthwhile about my life? What do I think my individual purpose is on this planet? Then stay as close to that purpose as possible, staying invested and connected to a sense of purpose.

Look at the "whys." I think, "Why me?" is a very appropriate question. I think people can assign meaning by asking the question, "Why me?" — not, "Why did fate get me?" as if it shouldn't have happened, but, "Why is this happening now in my life?"

(November 1980)

Michael Shorb

The Dolphin Messenger

Late afternoon & flawed sea unfurling
Wave on wave, diminishing sun
Sculpting copper roads of light on wet sand.
Walking, I came upon a beached dolphin
Battered by sand & the beaks of gulls.
First urged myself to walk on, avoiding
Dead things with white bellies mottled
Black by wind and talon. Not stare
At the zero of its stillness, blood
Tugging water washed from a hole
In its head, or touch the rubbery beauty
Of its lifeless fins, or marvel
At the jade serenity gracing its delicate
Mouth, the coral hues asleep there.

For I have never seen a richer smile
On friend or lover's face than this
The gangster of the sea gave back
So carelessly to the solar bell
Mushrooming on the dark water.

A wave came spattering around my ankles,
Reminding me that the sea had business
Here with one of its own, that no rituals

Shrined the reality of drying blood,
No Dolphin Father loomed & no songs sounded.

I kept walking, day used up, dreaming
A human love not of the sea
Or its shining casualties,
Guided by what seemed
An echo of the first unwrinkling stars,
Memory beyond memory, a dolphin's
Void & engulfing smile.

(August 1982)

Patricia Sun

Elizabeth Rose Campbell

I've spent too many years as an editor to let a writer get away with describing someone as "radiant." So I'll have to do it.

Patricia Sun is radiant. "Love without attachment is light," wrote Norman O. Brown. Maybe that explains her glow.

I wasn't especially eager to hear her, even after she was described to me as "the female Ram Dass." Not another spiritual teacher, I groaned, preaching what I find so hard to practice. And from California yet! I turned up my Eastern nose.

But being with Patricia was an intensely moving experience. Despite my admonitions not to be "blown away," I was. I wouldn't call her the female Ram Dass — that label is unfair to both of them — but she's surely one of the most extraordinary teachers in America today. In fact, not long ago she shared a stage in

In the freedom she has inherited by loving herself so totally, she is able to beam out unobstructed support for everyone to do the same.

San Francisco with Ram Dass and Jack Schwarz, another heavyweight of the American spiritual movement. During the discussion Ram Dass was asked a question by someone in the audience and, according to one published account, "Strangely enough, this man of so much eloquence only replied, 'I can't answer that. I'm too stoned on Patricia!'"

Seven years ago, Patricia Sun would have scoffed at this, or at the notion that in 1979 she'd be flying to the University of Madrid to teach teachers how to teach, or going to the Findhorn community in Scotland to speak on the nature of love. Back then, she was finishing up two degrees at the University of California in Berkeley, one in social science, and the other in conservation and natural resources. She was in the top two percent of her class, a highly motivated and highly successful Phi Beta Kappa student, ready to go on to graduate work.

But Patricia started getting more and more "intuitive" — disconcertingly, because she "didn't want to get into this funny stuff," but not knowing how to get away from it either. She took some tests given to several hundred people at a parapsychology symposium in Berkeley, and was one of a handful who scored 100 percent.

Patricia went to see a clairvoyant, who insisted she was a psychic healer. Again, Patricia balked, but was impressed by the accuracy of the woman's account of her childhood. Toward the end of the reading, the clairvoyant said, "Patricia, now is the time for you to really come into that which is yours." As she said that, Patricia was struck by "a gold white light . . . that went through my whole body, through my feet, right down into the earth, and it filled my hands, and I drew in a deep breath because my hands were so thick and full of energy. I couldn't put them down. . . . Tears came to my eyes, and I heard, 'I've come home.'"

Today, at thirty-eight, Patricia is increasingly in demand as a lecturer, healer, and teacher. Looking at her, it is hard to believe she has three grown children — the oldest a twenty-year-old son. She's been married ten years, to her second husband. She chose the name Sun a few years ago, "or rather it chose me, and when people say, 'Is it your real name?' I want to say, 'Most definitely yes.'" Well, I don't like people changing their names, either, but in this case, I won't quibble. The shoe fits. And it leaves tracks of light.

— Ed.

The ordinary is not one of the more heavily advertised images in the New Age. Promotional material for speakers, workshops, and communities emphasizes the grandiose, with an insistent sweetness that's an easy target for the satirists and cynics: Transformation! Self-Metamorphosis! Rainbows! Sunsets! Joyous Life! Oneness is All!

My prejudice against the emphasis on the glorious is this: unless the ordinariness of the moment is included in the job description of life — with all its beauty, boredom, missteps, and broken bones — then the point is entirely missed.

And despite the widespread acknowledgement that becoming whole (as a person, or a planet) will take time, there's often a determination to portray the vision at fruition *now*, no matter how inappropriate that might be.

I was reminded of that prejudice when I walked into the Guilford College auditorium where Patricia Sun would speak, because the people there fit my worst stereotypical views of what I'd find. They seemed giddy, over-confident, lots of them making their way to the most visible place down front and engaging in dramatic goodwill, ecstatic embraces, not a single person looking blasé, chomping gum, or acting even vaguely unconscious.

The program was sponsored by the Spiritual Frontiers Fellowship, and began with a meditation, led by an emcee who had participated with most of the audience in a week-long series of workshops.

The meditation was led like calisthenics, with show-biz style and near cheerleader antics; it was over before I'd had time to begin.

Afterwards, everybody sang enthusiastically: "I'm not the same anymore. I found the truth and it set me free. I'm not the same, I'm not the same, I'm not the same anymore!"

I'd heard Patricia Sun stood outside the glitter of the spiritual movement, and that was why I'd come. My doubts about her were superficial: I couldn't figure out how anybody who looked so young could know so much. I was mildly suspicious of her beauty. (TV makes pretty faces into stars, why not the spiritual movement?) And she was from California, where gurus rise and fall daily.

The tall blonde woman who walked onstage and murmured *thank you* into the microphone as she waited for the thousand people to stop clapping looked even younger than in her pictures. But her stage presence was well-developed, relaxed and focused; she seemed at home in this circumstance, attentive to her audience, and secure in herself, wearing her big-boned frame like a grounding rod.

It was only after the crowd settled down that I could begin to feel who she was. She won me over easily when she said:

"I'd sometimes almost rather not talk to New Age groups, because they've got all the words down now. They say, 'Oh yeah, I know all about that. Oh, I heard that. . . . Yeah, I know. . . .'" They won't be innocent and they won't be vulnerable. They won't say, 'Is there something inside the word *more* here?'"

Patricia spent the next three hours, and then another three hours the following Sunday at Melloweden, encouraging people to experience the *moreness.* "Until we begin to know that we don't know, we don't have any room to get full," she said. She suggested that we can embrace the unknown, and simultaneously learn to make "the power in us that is ours more available ordinarily."

The obstacle to all that is your conditioning, your programming, your "tapes," as Patricia called them. "Especially when you feel powerless," she said, "let a flag come up and tell yourself, 'There's some governing principle I've taken on here for my survival that I don't need, and there's some truth right in front of me, and I'm about to see it, and that's why I'm going into this crazy circular painful place.' And the solution, the key, will always be paradoxical."

Patricia addressed the parts of each of us that refuse to allow for our craziness. "We are all nutty as fruitcakes," she said. "And until we can know that there isn't anybody in a body who isn't programmed with some craziness, we can't really relax and work on it, because we're all going to try to look cool . . . we're all going to try to look like we've got it figured out. And all that's going to do is block your process of actually doing that."

Her emotional savvy was like any good therapist's. She knew how to relieve the tension, how to love the parts of us that fear and fight. And her total belief in the enormity of one's potential encouraged us all to risk more, to give up a little control, to stop trying so hard to be good, to discover our most genuine selves, and comprehend that it is unnecessary to deny your own power to stay in God's good graces.

She pointed out that if we all did everything "right," it would have a sterile quality to it, and only if we're willing to experience being "off the mark" will we come to know what it is to be on target, to find our center. "Finding your center," she said, "is finding a sensitivity in you that lets you be vulnerable and open and let everything in, and simultaneously saying 'yes, no, all right, nope.'"

What made Patricia so accessible to me was the equal footing she put herself on with the audience. Her emphasis, repeatedly, was on supporting *everyone*, in all their power. In the freedom she has inherited by loving herself so totally, she is able to beam out unobstructed support for everyone else to do the same. This is her intention and her success: "Love is for giving. Love is forgiving."

The language she used had an open-ended quality, necessary to carry the telepathic surge of meaning one can feel before the words are spoken. I was pleased that she spoke in terms that anyone could relate to. No cosmic code words. The words she used to describe our destination were simple and universal: "We are coming home."

And when she said it, everything that home could ever mean bubbled up from deep inside, and I knew she was right.

At the Melloweden workshop, a few days later, the group was small, no more than a hundred people gathered in a small chapel. Patricia talked about relationships, child-rearing, nuclear power, sex, illness, and about her transition from an academic perspective (as a psychological researcher at the University of California at Berkeley) to where she is now, deep at the heart of the human potential movement. "At one point," she said, "my rational mind convinced me, and showed me that there was more than rational mind. And it was like I broke a seal, a barrier, and that's when I opened."

Her psychic and healing abilities developed very rapidly after that, and eventually she shifted from private healing sessions to the workshops she does now, "because the same energy I'd use in an isolated way to work on somebody's illness, I now use in a bigger way to work on everybody opening up."

She asked us not to take a break during the three hours of the workshop because it would interrupt the rising energy among us, which was very definitely building.

To close the session, we all sat quietly and Patricia made her sounds — hard to describe, something like a cry or a chant, at first sounding like one voice, and then like two, with an electronic resonance that you could feel in your head.

I opened my eyes and looked at Patricia. She was standing tall, her eyes closed, her feet firmly planted on the floor and her arms spread, the palms of her hands facing one another. Her open arms seemed to support, hold, or guide the sounds they opened to, and encircled an energy vortex that mounted as the sounds did.

I could feel her making a creature call to each individual in the room. I could feel us helping her make the sounds without knowing how.

All she said when it was over, was, "I love you very much," and I struggled not to burst into tears. I was so grateful that Patricia was patiently weaning us from our need to fear — for the moment — and letting us experience this openness within ourselves, where un- dreamt of connections were giving birth to more beauty, more fullness than the mind could comprehend. And all of it available or- dinarily.

□ □ □

Patricia on . . .

These comments were excerpted from Patricia's talks at Greensboro and Melloweden. They should not be reproduced or used without her permission.

Two notes: Patricia, whenever possible, uses "they" instead of "he" or "she," so as to be "inclusive of both sexes." Also, her use of the word "tapes" refers to "your programming and survival conditioning from family and culture, both conscious and unconscious."

Our thanks to Patricia for going over this material to make sure nothing was garbled in the transmission.

— Ed.

The Boogeyman

The thing that I've noticed, everywhere I go, is that in every per- son, no matter how evolved, there is a little dark, sad, anxious place inside. No matter how cheery they are, I look in and I see that place.

Jung called this "the shadow." Perfect name. That little shadow, that part of you that is unconscious, is the part of you that doesn't love you, but judges you; it's the part of you that suspects you aren't good, the part of you that remembers when you wanted to do this bad thing or that bad thing or did it. It is actually much more than that. It is like an ancient taproot through humanity, it is all your ancestors, all the collective unconscious, all the ancient human experience, and we are, as a part of this evolutionary leap, about to make that taproot conscious. When it comes into the light, which is what consciousness is, it vanishes. It's not real, yet it's real. So it's true, you've got all that dark stuff, but it's not real.

I like to sometimes talk about that in terms of the boogeyman. I like that expression, because when we're in a dark room, and think we see a shadow move, we're filled with fear. The terror is real, the fear is real. The source of it is not. There's no boogeyman in the room. The self-doubts you have are real, the source of them is not. And the only way you will know that is to face life, dark corners and all, to look at it, and know that the whole point of life is to be here, to make life that light, make life conscious.

You know the bad stuff about yourself from when you were two years old and you stole a cookie, let alone anything else you did. You know it all, and it's accruing in there, painting an image of who you "really" are. What's also in there is all the judgment: "if ever you have suffered, you are being punished, and you deserve it," which is a cause-effect consciousness about discovering reality.

Suffering is there to tell you: if you keep trying to walk through this concrete wall here, because somebody told you there was a door here, and you try again and again, and you can't get through where everybody else says you can get through, and it hurts, well, the pain and the suffering are telling you something. Eventually, you'll stop and say, "I don't think there's a door there." And at that moment, there is a moment of incredible power, because you have let go of the tape.

Now it's scary, because then you go, "But how do I get through?" But once you know there's no door here, you stop trying, and you look around. And there's lots of avenues of maneuvering. They are unthinkable, as long as you're buying the tape of "this is the way to do it."

Life is like going through point A and point B and there's a big corridor and in this corridor there are lots of doors. There is one door that says, "Boogeyman." And everybody told you there was something terrible in there. And we spend our lives trotting from A to B and then you go, "Oh, I'm getting near that door," and, "Oh

God, I'm getting close to it," and you worry as you get close, and then we go past it in a panic, and we worry about something sneaking up and getting us from behind. And when you get far enough away, you breathe a sigh of relief, and you get worried about something else, you look at another door.

At some point, the job of growing up becomes clear. You get fed up being run by the fear every time you have to go by that door. You get sick and tired that every time you get to that kind of situation, or relationship, or portal — ugh. Terror. The only choice you really have is to go in and open the door and look. Booga, Booga, Booga! What I can guarantee you is you'll find each time more room to be, more power, more awareness; it's another beautiful place. It's just that someone didn't understand it. Someone was afraid of it.

Fear is the obstacle to knowing God, to feeling love, to being who you are, to having all your intellect, to having all your talent, all your power, all your ability, all your radiance, all your juice, all your uniqueness. All your connections. Your brain working whole. Your body working whole. Moving to holiness.

The Brain

You have two hemispheres in your brain, right brain and left brain functioning. The right brain rules the left side of the body, and the left brain rules the right side of the body. Throughout history, especially in the Orient and in Egypt, religion, philosophy, and medicine were extremely and complicatedly involved with being aware that there were different energies that affected the two sides of the body.

In Chinese language, the yang side is the right side: the linear, the rational. Modern technology now talks about that hemisphere as the major hemisphere, though it has the same mass and size. It's called major because it's what our culture values. The yang is the thrust-out, the categorizing, the rational, the linear, the verbal, the linguistic, that ability, that function asking, "How do you do it?"

This rational linear side is very essential. I ask you not to do what I call a "duality flip," where if I make one thing good, don't make its opposite bad, which is a very logical thing to do.

I'm trying to get to a place where our minds will function differently, where they will be amplified. A gestalt is more than the sum of its parts. All the different separate parts are one thing, separate, but then when they come together there is more, something else that's entirely different. That's what we're going to be able to do with our thinking. Right now we're jumping from one hemisphere to the other. And being very uneasy about what we get out of the intuitive mind. And going back to the logical, rational side.

We have equated reality with logic. That is not so. Reality is discovered through the tool of logic. Logic does not equate to reality. Because also included in reality is the mystical state, the divine knowing, the other whole hemisphere of your brain, which is called the "minor hemisphere" in our medical profession because we don't know what it does, so we don't value it. But it's where Einstein got $E=MC^2$. Energy equals everything. It's where Chopin got the music. It's where you get divine revelation. It is the acausal thinking brain.

Now for Western minds to consider the word "acausal" is mind boggling if you really look at it. That means "without cause." That's worse than infinity. It just does not compute.

There is, in the act of creation, in the experience of God, a whole component that is: it just happens. And we're getting ready to own that part, simultaneously with the rational, letting them both work together. And that is, in fact, centeredness, when you get both hemispheres working together.

Duality Flips

Absolute power does indeed corrupt absolutely, if you do what I call a duality flip. And that means you assume that the person is saying, "One person has absolute power and everybody else has none." That is, of course, evil. But if you didn't do a duality flip, and make it contrasting that way, and you just said, "Everyone has absolute power," then we would be in heaven. And as much as we fight and argue, and fear, and feel powerless, we create evil. Non-living. Non-life. Off. Off the mark.

I call it crooked energy, because you know how a hose gets twisted, and the water can't get through? That's how we are, we have a lot of little crooked bends, that we've been programmed with, that we've taken on. Fears we haven't figured out. Our energy can't get past it, and so we feel bad, we feel depressed, we feel powerless, we feel angry, we feel hurt, we feel jealous, we feel grief, we feel remorse.

"It's happened. Nothing can change it!" It's one of the great big dualities that locks us into a lot of suffering. "Well, as everybody knows, the past is over and done with, and there's nothing you can do to change it." Isn't it fascinating, that in a certain sense, though obviously we are the total sum of all past, we are also the total sum of all future? Because there is no such thing. There is always only "now." And you can transform the past, by your awareness of *now*. If it's a little hard for the rational mind, I can give an example. For instance, you have a memory, as a child. Your memory is true. It was your experience. Everything you remember is true, yet there is something missing. The other truths are missing. When the other truths are missing, what you experienced as true isn't true. When you know what is missing, you will be, as the Buddha said, awake. Now this is the paradox. And this is what we need to be able to hold and see.

You are correct and all your experiences count. There is no need to invalidate any of them. Merely stay open to the rest. And when the rest of it comes in, there is an alchemy, there is a leap in consciousness, and everything is different. I'd love for you to feel that, over and over, because that's the release place. That's the leap place. That's where it is, that's the next level of consciousness.

When we all have absolute power, then it is, "Thy kingdom come, Thy will be done, on earth as it is in heaven." That's when, as it says in Jeremiah, we will not have to preach to each other any longer in the days to come, we will not have to remind each other about the laws of God, we will not have to keep telling our brethren how to follow the laws of God, because it shall be written on the inward parts of us all, and all will know God. So, we're coming home, and when you genuinely support someone in their power, you bring it all home, and you have acknowledged your own, because if you stop to think of it, what is the most powerful position you could take in the world? One of totally supporting everyone in all their power. Because you have no fear of loss.

Do We Create Our Own Reality?

The thing in the New Age now is to talk about how "you created it." It gets a little annoying, on occasion, when someone says, "Well, you created it," and one of the reasons why that is annoying is because there's something missing there. While it is completely true that you do create the reality around you, it is also completely true that you are an effect of this universe and that you are completely in response to it, receptive to it. Yes, you created it, and simultaneously we are completely an effect of the universe. Now, if you can hold those two things together, simultaneously, you can find a growing edge of power that you have in how you have chosen to be here and joined in on your destiny and the unfolding of things. Yet, part of how you've chosen it and joined in is through not knowing.

Everytime you are in that ambiguous state which we often hate because it's equated with going crazy and danger, and not being able to figure things out, and insecurity, every time you are in an ambiguous state, you're right up against the paradox. You are at a place where you can make a great shift in consciousness. And to the degree that you refuse to make the leap, trying to figure out, "Is it this way?" or "Is it that way?" you will run back and forth and feel a lot of anguish. Sometimes what you'll do, instead of picking the leap, is pick one. Just because you can't stand to keep going. And then you'll pick one, and you'll do a whole dance of being stuck over there, and eventually you'll have to get stuck on the other side, and that's what life has been since Adam and Eve.

As a matter of fact, Adam and Eve began the duality dance. That was the original sin. The fall was them eating from the tree not just of knowledge, but the knowledge of "is it good?" or "is it bad?" and then we knew suffering, and then we knew shame.

Men and Women

In the duality plane, we make things wonderful, or terrible. So some doors are labelled awful. And the awfulness is fed. Nobody knows why anybody's terrified there, it's just "Ahhhhh."

And one of the biggies on that particular issue is men and women. And men fearing women and women fearing men.

There's a tremendous amount of programming and conditioning that is almost biologically oriented in the way that we happen to be born. In this duality plane of either/or thinking, there's one extremely lopsided thing that happens. And that is that every single human being who exists has been born only of a female body, has lived parasitically off the flesh of that body, inside of that body, for about nine months, and then for most of humanity's history, off of that body for a year or two or three or four more. For something of an animal body in a four-square reality, that is powerful stuff. You don't live if Mom doesn't let you grow in her body, or take care of you afterwards. Plus, in duality thinking, if someone has the power of life, they then, of course, have the power of death. Stop to think what this does as a setup for men. Because, while women certainly get programmed with a ton of junk, on that particular issue, whether they have children or not, they know: "Oh, my body is one of those." "Oh yeah, I'm one of those, like Mom." So with women, for whatever your hassle is, whatever your fears are, whatever your dilemmas, whatever programming you have to work out, you at least have the "I am one of those" identification.

But for men, it remains always an otherness power. When you are strictly four-square reality thinking, that's something else, and that's why throughout human history, women were, in prerecorded history, dominant, and had to give it up because the men's terror was too great; and they became submissive, and owned by men. Then, it was the father owned the daughter, and handed her over to the husband, and there was the virginity thing so that nobody else got in there to tap that power.

Where did all that craziness come from in our cultures? We treat it like "well, that's just life." The fact that we come in two kinds of bodies and only one kind grows new life has a profound hookup to conscious evolving, and to the nature of the duality plane, and the nature of our trying to comprehend it.

Now there's also a biological thing of women feeling very "at effect" of their bodies. Giving birth often meant death, it certainly meant hardship, and you were extremely vulnerable for a long period of time. That set up one of the big programmings and conditionings that women have — they need to own men, to get them to take care of them. "You need to have a man. You need to get married . . . ." All those images come from the same biological thing from the time we were running away from saber-toothed tigers. The fact is that we no longer need to do that. That's not here anymore. Now we're here to connect. To use what we've each learned. To share feelings. To get to sense the other person, to break down that barrier of fear.

Once I was with a few women at a picnic dinner at somebody's house; the guys were out playing volleyball, the ladies were inside talking. And they were all talking about the men. They were all being very lucid, very clear, very accurate, and very complete in their understanding of how those men were, what their relationships were, what the problems were. They were very clear. And I thought, "Wow, these ladies really have good relationships."

Then the men came in. And the women who'd been speaking very clearly suddenly went (laughs embarrassedly). And everything went iiicchhhhkkk. It was like a wave that went across the room, and the men felt it, and their reaction to that yuck was to get yucky the other way, and then there was this *ohh*, in the room, and I thought, "Oh my God, that's what it is. Men are terrified of women. And women are terrified of letting men know they know they're terrified."

And that's the why to all this crazy song and dance we do. And why women are terrified is because throughout history they've gotten murdered a lot whenever they'd say what they thought or used men's fear. When you get that imprinted in your genetic memory, you get very evasive.

So it's been the way we've done the dance, to figure out who we are. All of this hasn't needed to be happening for a long time, and it's the hangover of the unconsciousness of the energy, not really founded in the realities of survival except as we create self-fulfilling prophecy. What we're about to do is really look at how we have the unfinished experiences . . . it's the real meaning behind ancestor worship. You must respect your heritage. Not in an exclusive sense of being better than anybody else, but in knowing that all your ancestors have been working on different pieces, and you've got assorted little vulgarities left over programmed into you that you have to become aware of and straighten out. And bring your consciousness into freedom, bring it into light. Bring it out of the shadow.

Matching Energies

When you say, "I'm right and I have to make all those people agree with me," you act out of powerlessness. You are not trusting the universe, you are not trusting the God within others or you, you are not saying, "I'll let you figure it out when you get it," which would be *real*. We want them to say they agree even if it's not real for them.

Now the greatest power there is, is love. Somebody can come up to you, opinionated, defending a position, and if you don't match energies with him, your resistance smack up against theirs, but instead, if you find the piece of truth in what they are saying (there is always a piece) — if you would let that come into you and feel that with compassion and return that to them verbally or psychically, then they are not so desperate for they will then *feel* you recognize the part which concerns them and then they will be more able to hear you. They can't keep doing that. You can only be desperate when desperateness is being matched. When there is room, when there is space, it all goes plop. They hear themselves. They can't have a real enemy out there, because you are not playing.

The Sounds

Question: What's the history behind the sounds you make, how did it start?

I didn't sing. I wasn't interested in sound at all. There was a psychic friend of mine, a very good clairvoyant in California, and she makes something like Indian-chanting sounds. She told me when I first met her, "You're going to make sounds that are going to heal people." And I thought, "Not me, I'm not making funny sounds." So I had no interest in it, at all.

Then one day a few years ago, when I was working on myself, I had a tremendous amount of grief in my pelvis, and I could feel it. Everything had sort of ripened, and gotten to the place where I was crying; the grief was really pouring out, and I thought, "Oh God, I think I want to scream." Then I thought, "Well, why not? Gone this far."

When those emotions line up and are going to come out of your body, there's a part of you that goes, "Oh my God, control yourself, what are you doing?" and then there's another part that says, "Oh thank heavens, I can't wait to get this out," and then there's another part that says, "Isn't this nice?" I ended up turning in with the part that says, "Isn't this nice?" and decided to scream. I felt like a soft bolt of lightning go up through the soles of my feet, and it went up through my body, and it hit my throat, came out my mouth, out my eyes, and out the top of my head, and when it came out my mouth, the breath I had taken in came out making one of the sounds. It was like I got caught in it, and I made the sound for a long time.

There was a woman there who had a slipped disc in her back, and the sound had gone up her back and hit the disc, and popped through, and her back was well. So I said, "Well, they seem to do good things, I guess I'll keep doing them."

For about a year, I did them strictly in that sense, as healing, as something which moved energy in people's bodies, helped things that were stuck, move. Not just physical things but emotional things. It's almost like it put everything on another vibration level, letting the whole body, all the cells, everything, tune up. That was my perception of it.

A year later, I was doing a workshop in California, with about eighty-five people, and afterwards and during it, people would ask me what the sounds were, and I'd just say, I think they're very primordial. They somehow remind us of something very ancient in ourselves, and I always see it as a light connection, to ancientness.

After that workshop, there was another one going on at the same center, and it was a recording of workshops done with Jane Roberts. She's a trance medium and goes into a being called Seth. I haven't read those books except a few chapters here and there but I had a sense that it was good stuff; it wasn't literally true, but it was something that caused people to shift. So I was interested in hearing her become someone else, I was curious about that.

On this particular class tape, she went into a being called Seth Two, a being that they call that for want of a better name, a being that has never been physical, never had a body. Her voice changed drastically, she spoke very monosyllabically; one syllable at a time was a word.

The first two words were "perceive us" and it was (in flat nasal tone) ppeerr-ceeiiivvveee-uuusss, very strange sounding. What it said was, "Forgive the difficulty in communication. For untranslatable knowledge is difficult. We are not physical, yet have we seeded your God. Experiments begun in the past shall be re-initiated. Perceive us as you can." And "perceive us as you can" came out, pppeeerrrCCCEEEIIIVVVEEE*uuusss*, and it started to get that sound in it.

I went into a trance when I heard it; everything turned like a negative, like a black and white photograph. I was just stunned, and a lady next to me said, "Oh! It's like your sounds!" and she hit me on the arm, which felt like a great shock, and I just got up and walked out and sat in my car for three hours.

For about three days, I was just really stunned. It was as if my personality had no way to digest that experience. Here I was making these nice sounds that made people feel better, and I knew they were good, and they made me feel terrific, but I really didn't like them being any of "those other things," and I don't know what those other things are. I'm really telling you as closely and accurately as I can what the experience was, and obviously, somehow it is related.

What we need to do is take experiences as they come, take them open-heartedly, and as clearly as we can, share them with each other as it feels good to do so, and as accurately as possible. Not embellishing or reducing, so as to make it more acceptable to some tape. And in that way, we will find the common thread of the next place we're going, and we'll begin to get the truth. Let your conclusions keep moving.

Another thing I can tell you about the sounds is that a psychologist who had done some work on these Peruvian whistling jars came to one of my workshops. I'd never heard them, but you blow several pipes or pots at once, and the combination of sounds makes a sound like the sounds I make. A number of sounds are simultaneously in the sound I make.

They found that those pots caused the right and left hemispheres to synchronize and when he was in my workshop he was pleased and so was I because so much of what I was talking about was left brain and right brain being able to work together, and what he perceived was the sounds helping that happen.

Craziness

We are all programmed, incredibly, with all kinds of craziness. In other words, we are all nutty as fruitcakes, and until we can know that there isn't anybody in a body who isn't programmed with some craziness, we can't really relax and work on it, because we're all going to try to look cool. And we're all going to try to look intelligent. And we're all going to try to look like we've got it figured out. And all that's going to do is block your process of actually doing that.

If you can't let somebody be in their crazy place, because you can't let you be in your crazy place, then you will have to cut it off and come to a conclusion before feeling out completely what is going on. I think it was Longfellow who said (I am paraphrasing), if we could but know the hearts of our enemies and the quiet desperation that lies in there, we would be relieved of all hatred and anger, that if you could really sense what's making someone run the way they are running, if you had dealt with your own despair enough, if you had enough experience facing it, and enough feeling compassion and enough feeling okay about you, you would let yourself feel the other people and feel where their despair was, then you wouldn't need to hate them. You would then know how to send love and when not to say anything but just step back and not judge. If you observe the truth, you observe the truth. If they don't know it now they will know it later.

Illness

Question: Could you comment on physical illness and its relation to getting conscious?

We keep energy from our conditioning and programming locked in the body in sort of a deep-freeze state, so you can be quite unconscious, and run around with all this unconscious stuff and be pretty healthy and be okay. The minute you start going for getting conscious, you start defrosting these packets of unconsciousness, and as soon as you start doing that, you get symptoms, you get feelings, things start to happen.

We've got it backwards. We've laid blame if you feel bad, or you feel sick, like you're doing something wrong. You're merely bringing into consciousness something that everybody else, and you, have taken on. That puts you in a different relationship to the illness. A lot of illness is staying stuck because people feel guilty they have it. And they can't get through that one enough to process it out. Because they keep introducing to themselves, "You're a bad person." And that's the part you have to forgive. That's the whole point.

The location is very important. A lot of women have bladder infections, cystitis and so on, and often it is connected to sex, as it is mechanically related in that the urethra is short and bacteria can get up when you have sexual intercourse, but that isn't the whole thing. It is the trauma of the intimacy of sex, when you begin to open up. And when it then shifts to female organs that compounds it. The trauma is one of female role, in the sense that it's in the chakra of clear sentience, clear feeling, knowing, gut-level knowing, all kinds of knowledge we have about touch, sensation, and feeling.

Whenever there's a dis-ease in that area, that means you are working through the frozen energy there, it's starting to become conscious, and you are in a state of anxiety, so it's difficult to handle.

The more you can be so sensitive to your body speaking to you, the less drastic does it have to be to get your attention. I don't get sick anymore, and that doesn't mean I couldn't. But I don't, because I feel it all coming, before I'm sick. I feel the energy moving. I feel when I've taken on a trauma, when I've gone unconscious on something. Or when I am not prepared, something's come up and I didn't see it. And I sort of didn't want to see it because it was painful. So the more conscious you let your body be, the better you take care of it, the more insight you can get. Look at it as a metaphor; look at the organ, the function of the organ, the site, and when the disease occurs. The bladder holds system poisons; it holds them before releasing them from the body. What a metaphor for psychological process! And then, if it goes to the ovaries, it has very much to do with the egg, the beginning, and it also has very much to do with feelings about being a woman. If it's on the right side, it has to do with asserting, and being yang, and fear of yang energy, or difficulty with over-asserting in a strident way, because of fearing loss of power. If it's on the yin side, the left side, it has to do with being penetrated.

California

It's funny how we worry about the West Coast falling into the sea. I think it already has. We have to realize that all intuitive speaking and visions come in a metaphor. There's no more perfect metaphor than the eruption of the earth's energy and that this area of the world has fallen into the collective unconscious, which is what the sea is always a symbol of, the mystical, the depths, the collective. And that's why California is crazy; it is mystical, and it is a growing edge. People all over the world are looking at their own shadows. California is deep in this process. This is reflected in the growth of the consciousness and the environmental movements, as well as drug and cult movements, as people risk, make mistakes, and *learn*. We are learning. Economics is part of what we must learn, too.

The first depression occurred right after we hit the end of the frontier. There was no more land to take, so unlimited growth based on the capitalistic process just couldn't happen anymore; it had to start reverberating back. All our economic problems are very much related to our lack of consciousness. The minute we get conscious, the economic problems will stop. It's inevitable we'll have all of it: recession, depression, everything, as long as we keep doing work and living unconsciously, living out of the flow, which isn't trusting. We're going to have to find out, in some measure, the hard way, because the hard way is how you find out for sure. I'm not so worried about it. And the same is true of California. If it falls into the sea, then it falls into the sea. [Patricia's home is on the fault in northern California.] I just don't think that's going to happen.

Continue to grow and work on one's self, rather than trying to make the external organizations take care of it all, which is what we have done through all human history, and all it has ever done is caused war, because we argue about who knows the right way to do it, and it doesn't work because it has to be an internally directed truth as well. You can't make people obey laws. But when the truth comes down to it, we are all good, we are all part of God and we are all coming home. And to the degree we deny that truth, we make it more difficult for that to happen. I know that sounds very idealistic; I'm sure it is. I also think it will happen and whether it takes twenty years or twenty thousand is up to us. I think it is inevitable that we shall evolve and remember who we are.

Sex

There is an intense sexuality that goes along with being alive. And the more alive you are, the more into your vital processes, the more creative you are. If you're of the artistic bent, you try more or less to get lost in the collective unconscious and bring up archetypal images and to *allow* yourself to *receive* that which comes from the acausal mind, which is really what creativeness is. The operative words here are *allow* and *receive*.

The same kind of process has to go into effect for good sex. You step aside of the persona, the chattering personality, the checking it out personality, and let the higher self personality feel, surrendering to the yin flow of the experience, being penetrated, penetrating, simultaneously, emotionally, physically. You let that happen; with everything really wondrous, you have to *let* it happen. You don't really *make* creativity. You don't *make* healing, you don't *make* great sex. You let it. And this is the great hassle that Western minds really have with everything divine and wondrous. We're always trying to figure out how to teach creativity, how to make people creative. It doesn't work; it turns into "arts and crafts" which is okay, but that's technological and doesn't tap the place where it's the growing edge, the creative place, a catching thing that calls to that other place; that's what great art is.

Suffering

Question: Could you comment on the Buddhist saying that all life is suffering?

I think that the Buddha's statement suffered in translation. In being alive one experiences suffering. In being in this first stage of evolving consciousness one experiences suffering. That is there. The minute you own it as a part of the unfolding process of life, in a funny way it is no longer suffering. The thing that you called suffering is there, but it is not suffering. It's got a giggle in it. It's got the cosmic joke leaking in on it. I think that's what Buddha said. This process is intrinsic in life; if you seek to escape suffering you lose in the process.

You can grow wonderfully in the beautiful spots. They are magnificent, healing, expanding, terrific, and inevitable. And, if you try to hold on to one, you get hit in the head. The universe rules: yesterday's ecstasy is today's garbage.

You have to keep being on the growing edge and keep going for being alive. Lace it with a little kindness, do the best you can, keep your eyes open and remember. And keep breathing. That's all you have to do.

When you are down, let a little part of you giggle. A part of you will resent it: "I don't want to giggle now. I want to be mad." That's okay too, they will both be there.

The Future

People used to get really frightened when I healed them; they were really grateful that they didn't have pain anymore but they'd look at me really funny, and I could see all the witch pictures, all this scary imagery come up in them; it feels like demon power to them because they don't feel any connection with it. So I used to tell people, "You did it too." Only I didn't mean it because I knew I did it. I knew how I concentrated, I knew how I found the place, I knew how I shot the juice, I knew what I was doing, and I knew I did it.

And even when I didn't know what I was doing, I knew I was letting that happen. So I would say, "You did it too," because it was the only thing that came to me to say.

Then one time, I was meditating and it came to me that the reason I always had miraculous healings is because I create people coming to me who are willing to have miracles. And I totally realized how they did it. I did it completely; they did it completely. It's the paradox again. No loss. No one powerless. The paradox.

So after I realized that, I said, "Well what am I supposed to do then?" Then, I felt the question, "Would you be willing not to have miracles happen, when you do healing, because the important thing is the energy, not the healing. It's important that you do generate this energy with people, but not necessarily that they be healed." And I thought, "Well no, then they'll think I can't do it!"

It took me about three months to realize, "Of course I would do that," and it didn't matter. So I meditated and said, "Okay, now what am I supposed to do? I agree I'll generate the energy. What am I supposed to do now?"

I went into deep meditation, and the words came up very clearly, "end wars." It was hard enough being a closet psychic, so what is this "end wars?" And I thought, "Just a minute. Find out what that means." And what I saw then was a beautiful vision of the planet. It was blue and white and green, as though seen from outer space, and these gold white lights were coming down, all the way around, and as they came down, I realized that they were beings, coming to this planet. The words came out "The Age of Avatars." And that's like Christ or Buddha. And I thought, "Yes, that's true, this is the Age of Avatars."

As I was looking at these lights, I saw a face in one, a countenance that was not male or female, but very beautiful, with golden white light around it. As I looked at that face, I realized that person had learned how to love themselves completely, while in a body. And they turned and looked at someone who was standing next to them who was not lit, and looked at them with such complete acceptance and love that they became light. And then that person looked to someone next to them who wasn't lit, and looked at them with such love and acceptance, that they became light. And then this critical mass of energy was reached, and the whole world was lit, and then the words came: "Twenty years." And that was about six years ago.

Remembering and Forgetting

We all know and we all forget, and we're in the moment of quickening right now. We're going to forget completely, remember completely, forget completely and remember completely. And it's going to go on all the time, and it's going to get bigger and bigger, you're going to forget deeper and remember clearer. You will know and you won't know simultaneously.

As you paradoxically let yourself be empty and say, "I don't know," you make a wonderful space to be filled, and as you are filled you expand and you are greater. And in that greaterness you say, "Oh, there is more I don't know." This then creates more room to grow. In contrast, the duality thinking would say, "There is this much to know — everybody run and bottle it up. And you're not okay unless you've got it all." You're condemned to hell when you buy that, because you can't win that way. You win by simultaneously knowing you are a pipsqueak in the universe, you don't know anything. We haven't even begun to see what is in the universe. And the minute you realize the paradox inherent in our perception of the universe, you will have broadened your ability to perceive the universe.

(December 1979)

Alan Brilliant

Oil

I

I use grease
for the axle of my wheelbarrow
the track of my printing press
the nipples of my car's pinions
lubricating oil for the tendons
    of my typecaster.
I use heavy oil
for the gears of my printing press
and the great pressing wheel
    of my bindery boards
penetrating oil
for the hinges of the house doors
the car doors, the typewriter keys
oil to keep the hoe from rusting
    and my rake and my little trowel
linseed oil, boiled to keep
    the paint from drying
        raw to keep
    the outside steps from rotting
neatsfoot oil for my old shoes.

II

When I was born
they had the oils all prepared
chrism for my confirmation
oil of the catechumens for my baptism
"Be opened," they said and rubbed oil
between my shoulder blades
so I could be supple and strong
and oil for the sick
for my eyelids and earlobes
for my nostrils and thin dry lips
for my stained hands and tired feet
food for a long journey.

III

They say that oil and water
    won't mix
but when I was born
they put olive oil scented with balsam
in the sea water of my mother's womb
they put ink there and pads of paper
a hammer, a ruler
a type case full of lead
and when I was thirteen
they added drysand and woodash
they sprinkled limedust and sawdust
in my amazed mouth.
When I was a man
they heaped flaked soot
from the ovens of Germany
splinters from the coffins of traitors
they dug out rotting books
from the burned libraries
and made me lie there.

IV

But I went to work
and took care of myself
discovering cracks in the shank
of my potato hook and the dibble

I use to prick holes in the ground
    for fall bulbs
I heard my lawn mower squeak
and worried about tar on my saw.
Soon I was oiling everything
I know I use too much:
mineral oil for my stomach pains
wintergreen for my bent neck.
They say there is a shortage of oil
    in the world today
soon there won't be enough to go around
and I worry with everyone else
about our needy shovels and
our neglected lives
and what to sustain us
on that last abrasive journey
through the treeless sand.

(July 1983)

This poem previously appeared in Paintbrush.

Fugitives

Carol Hoppe

I arrive late, as usual, paper ends flapping from my briefcase, crumbs clinging to my coat after a crackers-and-cheese lunch between stoplights. Picking my way across the muddy yard from my parking place in a tow-away zone, I glance at the glassed-in central staircase of the high school to check the time. No students are passing, not even dawdlers, so the third period bell has already rung. My Vietnamese pupils will be sitting in the Humanities Resource Room, patiently awaiting me, their teacher in transit.

It is my job to flit from school to school each morning, tossing out English sentence structure on the run to foreign students of all ages and origins. One stop at a bathroom or the principal's office is enough to delay me. Then I frantically stuff papers, gather supplies and step on

Sometimes I shudder when I consider the day my students will understand English.

the gas.

On my way to the elementary school class, the one which preceded this one, my students passed me. Little foreign faces sailed by in school bus rows, waving at windows high above my Pinto level. They, too, were on the move, despite their immigrant parents' hope of finding a point of rest in America. But when I straggled into class in our windowless store room, tripping over recording equipment on wheels (that, too, is moveable), they were already settled on folding chairs. I jabbered; they talked quietly among themselves. I was red-faced and distraught; they were shy and helpful. I tell my friends how satisfying my work is because they need me; the truth is, I need them.

The older students I am now approaching are more reserved but no less cheerful. They brighten the dreary building, in fact — that curious, flat-roofed structure on a barren field, whose leaky tin roof is now dripping all over the connecting walkway it was meant to protect. As I heave open the steel door with chicken-wire reinforced window slits, it occurs to me that its garish orange paint was probably intended to have a similar, cheering effect. Whatever happened to wood, I wonder.

As I proceed up the stairs the old, familiar uneasiness enfolds me just as it did when I was seventeen, helplessly entering my own high school. Others, like me, are robbed of personal force here. There are signs of their frustration along the way: thin grey carpeting slashed by a straight blade and later patched over, graffiti on the orange steel fire doors, not painted so that it could be washed off but gouged into the finish to assert — everlastingly? — well, till graduation at least, that "Brenda Jean has brown sugar." When the bell releases its reluctant audience for a measly five minutes, lockers will bang open all along this hall to reveal further assertions of identity. Aggressively, defiantly, this year's cold green cubbyhole is staked out with pin-up girls, rifle posters and the assurance that "State sucks." Even those who have made it socially — the slim cheerleader tossing blond hair in her tomboy letter sweater and leggy short skirt, the beautiful couple holding hands, curled up safely for the moment in each other's popularity and furling it like a banner — even they glance over their shoulders at the shy outsiders to make sure they are watching, as though awe could validate their own existence. How will my girls ever adjust to the desperation I feel on all sides? Or, coming from the heaving devastation of war, haven't they noticed the shifting ground yet?

They aren't girls really. As I enter the humanities library and find the first one, the younger one, I'm reminded of her woman-hood. She is alone again. I have never seen a student at her table offering conversation or help, and today her Vietnamese companion is absent. She lifts her calm full face to take me in and acknowledges me with a faint smile. I wave brightly, stupidly.

As I rummage in the proctor's desk for the key to yet another storeroom the intercom switches on. My hand stops in mid-air. Even before the piped voice starts speaking I know the air is charged with an outside presence we are powerless to keep out. Talk at other tables is interrupted, animation wiped off faces. Heads rise like caged mice responding in a daze to the opening laboratory door and the expected dole.

Once, last Winter, the announcement was startling. "I'd like to say a few words about snowballs," it said, brightening the face of every student except Tan, who didn't understand the language, much less the issue since bombs are the only kind of warfare she knows. But eyes flashed around her, full of mirth, checking each other's readiness to pounce even though they couldn't locate their prey. He must have been pacing behind very thin walls, to judge by his nervous tone. In regular classrooms teachers were studying their empty desk-tops or staring intently over their pupils' heads to avoid recognizing the glee.

"Now I know we all used to enjoy throwing snowballs when we were kids," the voice went on, ingratiating. "But I've noticed quite a few of them flying around the entrance lately, and I don't see any children." He would have laughed lamely at this point if he'd had real faces in front of him. But his only accompaniment was static. The voice of authority was growing thin, and he was backed into a corner, so he lashed out with sarcasm, a teacher's last resort. "Act your age, will you," he snapped, in tune with the control switch. And it worked again. The students were disarmed, exchanging more timid glances this time, trying to laugh it off, seeking cover in their books until the next display of grown-up frailty drew them out. I tried to imagine the man behind the voice, whom I had never seen. He would be shuffling papers with a vengeance, barking orders to a secretary, perhaps, dissatisfied with his own distance, isolation and lack of effectiveness. None of their lives is easy, I tell myself as I approach Tan, who bears the burden of all this frustration.

She gravely stands to meet me at her vinyl-topped table surrounded by shelves of *The Red Badge of Courage* and annotated Shakespeare. Her dark hair falls forward to conceal her face as she reaches for her books; sand-colored arms enfold them to herself like a flower gathering its petals in the dusk, fragile, intact. Lips closed, she smiles on me kindly with the corners of her mouth as I lumber across the room, lopsided with my heavy briefcase.

"Where's your friend?" I ask.

"Not here today."

"Oh, is she sick?"

"No. I know where." She is full of the pleasure of knowing something I don't and being able to lead me to the spot. "The ma . . . maf room," she states proudly.

"That's right. She's good at math." I remember then that it's the only subject either of them can be good at and ask her to take me to the lab, where Gai must be working with tapes.

As we leave the room a fat girl with her shirttail out blocks our way. Her hair is short and brown. It retains the ridges from her rollers. There are creases in her white blouse where it's tightly stretched across her middle. She lifts her arcs of eyebrow and stares ironically at Tan, who hugs her armful of books closer and lowers her head, creeping, it seems to me, into the tiniest possible space beside the door. "Excuse *me*," the girl hisses, then steps deliberately into Tan. I watch paralyzed, suddenly aware that she is used to this sort of treatment.

When I join Tan in the hall, she doesn't look at me, so she doesn't see my indignation. Even if she did, she is too modest to associate it with herself. Instead, she hovers round-shouldered over her books, as though she were meditating on their closed covers. Vulnerable, I repeat to myself, walking beside her swaying, compact form and examining her out of the corner of my eye. Tennis shoes. No protection in them. And no warmth in that discolored, synthetic T-shirt. A well-meaning Christian sponsor must have dug it out of the Boys' Tops bin at the thrift shop before she knew the sex of the "poor refugees" coming to her church. She probably hummed contentedly over her loot all the way home. Why didn't someone tell her Tan would need armor? And where are all those tough young high school boys who squander their masculinity on teeny-boppers with braces on their teeth? Don't they notice how graceful she is under this track team guise? Idiots, I sputter. Then I force myself to remember that they must cope with this seething school, the squared-off lots of their parents' suburban homes, the false gardens of our shopping centers under glass. And their only refuge is the assurance of each other's liking, which is just as transient. How could they possibly risk having such an alien friend? Besides, their mothers wouldn't like it.

We open the door on Gai and find her impassive in the midst of chaos. She is wired into the central desk, intent on the messages from her earphones. The rest of the class resemble caged-up monkeys, hyperactive under the influence of the bars and the absence of their keeper. Two of the boys are walking a narrow ledge beneath the window while their friends whistle and shout encouragement. Three girls circle the teacher's empty desk and watch as, above them, an innocent looking redhead with braids and freckles ties a note on a string to dangle from the recording apparatus overhead. A group of students are busily scribbling on the board at the back of the room. A few of them are pointing at Gai and snickering. She is totally unaware that her behavior is unusual. Sometimes I shudder when I consider the day my students will understand English.

When Gai finally notices my teacher-like, attention-getting gestures, she jumps up with her headphones on, trailing wires as she stacks her papers. Stumbling over cord, she unwinds it from the legs of her Levis and comes over with a worried expression on her round face. She barely reaches Tan's chin.

"I fought you aren't coming," she says, leaving me to fill in the rest of her reason for being here.

"No, just late again," I assure her, watching the relieved smile widen her face and narrow her dark eyes.

Silently, they fall in with me and we leave the jumbled classroom with its dislocated students. I stride at first, as befits my teacher role, but I'm slowed down by their tiny steps, quieted by the soft flurry of explanations in Vietnamese that pass over me, comforted to know that their words contain no malice. Walking between them toward our English class, I forget the locker-lined halls and the fear that they contain. These are survivors of a far more terrible fear, and they can afford to shelter a fugitive like me.

(August 1980)

There Is No School On The Sixth Floor

Ron Jones

L ast summer I found myself unexpectedly teaching school. My classroom was a hallway on a deserted floor of a mental hospital. The students were five adolescents hospitalized for psychiatric treatment and eight "street kids" paid to attend school. The school program was a part of an unusual experiment to prepare psychiatric patients for the real world.

The inner-city street kids were hired by the major's office as part of a summer employment program for disadvantaged youths. It was hoped that they might serve as therapeutic models for a peer group of severely disturbed young adults.

This introduction of the real world into the hospital setting was a unique situation. Most psychiatric hospitals attempt to help patients resocialize through companionship or

This is excerpted from Ron Jones' There Is No School On The Sixth Floor (Ron Jones, 1201 Stanyan Street, San Francisco, California 94117).

volunteer community helper progams. But these efforts to ease the patient into the outside world take place *after* the patient is released. This care is comparable to "here's the name of a friend, and here's a new coat" given to individuals leaving a prison.

Of course, it takes more than a new suit to catch up with what's current on the outside. Especially if you're an adolescent. So a special summer school was initiated. Kids called "street wise" were paid to help kids called "crazy" face the eventuality of leaving the hospital. It was an adventuresome idea.

The street kids were an amalgam of personalities. The self-proclaimed leader of the group was a young Chinese woman named Mary. Ideas shot from her like darts. As she talked, she literally painted words with her hands. Another kid named Johnny T. fielded Mary's enthusiasm with a gold-toothed smile. Johnny's radio and knit cap gave him away as a kid from South Hampton Street. He was one of those rare "tough" kids who could go anyplace.

Georgia was simply big. She was a large black woman who looked and acted as if she was in continual choir practice. She glided quietly into any setting and then anchored. She didn't say much, but she hummed a lot and you felt good being in her company. Alyce was also black, but she was different from Johnny T. or Georgia. Alyce's middle-class background kept showing. She was always acting to please, to find someone a chair, to share her latest accomplishment.

Whereas Alyce moved to accommodate the world, Vicki, Lisela, and Philip gave it color. They were from the city's Latino neighborhood. Their words overlapped and spilled into the air like machine gun fire. Staccato expletives about boyfriends, marriage, El Salvador, and a hundred incidents were ignored or absorbed by most of the kids. For Richard Lee, a tall Chinese kid, the salvo of words was something to dodge. With each surge of verbiage, Richard would wince and back up then spin and sit down, only to stand and turn again. Richard was a matador turning away from words and motion cast in his direction. Like a wind-up toy twisted too tightly, you wanted to hold him for a minute and let the extra juice whirl away.

The final outside student was Ellen. She was the only white kid in the group. Shy and boyish in her heavy jeans and sweater, she was unique in one respect. Her younger sister was one of the psychiatric patients.

Although the city kids reflected a tremendous diversity in style, they held similar opinions about working with peers who were mental patients. They expected the patients to be "bedridden," "mentally retarded," and "unable to make sense." They felt the patients would be "talking about things that don't exist," "constantly running around tearing things up," and "always yelling like on TV." The greatest concern held up by the city kid was of "being beaten up by a crazy patient."

The patients in the school program were also quite diverse. Leona was the group cheerleader. With her broad shoulders and her "rocker" walk, she looked like she was skating for the Bay Bombers. Leona was hospitalized for aggressive hostility. Her sister Ellen explained that Leona hit people, was always in trouble, that her stepmother couldn't stand her — "she could never come home." Leona's closest friend was Danny. Like most of the patients and outside kids, Danny was sixteen. He looked about eight or nine years old. His hair stuck up in the back and down over his eyes in the front. He looked like a Cub Scout in pursuit of merit badges. His body could run and jump over fire plugs, but his mind seemed fixed on questions of sexuality. Like a stuck record, he'd ask, "How long is your cock?" To the girls, he'd smile and ask, "Can I squeeze your tits?"

Lynell was one patient who never heard Danny's question. Just as Danny's speech repeated, Lynell's every movement was ritualized. Her frail body would crank to a standing position, only to reseat, then stand again, and sit again, and stand again. Her walk was several steps forward, followed by a pivot and steps in another direction. Every action was methodically traced over and over, a process called "perseveration." A crusty webbing of dried tears covered Lynell's eyes like spider webs. Tobacco stains crawled over her fingers. Her uncombed hair and disregard for clothing made her look like an aged woman.

Of all the patients, "Zero" was the most mysterious. He looked like an average suburban senior high school student. In many ways, though, he was anything but average. Zero was an electronics wizard. Dying TV sets came to life under his care. At his command, hospital elevator doors would open to an exposed shaft. He could listen in on any phone conversation coming into the ward. And with little trouble he could vanish. In a ward charged with emotion he had found the secret of quietly blending into the scenery or exiting through an unnoticed door. So he lived in an electric world and played ghost to the real world.

Rella also hid from reality. Her escape took the form of silence. She never spoke. Periods of silence were interrupted by periods of severe vomiting. Her life swung back and forth from silence to physical illness.

Just as the city kids shared certain expectations about patients, the patients expressed a set of opinions about their counterparts out-side the hospital. Generally they felt the city kids were "loud," "hard-looking," and "very dangerous." That "those people will pick on us," that "they'll make fun of us," that "they don't know about a hospital like this." And, "they'll probably hurt us, kick us and stuff."

They were two groups of kids separated by worlds of experience. Kids from city streets, called "disadvantaged," being asked to work with kids called "crazy." Both fearful of the other. Both willing to risk abuse and danger in order to attend an unusual Summer school on the sixth-floor hallway of a hospital. What happened when these two groups actually met was the basis for some unexpected learning, some surprises, and a new definition of the word "mental."

School didn't exactly start with the pledge to the flag. In fact, we didn't have a flag, much less desks or books. What we did have was a huge billboard depicting a fanciful spaceship. It seemed like a natural introductory activity. We had a roll of tape, a paper billboard, and lots of arms and legs. The perfect educational plot. City kids and patients would meet each other — help each other — and share in the success of covering an ugly wall. Everything about this plot was perfect except for one thing. The tape. It stuck to everything but the wall.

Like learning, chaos can start quite innocently. In the case of the billboard, it started with Georgia.

Georgia used her massive size to tear delicate pieces of tape and affix them to the floor. They stuck up like grass. Actually, it was Mary's idea. She directed everyone to start taping the edges of floored paper. Johnny T. smiled. Alyce tried to help by passing tape to waiting hands. It stuck to her and those she touched. Vicki and Lisela rolled the taped paper against the wall and continued talking. Richard and Ellen dutifully continued taping.

And the patients? Well, they were really needed. They greeted the sight of the street kids struggling with tape as a worthy adventure. Leona used her roller derby strength to hold up the top of the billboard. Danny used the moment to chase after Mary. His pursuit left a trail of sticky tape. Alyce stopped handing out tape. She sat down. Found herself taped to the floor. And was too embarrassed to get up. Lynell, the patient of a thousand directions, held out a corner of paper and wouldn't let go. Rella just watched. Zero gave a nervous laugh and disappeared into an empty room. Johnny T. and Philip formed a human ladder to hold and tape the upper edges of the billboard. They demanded more tape.

Bodies pressed and sprawled against the paper. Tape was passed from hand to hand to wall. Tape hung like fringe from shirt sleeves and grabbed at unsuspecting feet. It did everything but hold the paper against the wall.

Suddenly the paper spaceship unraveled like an avalanche. It buried its tormentors. Covered them like a tent. No one escaped the falling paper and its tangle of tape. In slow motion Johnny T. and Philip cascaded downward with the roll of paper. For a moment there was nothing but silence, then a giggle, followed by yelps of laughter. Feet kicked to get free of the paper maze. Bodies scrambled into a stance. Tape was everywhere. It would take another hour to put up the paper spaceship. But it did get up. One spaceship flying through the hallway. It signaled the start of Summer school. A fragile alliance between street kids and inside patients had begun.

The impact of street kids on patients was immediate and dramatic. In the first few days of school, Danny was the subject of all our attention. He was in love. In love with Mary and Georgia and Alyce and Vicki and Lisela and Leona and Lynell and Rella. He displayed his passions by squeezing girls' tits, often by a surprise maneuver. He would spring from a hiding place or run full tilt down the hall to embrace his victims.

The girls went bonkers. They threw words of warning, "Cut that out!" Then words of consequence, "I'm going to smash you if you touch me again." Danny took these taunts as encouragement. Mary finally explained — "It's not that we don't like you, it's that we don't like what you are doing." Danny greeted Mary's explanation with a smile. He put his hands over Mary's breasts and tickled with his fingers. Mary grabbed his hands and pulled them gently to his sides. And held them there as she continued. "Boys don't treat girls that way. My boyfriend doesn't treat me like that!" And so it went. Danny received daily doses of street etiquette. The message finally got across.

We were doing some improvisational drama. Each student was given a statement on a piece of paper saying "you are robbing a train" or "you are washing a car." The students were asked to find others holding a similar statement — and they were to conduct this search without using words. Danny started to follow Mary, then suddenly stopped. He became busy writing on slips of paper. In the midst of people acting out the robbery of a train or washing cars, Danny circulated his directions. Georgia showed me the result of Danny's labor. He was distributing his version of the assignment. It read, "Grab Danny and give him a kiss." Mary reacted by walking straight at Danny. She didn't speak or hesitate. She kissed him gently. Danny had met the real world and found a way to touch it without being hit in the face.

By the second week of Summer school, Vicki and Lisela institutionalized the idea of giving. They called it Kriss Kringle. Everyone put his or her name in a hat and then we drew names. I pulled Georgia. In the week that followed, it was my Kriss Kringle responsibility to give Georgia a gift each day. I was not allowed to tell anyone whom I had drawn. At the end of the week we were to tell that secret. Gift-giving graced our presence for five days. I arrived one morning to find that my Kriss Kringle had prepared me a complete breakfast. An unnamed poet posted his (her?) work as a gift for everyone. Alyce received a lace fan. Someone gave Danny a copy of *Penthouse*. Lynell, the patient who looked so feeble, was given a bright ribbon for her hair. Johnny T. got a supply of batteries for his radio. Rella, the girl who was almost catatonic, found a daily supply of chocolate chip cookies. She began to share them. Several girls were supplied with perfume and makeup. Patients unaccustomed to using cosmetics and trying to look good suddenly started coming to school in eye shadow and traces of rouge. Lynell wore her new hair ribbon with a beautiful cameo. The cameo was something her grandmother had given her. Something she had kept in a bottom drawer. Something she now wore with a glow of pride.

Richard, the shy outside kid, took a Polaroid picture of Lynell and her finery. Lynell smiled. It was the first time I had seen that.

The photo caught that moment. Lynell looked with disbelief at the photo, then walked away without saying a word. In a few moments, she lurched back down the hall. She was walking in a steady gait. That's right. She was walking in a deliberate direction. No turns. No steps forward and back. She walked straight to Richard. Then she spoke, "What's 'photogenic' mean?" Richard answered, "It means you're beautiful." Lynell smiled broadly. "The nurses downstairs said I'm photogenic." Richard was as pleased and as rewarded as Lynell. The chemistry between street kid and patient was beneficial to both.

Perhaps the greatest gift provided by the street kids was the freedom they offered. Prior to the Summer the patients had not been allowed on field outings. For many patients this meant they had been confined to the hospital ward for more than a year. Midway through the Summer, Mary argued for control of our budget. It was given. With the money, the students planned an outing to a roller rink. I was surprised to find that the hospital had no outing policy, and therefore had no outings. When Mary pursued this matter she found that the hospital insurance regulations prevented our use of private cars. Or buses. Or taxi cabs.

Mary found a solution — a form of transportation not stipulated in the insurance policy. She argued, if it's not in writing, it must be permissable. Her solution was a joy to all. She rented a large black limousine from a local mortuary. On the designated day for our roller skating trip, we found a slinky Mercedes limo waiting in front of the hospital. Mary ushered everyone into the limousine. Three nurses volunteered to go along. The psychiatric ward had its first field trip. And much more.

It turned out that Lynell, the girl who could barely walk, could roller skate. And Rella, the patient who never spoke, asked to go along. We had rented the entire rink for ourselves. The manager was delighted with his early morning customers. We zoomed about. Johnny T. was silk on wheels. Leona, her sister Ellen, and Georgia inched around the arena wall. Alyce could skate backwards. Mary, Vicki, Lisela, and Richard formed a whip that sent both ends crashing toward the middle. Most of us practiced graceful falling and surprise stops.

After a few minutes of skating, it became obvious that the manager liked us. From his booth at the end of the rink, he announced, "All right, ladies and gentlemen, I have a special surprise for you today — haven't done this in years. We're going to do the Lindy." A scratchy record came on. It sounded like a rhumba. The manager placed a bar in the middle of the rink. Our mission was becoming clear. "All right now," the loudspeaker cracked, "everyone up for the Lindy Low. How low can you go?"

With the manager waving encouragement, we skated kamikaze style toward the bar. The object was to duck under the bar and still stay on your skates. Johnny T. whizzed through with a graceful dip. Danny and Richard approached the bar in a gale of laughter. They both crashed through it. Alyce skated full speed at it and then ducked into a ball that flew under the bar in a blue. Everyone clapped. Georgia and Leona walked up to the bar in a stagger, grabbed it, and walked through. More clapping. Danny raced toward the bar, again, and slid under like a baseball player sliding home. Zero circled the rink, then dashed at the bar. At the last second, he stooped into a crouch. The crouch exposed his invention; Zero had tied skates to each hand. They worked like the landing gear of an airplane. He swooped under the bar, riding on four roller skates and a grin. His victory was contagious. Everyone was rooting for everyone else. We enjoyed the greatest freedom of all — play.

Exhaustion finally took its toll. Skates were gingerly pulled off and stuffed back into boxes, rear ends were rubbed, the candy machine assaulted. As we were leaving, the manager of the rink moved to hold open the door. He was obviously pleased with the day's events. In a final gesture of goodbye, he declared, "Nice group you have here. You're good kids, not like those crazies that usually come here." A secret smile traveled across twelve faces.

Summers don't end. They tuck away someplace in your memory. And wait to be recalled. For me, this was a special Summer. It was one of those Summers when your ideas about things get tested and sometimes change. This had been a Summer of change. At the close of school, I asked the patients how they felt about their counterparts from outside the hospital. They responded, "I thought they'd make fun of us, but they didn't. . . ." "They don't feel sorry for us. I like that." One patient acknowledged, "I still feel embarrassed in front of them about being in the hospital." The same patient then summarized how the patients generally felt: "We all blend together; they don't seem all that special."

As for the outside kids, their opinions about the patients also changed. They noted that patients came across not as crazy and destructive, but as quieter, less confident, and more reclusive than their community peers. They expressed surprise that the differences they expected to encounter were not as radical as anticipated. "They seem normal to me." "The kids are different, but they're not bad." "I've kinda enjoyed their company." Perhaps Johnny T., with his gold tooth and constant smile, summed it up best: "They're a little mental — you know, like me."

(July 1979)

Looking Back

Tuli Kupferberg
On The Not-So-Bygone Sixties

Howard Jay Rubin

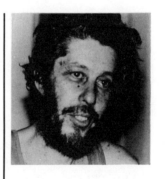

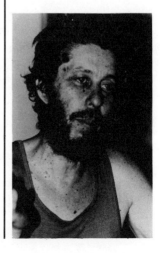

At a time when radio stations clung safely to bubblegum rock, The Fugs — Tuli Kupferberg, Ed Saunders, and Ken Weaver — were to music what Lenny Bruce was to comedy. With songs like "Slum Goddess of the Lower East Side," "Coca-Cola Douche," "I Couldn't Get High," and "The Nothing Song," they were catalysts of what Tuli Kupferberg calls "a kind of beat-hippie-bohemian defiance of the status quo, the establishment, and the America that sucks." That was 1965. Seventeen years later, it seems an era that has come and gone. Or has it?

We'd printed some of Tuli Kupferberg's recent cartoons but knew little else about him since his years with The Fugs. I was planning a trip to New York, and Jeff Badgett, **THE SUN's** assistant editor, suggested I give Kupferberg a call. He agreed to the interview readily, *adding, "Of course, I'm a bit different from your usual subjects. I don't buy that New Agey spiritual stuff." "Good," I said, "my cynical side could use a little prodding." "Well, let's not call it cynicism," he suggested, "maybe realism. . . ."*

When we arrived at his fifth-floor apartment Kupferberg said, with a mischievous smile, that I'd caught him in a vicious mood. He was ready to "let the readers have it." We spoke around the kitchen table, by the aisles of books that were most of the room's furnishings. His wife Sylvia finished the dishes behind us. "You know," she said, "the last article done on Tuli spent more time describing our unfinished bathroom than anything he said." I promised to include both. Through the opening banter his voice was a reluctant mumble, then as talk grew livelier, a livelier mumble. His wit was quick and abundant, good-humored though sarcastic.

Again and again the talk turned to politics. When asked by Jerome Rubin, my father and photographer, to define his own, he had no easy answer. "I'm a man who's still looking for an effective radical politics." It's a search he began more than forty years ago. He's felt the frustration of watching the fall of countless promising movements, and seeing the inability of leftist thought, thus far, to provide workable alternatives to the inequalities of capitalist culture. He's wise enough to see the faults in all the perfect theories, the clay feet of all his heroes. Still, his sincerity shines through.

I found our talk fascinating, especially as we role-played the old argument about the relation of politics or work in the world, and spirituality. Are the ideals mutually exclusive, or intertwined and inseparable, one lending strength to the other? To me it seems that a sharp distinction between the two denies an essential connection: political action is impotent without a keen moral or spiritual sense, spirituality dead-ends when divorced from action. Tuli felt that the other-worldliness he's seen labelled as spirituality is a cop-out, a placebo. We felt it important to air his view, though the discussion seemed more semantic than substantial. "I suppose it's really the same thing," he said, "but I prefer my kind of social activism." He summed it up well: "It's not so much what you think you think, but what you do and how you really feel."

— Howard Jay Rubin

SUN: Who is Tuli Kupferberg?
KUPFERBERG: He's as yet undefined. That was pretty helpful, wasn't it?

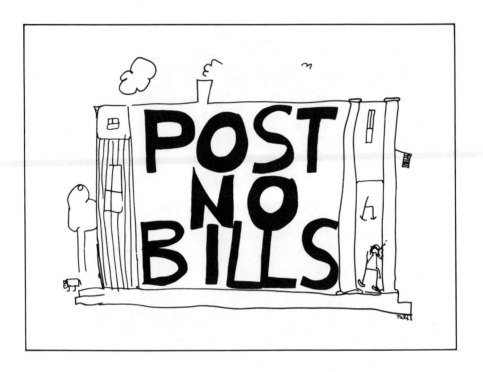

SUN: That was fine. A couple of facts: you have a wife, what's her name?
KUPFERBERG: This is my wife, What's-her-name. Sylvia.

SUN: And a daughter. How old is she?
KUPFERBERG: She's eight. And I have a twelve-year-old son, and a thirty-three-year-old son, who's not here, by a previous engagement.

SUN: In an old **SUN**, you were described as an artist and a writer. What are you working on now?
KUPFERBERG: I don't like people who define themselves as being artists or writers, or even, by extension, by their craft, unless it's a very down-to-earth one. I think those are very egotistical descriptions.

SUN: So, what kind of stuff are you doing these days?
KUPFERBERG: I'm taking care of the children and drawing cartoons.

SUN: A lot of cartoons?
KUPFERBERG: Yeah, they only take me about three minutes each. See, I don't know how to draw, but I'm a good cartoonist. It's really a literary form.

SUN: Let's look at the Fugs. What were things like when they started, and what were the Fugs about?
KUPFERBERG: Well, things were more exciting when they started, now things are more depressing. We were at the beginning of a kind of upswing then, in '65, and now we're at the depth of a downswing, and some think that it's the beginning of an upswing.

SUN: Do you think that?
KUPFERBERG: Well, it may be. It's not the end of the beginning, but is it the beginning of the end? People have always had these end-of-the-world feelings about their period, especially when they get more than fifty years of age.

SUN: So, what brought the Fugs together?
KUPFERBERG: Fate. You want to know the specifics? We were reading our poetry, and reading poetry is a kind of sedentary thing, although the beats tried to liven it up, making it into a more

dramatic art. We'd sit at a cafe on Second Avenue, which was run by someone who gained most of his income from a bookie operation at the same place. Maybe it was a good thing. I mean, at least it was a lively venture. After our readings we would go around the corner to a place called the Dome. There was a bar with a jukebox that had Beatles and Stones records. And the fat-assed poets would be shamed by all the others into dancing. Ed got the idea for forming a rock group that would have lyrics that were a little more meaningful than the standard known at the time. I picked the named Fugs from Norman Mailer's expression for the word fuck in *The Naked and the Dead*, and we were on our way. Ken Weaver was in there too, so we three started the Fugs.

SUN: Can you think of any of the lyrics that seem representative to you?

KUPFERBERG: Yeah, it was Ted Berrigan who gave us what I thought was maybe the best Fugs song. It was called "Doin' All Right," and it goes like this: "When I walk down the street, the people that I meet hold their noses and say, 'How are you fixed for blades?' But don't mind 'em, I walk right on by, 'cause I'm high, and I'm getting almost as much pussy as the spades." I think he said more pussy, but that was revised as being too racist. And I think it's never sung that way anymore, because it is a kind of racist and sexist line. Then it went on, and if I had to pick two lines that represented the Fugs I would pick these two, "I ain't ever gonna go to Vietnam, gonna stay right here at home and screw your mom." I think it starts, "I got hairs growing around my nose and throat, I don't ever exercise the right to vote. When you see me on the street you yell, 'Jesus Christ,' but I'm getting mine, I'm doin' all right." So that was the beginning of a kind of beat-hippie-bohemian defiance of the status quo, the establishment, and the America that sucks.

SUN: What kind of reaction did the Fugs get?

KUPFERBERG: An amazingly enthusiastic and friendly reaction. We played for our friends at the beginning, and it was probably more fun then than it ever was. It was very communal, half the audience would come on the stage, anything could happen at a show, and sometimes did, although that was true all during our career.

We were basically theater, because we would act out each song. I would do a good part of that since Ed had decided I shouldn't sing, for good reason. So when you hear the records you only hear about a quarter of what we were. We would improvise every night, and I would construct a dramatic piece around each song, with a lot of costume changes and a lot of weird things, props.

SUN: Were you ever famous enough to have to deal with people treating you as a celebrity?
KUPFERBERG: There can be ten people who know you and you'll still have to deal with that sometimes. The first way you deal with it is by accepting it all, because it's such a welcome relief from being a nonentity and a piece of shit the way society treats most people. But then you realize that it has its built-in stupidities and drawbacks, which is that you get to believe, if you're stupid enough yourself, that the adulation has some sort of proportion to what you really are. The other bad thing is that so much is expected from you by these people who want you to fill out their lives. I know this because I've been at both ends of it, I've hero-worshipped myself so I know what's involved.

SUN: Who were your heroes back then?
KUPFERBERG: Oh, the usual. Dylan, maybe. I've had literary people I've admired. I can't remember them because they soon devolved into being less than heroes. My latest hero with clay feet is George Grosz, the German cartoonist. Cartoonist is a very mild word because he was an incredible social critic of Germany in the period between the wars and then he came to America and sort of mildly attacked everything he stood for. He called the people — meaning the masses — idiots. Maybe they're not the brightest, but. . . . Then he was asked to draw by some left-wing magazines for no money and he said he'd had enough of that, as if the people who make these magazines were making money off him. I'm sure they weren't. They were also working for nothing, almost nothing. So he was the latest hero to go, but woe to the land that needs heroes.

SUN: Were you part of the Yippie myth?
KUPFERBERG: Myth? The Yippies were not a myth.

SUN: Then what were they?

KUPFERBERG: They weren't a myth because they knew they were a myth, you see. It's hard to say if there was a Yippie myth because it was very effective for a period. Something that was effective can hardly be a myth. It maybe wasn't what it seemed to be.

SUN: What was your part in that?
KUPFERBERG: Well, I was in on it from the beginning, almost. I went to Chicago during the '68 convention and the Fugs were supposed to play there but part of our band was in California and they were too afraid to come. I was afraid too, but I figured we promised to go so we should go. I wasn't quite sure it was a smart thing to do, because I thought people would be killed there. I think it was a wonderful idea to disrupt the convention, but not at the price of a lot of dead young people.

SUN: What was your experience there?
KUPFERBERG: Horrible. We came a few days before it was supposed to start, and were informed that a young Indian boy had been shot to death on the streets. I don't know if he had a weapon or not, but the cops said he looked like he had a weapon, and he was just shot to death. That was the only death in that period, but it certainly cast a pall over what was going to happen for me. I don't claim to be a physically brave person, and I was terrified of the Chicago police. They looked like brutes, like caricatures of policemen, and they certainly hated any young person who seemed to be having a good time or who showed disrespect for the institutions they thought made America. I was in the park those nights, and I was in some of the demonstrations, but I had the misfortune to take something — it's argued whether it was the first THC or a horse tranquilizer. There were provocateurs there from about ten different government agencies, some of whom I'm sure were spying on each other. So that would have been something that one of those agencies might have put into this stuff that was being passed around. Anyway, that incapacitated me for three or four days during a lot of the action. I was just out somewhere, at a couple's house who had come to Chicago to do some sort of social work or maybe as part of their school term, some Midwestern, liberal, progressive college like Antioch or Oberlin where you did a term's work outside, and they had become early followers of Mahara-ji, and they insisted while I was trying to come

out of my fog that I visit them in New York and visit Mahara-ji. And here while the world was being turned upside down in Chicago, while the whole world was watching, they were interested in the perfect little master. I couldn't believe it. I'm sure the readers of THE SUN will be taken with my observation.

SUN: The PEN club just released a report about the harassment of the underground press back then. Do you think the underground press was effective?

KUPFERBERG: That was released a year ago, and none of the major media covered that story at all, and here was something that was compiled specifically to show how the press was being harassed, seduced, framed, sent to jail. You remember the reports that the *Times* had its reporters working for the CIA? Well you see, the *Times* doesn't work for the CIA, the CIA works for the *Times*. So, your question was?

SUN: Do you think that the underground press was effective?

KUPFERBERG: Sure it was effective. It was as effective as the movement. To the large extent the Sixties movement was one of ideas. And to a great extent the movement was the media. If you count the concrete accomplishments of the Sixties they were a speeding up of the end of the war in Vietnam, and a lot of young people changing their ideas about what their lives were about. The effect of the Sixties is still with us, especially in people who are now 30 or older. To the younger people, because of the media, it's as if the Sixties had never happened, as if Vietnam never happened. It's parallel to what I'm sure happens in Germany. The young people there know very little about Nazism and our young people know very little about what happened in the Sixties. See for me, the Vietnam experience for America is typified by what happened to Nixon. Nixon was thrown out. He was a mass murderer — I think he was responsible for the murder of hundreds of thousands of people — and he was impeached for wire-tapping, that's why he lost the presidency. He was a wire-tapper, a very serious crime, almost as serious as littering.

SUN: Where do you get your news? How do you find out what's going on?

KUPFERBERG: In very difficult ways. But first you have to have some sort of analysis of what society is about. My analysis is very simple. Basically, there is a ruling class that controls the state, the police, the army, the educational system by and large, and they control all the media. If you realize that, you realize that they will be lying a lot of the time. So you just proceed on that basis. Occasionally things come through, of course. There is an interesting article in Cockburn's column in *The Voice* this week about a *Times* correspondent in Beirut. During the longest period of bombing by the Israelis, he wrote in his lead that the Israelis had bombed Beirut in an indiscriminate manner for the first time. They took out the word indiscriminate. And there is a long series of cables between the correspondent and the editors at the *Times*. This is what the *Times* does, and it does it much less obviously than that. If you look at the *Times* everything just seems to happen. They have no theory of society, except they do, they have the theory that everything is in general going pretty well and we just have to fix a few things, and I'm okay Jack.

SUN: If you were to pick up a magic wand and fix something, what would you fix?
KUPFERBERG: I'd start with the important things, like the toilet and the sink. OK, the people in control of industry and the schools and so on are also in control of all the different media and the means of education. So it's a cycle. Now if you can break in at any point, for example, if by some miracle you could control industry — say there was a very radical labor movement that by a general strike took over industry, then by their very nature they would, for instance, take over newspapers, at least they would share the power. They would be able to publish what they wanted and get it distributed, instead of the owners now publishing what they want. There isn't any one magical thing you can do. The point is that you have to get in at a particular place. No one has been able to figure that out, how to do this, otherwise we would have had the revolution. So we don't know what to do because it doesn't matter what kind of perfect theory you have, if you can't effect it it's not a perfect theory because a part of it is missing: how to get it into action.

SUN: New York is a place that is extremely media conscious, media overridden. What effect do you think this has on the culture here?

KUPFERBERG: What effect it has is to give a lot of people work. Most people in the media are not doing anything worthwhile, they are just perpetuating the system. Sports, for example, serves two functions, one to dull and use up people's time and energy, a sort of idiot-making function, and the other is as a rehearsal for capitalist struggle, the army. Football is a perfect paradigm of war, and all the other sports, they're sports, that means someone wins or loses. Boxing in Rome and Greece was boxing to the death. Boxing is banned in Sweden, but in America people go to a ring to see someone get the shit beat out of them. That's the same reason they go to auto races, to see a car crash. In tennis matches they may go to see someone win, but someone always loses when someone wins. It's funny that it works that way.

SUN: What are your feelings about living here in New York?
KUPFERBERG: New York? It's the most exciting cesspool in the world. I have this cartoon I just did where someone's interviewing Mayor Koch and he says, "Mayor Koch, what do you think makes a New Yorker the remarkable person he is?" And Mayor Koch says, "I think it is his uncanny ability to avoid all the misery around him." Everyone comes to New York for a different reason. I didn't come to New York, I was born here, and it's just been hard to get away. But I can honestly say, in the more than fifty years that I've lived here, there's been a steady decline in the quality of living. I grew up in a working-class tenement. It was clean, safe, and comparatively friendly. It was no paradise. New York was never a paradise. And a lot of the mugging and violence existed in the nineteenth century, so it's sort of being recycled now. But people don't come here to be in New York, they come here to do a specific thing. If they're young and attracted to the arts, this is the place to come. If they need a job and they're Puerto Rican or black, this is why they came, and millions came. And for a while there were jobs and then they were left high and dry, so New York has almost two million people on welfare. That means Puerto Rico and Georgia and Alabama and North Carolina have less people on welfare. But now the new federalism is going to spread the welfare all over the country so there will be more people on welfare but they'll get less. I think that Reagan believes in sharing the misery, at least among the welfare recipients.

SUN: What are the big changes you've seen since the Sixties?
KUPFERBERG: A change in the attitudes between men and women. First, the admission in the early Sixties that there were men and women, two different sexes, a kind of freeing up of sexuality, a lot of it not perfect, that struggle is still going on of course. Also, a realization that the authority of institutions is not God-given, inevitable, or even desirable in American society, that there are a lot of institutions that are horrible, like the justice system, the military, capitalism if you will, parts of it. Thirdly, the idea that it was possible, at least theoretically, to step outside the entire structure. The young people in particular were able to do this because they had no responsibility, they had some financial support, and they had the traditional freedom of being a student or just being young. And to step out of it and not automatically follow the nine-to-five path to oblivion — which meant go to school up to a certain age, get a job, get married, have children, pay your taxes, go to war, be a good citizen, retire when you're sixty-five and too old to enjoy anything, get drunk on Friday night, watch TV, and die, and pass this way of life on to your children.

SUN: How have your ideas changed in recent years?
KUPFERBERG: They haven't changed (laughs). Because my ideas are correct (laughs). Well, they've changed in that I once thought that we were closer to the realization of better times. I think radicals have to believe that, because it's pretty hard to be a radical. I guess I've been disabused of that, although now that we have Reagan we have another shot at it. But at the same time, the catastrophes and the potential for destruction have become even more immense, and the misery just permeates all of society, the whole world, so much that you don't know what to do.

SUN: Have your views about yourself changed much in these years?
KUFERBERG: Well, when you get older. . . .

SUN: How much older did you get?
KUPFERBERG: I'm fifty-nine. You get sort of impatient and you realize that you shouldn't waste any time. So, I've decided that getting even is a worthwhile motivation, which is what I do in my cartoons, in a very gentle way I suppose. But I feel I want to get it all

out. Older people are more direct because they have less to lose. They don't have to kiss ass so much.

SUN: When we spoke on the phone, you said you were probably different from most people I interview because you aren't "New-Agey." What is New-Agey?

KUPFERBERG: First of all, I am eminently qualified to speak about it because I know very little about it, but I'll give you my impressions. I started off from a Jewish rationalist point of view. We Jewish rationalists were lucky; when we rejected religion we did it wholeheartedly and a lot of us became the radicals of the world, from Karl Marx on. I myself am an agnostic because I'm a coward, I want to play both parts, you know. What have I got to lose? As far as the New Age, I'll analyze it into two parts. One, the afterlife. Also the rebirth, the reincarnations. Reincarnation is very big, it exists in some of the Eastern religions, but it's big in America too. But everyone was someone like Cleopatra, Frederick the Great, Moses, hardly anyone was this poor schmuck that was building a pyramid, or a peasant, or a murderer, hardly anyone was ever reincarnated like that. Some of this is pie-in-the-sky. This is a standard part of religion — you delay all of your satisfactions until the next life. This is a religion for slaves. I knew this would come up, so I have this book by a Greek who was captured by Romans and taken back there, sold out and became a historian at their service. This is 125 B.C.: "Since the masses of the people are inconsistent, full of unruly desire, passionate and reckless of consequence, they must be filled with fears to keep them in order. The ancients did well, therefore, to invent gods, and the belief in punishment after death." So that's the afterlife. Now. . . .

SUN: Let's stay with that for a second. Without that particular sustenance, those beliefs, how do you think about death?

KUPFERBERG: That's the other part of it that I was going to discuss. That takes care of the afterlife, but you still have to adjust to life today, so what do you do? You need something to keep you going now. I suppose it's really the same thing, you throw yourself completely at the mercy of a god or a system of help or a great teacher. But I prefer my kind of social activism, my radicalism. It's the same sort of thing, really, except I believe that mine is more in touch with the real world, the problems of the real world, whereas a lot of people who are defeated in their attempts to solve the problems of the real world opt for this otherworldly solution. And it's understandable, and who am I to forgive, but it's forgivable. They have the solace of their religion. For some, of course, opium is the religion of the people. This is another way out. These are ways of confronting the horrors of everyday life. So there's religion, New Age and Old Age, dope, art, and revolution. Money is just power, and you have to define what you want power for, some people want it for sex, some people want it for sadism, some people have forgotten why they want it. Then there's the family, and there must be other things that I don't know about. These are various solutions to the problem of living.

SUN: When you come up against something that scares you, what's your support?
KUPFERBERG: Well, my family, I guess, my beliefs, and sometimes there isn't any support. Sometimes you're scared shitless, you don't know what to do. That's why I say these are all understandable as long as they are not taken for what they are not. I don't think believing in God is a way of solving the problem of the twenty million people who are on welfare. It's important not to get the categories confused, and there are some church people who don't get them confused. There are a lot of very respectable religious radicals in this country. And there are very weak, foolish, crazy, and impotent political radicals.

SUN: If you could get one thing done, in any field, what would you do?
KUPFERBERG: (Laughs.) I wouldn't say I'm at the zenith of my political, moral, ethical, religious strength at this point, so if I could keep the subway from making so much noise. . . . I'll tell you why that's so hard to answer, because there isn't one thing. If I could get one thing, if I could get this subway noise stopped, someone else is going to have to pay higher taxes to put rubber wheels on the subways, and it's probably going to be me. So I'm not willing to spend a hundred dollars a year to get the subway quieter, because there's still the auto noise out there. Let's put it another way. What are the important things that need immediate fixing? I'll tell you what pisses me off more than anything — the incredible stupidity of armies. The

very fact of nation-states. If we could get rid of them that would be nice. But there are a few states that don't have any armies, that have almost no armies, so it's possible even now. But the world's armaments cost maybe a trillion dollars a year, and it's trite and commonplace, but if you would spend all that constructively. . . well, we don't. I have another cartoon where a reporter says, "Mr. Reagan, you cut the welfare program, you cut all the social programs and nobody complains about that. People complain about taxes, but they never complain about taxes for the armed forces. Why is that?" And Reagan answers, "I guess everybody likes a good murder." The fact that this is institutionalized and accepted in America and all over the world is incredibly disappointing. People oppose the draft, but they don't oppose the army. We should be talking about unilateral disarmament in every country in the world. When they tell you to join the army and learn a trade, the trade is murder. They don't tell you that in the commercials. The trade is how to kill people in different ways — hand-to-hand, chemically, electronically. So, if you could arrange for **THE SUN** magazine to get rid of the U.S. army. . . .

SUN: I'll see what we can come up with. Have you read **THE SUN** ?
KUPFERBERG: I read it, but I can't take New Age materials so I don't read it very carefully. I gave it a chance. I know that there is worthwhile stuff even in New Age material, but it's like my reading of poetry. I don't read little magazines anymore because I know that one out of 500 poems will be really great. But I don't have time to read through all the mush for the one gem.

SUN: There is an attempt in **THE SUN** to cut through a lot of the New Age mush. It's hard to say how well it works. . . .
KUPFERBERG: Well, I'll let you be the judge of that. To me it still seems too spiritual. If I would ask you to define that word, what would you say?

SUN: It's a hard word to define. Everyone has a different definition.
KUPFERBERG: But you have to define it. It's used all the time in the literature. In fact, it's what distinguishes it from the materialist or the practical. I could define materialist.

SUN: Go ahead.

KUPFERBERG: It means one who deals with everyday life, dealing with the basic necessities which I would define as food, shelter, clothing, companionship, the ability to work at something that is satisfying, the freedom from terror, the freedom to self-actualize, to use the jargon, in the arts or the spirit. I'll even use that word, but that comes at the end because it's hard to be very spiritual in the concentration camp, some people can, but I don't think we should ask that of everybody.

The spiritualist, I would say, is someone who doesn't have to worry about taking care of the basic necessities, and starts to think about how he can develop himself while ignoring everyone else. In other words I think that it really helps to be upper middle class if you're going to be New Age. There are a lot of upper middle class anarchists too, but a higher proportion of New Age people.

SUN: My problem in defining spiritual is that any definition I would find workable has to include all of that — taking care of necessities, relationships, responsibilities and so on.

KUPFERBERG: I'm sure that there are some thinkers whom we think of primarily as spiritual who agree with that, but my impression is that they are in the minority. Trotsky said that after the revolution people would not stop having problems, but that the problems would be on a higher plane. So, I would accept that. That's why I resent people who think of themselves as artists and above it all. I wonder whether they have the right to ask society to support them when others are passing through hell and starving to death. I always try to spend part of the day working on something menial. I don't think you should lose touch with that which other people have to go through every day just because you consider yourself a superior person.

JEROME RUBIN: You're fifty-nine, so you were around in the Forties.

KUPFERBERG: I was around in the Forties, yeah.

JEROME RUBIN: So you were around forty years before the Sixties came around. How did you, born in the Twenties, become a child of the Sixties?

KUPFERBERG: Interesting question. In 1932 I was nine or ten, I remember the Depression well. And I remember that in Central Park there were shanty towns, I remember visiting them. Homeless men covered the wide part where the reservoir now is. And I remember problems in my house with money. So I became a Communist, a radical, and I attended my first political meeting in high school when I was thirteen, some sort of Commie-front organization. At eighteen, when I left my parochial immigrant's family, I discovered there were different universes. I discovered Greenwich Village and bohemianism. So the link between me and the Sixties is the double link of political radicalism and bohemianism, which have always been linked. It goes back to the France of the 1840s, 1860s. Then the war came and wiped everything out, wiped the slate clean. Then after the war came the Fifties, which were death, death to everything. America became normal again. And the beats were in a direct line from the bohemians, and all these lines meet in the Sixties. So the Sixties were nothing new to me. The only thing new about them to America was that it was on a huge scale, and it seemed as if it might work, it was coming together. In the Thirties a lot of artists were radicalized, the Village was radicalized. The streams were always together, and the Sixties seemed to be a real fruition of this period. It seemed as if it was going into the mainstream. The mistake, of course, was that it was just a youth movement, and it made no contact with anything past student life. And when the main student issue, which was the war, dissolved it was seen to be organizationally and theoretically a weak movement, because it was not able to link up with the rest of the country, the working class, the middle class, and with the older age groups.

SUN: How do you feel about the idea that to create any effective change in society you have to start with a change in yourself, and that the two go hand in hand?

KUPFERBERG: That's always been a cop-out as far as I'm concerned. Now I've often found people who had my political ideas who were horrible, and if they ever attempted to put them into actuality they'd only fuck things up worse. And I've met people who I supposedly differed with politically who were very charitable and good people. So it's not so much what you think you think, but what you do and how you really feel. It's a chicken-and-egg question as to which comes first. But I will say that if you think you're going to wait

to become a perfect being before you start to live in the real world, you're going to have to wait a long time.

SUN: Anything else?
KUPFERBERG: I hate to end on a depressing note. I will say that what we have going for us is our biology, or nature, which has a lot in it, not all completely wonderful, but we do have the potentiality for a much better world than we have because we've seen glimpses of it all the time in our personal life and even in periods of history that have been short but have existed. I leave you to find out which ones they were and to make some new ones.

(December 1982)

Kicking The Corpse — Or Is This Love?

Sy Safransky

The Long Island Press, bowing to rising costs and increasing competition, ceased publication yesterday in its 157th year. . . .

Mayor Beam said the closing of The Press was "indeed a sad occasion." From its beginning in 1821 as The Long Island Farmer, a weekly, to its rise as a great metropolitan daily, he said, The Press "has been an enlightened voice serving its readers. . . ."

— The New York Times,
March 26, 1977

I'm having a hard time writing this. I think I've figured out why. I want it to be a eulogy, but I can't stop kicking the corpse. I want you to care that another American newspaper has expired. But I wonder if I care.

I knew it, intimately. I can recall it, like an old lover: how it looked, and felt, and smelled, its rhythms and horrors and inside jokes. But that is

If we saw a world made up of separate objects and events, rather than the separate features of one event, that is what we reported.

nostalgia, not love. And since I'd fault it, first of all, for its lack of love, you can see my predicament.

Why bother, then?

For one, I feel a kind of allegiance. It was the first daily newspaper I worked for. That seems more important, after all these years, than its shortcomings. (In just such a way, I felt patriotic about America when I lived in Europe, and more my father's son after he died. Whether the common denominator here is self-deception or true generosity, I do not know.)

For another, I'd like to resolve the conflict. (David Guy wrote in last month's SUN that Paul Goodman "was the kind of person who says what he wants and then wants it." I'm the kind of person who writes what he thinks and then thinks it.) Anyway, my ambivalence about The Press applies to the press in general: for example, I would defend (to the death?) the right of a newspaper to print something loveless and worthless. Is this the measure of a democrat, or a fool? I cheered Woodward and Bernstein in "All the President's Men," but they lied to get the story, elbowed other reporters off the track, and, even at their best, treaded the same old journalistic mill that grinds life into Events and Personalities, reduces the world to a sadness of contradictions — reality, if you will.

When I quit The Press in 1969 I told my editors why:

Our obligation to the reader extends beyond stringing together quotations (which any reasonably intelligent stenographer can do), yet our "hard" news accounts are based on a distorted notion of objectivity which demands that equal weight be given to truth and untruth.

. . . trained reporters must write captions, make photo assignments, rewrite publicity handouts, read page proofs, write high school graduation stories, perform clerical chores such as typing the names of lottery winners, and rewrite the copy of beat reporters and bureau chiefs. . . . It is not surprising that even the most enthusiastic reporter soon becomes demoralized and sloppy. It is because of this, and not low wages, that The Press does not attract, or long retain, good talent.

My first major political piece was a closeup on the Congressional race between Republican Sy Halpern and a Democratic and Conservative opponent. Having been warned by some colleagues to "be nice" to

Halpern because The Press *traditionally backed him, I was still somewhat surprised to find we had run dozens of stories on his campaign activities but had mentioned his opponents only once. My article, a balanced account, drew a chuckle from an editor, who said he would run it "just to see how Sy (Halpern) reacts." I later found out that Halpern himself was amused that* The Press *had finally run a straight story about him.*

One reporter boasted that he and a colleague had nearly every local politician tied up in public relations "contracts." Perhaps he exaggerated, but how does one explain the comment of an editor, after informing me that yet another editor did public relations for a local Congressman, that "you're getting into higher politics now, son."

Sometimes we will use quotes around a word in a headline when the word doesn't even appear in the story. When I asked an editor about this once, he explained that "we're quoting ourselves."

My memo had all the impact of the surgeon-general's warning on a two-pack-a-day smoker. They kept right on doing it — out of habit, or pleasure — and I kept right on until I reached Morocco.

The Press was worse than a few papers, but better than most. This says a great deal about American newspapers. But to most publishers, a newspaper is no different from a shoe factory — except, regrettably, with rising paper costs, a newspaper makes less money.

But I'm dancing on the grave — and all I meant was to say a kind word: for the grease and the cogs, America's bent back and broad middle. For *The Press* was a servant of the Middle, its bland face reflecting what its eyes perceived: the blessed mediocrity of the daily round. It was the newspaper of the Archie Bunkers — the small homeowners with mortgages and kids, those for whom the American century was the dreary armpit of the late shift, Church on Sunday, letters every week from Vietnam, night school, taxes — and it was American through and through, in its heroes, and hypocrisy, and democratic smile (strong in the corner, roguish in the curl; search my face, you'll see). I was armed against it from the start —

"Tomorrow is the day, shoppers," began a page one story recently, "What day — Why, the day to pump new life into your worn and weary budget — the day you can't afford to miss. It's the first of the Spring

Jamaica Day. . . . Whether it's shoes, stockings, sofas, shorts or shampoo you need, you'll find it at bargain prices in the savings spree sponsored by the Jamaica Chamber of Commerce. . . ."

— seeing, out of my own narrowed eyes, an institution given over to profit and the easy answer, even as I quivered with my own solutions and success. I'd been polished by the Columbia Graduate School of Journalism, and so brought with me an arrogance equal to my skill — which, in the Sixties, we called idealism. I'd become a journalist not out of some abstract love of the craft, but to change society. Thus, my impatience with any assignment I could not turn into a polemic, however veiled, against the status quo. And there was nothing I hated more than the status quo (except, of course, myself).

Bent over my typewriter — a big, old-fashioned Royal, anchored to the well of my desk — cradling a phone between my shoulder and my ear. . . . There's a pipe, or cigar, or cigarette, in the ashtray beside the coffee. No that's wrong. We didn't have ashtrays. Magazine offices had ashtrays. We had floors. Grimy floors. To match the windows and the walls. The desks were the sad steel-gray of tanks and Winter skies, with histories written in coffee spills, sandwich crumbs, eraser flakes, pencil points, ashes, God knows what (one legendary deskman kept to himself, until the night he quit, when, upon finishing his shift, he walked to the editor's desk, unzipped his fly, urinated, and left). There was a perverse romance about the dirt; it suggested the "real world" more accurately than polished mahogany and chrome, at least that world of crime and strikes and social malignancy we judged most real. . . .

"The news" was a romance, too, shaped by our assumptions about God and country, death and birth, the seasons of the planet and the race and ourselves. If we saw a world made up of separate objects and events, rather than the separate features of one event, that is what we reported. Marooned on our own dry sands, we saw an island universe, with walls and boundaries, and lives signed in grief. We drew our own line, between "in here" and "out there," made the cops and politicians arbiters of one and the columnists and editorial writers the priests of the other — all the time ignoring the vital intersection where "objective" and "subjective" flow endlessly into one another, and thoughts give birth to worlds. Right now, I'm reading a book by Jane Roberts called *Psychic Politics*. She puts it this way:

> There is an inner landscape of the mind that produces dreams, experiences, and events, and this correlates with the exterior landscape. It's extremely difficult to map this interior land because we confuse the brain's activity for the power behind the brain, and because we do not consider the interior landscape as real as the exterior one. We're also so immersed in the interior world that we take its natural elements for granted. Dreams, thoughts, and all mental experiences compose the natural phenomena of the inner reality. We travel through the psyche as we travel though time and across the face of the Earth. When we encounter events, they will appear differently according to our position within the psyche.
>
> Many dream events are versions of waking ones — not distorted at all, just the dream version as the physical event is the waking version. While we accept the waking experience as the real one, it is no more or less real than the dream event.

If, on the front page, this was never acknowledged, in the city room, at least, dreams were as large as "life," personalities were worn inside out. We were more naked among ourselves than before any reader. . . . *The dayside editor's note to the night editor with whom she shared a desk, complaining about the cigarette butts, and he going from room to room that night with a big trash can, filling it with every butt in the building, and dumping it on the desk before leaving. . . . The nervous editor who chewed paper when he was under pressure and one night accidentally ate the lead story. . . . The reporter who was a chronic liar, going so far as to use his father-in-law's death as an excuse for staying out of work — a good enough excuse, if he had died, which he hadn't. . . .* If we had abandoned our static writing formulas to reveal something of the real newsmakers — *us* — what copy we might have turned out! How many more newspapers we would have sold!

The Press is a ghost, but I still live with The Deadline. I court eternity, but the seconds tick away; the press next door is rolling and it's time to end this, as abruptly as I began. Would more anecdotes have told the tale? No more than *The Press'* ten thousand facts explained anything. *The Press* tried to stretch those facts, like a pale skin of meaning, over the bones of the world. But the bones of the world are too big for that. The real story keeps poking through.

(July 1977)

US/Readers Write About . . .

How To Really Change Society

On Hiroshima Day, I was at a small demonstration in front of the General Electric headquarters in New York City, protesting nuclear power and nuclear weapons. At 8:15 a.m., the moment the bomb was dropped on Hiroshima, we sat down in front of the entrance and observed silence. We were arrested almost immediately, taken to the First Police Precinct and kept in a holding cell for about an hour. During this time, except when I had to walk, I meditated.

Meditating didn't "protect" me from what was happening, but made me experience it more directly. Certain moments filled me with blind terror: the handcuffs being snapped on my wrists, the door to the cell clicking shut. What scared me was knowing there was No Way Out.

Of course there is a way out, and that is internal. While meditating, I realized that I didn't really want to go anywhere. I was just attached to being *able* to go somewhere. Meditation enabled me to overcome this attachment, to channel my energy from the ego center to the heart.

This is the true alchemy — the transformation of fear into love. It's available to all of us. It can save the world.

But on the physical level, putting one's body in front of the entrance to General Electric — sole producer of uranium for the American military — is a good start.

Sparrow
New York, New York

Society is *us*, not some remote or abstract entity "out there." Our thoughts and feelings this moment are making the world what it is and creating our perception of it. No matter what we may like to think, we are always equal to what we judge. In the spirit of this recognition, changing society becomes the moment to moment play of changing ourselves, of becoming the good we wish to see. As we embody the change we seek, we give it substance, we become part of its foundation — a foundation that can last where words, programs and legislation cannot.

What is important then is not so much what we do, but what we *are* — our willingness to be animated by Truth. In letting freedom in, in doing 100 percent what we are best at, without reserve, in being ourselves, we fill our places in the dance of the Whole. As the colors and shades of a great painting radiate their part, the whole painting brightens. It is ever so simple. It is *us* and up to *us* and the time is now.

Bruce Terrell
Mill Valley, California

□ □ □

Things fall apart. We might as well be reconciled to that.

I think of the missionaries who come to my door and come in to talk, who remind me of something in myself. Something in me sees the safe world, the known world, crumbling, and wants to hit the problem of changing society with a blueprint, a textbook and a technique. To do it like an engineer, build a good structure and walk away, problem solved.

But the problem isn't solved.

Society isn't just a hunk of metal. It's us, it breathes. Maybe we'd do well to treat it like a person, not be hitting it with hammers all the time, give it space to be what it is and appreciate it for that.

Things have been going downhill for as long as anyone can remember, probably since the beginning of time. That viewpoint is always available.

But life is not a situation where I am building up and evolving while society (that is, everyone else) is breaking down. I share the whole breakdown. Day after day, my life falls to pieces! By reflex I rouse up all the king's horses and all the king's men to fit the smashed egg back together. Occasionally though, I accept the catastrophe and something surprising happens: something strong and new stands where the mess was. Humpty Dumpty becomes a beautiful omelet.

This past Summer the course of my relations with the opposite sex was driving me crazy. All these grand, saving relationships were failing, one after another, before they'd even begun. It was breaking me to pieces. One day I finally let go and began to watch, as if at a picture show, popcorn in hand. I still felt drawn to my big dreams, but I had gained a freedom from them. I've laughed and cried, watching a few more go.

What drives us crazy about society may be just what we need to grow. Sure, the world is a damned mess. But there's a smile down there, on the other side. It's all working out by falling to pieces.

I'm not saying death to engineers. Let's improve roads, sewers, administrative efficiency, minimum standards of living and health. But the project doesn't end when the engineer's new structure is built. The slow disintegration is as true as the quick integration. Why so desperate?

Maybe we can relax a bit. Maybe society saves itself, and we can love it, let it find its own way back home. Wherever, whatever that is.

Gerard Saucier
Austin, Texas

(October 1981)

After quitting his job on public television last year, David Grant decided to maintain a month of silence. This journal was written during the last two weeks, when he travelled on foot, carrying a petition calling for military disarmament. His only companion was his goat, little Iowa, who carried provisions.

The petition, calling for all governments to "totally and unilaterally disarm," wasn't mailed to anybody because, David says, "I don't feel like it's finished. I might be off again. Besides, the act of assent is what really counts, not the supplication of the nation-state.

The title is David's own.

—Ed.

Peace Nigger's Long March

A Pedestrian Journal

David Grant

DAY ONE   Morning

In Japan and Korea it is Buddha's day.

Hillwalking. Aries new moon, under-cover-of-darkness, wordlessly.

Deer manitou the first red-blooded being seen — off on the other side of our land cooperative.

Through the wild azalea blooming swamp, fearless. Deer my friend from long ago, totem power, protector and guide.

Unyielding dogwoods immodestly white, trees of crucifixion.

One simple-minded herd, its bovine flatulence silenced. Blumbering lummoxes, droopy-headed and bloated, they frolic in Queen Iowa's footsteps. They fling their heels high, twisting all that blubber and homaging her caprine independence.

Iowa traumatized but quiet, pant-

Yesterday afternoon, first signature on disarmament petition! Young man pulled his car over, said, "I saw you walking. . . ." I handed him my note. . . . He, as dumbstruck as I, then asked to sign it.

ing, too tired to eat. Still ruminating on this event's significance. Looking back and back for her baby. Out now of her elemental home, my slave, and not so sassy!

("Missy Miz Iowa, ah does fo' you jes' lak you needs. Yas'm!")

Midday

Our little Iowa is so slow. Buck Lake Road, only half as far by this time as I had hoped. Weak from a year penned, she pants pitifully. I take heed, meander, nowhere but here.

She is learning to follow, perhaps in spite of my corrections. The rope stretches full length to her choke collar. She falters, I jerk. She falls behind less and less. Until panting, mind-wandering, more jerks, we stop just before she's pooped.

Four cups of milk already from her today! A lot I am asking of her. She teaches patience. I teach her not to be afraid of, nor to shy from, drinking near the noisy waterfall sheen. When she begins bleating with wistful backward glances, I know she has rested long enough and it is time to move on.

Dark Night

Flashlight pen, "Nightwriter," first use of my gaggle of gadgets.

Iowa, even doused with Oil of Citronella, keeps swatting mosquitoes. She has been as perfect as I could ask, keeping her rope's distance. Here in this bramble field she is quiet and unafraid, just knowing I am next to her inside the tent.

Evening meal: hard boiled egg; couple of cups of Iowa's sweet milk — with nutritional yeast added; Diann's holy love gingerbread.

Fagged out! Just past Chaires.

DAY TWO

Iowa remembers the way to return, scorns the march forward. Mournfully mutters with her face turned back.

The morning's farmer, gathering his mail, "You've got your goat loaded down, same as yourself!"

There were two weak points in our system of which I knew before leaving. Both manifest immediately. A half-hour spent, a waste, looking for hand-rope this morning . . . hadn't drilled a hole in the dogwood staff. Also: the night's sleep on cool hard ground, deflated. Of course the air mattress had a hole, I knew it, but couldn't find it in the rainbarrel back home. My raft for swimming the Apalachicola is, therefore, not. Repair must be ahead somewhere somehow.

These holes in my plan remind me: self-employed now, no longer within the safety of salary — that time has been torn; the order of the day is order; doing it right the first time, while insisting on not doing it, what they call, "right."

Yesterday afternoon, first signature on disarmament petition! Young man pulled his car over and said, "I saw you walking. . . ." I handed him my note: *I am silent, walking westward, carrying petition for military disarmament.* He, as dumbstruck as I, then asked to sign it.

Late dusk

Oh what blessed relief to be inside this mosquito-proof tent with a steady high hum all around. Iowa, sitting silently outside, is swatting some. I massage her udder with repellent, and her face and her rear end, too. A few sand fleas inside . . . they had driven us away from the day's last stop-and-rest place.

Iowa is giving more than six cups a day and though I gave her all the grain she wants, she nibbles less than half of what she would eat at home. She's a kidless mother, lugubrious and despondent.

I eat the love-filled gingerbread over her dish so that, with the crumbs, she is infused as well as I.

Sleeping in the devastation of a clear-cut area. Before the packbags can plop, an immediate attack: a twinge of terror creeps in during the rush to drape mosquito netting over the hat.

("Diann, I missed you with that first thundering step.")

First person I met today, ex-Sheriff Raymond, recently deposed (the county is edging towards liberalization). There's no denying this ole boy's one-time shrewdness. But now, out to pasture with his big shiny roans and Appaloosa crosses, I really bamboozled him.

"Uh, hey, ah, you lost?" rushing out — was he walking straight? — from his house set a hundred feet back off the road.

I gave him my note: *I am silent. Walking westward. Carrying a petition for military disarmament.*

A quick glance at my pack goat, a cock-eyed twitch in his brow, "Well, uh, the pavement ends a couple miles on!" Before I can evince not a care, he catches himself, "Uh, can you read?" I can practically hear his mind add, ". . . boy-ah?"

Dutifully I nod yes. Does he see, can't he see, my smirking?

He takes my notebook and writes: *Pavement ends, two miles.*

So I write back: *Tram Road West.* I'm not really going west at that approaching intersection, but it will make "sense" to this good ole boy, and I do have some mercy.

He ingests this information, plots the coordinates and waves me on.

DAY THREE

Dreams: of a movie starlet explaining how many outfits of clothing she takes when filming on location.

I take note of my own clothes: T-shirt batiked by Sanjit with big green letter "e;" the land co-op shirt we designed, sky blue, silk-screened by Glenn with a ferocious mosquito and the cryptic words "I Gave;" the stencilled T-shirt with the light-hearted deep blue sea dance from "Blueberry Hill" by Linda; longsleeve Army surplus green mosquito-proof over-shirt, a size or two too big, from mama-in-law Janice; long-tattered royal blue monk's hooded sweatshirt for the cool short-haired one from long ago at Notre Dame; Summer straw Carribean wide-brimmed hat left behind at our house by unknown and unclaimed friends; mosquito net hat shield presently acting as hatband made in the last hours of rushing new moon duress by my long-suffering wife; wheat brown thank-god mosquito-proof getting dirty corduroy pants from TV money new two years ago; light seas green too thin Bargain Box threadbare corduroy pants now wonderfully pajamas clean cotton feel in nylon sleeping bag; one pair thin white inner cotton socks; two pair thick white outer cotton socks; one mismatched one blue one black "dress" cotton socks; one pair Yukon leather insulated recently black-gooped, dirty yellowed shoe-stringed, Vibram soled twelve years old, three inches over the ankle, waterproof and now black-brown, softly wrinkled bought-in-Whitehorse, Hudson Bay Company take-me-anywhere-I-want-to-walk, my dear dear boots; not-yet-had-call-to-wear nylon strapped tan leather inner-soled and cracking rubber therefore black-gooped outer soles, Rainbow Sandals, TV work shoes for the last year from the Tallahassee Taproot Juice Bar, my dress up (ha ha) relaxation shoes and, also to be, fording-the-deep-rocky-bottomed stream walkers; not including the lightest weight sky blue nylon swimming trunks and the two pair of cotton boxer undershorts; but including the all-but-forgotten on these unceasingly sunny days and star-filled nights (three weeks now since rain) forest green nylon poncho and powderpuff blue nylon rain pants.

That makes seventeen various external apparel. In my dream I was mocking the actress for her six extra dresses!

Second Dream: Talking with Tanzanian president, Julius Nyere; observing his plans for pan-African socialism.

Been writing this sitting in the crotch of a tupelo tree in a small tupelo swamp. Stopped here to let Iowa drink. She's traumatized still — though beginning, I think, to accept her fate. I can see her ponder, "Why me?" She refused all but a mouthful of grain this morning; hasn't eaten much greenery; is now refusing to sit down and rest, been standing the whole time.

Not any mosquitoes or sand fleas here, curiously. Time to drink from the canteen of yesterday's lake water. Move on.

Woodville, Early dusk

Teeth rattling shepherd. Ex-urban density. Double slow time. All OK and fine.

Postcard request to Diann to mail food to one of three dots on the map — Scott's Ferry, Gaskins or Broad Branch — all on the other side of the broad Apalachicola.

The message to her ends: "Picking up pace, strengthening, you take care. I love you."

DAY FOUR   Next morning

Bad blew the night away, whew.
Screaming dust spewing headlights.
Human shadows yelling "Go away!"

"Get on out of here!"

The two of us, Hulk and Cerebrus, despised.

Air mattress, Apalachicola ferry for backpack, leaking. Night on the cold hard ground.

No hairshirts for me yet, no thanks. Despite all good intentions to the contrary.

Iowa girl appears more and more camel- or lama-like, a beast of burden. Her drooping eyelids and dully bobbing head. Oh woe, oh woe! She is learning to heel well though — even in the faces of dogs, horses, motorcycles, sand fleas, horse flies, dark splotches in the pavement and all the other myriad capriverous creatures.

Midday

Dream: Climbing on and through the roof of Scotty's huge hardware warehouse. There seemed to me to be no other way to get in. A store manager chastised me for my unorthodox entry, but because I was maintaining silence, I could do nothing but shrug, signifying that I knew no better.

The dream came straight out of last night's confusion in finding a sleeping place.

There in the fast and dirty highway nightlights, I was looking for an air mattress patch. Entered Winn-Dixie and 7-11 neon everyday-everyday just folks. I retained my food chastity despite the allure of fresh carrot's orange seductive glow. I am relying solely on what I have and can forage: dandelions, grape shoots, smilex, young black-berry leaves, cattails and on from there.

Ended up the night by befuddling three old beer drinkers and their yelping shepherd. Without their absent eyeglasses, none of the men could read my note, *Where is two-sixty road west?*

Throughout the slouching shrugs and confused silence, cricket masses screeched and scratched maniacally — caged in old freezers next to us, doomed to drown for lurking fish gullets.

Finally, in desperation, this choking town an unlocked maze, a note written while standing outside a humble shack: *Do you mind if I put my tent up and sleep in your yard?* Opening the ajar picket gate, to be met immediately with near hysterical cries, "Go away! Go on!

Get out of here!" Me gesturing in the barely lit edge of darkness. ("I can't speak.") She, young, alone inside with her children, "No, no, you just go away."

I leave immediately, slip sliding away, all deference and humility. ("I am so sorry to have frightened you, please forgive me.") Bowing and scraping into the darkness. Soon thereafter to flop over a tree farm fence, sleeping in the soft sand of a plowed fire lane. No tent, just hat and mosquito netting. Sweet sleep solace.

The Dangers: Half dreamt I'd got amoebic dysentery. Scratched my itching rectum. Could even see the slimy worms crawling out, damn them.

I remembered the canteen, fully drunk, of untreated water from "Big Lake." "Big Lake." Ha! Nothing but a Big Swamp. It was, however, deep enough to open its reed choked heart to the sky. Out there in the middle stood one lonely, stripped bare tree. Perched at its tip-top, immobile and glistening, a large pure white heron, guarding his waters. The bird said the water was safe.

Then yesterday afternoon, very thirsty and empty, drank clear but algae-filled ground water from a fifty-foot wide pond. It looked like an occasional pond with grass still growing underwater. The pond was within a barbed-wire tree farm. Cattle had not been there recently. But then again, I thought, what's recently? Took some chances there.

Also remembered the qualms over potential dog shit bugs. Eating those dandelion greens at the church near Bradshaw's on the first day out.

After briefly taste-testing a few, I washed a whole bunch. ("Mmmm! Hey, them was some good greens, too!") Saw them next day in my own shit — a two-inch length of gnarled greenish-brown, sort of like Iowa's dainty pellets only bigger and all smashed together like twisted rope. All my other shit is light yellowing-tan, smooth and mushy — the fecal results of my dietetic simplicity: granola and "magma" (my personal concoction of dried fruits and nuts.).

I prefer the stuff that drops out and hangs tight together. It's picked clean and well-packed for delivery back to the source. I'm on the lookout for more dandelion greens.

The upshot of these scatalogical concerns coalesces in the decision to start using halazone tablets in my drinking water. Today I read on one of my plastic Wilderness Cards: "Tropics & Swamps: standing water generally unfit."

This is all a bit of catch-up since I didn't get to write in last night's confusion. For the real clincher regarding sanitation, we need to backtrack to yesterday, midday.

Finally clouds! And a good breeze and me smelling myself, wafting funk to high heaven. I resolve to bathe and launder at the next opportunity.

Early in the day, we come to a stream, nice size, full up, waist deep, heading south under the highway. Oh water! Scrubbing salvation! no more stink-o-me.

The stream is fifteen feet wide, shaded, with no mosquitoes to mention. As fast as I can, I put on blue nylon swim briefs. After all, what eyes linger from yonder jungle? From highway bridge? What mean little thoughts lurk shadowly therein? Perforce, a patrol car is the first mobile by.

I wade in, dragging Iowa along for her first swimming lesson. She swims well on this, her first time out. It's not hard to see, however, that it may not be her favorite sport. She quickly gets her feet back on solid ground, drinks her fill and unceremoniously abandons me to my folly.

I begin laundering the clothes, amazed to find how the water alone cleanses. I use a little of the precious soap on the utterly dirty spots; the soaping is done up on the stream's bank — no suds in the water.

As the water's euphoria begins to wane, I notice a somewhat sickly odor from this stream. A vaguely familiar smell. Nonetheless, to be re-beginning again! To wash all the sad grime behind. Ahhh! I begin wondering just what stream this is. Still dazzled by all this clean clothing, I lay out the patchwork flat. The dried green grass, a frame for cloth colors catching a hide-and-seek sun.

The stream has a peculiar fetid odor, a negativity about it. Still, the water cleanses. I jump all in, jump out and soap up. Oh, the head gunk loosens, crotch lint fades, the arm pits dissolve wondrously clean.

Finally, I remember: our garden's first fertilizer, years ago, that smell so distinct and definite in the rain. This is Munson Slough, Tallahassee's major cesspool outlet, running from only a few miles north, directly out of the only sewage treament plant in town. Oh that familiar sewage sludge smell!

And so, water danger and water need. Water is food and water is clean.

As an addendum, perhaps as further warning, while finishing the last few sentences, a fast four-foot black snake slithered up to within three feet, checked me out and then slipped straight over to check out resting Iowa, fifteen feet away in the shade. The snake must have decided we were OK, but not being a friendly sort, headed back into the underbrush.

Late Dusk

Using this flashlight pen gizmo that I bought for *her* Christmas present. My rampant gadgeteer greed.

Many self-referents, correctors. Munson Slough debacle for one. Later today, another:

Walking up a quarter mile stretch of ferocious U.S. 319, heading for the dirt road into the National Forest. Am walking way over by the fencerow at the edge of the easement, nowhere near the road's shoulder. Iowa is heeling nicely. She heels right side or left, depending upon which leg I slap before we walk. I also have a few non-verbal, non-voiced signals — whistles and whirrs. She "comes" now and recognizes her "name" as a three-note whistle. Anyway, there we are walking as usual AND. . . .

Speeding shiny, somewhat souped-up, metallic blue pickup truck swerves way off the road, pulls up to us and the driver, all burly, gruff and indignant: "Hey, is that legal? I'm from the Humane Society!" He's pointing to Iowa and her bulging packsack.

I look back at him, past his fat stupidly grinning daughter, I guess. Plaintively I place my hand over my mouth and shrug my shoulders.

"No speak English, hey? *Well, mucho malo! Mucho malo!*" again pointing at the goat.

I smile politely, somewhat obsequiously. I bend over, stooped down under the weight of my own truly heavy backpack. I point to my load, then at Iowa's back and finally back and forth between us both.

Confounded he sputters and fumes. With one vehement gust,

"Aw shucks!" he peels out, defeated.

Later I consider notes I could have written to him: *Is horseback riding illegal?* Or, *We both carry twenty percent of our weight, even-steven.*

However, I'm glad I didn't and glad that it happened the way it did. Made me reconsider my attitude toward Iowa girl.

He made a point because she's not here of her own free will. It's fine for a human like me to be as nutty as I want: carrying this heavy load, maintaining silence, eating weeds . . . and occasionally striking the poor little girl with my dogwood staff . . . yes, I am Iowa's crucifier.

But (always *buts*), she does need to stay near under duress. Without me, she's dog-meat or highway gore. I wish I knew a painless way to teach her, but I don't. As it is, she is heeling near faultlessly after only two full days of training.

Nonetheless, she's not here by choice and I am. The man's concern was justified and instructive. My silence turned a potential encounter into a two-way learning street.

As a result, I make the following adjustments:

1) From now on, at every rest, Iowa's pack comes off before I remove my own. And as we leave again, hers goes on *after* I have mine all set and mounted;

2) I remove half of the weight from her pack and place it in mine. I have stupidly made no allowances for her year of being penned. Will seek a weight ratio which is based on tiring us at about the same time, rather than one based strictly on percentage of bodyweight carried;

3) I do whatever else I can to ease her trials. This evening it meant getting out of the tent — and opening the door to sand fleas and mosquitoes — to rub more citronella on her face and udder.

DAY FIVE   Mottled overcast morning

Upon waking, decided that the man in the blue pick-up was actually BILLY GOAT GRUFF, also known as BILLY GOAT BLUE . . . the Great Protector of All Nanny Goats. I have known this character since my early childhood when my mother tells me of interminable listenings to the 78 r.p.m., "Song of Billy Goat Gruff."

Midday, Rainy

Trout Pond Recreational Area for the Handicapped

Why swim the Apalachicola
Why climb Truchas Peak?
Why seek "Mountains and Rivers
Without End?" Why?

First bowl of popcorn
Hot cup of soup
State park rain shelter
Safe fast fire grill
Decent pasture, too.

Thank you, Lord
Thank you, Lord
I want to thank you, Lord
For helping me make good
On my chance!

DAY SIX

Night, quarter moon

I hope Diann will hit "The Bargain Box" for a little rain hat for
Iowa. That would be the crowning touch, the *ne plus ultra* of goat
mod. If you think we're a pair now, wait until then. Besides, she
would really like something to keep the rain out of her eyes.

Rattlesnake Riddle-Ramble:

Rattlesnake I've eaten, fried alone in oil, shot by neighbors,
tasted better than fine, lean white chicken meat. Wanting to live off
the land as much as possible and to carry as little as necessary and to
go for steadily longer periods without needing a mailstop "care"
package of magma and granola from Diann. At the same time
wanting to live according to the precepts of Buddha who abjured
killing though did allow his monks to *accept* meat as long as it had
not been killed specifically for them. Having one winter caught a
baby rattlesnake at our homestead; having released it unharmed
after three days of continued hibernation in the refrigerator; having
encouraged its own venomous intentions towards rodents and
others; having re-enforced its natural harmlessness — or more
probably its fear — towards humans. Knowing how easy it would be
to club one to death with the dogwood staff; knowing that vegetable
foraging usually costs more than it gives; knowing that lean unbled

meat is the most efficient and complete source of metabolic wilderness energy. Considering that the Buddha lived in a more southerly clime where meat spoilage is a more serious year-round hazard and where vegetation is sufficient to provide all protein needs. Noting Buddhism's ethical pluralism and the Right Perspective of eating from where you are. Wondering if rattlesnakes, then why not blue racers, kings, corals, armadillo, possum, wood lizards, turtles, grubs, stray children? Realizing that today at Lost Creek, upon casting this trip's first fishing lure, I had become a hunter — and at that very moment listening to the ominous hoots of owls in the daytime. Reflecting upon the life of a nomad — its dull anti-romanticism, its meanness. Remembering the cloudy cruel eyes of the Greek shepherd I met in the grown-over ruin of a hilltop Turkish fort. Knowing full well what real red-blooded Americans think of panty-waists; cow-towing, perhaps, to the no-bullshit of he-man hunters. Visualizing the brutal violence the act would require and knowing how little courage it would take and how small a part of the potential violence in me that it would require. Trying to determine the implications of such an act relative to the petition for total and unilateral military disarmament which I am carrying and for which, partially, I am suffering. Considering the relation as well to the dogwood firestick that I burn little Iowa with — as corrections, of course, "for her own good." Pondering whether to consider my nibbling of grape leaves, cattails, dandelions, smilex, partridge pea, blackberry leaves and all the food I carry on my back . . . whether that has anything to do with it or not. The same old questions of suffering. Wondering, finally, whether the native Americans, for example, weren't simply fooling themselves in saying they only took from the animals what the animals gave of themselves.

Is there a question now (once there was): to walk softly or to tread?

DAY SEVEN Friday Night Hoopla

"Chuck will's widow! Check Will's will! Chuck willow's will! Chuck willow's real! Chuck what is real! Check what is real!" First from a tree close to the left, then in the distance, then close to the left . . . temporarily competing with, but successfully ousting, an army helicopter droning eastward.

These metaphysical, and yet practical, not to say necrophiliac or avaricious . . . no, simply to say: these gay Friday night bird blades out for a hot night on the ole national forest.

We're in thick bear country now, set up about a quarter mile from an electric-fenced apiary, about the fifth we've seen. Tall pines interspersed with scrub oak and the dense ti-ti. Those hammocks are the daytime lay-up home of the black bear. Dense ti-ti a couple hundred yards from our tent site here.

This is our third night in the forest. No signs, no spoor, no prints of bear. But lots of smells and tracks of deer, possum, coon, some big birds. All the flowers are yellow! Is it the season or the soil?

While sitting in zazen today, I was given a blow to the head by an errant and bezoomy enlightened grasshopper. I immediately awakened to the exquisite reality of a tiny hiding yellow flower. For fifteen minutes I had been staring without seeing.

Saw three vehicles all day: a National Forest truck-van, a road-grader (three times, back and forth) and a glimpse of a pick-up truck.

The road-grader stopped on the third return as we were resting by the road. The man leaned back, took out a cigarette. Before lighting up he said, "Sure looks like it's warming up today."

So I smiled back as he stretched and loosened up in his high seat. I walked over and handed him my note. Either he was an extremely slow reader or he was just confused and sat there for a long time, cogitating.

Then he looked at me kind of funny, sort of smiled and shook his head. From up high there on the throne of his Cat, he threw on the ignition and went bulldozing on down the road.

He never did get to light up that cigarette.

Because I am walking today mostly within a wildlife management area, I have not passed many clearcut areas. But walking back of Woodville on paper company land, I certainly witnessed the desolation.

Mile long three-foot wide ruts as deep as my knee, every ten feet for hundreds, thousands, of acres. Struggling bits of green arms and legs, pitifully reaching from the graveyard to the sky. Bare gray sand, torn stripped limbs jutting grotesquely, never acceding finally to publishing's tramp. The flattened mashed and soppy desert. Everywhere within it, sand flea heaven. Near a bit of marsh, mosquito nirvana. What price the daily news?

DAY EIGHT Halfmoon, full Swampnight

OK, baby, I'm ready for you to come get me now.

Sheer and utter exhaustion.

I've had my day in adventureland and no thanks, no re-ride.

I couldn't finish what was begun "In the Heat of the Fray." There were too many mosquitoes and I was not resting, thoroughly dejected, on the wrong side of one more swampstream to cross.

So to continue from there . . .

All right, so the Ochlockonee is no big deal of a stream. Just some sort of stream of consciousness, about which more later.

I had decided to test our stream crossing abilities. There were unanswered questions: Can the sleeping bag's air mattress effectively float our fifty or so pounds of gear? Will it capsize? How will Iowa handle swimming a river? What will the currents do?

So instead of heading south for the bridge, I go north to Pine Creek boat landing. A beautiful day, as I said.

We get to the landing about midday. The usual gawks from the dozen or so people there. I immediately head upstream into the woods to avoid the stares and impending questions. And to prepare.

Of course I'm worried that I'll lose all my gear. Or that Iowa will give out in mid-stream. Or at the very least something will happen to make me look ridiculous to those people who will be onlookers as soon as I leave the river bank.

I'm apprehensive and nervous, but thorough. I take my time, one step, one step.

I get the air mattress raft all loaded and tied and floating, say a brief prayer, pick up Iowa and cradle her into the water. We're off!

The raft is a dream, buoyantly trailing about ten feet behind, tethered to my shoulder. Iowa paddles like Esther Williams and, but for my silence, I would let out a Johnny Weismueller yell. Ah it was slick as a whistle!

Climbing out on the other side, I hear the kids who were fishing with their father finish exclamations of excitement and glee. As we're beginning to dry off I hear the camper-tent fishermen's words deflect across the water, "Yeah, but what's he going to do on the other side? There's nothing but mumble mumble mumble." And another: "Yeah, well he sure did a good job!"

After the half-hour of putting everything back into walking order, I take out the *Tao Te Ching* and read my daily homily, today number eight. The first sentence is "Goodness is like water." How can I not laugh and smile in wonder! While gliding through the sunshine glimmmer, I knew we could have kept swimming downstream forever.

But a few lines later, there's a sentence of warning: "Water goes where men do not." Oh, that old Ochlockonee of consciousness.

I know that there is a north-south highway only a few miles due west. So I take out my compass just to double check directions (it still being midday) and face the dense tangle west.

Iowa becomes difficult to guide through the labyrinth of vines and stickeries.

I soon find that the river's not finished. No, not by a long shot. First I go west til I hit water, Then I go north til I hit more water, then . . . I come finally to a big evil swamp lake. Jittery. Nobody knows where I am, me included.

Back at the river, with an audience, with boats and people nearby . . . a little nervous then, yes. But basically all fun and games.

Now, at this impassable 150-foot wide swampstream lake, we must raft it again. Not fun. No game. Serious stuff.

Humbling virgin cypress, draped miles high with moss, motionless. Thin black bottomless soup. Moccasins?

I make three stupid decisions. First to try and swim with my sandals on. Second, I swim wearing my green "e" T-shirt. Third, I do not remove Iowa's harness. (A catastrophic fourth decision would have been to leave her pack on — to use it as "water wings," filled with empty plastic containers and inflated sleeping bag sack.)

Luckily, with the first two strokes the sandals come undone and float. I recover back to shore, but the mis-start adds to the confusion and worry.

The T-shirt is more leaden than I expect and the drag tires me.

Iowa nearly drowns. She goes under twice. I rescue her, towing her across with my hand under her head. The raft floats OK. I'm weary and afraid. I begin silent cries of "Please God, no more water." I put on my dry walking boots, hopefully.

Within a few feet, more water. Smaller swamps and streams, all wadeable — but Iowa hates even to wade. It was so sad to see her stand trembling after the near drowning, knee deep in water. She stood there the whole half-hour I took to repack. She was so tired and shocked.

Just at dusk, we come to yet another deep swamp, though not as wide as the other. I rightly decided to swim it before dark. We can start the morning with at least the hope of heading upland.

So that's where we are now, within easy earshot of the motor-boats having their Saturday night fishing parties. At a much greater distance, but audible, an occasional muffled truck to the west.

We hear deep throated alligator growls; they sound like a couple hundred yards away. At the end of the day, we followed deer trails and that always makes us both feel better.

We're about five feet higher than the swamp we just crossed, sleeping under sweet gum.

We saw some fearfully big birds.

Iowa's finally just laid down. She won't lay down till she's dry. I dried her as much with the handkerchief as I could.

I hope we make it out of here alive.

("I'm sorry, Mother Nature, I didn't mean to challenge you. Hey, just a joke. All in fun, huh? Now, how about letting us out of here?")

Oh to be safe at home in my honey babe's arms.

Twigs crack outside, strange growls, Iowa acts a little like something's approaching.

I'm going to sleep. It's the only way out.

DAY NINE   Middle of Moonless Night

Intermittent sleep. Full-blown hemorrhoids. Hobbled to piss.

It's the nervous tension. It's all that dried fruit. It's the lack of desire to drink the plastic-tasting halazone-treated swamp water I'm carrying. Besides the halazone is two years past its expiration date.

All I can hope for is that, for some unforeseen reason, it should be this way.

Beginning to wonder why I left at home the emergency whistle I used to carry. If necessary, it could be heard by the boaters.

Morning freshness

One of those laughing hyena birds overhead.

A woodpecker drumming on a thick dead tree — deep staccato bass, blazing away at twenty blows a second.

A ray of light through the eastern window. Motor boat drones.

Numberless twitters, tweets and whistles.
What to do about this pain in my ass?

Dream: I am a prison guard. There is a minor but significant flare-up. I'm new on the job, so I write it up, not wanting to be seen as an easy mark. A few days later I am accosted by one of the inmates involved, a tall thin jet-black gleaming-eyed man: "Hey now, why did I get a negative report so bad? You know what that do to my record, Jack." I hem, haw and shuffle. I don't know whether it's *my* report to which he's referring — it might not have gotten to him yet. Stalling for time, I telephone Central to see what report they've got out on him. While the operator puts me on hold, I ask the prisoner if he knows who wrote the report. "Yeah, *you* did, man!" implying, "Why you jivin'?" I hang up the phone and turn full face and say, "Well, it was a truthful report." He responds, "Yeah, it was honest, right on, but you know what it does to my record!" At that point I feel relieved.

I've only once had hemorrhoids so bad that I didn't want to walk — during the mental hospital bit and then there wasn't much cause to move around anyway. But two weeks ago, for the first time since then, they flared up enough to call in sick, one of my last TV working days. I attributed that flare-up to the stress of change.

Now again, here in this wondrous but severe backwater swamp.

I'll tell you one thing. My experience yesterday convinces me that swimming the Apalachicola would be a snap.

The only reason Iowa nearly drowned on the second crossing, I discovered, was because I had not removed her harness. She hung up her front leg in a strap and panicked when she found it useless.

So swimming the Apalachicola would be no sweat. But crossing through the swamp forest on either side would be hell. Much worse than this. The flood plain is wider by far.

So I think I'm going to stick to the roads and bridges. I've had enough cross-country swamp experience. And have yet more to face this morning.

Midday

Still in this swamp. Same woodpeckers, same big owls, same noxious mosquitoes. A few false survey markers, old logging trails which disintegrate into deer trails, alligator mud holes, swamp-streams forever. One more rafting swim, a couple of waist deep wades and lots of slogging. After a long quiet period at breakfast, we heard a big animal splashing behind us for a brief second, then no more. It was our rafting spot — and though I was so slow and careful, hard to believe that it is, I forgot to remove Iowa's harness. Fortunately it was only a short fifty-foot swim and no harm was done.

Whatever it was behind must have heard us and quieted for us to leave. I figure it was a deer manitou checking to see we were careful.

Hemorrhoids seem to be somewhat better — definitely better than last night. Never has the sound of the internal combustion engine been so appealing. I hardly can hear either boat or truck. Just heading west, I know there's a road out there somewhere.

Lying here resting, head propped up on pack, covered with mosquitoes that, thank God, cannot bite through. A few extras are thrown in — tiny biting flies and some buzzbomber horseflies, too. Ah, the beauty of nature! Once again, technology protects via this long sleeve sweatshirt with hood and mosquito net hat.

I keep putting on my dry walking boots after these waist high slogs, hoping that I'll not again need my wading sandals.

My granola and Iowa's goat grain both ran out this morning. I fed her some sweet condensed nut and fruit magma. She gobbled it.

Iowa's giving a solid five cups a day and, oh, so grateful am I.

Dusk just past

Well, if you're reading this anywhere but as part of the deceased's remains, I survived. But first, right here:

Tent pitched on a small ridge not far from "Yellow Creek." The bombastic burps of bullfrogs; cricket's clacking canopy; from the tree's overhead: "What is real? What is real?" Frog songs sporadically punctuated with a streak in time — a long sucking gasp broken in mid-whine by thumpity-thump-thump, an automobile across the bridge a couple hundred yards east. The distant dog bark — I thought it was aimed at us. But it continues whether we're silent or not — and we are now. The salve of this half-lit night's symphony soothes even as it flows away.

After the last entry: We had just waded through one more disheartening swamp-stream, thigh-deep. Sodden and forlorn, despite the shining sun, faithful Iowa and I began once more to trudge west.

Onward and upward and up and up! and out! of that stinking slimy sluggish backwater goo. "Hey, Mr. Black Bear, Mr. Cottonmouth, Mr. Razorback, Mr. Gator! You all go on, you can have your never-quit skeets, your webs of jungle thorn, your creepy-crawly stingarees! This boy's heading for high and dry.'"

I first really knew I had it made when I stumbled onto a beatific bonanza of crumpled beer cans and "Posted" signs tacked on every tree. When we finally reached the road, we faced the blasted land-scape of yet another paper company harvest. Even though we were out of the muck, we were still pretty low and depleted.

Out of the blue, an old man in a medium blue car pulls up. "You Puerto Rican? Cuban? Latin American? From right here, huh?" I'm handing him my little note as I notice on his windshield "Help America something-or-other" over a waving flag. So I guess he's an American Legionnaire and I'm glad he's obviously too feeble to hurt me, if that be his wont.

"Hell, I'm for doing away with *all* arms! You want me to sign this? Hey, I'm going down the road, be right back, see you then. You won't take a ride, will you?" Forty-five minutes later, he returns, I'm resting. "Here, take all this feed for your goat. I've fed my hogs and calves, the rest is yours if you can carry it."

Goat feed is the *one* thing I have concern for at the moment since I'm all out and there's nothing but paper company land for at least another day.

"Sorry, I don't have anything for you." I hand him the petition; he signs as I'm taking the grain bag. It's probably near fifteen pounds. I fill the grain jar and empty the granola container. How can it be? It all just fits, right to the brim.

That guy was some kind of savior to me. He didn't say much. Of course with me not talking they rarely do. He offered to drive down the road to a tiny store just barely in sight. Said he'd return with a bottle of soda for me to drink. I motioned no and thanked him with clasped hands for the goat grain.

When I got to that little teeny tiny store down the road, I met my grandma, Lyda. O, she was suspicious at first to be sure. Kept her hand on that screen door lock a full couple of minutes looking at Iowa and me.

But she warmed up quite a bit. In response to the last, recently added, line to my note — *You are welcome to sign* — she responded, "You know, I just don't know what to think about that."

I bought some sardines and crackers. Went out back to the spigot and drank a quart of water on the spot. Stood with her a while admiring her azaleas and gray-beard.

Filled up canteens with good well water and went on down the road.

North to Telogia, giving up on that Apalachicola swampland slog.

Last encounter of the day, two young rednecks brazenly blowing a joint. They zip past us going to opposite direction, nearly breaking their necks craning to look around. They throw a quick u-turn and skid on back. "Wha' tha'?"

I hand over The Note. Driver, gruffly, "Well, no, I don't think I want to sign that." ("OK, OK, no need to huff.") "Here, you want some of this?" ("No thanks.") "Just walking around the country, huh? Can't talk, huh. Well, that's too bad, I'll bet you've got some stories to tell."

One goal of this walk — and of this life — is to learn to treat everyone fairly, equally. On the inside, I didn't really do right by Sheriff Raymond; though on the outside I didn't do wrong either. Silence increases a tendency to shun. As usual, there is a fear and a fright.

A newly discovered walking quota; one signature a day. I now have seven. Self-criticism: an indulgent massage for my psyche? Cheap, lazy theatre? A trumped up and trendy frivolous game? All of the above? Oh, I suppose. Yeah, some.

Dangerous? No, not really. People don't want to harm. We are protected. Also in the stronger position. The less one has, the more.

We're just a pebble-sized image, slung with a laugh between the eyes of Uncle Samson.

DAY TEN   Here and There
     "And God Said: 'SHARE THE POPCORN!'"

("Aw, God, that damn goat! Shoot, all she ever wants to do is eat! Damn it all, look at all this green stuff here — grass and vines and brambles. Her favorites! Plus we've got all the water she wants here at this little nameless creek. Hey, man, this popcorn is only the second batch I've made on this trip. Naw, God, there ain't no good reason in the world I got to share my popcorn with this walking belly. Or, maybe, you just don't know how I feel about my popcorn.")

So, having affirmed my decision — and having expertly popped a potful on the open fire — I pick up the pot with bare fingers and YEOOOW! Dropped the pot right there on the spot. Spilled half the kernels for guess who.

Moral is: God, too, is a Billy Goat.

Heading north on 67. Not too far to Telogia. Taking my time, long sunny days. Not going anywhere.

A plush Malibu Pontiac practically screeches to a halt. Two older ladies, both well-dressed, one with hair dyed red, the other streaked in silver.

"Where'd you get that cute little goat? How old is she? Where you heading? Ah . . . ???"

Before she can run out of questions, I hand her The Note.

Before I can brace myself for any kind of response whatever: "Well, let me sign it!" the driver says. The passenger signs, too.

I'm probably more dazed than they are. They leave us with, "That sure is a pretty little goat. Good Luck!"

Ten days ago, as Diann and I parted, I held up three fingers. She said, "Three months?" I shrugged ("Yeah.") But as far as I'm concerned now, it could be three weeks or thirty days.

I'd like to help her put in the cistern, keep up the garden, be her helpmate.

Mid Dusk

"Tiger Rose, Tiger Rose, come in please. This is Peace Nigger calling Tiger Rose. Over."

"Come on in, Peace Nigger, this is your sweet Tiger Rose."

"Tiger baby, took our first flak today. Over."

"M-m-m, what kind babe?"

Sitting in zazen barely in sight of road. Officer-of-the-Law pulls over, rushes up. Stentorianly: "Do you have identification!"

I pass The Note.

And I feel him crumble. It's amazing what that note can do.

Regrouping somewhat: "Well, you can hear, can't you? We've had complaints about you."

("Me?") I gesture surprised, genuinely hurt.

"Yes, this is private property."

We're about fifty feet off the road, no fencing, just dirt and pine trees, nothing much else. Oh, one little wood rat peeping out of a tree trunk hole as I slowly completed one yogic asana.

I write a note, *You've had specific complaints about me?*

He says yes, about being on private property.

All I can think of is that long half-day relaxing at the creek, laundering clothes, popping popcorn — and sharing it, however accidentally, with Iowa. Just lolled about there, even got self all spic 'n' span clean, ready to go through Telogia.

Of course at that creek there wasn't a house within a mile or more. We've been walking primarily through forest, some owned by paper companies, some of it national forest, some private. Nearly all of it unfenced.

But I do remember one custom pick-up truck which made a big point of cruising the bridge to see what we were doing there.

"You've been on this road for two days," The Liberty County Sheriff's Deputy says.

I'm not surprised that he knows that. There have been several vehicles I've seen three or four times.

But it is kind of interesting to know that Big Brother is watching.

Shoot, that's no news. Everyone, all of life, is watching.

After perusing *all* the cards in my wallet, "Well, if we get any more complaints, we'll have to take you in."

"So, Tiger Rose, baby, what you say to that? Over."

So he gets on his radio, "Black male, license number ———, blah blah blah. . . ."

No, I'm not wanted.

Yes, I was going to Telogia — which I overhear him report to the radio is only three miles north.

He tells me basically to get on through Telogia before dark.

I start on up the road, well aware that there is a potential darker side to all of this. But I do feel that the forest and swamp have honed me. Still, no need for useless confrontations.

So I go into evade and escape tactics. Instead of continuing on north, we head back into the National Forest, the public lands west.

I'd wanted to go to the post office in Telogia. It's late enough now that it would have been closed anyway. I'll take a "long cut" and get there on time tomorrow.

No big thing, this. But the private property issue opens a can of worms for me. I, too, am a landowner — as stewards, as well as others, are called these days. But now is not the time to go into it.

Sleeping in dense bush on national forest land, one hundred feet from the rails of the Apalachicola Northern. Will walk the tracks into town tomorrow.

Dealing with police as a neutral force becomes more difficult when they "attack." All one can do is react with honesty and harmlessness.

Liberty County — halfway, I suppose, between Freedom and License.

DAY ELEVEN

At the Telogia Post Office:

Telogia, nothing more than a crossroads, a cinder block one-room post office and a general store.

The postmistress says she doesn't know if there is a post office in Scott's Ferry, Gaskins or Broad Branch.

I'm going to cross the Apalachicola on Highway 20 over to Blountstown where I know there's a post office. Should take about three days. Will ask Diann to write me there. Would like to know what's been happening with her. I miss her and, as I said, would be happy to be helping her with the cistern and the garden and life.

Our reception here in Telogia is revealing in that no one acts surprised at my silence. They seem to have been expecting us. At the post office, a sheriff's deputy's only remark was, "Hmm, pretty goat."

Nightfall

"Beating the edge too fine dulls the sword!" — Lao-Tse

A flat wet day.

Why do I beat Iowa so?
Why can't she understand "please?"
Why doesn't she know r-o-a-d spells death?
Why are all my clothes wet?

Thanks, God, that Iowa is dry.
Everything inside is scattered,
Soppy, sloppy as it always is
When water-water comes down.

Now for a cold clear windy night —
Good for our garden and good for our soul.

Nothing left, much.
Eating less than ever.
Still enough milk.

"Why you and that goat are the biggest thing to happen in Telogia since the helicopter landed in the woodlot!"

"Can't talk, huh? Wanna beer? No, don't drink beer, huh? Hmmm, milk only, huh? Hmmm, from Jacksonville? Tallahassee! How long'd it take? Long time, huh? Hmmm, goat's pissin'. You've only walked one mile since eleven o'clock. Looks suspicious."

While letter writing back at Telogia just outside the post office, an old man crouched over my shoulder for several minutes, squinting to read as I wrote. He seemed to think it was a note to him. I was too involved in the letter to write him the contrary.

It is difficult to go into a post office, store, anywhere. Left without me, Iowa starts bawling within a few seconds. I must keep returning to reassure her every minute or so. No one will do but me, she's one hundred percent specific. She doesn't even care, particularly, for other people to pet her. Makes me feel right wanted.

Animal Trainers must need to suppress guilt feelings. Parents must, too. Training involves the infliction of pain. This requires, at times, the trainer to urge in heart and mind, "Pain!" It doesn't take long to figure out who the beast is.

Bought half-dozen eggs. Sleeping a quarter mile from county dump. Regroup tomorrow morn early.

DAY FOURTEEN   By the river

Two weeks walking and a month now of silence. The "purpose" has manifested: retreat and regroup.

Time now to decide the next decision. Today.

The river's unseen from here, in a pasture slightly beyond the bank. But the cool wet air and water birds flying tell me it's there.

Iowa girl: short, stubby, invariably "cute" or "pretty." Always preceded by "little." Should call her "Little Cute and Pretty." For days now, she's been supplementing her browse with forty percent protein hog rations. The stuff is primarily soybean meal. But it also contains fish meal and oxytetracycline. Not really the right stuff for a lactating ruminant.

Will call Diann tomorrow noon from Blountstown. Will break silence and telephone boycott at once. A full four weeks . . . Friday full moon noon.

Will ask her to come and get me. Mission accomplished.

Had to clear the slime from my receptors.

So now, clear road, which direction?

One day, one week, one month, one year, one decade?

Tomorrow: go home, rest, clean up, eat good, kiss and hug, look around.

Next week: a daily work schedule — one-third write, one-third homestead, one-third maintain.

A month: visit Koinonia; submit notes; mulch garden fully; build compost privy and drinking water cistern.

A year from now: more writing; livelihood of physical work outdoors; foreign work travel and language.

A decade hence: publishing, loving, parenting, boatbuilding, harvesting and sowing.

Last time I felt so high and clear and free . . . last place like this high cliff in the center of an oxbow bend, being eaten away as I write from under me; large trees torn below and with every breeze wondering if this earth here high will any minute give way; the predator birds — osprey, eagle? — twirling their way about the sun; the river itself, the roiling channel right at our toes, apex of the hairpin turn; fragile edge, windblown sky splayed and splattered, slobbering its beauty all over me. . . .

The last time I felt so high and clear and free . . . was in the Yukon where the summer winds were colder still and the high sky was just as thin.

So why return home? Because this same sky is there, because my wife is there, because — having recovered this sense of beauty — I want to bring it home.

That little girl at the store, her look! Total innocence, unknowing of guile, no mask, without seeking. She was beaming at me: "Man, you're beautiful! Goat, You're beautiful! You two are beautiful!"

Beauty seeing beauty radiating beauty.

Diann's first gift to me, *Navajo Wildlands*: "In beauty we walk!"

A fly of huge beautiful red eyes came walking here on this page, then flew to shirt, walked around a bit, and, for the first time I ever saw, shat on me!

An utterly appropriate last day first.

Tonight will sleep in Kerouac style — beneath the wheels of doom. Let God decide whether tonight is my night to die. If it rains heavy upstream tonight, this river cliff might cave. I'm sleeping right on the edge this last night. The view, the chance, is worth it.

Said I'd be gone three months. Damn straight, was too. A month in that swamp, two weeks in the rain, a couple weeks in innocence and a month walking. That makes three.

Silence — a sturdy tool, and surprise! a non-violent weapon.

Past Dusk Now

Looked like some kind of a weak cloud system coming in at sunset from the southwest. It engulfed the last of a red and billowy, smeary sky.

Thinking a lot about talking to Diann on the phone tomorrow. Hope this time has been as productive for her. Hope she wants me back.

Spent all day just watching the river run. Did move camp upstream a mile or so, much more secluded here. Higher cliff. Really can see well both up and down river.

The ionizing effect of all this running water must stimulate the magnetic field around an electric wire.

High here, wind all day and night, too.

Pray this cliff to hold one human, one goat and their gear.
The leaves whisper good night.

DAY FIFTEEN   Dawn

In middle of night, I wake up to hear, "Ker-SPLOOSH!" The
soft sound of earth sighing and heaving ho . . . part of the cliff not
far upstream had given way. My heart lept. I tremblingly rushed out
of the tent to note that Iowa girl was no longer sleeping near the tent
but was back out of harm's way. I could hear God laughing out loud!

With due respect to Kerouac and humbled again to submission,
in the full moonlight I move the tent landward twenty feet or so.

Besides, the sleeping bag's air mattress raft had deflated and I
don't float in my sleep without it.

Of course, having moved, I did hope that the cliff would justify
itself by crashing as my last footstep fell away. But alas, such an
event did not occur. Just as well, I suppose, for who could stomach
such melodrama?

Across the Apalachicola
Midmorn

Long long narrow bridge, the swamp four or five times wider
than the river itself. The bridge practically an overseas highway.

By a stroke of luck, or as Allah would have it (always the last
laugh), construction was underway and the bridge was one-laned.
Much less danger from speeding cars.

Passing one of the work sites, a burly bronze black-haired
worker grins at us in amazement. I stop, he pets Iowa, I hand him my
note.

He looks up, "Sorry, I can't read. I'm Greek and. . . ." I smile,
shrug and begin to walk on. Before I know it he has handed me a
dollar bill, while flipping his other hand up with his thumb to his
mouth. He signifies that I should go buy a drink!

So now I have been perceived as a mute beggar. That it should
happen at a literal and figurative high point over and in the middle
of the Apalachicola is more symbol and myth (and from a Greek no
less) than this poor melodrama can stand.

As these two weeks have passed I have at once descended and
ascended to that same status as the cruel-eyed but mystic brute of a
shepherd I met in Greece. At the start of this trip, Iowa girl would

never have been able to make such a run as we made across the bridge — not even without the goat pack. I goaded her much of the way, especially the last third when the traffic got faster and she had tired. In this context, "goading the goat" means to switch at and to thwack. Her rump was afire with the dogwood staff.

Waiting at the Wayside

Frightened myself walking through town next to big glass windows. Got a glimpse of self. Couldn't stand to look . . . and didn't.

No letter at post office. My silence is broken by a phone call contact with Diann. "I'm at your disposal." "Disposable?" "I'd like to come home." "Well, I'll come and get you."

Wild onion, garlic or chives by the side of the road.

Iowa's milk off-flavor, from the fish meal in the hog rations.

"Are you sure that's what you want to do?"

Caught in silence. The only way to go on with the petition . . . the only way to go on at all, would be in silence. And silence is a cage as well as a shell.

Thoughts of "normal living" at home for a while.

She should be here within the hour. She sounded real good.

Would still like to walk to New Mexico and farther some day. But not alone. Perhaps with a goat.

The trip's greatest personal failing revolved around Iowa's discipline. After a certain point she should not have needed further corrections, especially on slowly widening away from my side. I didn't know whether to persist in nearly constant minor corrections or only to inflict an occasional big thwack. In either case, she pulled down my mask.

I'm afraid I'd not like to hear her story.

(August 1979)

Michael Shorb

Chronicles
(March 22,1977)

Remembering formerly fallen nations,
Proud behind their wampum walls and calumets,
Never dreaming the sea/lake wild
Rice or the forty pound blue
& yellow forest turkeys would vanish
Over the rim of time's hoop,
I read familiar voices in the daily hieroglyphic:

'Persian Gulf Earthquake' crowds 'City in Space'
An Indian queen falls, dictatorial prophet's
Daughter, row upon row of Chinese farmers
Pass buckets of water hand to hand
To save the Winter wheat.
          (The narrative breaks apart,
A poisoned gene.) Advance of mongol hordes,
PCBs conquering the Hudson, economically
Worthless striped river bass
                lashing in a trough,
Senate debate over rat tumors
& aerosols, 'Russian Warning'. (More & more people,
In a small item inside, building homes
Far from cities and their salient catastrophes.)

& I recall a last letter from Stefan, who escaped

The Mekong War dated Kamloops, B.C., seven
years
Ago: how he listed all the tools scattered about him
Where he built his cabin; adze & plane, saw &
Hammer, weight of the nails he was pounding;
That, a signature, nothing more.

Or two years before that, taking acid
By the shore of Big Bear Lake in
                              Southern California
& the first fear, the no escape from
Swelling, death-bound planet
                              in the chest,
& then the colors in nothing but light
Streaming among pine branches
Stunning us, making us part of ripples
On the wind-driven water & the brute
Clouds of darkness formed
                              above the pulsing trees.
Or how a grey-blooded war in
                              television Asia
Made such holiness seem an insane novelty
Rotting in our blood as we tried
Staying high above our own lives
On alcohol and drugs, sex & hatred,
Racing through beachtowns the night they bombed
Tonkin Bay dreaming in a beat-up Jaguar
Of pure lands of highway strip & crashing
Waves, with no Christ or Marx,
Freud or Plato.

But what's a body to these forces?
                              Or a life in memory?
One night we went out with our friend Frank,
Who worked in the county morgue,
& saw, down a long row of glass jars,
The lungs heart & brain
                              from an old jeweler I had killed
In a traffic accident.

& the mysteries of time & death
With its trail of nations & men
Passed over us, & we stood there,
Before the jar, drunk & stoned,
Arms about each other's shoulders,
Swaying slightly, side to side.

(December 1982)

Going Against The Dragon

An Interview with Robert Bly

Sy Safransky

Some poets call from on high. Too high for most of us: the thin air of mind leaves us dizzy — what are they saying?

Robert Bly takes us down to the valley, and gets down with us in the dirt, and shows us this is where it starts — here in flesh, here in grief, here in memories we deny. His arms wave like big branches, as he tells us to face the dark in ourselves. His language runs like water over the dry bed, whether he's talking about what it means to be a man or a woman, or acknowledging the pain of childhood, or warning against the siren call of Eastern mysticism. Full of eloquence and extraordinary energy, Bly is one of the most respected and widely read poets of the age, as fully human as anyone I've met.

Born fifty-seven years ago in Minnesota — not far from where he still lives with his wife and three children (three

Stop talking about enlightenment for a while. The soul is not born ready for light.

older children are in college) — Bly has written nine books of poems, including The Light Around The Body, *which won the National Book Award, and is the author of eleven translations. His magazine,* The Sixties, *brought into English the work of many previously unknown writers from other countries.*

I interviewed Bly last February, when he was in Chapel Hill to give a poetry reading at the University of North Carolina. The reading was rousing, Bly's voice an instrument he has fully mastered, ranging through subtleties of volume and pitch from roar to whisper. His poetry readings are works of art. He threads together the arrangement of poems, the jokes, the asides, the curiously light movements of his big body, the seeming lack of self-consciousness, as he reaches out with his poems, known by heart, to touch other hearts.

We talked the next morning. He asked for the chance to revise and expand his answers. I'm glad he did, although he ended up omitting some of the spontaneity, such as him scolding me for asking him how peaceful he was, saying that was a "Barbara Walters question." Other times, too, he drew the line around "the private." I was disappointed at first, then I thought of him shuffling around his writing shack in Minnesota, alone for days on end, giving away, with each line, what is most private.

— Ed.

SUN: In one of the poems you read last night, you talk about longing for "the cheerful noises to end." You said, "When I'm too public, I'm a wind chime ringing to cheer up the black angel." What do you do to get away from other people's noises and your own?
BLY: Well, I can't get away from them when I'm giving poetry readings, but when I'm home I spend time by myself. Every once in a while a short time completely alone . . . three or four days in a woods cabin I have.

SUN: Do you do any meditation?
BLY: Yes, I've done meditation for ten or twelve years.

SUN: What do you do?
BLY: That's something that belongs in the private (laughs).

SUN: You talked last night about the difference between doing and

talking. What do you do besides write? What are your days made of?
BLY: I consider writing to be an intense form of doing, especially
when one is writing on a blank page. I usually spend six or seven
hours a day at my desk, in the morning and early afternoon, and
that concentration includes an hour working with a new stringed
instrument I have, a kind of old European lute, called in Greek a
bouzouki. I'll sometimes compose to that. I want to learn music. For
the past few years I've been struggling with the help of music to find
out how to measure time in language.

I have three boys still in school, and when they come home
about four, we may do some physical labor together, or, occasionally, hunt. Matthew, who is a sophomore, and I have been remodel-
ling the sauna this month; after school we'll work on that an hour or
two. I believe a lot in what Scott and Helen Nearing say about everyone doing two hours of physical work a day, just to thank the planet
for being on it. It's a good idea, though often we're too lazy to carry
it through.

SUN: Do you watch television?
BLY: An hour a week. Television is the most disgusting form of not
doing that we have. How can we have art if entertainment is
everywhere?

SUN: How long have you been married?
BLY: I married in 1955, and that ended in 1980. Then, two years
ago, I married once more.

SUN: How much at peace are you?
BLY: That's a new age phrase, at peace. What does it mean? I'm not
sure it should be thought of as a goal. If I were at peace, I wouldn't be
in this room.

SUN: Last night, you referred to Jack Kerouac as a wonderful writer
and an idiot. Why was he an idiot? What was idiotic — and what
wasn't — about the beats and the hippies?
BLY: What was very strong was their desire and knowledge of how to
escape from the conventional opinions and the collective stiffness that
dominated the Fifties. Ginsberg and Kerouac and Kenneth Rexroth
before them — they were all children of Rexroth — understood that

by going into the more spontaneous parts of the personality, parts that Blake, Wilheim Reich and Jung had already described, a certain freshness would come, a certain joy would come, feeling would return. That happened, but looking back one would say that the error of ignorance lay in falsifying the nature of Dionysus.

The ancient Greeks portrayed Dionysus as a being with his head slightly turned to the side and down, a lot of grief in the face, and a thin line of silence all the way down his body. When one centered "person" is present, others, they found, can be spontaneous without damaging themselves. But in America we often use Dionysus without his permission as a saintly cover for our childish, chaotic and destructive behavior. Kerouac participated in that deception.

Moreover, a compulsive cheerfulness accompanied the whole movement. When I went to Russia this last year, I experienced each day the perception that the door to feeling is grief. Russia accepts grief and is still grieving over the Second World War. The lack of grief in the whole American Sixties movement may be one reason why it petered out. It's as if grief is an adult emotion, and limitless good cheer and longing for chaos are childish emotions.

I don't believe people have thought enough about what it means that Kerouac lived so long in his mother's house. Long after On The Road, a writer went to see him and said, "Let's have a drink." He said, "Well, my mother doesn't like to have beer in the house." So they had to go out in the garage and drink. What I'm implying is that below the pose of independence many of the cultural radicals were mama's boys. Some sort of failure in male initiation was going on.

I have the sense that the writers in this movement did not answer the question: what is true masculine behavior? Is leaving people and rushing about the country masculine? Is drug-taking masculine? The result of the confusion the movement had about this matter is that many men left over from the Sixties are being dominated now by women. How often one meets a spontaneous new age man living with a fierce angry woman, whom he can't stand up to.

There's a longing in the culture now for that imbalance to end. I don't know if it will happen. Does that answer your question?

SUN: Yes.

BLY: That doesn't mean that Kerouac isn't a good writer. There's something marvelous in his use of language, and his wit and love of living things is tremendous. But his work lacks that quality that someone like Rexroth had, which was adult grief, and we miss entirely the mood of the great Russian poetry of the last forty or fifty years, in which you have deep form and deep grief together. Other people's sufferings is the issue, not one's own light-heartedness. Do you agree with that view of the Sixties?

SUN: It sounds right to me. Yet I wonder if the cheerfulness and the childishness isn't the edge of something else.
BLY: What?

SUN: Something that went along with a spiritual renaissance, nine-tenths of which is crap, but one-tenth of which is valuable.
BLY: I agree there was a spiritual awakening.

SUN: Cheerfulness may just be misdirected faith.
BLY: Or true faith may be a redirection of energy that once went into cheerfulness. The so-called new age can be thought of as a rerun of the 1860s. As you know, Emerson and Thoreau and Whitman accepted Eastern ideas, and those ideas helped them to blossom. Thoreau in *Walden* mentions Kabir. America has always had part of its head open towards the East. Gary Snyder ends *Myths and Texts* with a sentence from Thoreau: "The sun is but a morning star."

Yet that spirituality you mention fed itself, and still feeds itself, primarily on Asian food. We need the food, because teachers in our own tradition don't cook. I mean by that not one of the major Christian groups teaches meditation any longer, in a way that makes the discipline available. The Americans had to go to Asians to learn it. I am an example. I took instruction from Trungpa while he was still in Scotland, and later did meditation with Ananda Marga teachers. And yet that food is not quite right for us. The Asian emphasis on skipping over pain and suffering, such as one finds in Rajneesh or the Maharishi, seems to me dangerous for our psyches, and a violation of our deepest traditions. So I feel that if we have projected our interior spiritual guide onto Asian teachers, we should take it back now.

Many Eastern gurus suggest that our suffering and grief can be dismissed as Western neuroticism, and the student can go directly to bliss, or the heart, or the spirit. That idea is not helpful. Let me tell you a story.

Gioia Timpanelli from New York and I sometimes work together when teaching or telling mythical material. That happened recently when we both taught at the Summer session of the Rudolf Steiner people in California, at San Rafael. Steiner is a genius, but his disciples tend to avoid all negative emotions, and emphasize the spiritual nature right away. We found ourselves in hot water there.

When it came time for Gioia's performance, she decided to go ahead and present the other point of view. She told the audience that she would center her performance around the chakra system, and would begin with a story from the lowest chakra and move upward. To my astonishment, she told a dragon story for the anal chakra, which brought a lot of dragon-fierceness into the room, dragon greed and dragon brutality, and followed that with a dragon story for the sexual chakra and a dragon story for the stomach chakra. By now the audience was well off their feet, and they felt to me kind of desperate, longing for their usual nourishment provided by spiritual nature and the prospect of spiritual victory. She wouldn't give it to them. They canned both of us shortly after.

Let's talk about dragons a little. I have the sense that Asia went through its dragon-fighting stage hundreds, maybe thousands, of years ago. Krishna, who represents ancient Shaivite traditions, strangled dragons and giants when he was only one or two days old. He didn't have much trouble with them.

But we are still in the dragon-fighting stage; our dragons have not been defeated by any means. Do you remember that Beowulf's first battle was with Grendel, a giant, and Grendel's mother? And his last, from which he died, was with a dragon. That means we are not always victorious with dragons. Dragons come up again in the King Arthur cycle. Giants really won the Second World War in the sense that the Nazis got possessed by giant-energy and a tremendous cultural destruction followed.

I take all of this to mean that the giants and dragons are very much alive inside us. The light tone of the new age often implies that all you need to do is to meditate twenty minutes a day and if something negative appears "bring it up and bathe it in the heart radiance." I hear revolting statements like that every day delivered with full confidence.

It's very dangerous — this heart radiance attitude — because if the dragon material is not dealt with, a man or woman can suffer a breakdown, and the longer the dealing is put off, the deeper the breakdown will be.

SUN: What does it mean to you to deal with it?
BLY: First of all, we stop talking about enlightenment for a while. The soul is not born ready for light. Joseph Campbell declares that the human infant, to judge by his inability to function well apart from his parents, is born twelve years too soon. A kind of marsupial pouch called the home is necessary; if it is not present, the body's development can arrest, suffer distortion, or end. But the human soul too needs a marsupial pouch. This is called mythology; if that is not present, the psyche's development can arrest, suffer distortion, or even end in suicide. The soul then is not born ready for light. Mythology in ancient times acted so as to guide the young soul through regions of darkness; one can still feel "Hansel and Gretel" doing that guiding for children.

So, for us, mythology is more helpful than enlightenment or to put it chronologically, years of mythology need to come, accustoming the soul to darkness, before the soul is ready for enlightenment.

Some storytellers deal with dragon energy by memorizing stories and telling them: that is active, not passive, and so belongs to dealing. To take rage, anger, jealousy, envy seriously, while watching them, is a way of dealing with dragons. Rather than getting a massage in order to remove tensions from your body, you could say, "What's the matter with tensions in the body?" Rather than slandering your parents by taking an Asian name, you refuse to do that, and ask the Asian to take an American name. See if he'll do it. That will bring up a little dragon energy. Going back to your parents and trying to understand the grief in them, and in your relationship to them, is a good way. Dealing with dragons seems to involve moving backward or downward.

For the work with one's parents, and early childhood, Alice Miller has produced a superb book, called in cloth, *Prisoners of Childhood*, and in paper, *The Drama of the Gifted Child*. I think it's marvelous. It threw me into a depression for several weeks when I read it recently, but it was a *good* fall.

The "drama" is this: we receive a deep wound from our parents before we can speak and we spend the rest of our lives pretending we

had a happy childhood. When people can't remember their childhood, or when they say, "Oh, it was very happy! I had wonderful
parents," that is, Alice Miller says, the mark of a really deep wound.
I always answered things like that if someone asked me about my
childhood.

That our mothers and fathers gave us a wound does not stem
from their being evil — that's not it at all. It stems from their being
narcissistic. For our purposes here, that would mean that they
needed us for something, or they needed us to be something, or they
needed something from us. They weren't standing on all four legs in
the world, they weren't complete in themselves, they were needy.
But who isn't? Our parents too were born twelve years too early.
What do they need us for? Well, my parents were second and third
generation Norwegian immigrants, and felt, as many immigrants do,
insecure, inferior, perhaps a little savage, and they needed my
brother and me to be nice.

The nature we brought with us from the far reaches of the
universe, and worked on in the womb, using the threads of DNA,
and the genetic cross threads, was our nature, and our gift. But our
parents didn't want it.

Alice Miller believes that we each live with this tremendous
wound, which amounts to a rejection that is, because it is pre-verbal,
not accessible to encounter group tellings nor to confession. And
what do we do then, if we can't express it? We can respond to this
wound, acting it out and hiding it at the same time, in two possible
ways: we can work things out as we reject someone deeply — that
would keep us in unconscious touch with it — or we can work things
out so that someone else rejects us deeply. Both ways are good. I've
done both.

Let me tell you a story. A few months ago, on my way to a men's
conference, I rode with a man also attending, who was in his early
thirties. He was boiling with anger. It turned out that some months
before, after six years or so of marriage, his wife told him she didn't
want to be with him anymore and she left. His anger eventually led
him to a gymnasium, where he worked with body-building, and he
actually put on about thirty pounds doing that. But his anger was
still with him, and as he drove it poured off his shoulders. During
one of the sessions later, I brought up the thought of Alice Miller,
and a moment later when I happened to glance at him, I saw that he

was starting to melt. He realized all at once that he had set up the marriage with great care and finesse so as to get the maximum rejection, and he had gotten it. His is one way of living that out.

So one can live through post-verbally a rejection that one received pre-verbally. I suppose the important thing would be gaining consciousness of the procedure, so that one wouldn't go on being angry and offering blame for the rest of one's life. As the Buddhists say, when the pre-verbal is entered, blame disappears. But grief comes.

The work of realizing what one has done is an example of what is described in the fairy tales as cutting off the head of the dragon in the solar plexus.

SUN: Once you've acknowledged the deep grief, isn't there a way to bring it up to the heart, not superficially, but more profoundly?
BLY: I suppose. But some dragons don't want to be lifted up into the heart area. That's their place down where they are. You go down and meet them on their ground. "I'm going to lift you up and bathe you in the violet light of the heart." What do they care about that?

SUN: You said last night that going to a Jungian analyst was money well-spent. . . .
BLY: Yes, I said that learning to think intuitively is something our ancestors knew how to do. Fairy tales move intuitively from one point to another; so do myths. We've lost our ability to do that, so we have to hire someone to teach us to think intuitively, which teaching we mistakenly call therapy.

SUN: Is that something you've done, or do?
BLY: Well, no, my therapy, or my instruction, came through reading Jung, alone, in a field, while also trying to write poems. The intuitive intelligence and language appears in all dreams, in true fairytales, and in great poems. We have to struggle so much now to write poetry. I didn't publish my first book until I was thirty-six, and I would say that the ten to fifteen years before that were spent trying to understand intuitive language and sound. Frost says, "A man is a writer if *all* his words are strung on definite recognizable sentence sounds. The voice of the imagination, the speaking voice, must know certainly how to behave, how to posture in every sentence he offers." I didn't have an older male that I could apprentice to,

physically, in this world, but I did have one in the other world — Yeats. And he is a superb intuitive thinker; he is still my master, and I read him every day. I mentioned last night that I think the male needs to be initiated into the world of male intuition, but the initiator needn't be your father. He doesn't need to be alive. And I suspect women need and long for a similar initiation. Many women poets have been initiated by Emily Dickinson or by Anna Akhmatova.

SUN: Another thing you said last night is that it takes a lot of energy for a man and woman to have a relationship; you have to get it back from your parents. I'd like you to talk about what that energy is, how you get it back, how *you've* gotten it back.
BLY: Let's say the dragons ate it. We're going to suppose that an energy, invisible but potent, a sort of liquid fire, appears in us and with us at birth. Our body produces it naturally, even while in the womb. When we are tiny, we keep some for ourselves, but most of it we give to feed our mother's thirst for it. We exchange it for a similar substance our mother gives us. We also, after we are two or three, give some, exchange some, with our father, but much less. Around twelve we begin to give more to the father.

What am I saying? Most of a boy's liquid fire, because his mother's sexuality has tremendous magnetism, becomes pulled toward and committed to his mother. Another way of saying it is the dragons eat it. They become fat on it. Dragons are not idealistic or religious; they are usually guarding some materialistic treasure they can't use themselves. So when the dragons eat the liquid fire, the stomach becomes home for a complicated interweaving family of energies: self-preservation, love of food, possessiveness of the mother, and beyond her, all women, the impulse for sexual union now confused with maternal receiving, fierce longing for comfort, for home, for not leaving home. The main image is that the dragons eat it, and we can't get it back, because, fed by that fire, they get too fierce for us.

If we talk of early marriage, the young male doesn't have enough of that invisible fire energy available to sustain and feed a relationship. He has twenty percent or so at the most. And the girl? What she has not fed to the mother, she has fed to the father. The father dragon in her stomach guards his useless treasure, and fights her off if she wants to get the fire back. So she too has no more than twenty percent to give to a man her own age.

That's a gloomy prospect. I remember in my first years of marriage a terrific loneliness. I think the loneliness appears because neither the man nor woman can give; what each is thirsty for the other has already committed somewhere else. The committing took place unconsciously, that is, without the conscious mind being utterly clear about it, and so the conscious mind feels helpless. It's like a lawyer who can't find the papers for a certain case — what can he do without them? Nothing.

So reversing that means making things conscious. Writing is very helpful, Jung and Marie Louise von Frony are very helpful, imagining witches and dragons is very helpful, moving toward the non-maternal is very helpful. Using food stamps means participating in the state-maternal so that is not helpful. Drifting is not helpful. Joining a spiritual group usually means joining a reconstituted family, so that is usually not helpful. For a man in this situation, adopting feminine values is dangerous. I've tried all of these. I know that all my remarks need qualification, but each person can do that for himself or herself. In our culture now, the young male, being parted from positive masculine values by the collapse of mythology, and separated physically from his father by the Industrial Revolution, is often, in this new age, full of feminine values. Many of these values are marvelous, but their presence in his psyche are not well balanced by positive male values. It is the male, in both the man and in the woman, who fights the dragon — the dragon-fighter is not "a man" but the yang, whether that appears in a woman or in a man.

The young man in this decade, unable to get his fire energy away from the dragons, will find it difficult to support a relationship by the time he's thirty-five. To some extent, the young man, each time he leaves a woman, feels it is a victory, because he has escaped from his mother. But the woman feels it is a defeat. I notice that men, when around thirty-five, begin to feel the whole sequence as a defeat too. Then the time has come to fight dragons, or as *Iron John* or *Iron Hans* (a Grimm Brothers' story) says, "Get the key to the cage from under your mother's pillow."

I can't speak for women, but I suspect they have some work to do in getting the key from under their father's pillow. I think they do better on that in some ways than men do.

With men I understand the struggle a little better. During the struggle I think it's important to stop imagining yourself as spiritual. Spiritual people don't steal keys. You know that (laughs). I think the whole imagery of going down in the lower chakras and fighting the dragons has a certain quality in it that involves forgetting oneself as someone destined for higher consciousness. One doesn't consider oneself as someone spiritual, or someone nice, but one just does what men and women have done for hundreds of thousands of years, which is to deal with that material. It's good also to stop imagining oneself as part of the new age.

(November 1983)

Facing Fear

Dee Dee Small-Hooker

I have this perhaps incorrect notion that you get whatever you ask for. (It's just the delivery date that's uncertain.) The purer, more in-tune you become, the less the "you" exists. "You" become what is and always has been. Which is just a lead-in to the fact that I "asked" at some point to have this experience, since I am at a stage at which I would fear a violent death.

I had wondered off and on for years how well I would keep it together if confronted with the actual threat of pain and death. Confronting fear is a test that exists for us. A rite of passage. Just you and the powers that be.

I think it's important for people to pass along the mechanics of this kind of experience, like Carlos Castaneda does, like Ram Dass does in terms of experiences that the "layman" can hang onto. Guides. So the diagram

It's a matter of nakedness, ultimate nakedness. In Tibetan literature they say you must embrace your ten thousand horrible demons and your ten thousand beautiful demons, too.

can be recalled if the need arises to summon some courage.

The Tale: we had spent the whole of the July day crossing Pennsylvania's luxurious midlands, having camped south the night before. We were fasting, too, in an effort to amend the excesses of two previous days in Norfolk and to clear our minds of the unpleasantries we had encountered there. (We were visiting a disintegrating family scene; we felt, unhappily, helpless.)

I was slightly irritable and knew that Will was on edge just as I: the VW was just too tiny and cramped to make travel very lighthearted for long. A couple of hours before dark we entered the Alleghenies in northern Pennsylvania. The park curved around, crossing the New York state line, surrounding a monstrous reservoir fed by three rivers. I felt pretty certain we could find a campsite before sunset — if we could agree on one, which was uncertain.

The marked, legal campsites surfaced early on, but they resembled pictures I'd seen on TV of refugee camps: people cramped together, huddled around small cooking fires, children squabbling in the roads, clothes drying on a thin wire strung between camper and car. Neither of us wanted to pass the night there. Besides, as the sign indicated, there was no room.

I could tell from his face that Will would tire early today of the game of finding a campsite at the last minute. His forehead was pinched as he wheeled the car back onto the main road again. We were both aware that night was closing in at its leisurely Summer pace, but closing all the same. We were forever hunting campsites at twilight, but our luck seemed to be holding again as we spotted a decently graded dirt road that wound to the left of the main road and appeared to follow a ridge around the side of the mountain.

A few yards in and the steep gradient hid us from the highway. We had only the whole ridge of this mountain to argue over, I thought, as we rode into a deeply shaded, cool-looking forest, with no signs of other people. The forest floor was muffled with a thick mat of leaves and rotting vegetation. Any place we found was probably going to make a soft bed, although lumpy.

About a half mile down the road a stream flashed off to the right, its thin icy line disappearing around gray boulders and thickly grown-together cedars upstream. Will pulled the car off the road up from the stream and we got out to survey the situation. It was the same lumpy, spongy mat, trees growing more thickly together further away from the road. But here there were breaks in the vegetation and a few small stones lying around which could be gathered to ring a campfire. The stream was down a little rise and seemed OK to wash in and drink from. Deer tracks pocked the sand. There was a path leading back into the deeper woods, and all in all, it felt fairly safe in spite of a certain primeval heaviness. We agreed, in silence, that we would pass the night here.

We still weren't talking as we unloaded the tent and sleeping gear, although being outside and stretching made things noticeably more tolerable. I breathed in the air heavily scented with rotting, wet wood and cedar and black dirt and felt revived by the smell of such richness. Small things rushed about in the underbrush, tunneling through the layers of rotting material. Soft crackling background noises surfaced from pools in the stream.

We both felt a bit lost not having to prepare an evening meal; it filled in between activity and rest on these outings and was always a pleasant responsibility. But Will made a pot of tea instead and we sipped in silence, until he suggested a walk to clear the air. Take the path into the woods to see what lay beyond.

The exercise and putting some geographical distance between the two of us appealed to me, so we took off, not trying to stay abreast of one another at all. Down the path that led from the campsite, over more lumpy ground and rotting stumps. We passed under a fancifully arched sapling, as though through a doorway, and the vegetation got greener and a bit soggier. I noted with disappointment that we seemed to be approaching a swamp and promptly lost my enthusiasm to go further. We seemed to be intersecting the reservoir just where the water stagnated and contented itself with lying in still, slime-green puddles.

I headed for a knoll that looked to be drier but Will plowed straight ahead into some waist-high grass, going on to explore and be alone. He didn't bother to say see you later. I wasn't going to follow. Not me, boy. Snakes. I climbed to the top of the knoll and took a 360 of the slight view it afforded. I watched Will's back disappear around a bend in the tall grass in one direction. Just more slime out there, I bet. Soggy forests. Waist-high grass going God knows where.

I had just formed a picture of us as Bogey and Hepburn in the Congo when the hair at the base of my neck began to prickle. I became uncomfortably aware of someone or something watching me. The sensation seemed to emanate most strongly from the section of woods back toward the campsite. Great. And I had to walk back through that! I turned away from scrutinizing the sensation, calling it ridiculous, and busied myself with debating what kind of tracks those were on the knoll top; indisputably deer, but for the sake of time and courage, maybe wild turkey? (I envied the Indians their sure knowledge of that most formidable body language.)

Taking a few deeper breaths, I again looked up and around me. Things felt safer, somehow. The sensation had lessened. I climbed down from my vantage point and headed back to the campsite, stepping as defiantly and as heavily as I could upon the ground. When I passed under the sapling, most of my anxiety passed and I felt even more comfortable striding into the familiarity of the campsite.

No sign of Will. Oh well. I grabbed a book, one of the *Dune* trilogy, and blew on the coals of the fire inside the stone circle. Only a few minutes of reading time left and the sun would be completely obscured. I wished out loud for Will to hurry back, not relishing time in the dark alone. Things still had an uncertain, creepy air about them.

He appeared minutes later, striding up the road from the direction we'd driven in. As it turned out, the path he followed had curved back around and met the road a few hundred yards from the campsite.

Darkness settled in minutes after he arrived. I could make out stars through the tree cover but no moon. Maybe one would be coming up later, but it was going to be pitch dark when the fire died. Will didn't wait; he climbed into the tent and lit the tiny hanging lantern to read by. We were speaking now, the walk having served its purpose, and I slid into the sleeping bag beside him and zipped up the tent's screen face.

I snuggled closer and propped the book on my chest. He commented about seeing no snakes that evening, but seeing lots of deer track and some larger tracks alongside them. I tried to be absorbed in the book but was at a fairly involved place and really did not have the concentration it demanded; so I shut it. I wished to be horny, I said out loud. So try, my husband suggested gently. He helped. It was a strange new world, touching flesh after so much distance. Home away from home. I was nicely exhausted as I watched the muscles stretch in Will's shoulder as he reached up to hold the lantern while he blew the candle out.

He lay back and threw the sheet off his chest, and then it began. Footsteps. Coming from behind us, coming up on the back of the tent. They came steadily and quickly. One, then another, and a third. A twig snapped under the weight of one step. (How melodramatic, something in me thought.) Another step. They were heavy and man-like, not soft and meditated like those of a cat. Human steps. Stopping almost right on top of us. We both rose on our elbows and looked in the other's direction. I felt myself jerked into a very tight knot of fear. Will seemed fairly calm. What was that? he asked. I didn't know. My mind was wiped clean; it was difficult to breath. I managed to say that it didn't sound like a cat and that seemed to take all the energy from me. I didn't fear harm from any wild animal. (I remembered that there was no food out; I wasn't having my period; there would be no enticing scents.) But what if there was a crazy human out there who had watched us and waited all evening until we were inside the tent? My hand gripped Will's arm for comfort.

Outside it was completely silent now, completely silent and deeply dark. My breathing was the loudest sound in the universe. I raised my head just high enough to see out of the tent flap and there was nothing to see, just darkness and a small red glow from the ashes of the fire. Was it going to do something? What was it plotting behind our tent?

Then it screamed. My panic rose with the scream. A short, screeching hawk-like scream. It screamed again, and again. It was right there on top of us, outside the tent. Something was building, I thought, something terrible is going to happen and we have no defense. "Be cool," Will whispered, "be cool. Whatever it is, I'm not afraid. It doesn't make me afraid."

I heard his voice as from the bottom of a deep well. It was nearly hypnotic. I was just lounging there, waiting for something to happen. No sounds, no movements from outside. I imagined myself bolting from the tent and making for the safety of the car. Then I remembered locking it earlier. It was too far away, anyway. And we had literally nothing to protect ourselves with: blankets to wrap up in to protect us from claws, maybe, but I knew that whatever was out there was not a cat.

Suddenly an image crossed my brain. An image of a tall, dark man standing outside, behind our tent. Only instead of a human head, there was a hawk's head and a curved beak. The picture passed as suddenly as it had come and then every nerve in my body informed me that if I didn't do something, take some action, then it would be done for me by whatever was outside the tent. To take control, I thought; what to do?

For a minute my horror subsided and I remembered reading in *Grist for the Mill* about a mantra to repeat if ever you felt yourself in physical danger. Yes, that was it. The mantra. I started repeating it to myself: the power of God is within me; the grace of God surrounds me. Over and over. I was beginning to decompress. Whatever was out there hadn't made another move, but I could still feel its looming, dark presence, strong as ever, behind us, almost over the tent. Minutes stretched on.

Lights slapped the tent front. I jumped in the sleeping bag, my throat again constricting, but there would come no scream. Then I silently and gratefully cheered as another VW came chugging around the bend in the road, drawing closer, the lights growing brighter. The mechanical noises were music to my ears. The fucking cavalry, I thought. (How melodramatic, the voice said again.)

The car passed slowly, not stopping, turned farther down the road and passed on again. I savored the lights as much as I ever have anything. The thing . . . whatever it was, its force wasn't as strong anymore. It was as though a weight had been lifted somewhere in the darkness.

Will sighed and told me that he was going to sleep. Oh, good luck, I thought, going to leave me all alone stuck in this consciousness. I knew *I* couldn't sleep. He kissed me and drew the sheets up to his shoulder, turned over and slept. I just kept repeating the mantra over and over, feeling myself growing looser, my breathing becoming easier, hoping to keep the thing away through the night.

I hung on the mantra, trying to keep my concentration, even as sleep closed over me. The last thing I remembered was that it would be back in the morning: it was that much of an animal, I was sure. I slept.

At daybreak, a distant thunder woke us both. The morning was heavy with mist and the smell of rain drew closer with the wind. We debated sleepily, in light of what had passed in the night, whether to get up and move on pronto or to stay and take our chances with the rain and packing a wet tent. The urge to sleep won out and we decided to stay. After all, it was morning. We felt braver. Much braver. I climbed out of the tent behind Will and chose a spot to pee on. Everything seemed lazily peaceful; the woods were steaming and full of chittering bird voices. I wanted to see some deer emerge from the woods and come drink at the stream. I walked back to the tent, disappointed, and climbed in.

And then the footsteps came again, from the same direction, the same sequence, even the twig snap. It had been burned into my memory last night. There was no mistaking it.

It began its series of screams again and this time it had company that answered its screams from across the road. There was a curious gaming quality about the screams this time, almost a humor in them, as if they were toying with us, laughing at us, taunting us. But it was light, it was dealing in our realm now.

Will and I nodded at one another and then he unzipped the tent flap in one quick movement. We leapt out into the morning air. I turned to face the rear of the tent, to confront it. And there was . . . nothing. No drolling, deranged man, no animals, and no sounds of a hasty retreat. I looked up into the trees. Nothing. Across the road something flashed low and brown in the grass, about knee level, but after that, no other disturbance passed our eyes or ears. We ran across the road and searched the underbrush for the brown thing, for anything. Nothing. Nothing. I walked over to the stream and plunged my hand into the icy water. We packed the car and drove away.

Exactly what went on within me when I was convinced that we were dealing with a powerful manifestation that had threatened to do us harm? Physically, my blood pressure dropped immediately, my chest muscles froze and became rigid, the paralysis making it all but impossible to breathe. I felt a huge weight pushing down upon me and just could not get air into my lungs. My skin was clammy and cold on the outside; inwardly, I felt like I was burning up.

A book I consulted afterwards explained exactly what does happen in the body during extreme fear. Blood rushes away from the skin, causing the white pallor of people who have seen "ghosts." Paralysis, fainting, premature aging — they're all symptomatic of stark fear. The body makes what author Carroll Izard refers to as "prehistoric alterations": the blood undergoes a chemical change to make it coagulate more readily, in case of wounds; the sphincter muscles relax, to lighten the body. That makes it easier to run. And the digestive processes all but stop so as not to distract the involuntary processes of the body from total concentration on the problem at hand. Which is all well and good. But in Will's and my case, the object was to deal, not to run. The confrontation was staged as much on a mental level as on the physical.

I couldn't run because I had to stand my ground and deal with it, or, in essence, I would have defeated myself and, I think, the purpose of it all. (Not that I advocate not running; I'm sure there are times for that, too. This just wasn't one of them.)

Since we couldn't see our adversary but received only auditory and vibrational (tactile?) pictures of it, we had to deal with it on the *strength* of projections. It was all on the level of a mental duel. A serious bit of bluff calling.

My first thought — after deciding that it definitely was not a cat of some sort — was that we had no way to defend ourselves. No small knives, no guns, no stick; only a book to throw if it came to that. Ah, the book, *Children of Dune*. And then I remembered in my paralysis, which was the most marked thing about me at the time, that Frank Herbert had written: "Fear is the great mind killer; fear is the little death." And it truly is.

I was out of control, totally nonfunctioning. I was in a position to be handled, manipulated. This is where fear puts you. This is the way fear operates, which is to make the fearer inoperable. Then you're at the mercy of the fearee.

This is how fear operates even when it's present in milder yet more long-term degrees. For example, fear of failure usually prevents you from attempting that which would destroy the fear, be it taking a job in a field you really identify with, be it in confessing to another being that you love him. Fear seems to be a generally inhibitory state of being or non-being, whichever.

Will was either more on top of it than I or just better at suppressing it (as men are documented to be), because he had the togetherness to tell me that if it made any noticeable attempts on or toward us that we had to yell — great confident yells. In my current state I could have barely managed a croak. (Will has a great thundering voice, God bless him.) Which is another point about extreme terror.

It is a spell of the same order as experienced when you "get into" a movie, a play, a dance. You are bound, held. In cases of fear, breaking the hold with loud, abrupt, ridiculous noises is good. Yell, clap. Don't remain hypnotized.

After the creature's screams began, Will whispered to me to "be cool" and that he wasn't going to be made afraid. Later he said he did that because he sensed a great amount of fear emanating from me and he was trying to help me reduce it.

Which is another thing about fear: it is a heavy, unmistakable scent, a strong disharmonious vibration. It's real fuel for predators of any sort; they sense a weakness, an ineffectualness, and attack. It was then that I realized that the only way that thing out there *could hurt us was through my fear.* My fear was like an interstate, lined and paved, down which the thing could move all its weapons and do its worst; it was an almost tangible link with whatever was outside the tent, a tentacle it had lashed securely into my psyche. I had to break that link. I knew that if I broke that link it couldn't do us any harm. (So Churchill was right.) That was when I began repeating the mantra from *Grist For the Mill:* "The power of God is within me; the grace of God surrounds me."

Then, it was, simultaneously, like falling through cloud levels of space and ascending from the depths of a great heavy ocean. (So that is centering?) I began to breathe more normally again. My heart rate slowed. I began to believe that I was becoming stronger and more positive. And I was. It had to be that there was nothing going on in me but the mantra and that left no room for the fear. It became almost a sort of invisibility. Will was doing it also. The link, the tentacle, was pushed back by a slowly advancing wave of something light, yet something strong.

(It was at this time that the VW came round the bend. A little help from our friends? I certainly believe so. Heaven helps those who help themselves?)

The rational being part of me had this argument for the episode: you will not be harmed because you have done nothing to deserve harm. My intellect fought against this premonition of death with that. And then it said, but what if this is your karma to die here? (I wasn't thinking in terms of "ending an incarnation" then; I was thinking in terms of being ripped off.) I would feel some sort of peace, some kind of reconciliation, wouldn't I, if this was my time to go on?

About this time one of the stranger parts of the experience transpired: a distinct voice snaked into my brain; a thin, wisp-like voice, and it said distinctly, "Take your husband in your arms and lay down . . . to die." That confused me. Angered me. Was that my voice, the one I trust? Who did this voice belong to? My cowardice? Some instinct answered that the voice was too honeyed, too seductive (and it was seductive) to belong to a pure impulse. I denied it its request and repeated the mantra with even more determination. The voice never came again. I repeated the mantra until I fell asleep.

Will's reaction to the phenomenon was what he terms the "stupid man's reaction." Don Juan, I think, talks about this in his books, i.e., that many people are never confronted with and are invulnerable to "test patterns" from other levels, i.e., ghosts, the supernatural, poetry, because they just do not acknowledge their existence. Things obviously do happen to all people on many levels simultaneously, but if they chose to confine the reality to the material level, then that is where it happens for them. (So physicists explain the laws of karma in one language that never mentions the word "karma," and Buddhists explain it in their language using the word.)

The more you acknowledge other levels of existence and the extraordinarily beautiful multiplicity of life, the more aware and at the same time the more vulnerable you become to those elements of those levels that may be antithetical to your existence and well-being. That is why they must be confronted, at all acknowledged levels, or else they'll come back, and come back until they are confronted. Current psychology acknowledges this phenomenon: that you have to drag the ghosts out of the recesses of the mind, confront them with *you* and then they go away. That's life. That's growth.

That's what Don Juan means by becoming a warrior, I think. It doesn't mean being on the defensive as we know it. It's more a matter of reinforcing your existence and the spark of divinity that is within you so that when and if a confrontation becomes inevitable, you give just what you are. The thing in the dark was just giving of itself. It's a matter of nakedness, ultimate nakedness. In Tibetan literature they say you must embrace your ten thousand horrible demons and your ten thousand beautiful demons, too.

Anyway, Will's reaction after a while was to go to sleep. Which

Izard says is another effective technique for dealing with fears. He told me weeks later that he forced himself not to acknowledge that whatever was out there was not on the material plane. He knew that if he could control it (like you can control dreams sometimes, by just willing things gone or by willing that the existing drama in them not continue) then he could help me be strong. He focused only on the material reality, and through the mantra, quieted his fear.

We talked at some length about the experience weeks later during a bout of insomnia brought on by a strong full moon. Best as we could figure we were trespassing on an Indian burial ground or power place and got a very unsubtle hint to move along.

It was during this talk that it came to light (so to speak) that we had both shared the sensation of being watched during our twilight walk and that we had both gotten a distinct picture of an Indian man with a hawk's head standing outside our tent during the night.

(January 1978)

Lord Shantih

Thomas Wiloch

The Faithful Wish

One day the Lord Shantih threw a coin down a wishing well. He wished for another coin. Later, as he walked upon the road, he found a coin.

The next day Lord Shantih again threw a coin into the well, wished for a coin, and found a coin upon the road. This continued for several days — always Lord Shantih wished for a coin, found a coin, and used it to wish for another.

At the end of a week Lord Shantih cast two coins into the wishing well.

"I won't be able to come here tomorrow," he explained.

The True Fortune-Teller

The Lord Shantih saw a fortuneteller in the marketplace. The fortuneteller threw a handful of sticks in the air and examined the pattern they made as they fell upon the ground. From this pattern he divined the future.

Lord Shantih pondered this for many days. Finally he took a handful of sticks and threw them in the air. But the sticks would not fall down. They fluttered away like a flock of birds.

"If I were a true fortuneteller," Lord Shantih observed, "I would know this was something more than magic."

Flowers In The Sky

One day the Lord Shantih met a skeptic.

"And what if there is no paradise?" the skeptic asked.

"Then men would build one," the Lord Shantih replied.

"And what if there are no gods?"

"Then men would become gods."

"And what if men were not divinely fashioned?"

"Then everything was fashioned by the mind of man," Lord Shantih said. "And if there were no flowers on the earth, there would be flowers in the sky."

All Gods Answer

The Lord Shantih told the story of the farmer who prayed to the gods for a large harvest only to have his crop destroyed by flood. The next year the farmer again prayed for a large harvest and a drought destroyed his crop. The third year he prayed as before and this time enjoyed the largest harvest he had ever had.

"All gods will answer," Lord Shantih said, "if you give them enough time."

The Depth

There once was a river of unknown depth that flowed past the cottage of Lord Shantih. Those who sailed upon the river often lowered sticks into the water to measure its depth, but they could never find it.

Lord Shantih once asked a sailor why he sought to know the depth of the river.

"Because I sail upon this river," the sailor replied, "and I must know how deep it is."

"I walk upon the ground," Lord Shantih said, "and the ground is always paper thin beneath me."

Asking Directions

A seeker came to the Lord Shantih with a question.

"Where can I find the truth I seek?" he asked.

"When a leaf falls from a tree," Lord Shantih explained, "it always lands on the ground."

Another seeker came to the Lord Shantih and asked: "Which path shall I follow?"

"No one guides the river," Lord Shantih answered, "the river knows the way."

Yet another seeker came to the Lord Shantih.

"Where does one go to find wisdom?" the seeker asked.

"No!" Lord Shantih finally said. "I have been asked for directions too often. I can take no more questions."

"My Lord," said the seeker, "the ocean is always filled but never full. You can answer one more question."

With that, Lord Shantih rapped him hard across the ribs with his staff.

"Fool!" he shouted. "Don't ask me for what you already have!"

(November 1982)

Kali Comes Home

Elizabeth Rose Campbell

I

From the outside looking in, it appears that not only do I live alone, but I maintain a hermit's existence, an ascetic's search for bare basics, primitively situated in the middle of a heavily wooded forest, with no avenue of approach, no charming old road bed, nor a new one. There is only a dogpath, barely discernible in the daylight, which disappears entirely at dusk.

Once, there was a crudely-cut road, open for two or three months when building materials were being hauled in. Outsiders were hired to do everything I could not: turn the tiny box I'd drawn on a piece of paper into a house. It had two windows each on the east, west, and south sides, a carefully pencilled-in door, doorknob, and a final touch of a stove pipe

It is Kali come home . . . sweet hurricane horror with single purpose: to sweep away delusions.

chimney resting on a roof labelled "roof." It was all I could afford on any level, and it was my harvest come home at last — an 18x12 womb for one.

I helped as much as I could, a little embarrassed by how little that was, holding a board as it was cut or nailed, answering yes/no questions about the pitch of the roof, the matter of trim, any extras. But just in case carpentry was an art I could learn overnight, some skill flying home to its sleeping master, I hung around every time the house was worked on, squatting, squinting my eyes at the goings-on, thinking that some day it would be pleasant to become a carpenter myself, to learn the warmth of wood.

It is stone I am most drawn to, and if I could have built a house of stone, I would have. My walks in the woods off major paths are often magnetic pulls toward large boulders hidden in deep gullies or dense shrubbery. The forest has been touched only lightly by the logging industry, a twenty-five acre hill of five long, thick earthen fingers. They taper into furry tips which touch the valley meadow that marks the boundary. Boulders jut up out of the crevice's mossy softness, and increase in size as the slope climbs, a giant's stepping stone path to the top of the hill, where my land ends and a beef cattle farmer's begins. No one can own the view across the meadow. From this high point, one can see for miles, across hundreds of acres of farmland. At night, the illusion of standing at the top of the world is thickest, the forest behind you and the pasturelands all below, open and sweetly scented, the sky immense and accessible, the planets too bright to ignore.

Sometimes I crawl down into the crotch of the earth, halfway down the hill, and sit on the biggest, least jagged rock, look up at the old trees looming above me, and the ones below, and watch their simple leaning toward the light, the life in the leaves rustling to each other and, I feel, to me. Shades of brown, grey and green blur into one another and mirror the subtlety of sound, the wind, the distant caw-caw-caw, the insect's whine.

II

I park my car off my land and walk to it. In the beginning, this was due to a lack of money to build a road, no skills with a chainsaw, and an inherent confusion about where I actually belonged. Now it's a pleasurable privacy.

The cabin is accessible, but in no way public, and invisible until you are upon it, nestled in a rocky recess of the hill. It reflects my unfinished business, my budding into full view, my voice released. This house is made of cypress, of wood that will not rot, has no solid steps, but a precarious ladder before the door.

When I get home after dark, the dogs rush to meet me, and together we make our way up into the woods, winding like small ants through our tiny tunnel of a worn path past the subtlest of landmarks — this rock, that one, a sudden slant of the earth, a mossy crest. In the darkest turn of the path, I have hung a possum's bare bones from a branch of a tree, to reflect the beam of the light.

Every time I reach the cabin, catch sight of my cocoon, I feel I am wide awake in a dream I have been having all my life of such a place as this, where there is no fear, where families are built beginning with one, where there are no limits, no gravity, to ground my flights. Only a friendly burning lamp to mark the spot, to guarantee a safe return.

The cabin's contents tend to decrease, not increase, with time. It is a machine of distillation, this shelter, shrinking my life, sucking up loose ends, swallowing me whole, a mirror of priorities. There's nothing in it that is not at the core of my personal civilization — the essential furniture, a steamer trunk bulging with twenty years of letters to the self, and several shelves of dedicated friends: Jane Roberts, Seth, Ram Dass, the *I Ching*, Anne Morrow Lindbergh, and all my **SUN**s. Anything that collects dust was boxed and moved out.

Recently I have begun to appreciate my oldest companion again, my journal, seeing that it progressively touches what is untamable in me. For years it felt like a burdensome historical beast, appalling evidence of a self-centered fame, dark and untrustworthy, a potential embarrassment that would scald the hair off my body, making naked my ugliness for all the world to see. I knew it all along as the face of fear, forgivable by me if by no one else. Given enough time, I knew I could help it hatch, ripen; have it teach, not taunt. "Fire and fear — good servants, bad lords," writes Ursula LeGuin.

If left alone with an honest word, I could carve out a special place of tolerance where there was no need to judge, and set the fear free. In that ironic, splendidly human way, the fear balked at this, at the price I must pay: to give up judgment and keep discrimination, to give up waiting for the Second Coming, for the Messiah, for the

Saviour, for arrival of authority from the outside.

My journal tells me now: the fears have ripened, your riches are come home to roost. I no longer need to deny my past, to destroy the evidence, burn my journal lest I be "found out," dragged out of my conventional closet and crucified for thinking for myself.

So it sits there, this trunkful of journals, encyclopedias of every time I've traced my boundaries with the touch of a curious consciousness, set up a permanent post as a lookout for the tide to change. I love to defy time, to use the entries as gigantic levers of the imagination, to follow the careful tracking of the personality, as it meanders like an insect past that ancient elm, through this city gutter.

It has nothing to do with "writing," with typewriters, pens, paper, love of literature, good English or bad. Its functions are two: to let out and to let in, and to do either well I must be alone.

"The diary" is the letting out, the recording of events, impressions of my own reactivity racing through my fingertips in a longing to gossip, to tell the tale and find beneath it the truth, the unexpressed emotion.

What cannot be captured, photographed, recorded, everything that did not externalize in my day arrives when I "let in," when I fall into the silence that follows my worded focus, when I light no candle, have no holy intention, simply sit still, eyes closed, and face the emptiness. For a long time, the "letting in" was lonely compared to the "letting out," in which known personalities paraded past my inner eye, a sumptuous family gathering of my known loves, my daily details, immediate and accessible. The "letting in" requires endurance, a spiritual stamina that must be seeded with care. There must be enough self-doubt, enough hunger for the unknown, to pull me to my post, and enough self-trust to want to play with whatever I find, as an explorer in invisible worlds. It was a while before I could accept the practice of putting words on that space, of opening my eyes, fingers on the typewriter keys, and watch these friendly forces I found take shape — my own creations, I thought. After a time I began to suspect it was the other way around; I had touched ancientness, the sun that seeded my God, *me*, and the "letting in" was no longer lonely.

Sometimes I see images, sometimes I don't. The only one that repeats itself is of an Indian scout on a high hill, a lookout. I always see her from the back, have never seen her face, but I know it is my own, and she has been sitting there forever, letting me in, letting me out.

She reminds me never to leave my post, the top of the hill, never to abandon my silence, the focused power that feeds me. My journal will one day die, my post will not. I will look back on this skeleton of words and see a personal truth, with every partial insight, every piece of cultural propaganda ripening to a strong stink forgiven by the writer, bent over her life not out of narcissistic absorption but because the beginnings of largeness are there, the beginnings of a compassion for humanity.

III

Road-building reflects an enormous amount of energy, no matter how I look at it, as dollars, as duty fulfilled, a cleared passageway to destiny. One must be very careful when road-building. You'd better be sure you want to live at the end of that road.

I grew up at the end of "Meadow Lane," my grandparents' back acreage, on the side of a hill much like the one I live on now, with ravines and hardwood trees, honeysuckle, mulberries, wild plums and persimmons, a small stream surfacing after heavy rains. I built camp after camp, carving out paths through the thickest underbrush, wanting a hideout, some insulation from my little girl identity, where I could be the Indian that slept on dried grasses, carved cedar sticks, and collected feathers, turtle shells, snake skulls. On weekends and Wednesdays, my father was usually nearby, pushing his wheelbarrow from the rosebuds to the vegetable garden, playing with peanut hulls, leaves, pinestraw, building a winding walk. More than once, as night began to fall, he'd come looking for the clippers, a necessary tool for my compulsive pathmaking in the woods. I'd show him my camp, and, until it was too dark to see, we'd follow my paths and hack together at the deadends, the impasses I'd reached, the branches too big for me to cut, and talk of the long ago teepee, the one he built for his girls, an authentic wonder for rainy day games.

I'd forgotten all that until I began to clear paths again, fifteen years later, in my own woods. I bought a pair of clippers and wore wistful eyes, knowing what I wanted to do, but not sure I could, alone.

I was nineteen when my father died, his death a loss I didn't appreciate for years because I knew in advance, through dreams, of every step of his departure, and there was time for us to collect moments, for me to stroke his hair, for him to hold my hand and not hide his emotion, the end unspoken and invisible to the diagnostic descriptions of his "recovery." He lost a lot of weight after the first attack. A neighbor said, "Walker, you look like a gutted shad," but I thought he looked great, like a boy again.

Sometimes I see his old customers, strangers to me, who seem startled, moved: "Lord honey you look just like your Daddy," they say, as if they've seen a ghost. And I remember that last week, when the torch was passed, without a word: it was all that brown eyes, in their darknesses' fiery light, could ever say to each other.

I resented the beings that were waiting for him on the other side, the entities that crowded around our kitchen table after his head dropped, the bowl of soup still steaming before him, his napkin upon his knee. But beneath the resentment was an electrified awareness that I was in cahoots with them somehow, and they with all of us, and some mammoth door to nature had opened that allowed me to see where my father was going, which was not very far away, yet would require the deepest detachment to touch. My body shook convulsively, unaccustomed to the weather of that opened door, and I heard my voice say, as if from very far away, "many came to take him." And then they were gone, my father too, like genies out of a bottle.

Then there was a simple void, some vacuum in space, the door still partially open, and just as suddenly the void was eaten up by the molecules around it, like water filling a pond. This was some sacred ceremony, more awesome than a death could ever be sad. I was exhilarated, numb, a robot rerunning some old familiar record, and I said it again as the rescue squad arrived — "Many came to take him." My head was full of noises, urgencies, soothing sounds but I couldn't sort out the levels. The only distinct voice was my own, telling me to take the curlers out of my hair; company had come.

I'd never felt so free. Some chapter was forever over and the "real" work was about to begin. My father's departure signalled the start. His finger was in the pie of this design, I was sure, but what I did not know was that I could never reach my real work, whatever that might be, until I grieved the man that had died, the father of my male self, my female self, of all of my duality, find out what we still expected of each other and why. Until I did that, I could build no road to my own completion, develop the discipline I wanted in my life — not as a controlling, authoritative force but as a firm field of fearless love, where I was not subconsciously searching for my father, and our unfinished business. Until that was done, I'd need more than a pair of clippers and strong preferences to prepare for the path that led home.

IV

I smile when I come upon old foot paths in my woods, some of them seeming to go in circles, some of them deadends, lost in several seasons' leaves. When I worked on each one, I had a man in mind, struggling to get to him, or struggling to get away. Out of the ten years since my father died, nine of them nurtured a constant male presence, a wooing with all of my innocence, my scheming, my will to have my way. The first one went from his mother to me, three days after my father's death, still a baby at seventeen, with a yin sweetness and a way with children not unlike my father's. We grew up together, he and I, through the prolonged adolescence of college, as privileged children who played well together. After six years, he wouldn't fight with me, so I went straight into the arms of someone who would.

It wasn't just fighting I wanted, or needed, not confrontation but creative conflict, something to wear down my defenses with style, some playful jousting, the kind of contact that encourages strength, not dependency or grudgeholding.

We were both married when we met. Enter: taboo number one — fascination with the forbidden. Taboo number two — sex.

I never thought much about sex until my menses began and my breasts blossomed. What I did with my own body was a goodie from God, and I was left guessing when I heard at age eleven from a know-it-all friend that married men and women made babies by "sticking their fannies up each other's fannies." Sometimes they did it on the bed, "and sometimes they even do it on the living room floor, or a living room chair, sometimes the sofa." I envisioned myself ringing a doorbell selling Girl Scout cookies, and seeing this spectacle through a peephole in the door. I couldn't imagine how they did it, or why they did it. I just knew I didn't want to do it. And then suddenly a few years later I did want to. But every imaginable cultural lie had wormed its way into my mind. "There are some things worse than death," said an aunt, when she told me of an unmarried cousin who got pregnant. "Save yourself," said my mother. "Men marry one kind and not another."

So I locked in what was screaming to get out, with every other female friend. "Your reputation is everything," we were told, and so we saved ourselves, prolonged little girlhood as long as possible, graduating to women's colleges, institutions to take over the job, finish us off, keep us cut off from the knowledge of our fertility, our power, from owning the bodies only our fathers could give away, from access to men under any potentially sexual situation.

Sex was an "it," but a reward, or a punishment? I knew it was craziness, wearing sexy underwear underneath, and an armor of virginity outside; something in the psyche had to split. Just as my peaceful world split when I turned thirteen and learned: sexuality is a sin for the girls, a sign of maturity for the boys.

I felt the fear in my mother, that I might live out what she had not, an openly sexual side as a single woman. But if that was what one had to give up to have the kind of marriage she and my father had, I'd do it. I wanted that richness, the mutual lack of self-seriousness, a partnership in joy so successful they attracted children to them that were not their own.

Joy breeds generosity and my parents' doors were open. I was proud of them, sure I'd handpicked them. They were the only "old" people I knew, or any of my friends knew, whose house on weekends and in the Summer might be full of young people who were there to see them, whether or not my sister or I were home. The pool table in the basement had something to do with it, the fireplaces, the free food, but the nectar was the blended personalities of my parents, the matching graciousness, and the distinct appeal of a liberal and intelligent approach to life compared to the Old South's. The Summer I was fifteen, sixty young people presented them with a silver engraved platter, from "The Basement Crowd," for opening their hearts, for opening their home, for not sending the kids away when the police chronically came to ask them to move their cars. In the Summer of '66, after 7 p.m., the street in front of our house was often blocked, or noisy.

Being open-minded was one of the values my parents were most proud of. Few of them were phony, with the exception of their sexual rules: what was permissible and what was not.

If it'd been anybody but them, I wouldn't have saved myself, wouldn't have bought such an expensive package even though everybody else was pretending to buy it, to stock up on purity, to make marriage pay — one's ticket to happiness, to unrestrained love, a planned-for sexuality, at last.

I was well into my twenties when I gave up all pretenses, my mother's widowhood as the end of an era, a happy marriage obviously not enough for me to hope for in my life, to stake my salvation on. Your mate dies, *and then what?* You saved yourself for him but what did you save for you?

I began to trust my sexuality, that mysterious and magical arena of magnetic energies, of surrender to the spirit in all its sensuality. But it was with my forbidden lover, which complicated the creative conflict I'd wanted, the playful jousting, the team of two that would take on life, let loose what was petrified between the sexes, and heal the world of duality.

We nearly killed each other. We stepped in every stump hole, tripped on every piece of matching junk between us, and the majority of it had to do with sex. Our spirits were twin towers of belief, stately and tall, often untouched by the sexual war between us, but increasingly saddened, as we drew closer to our separately steamy rooms of repression, our necks wound round one another, contracted in a constrictor's starving tension, our free arms flailing, hands gripping knives, stabbing each other in a desperate gesture for freedom. We both were blinded by the slander that there was a limited supply of love; we both had too much of a heritage of hoarding sexuality, separating ourselves from the Creative power, each imagining its opposite held the keys to that inner wealth. Our sexual relationship died a powerful death, after dragging its mutilated body around for a full year, dying slowly and indecisively as the two of us blamed each other for being unable to give a strength and support that could only come by setting each other free.

For three days I sat in the cabin, staring at the walls, unable to sleep, witnessing a death of delusions, and in a forbiddingly empty space, totally new territory. I was not with a man, as daughter or mate, for the first time in my life, ever. I would be again, I knew, but never again without owning my own body, my spirit, without confusing genuine need with neurosis, love with manipulative gifts, sex with sin. It was a triumph, a transforming configuration of all the painful details, but it only soothed me in the situation temporarily. I felt I'd let go of, at last by choice, some subterranean sea that had been blocked off for eons from my expanding ocean, and now it had reached that largest body of water in my spirit, and merged with it, an integration so profound that everything shifted in me, everything, and the intensity of the new world rang in my ears until I couldn't bear it.

It was about three in the morning and I was facing the windows, sitting there like a live wire, electric and straining with the size of the stretching. Bigger, and bigger and bigger and then I felt, like a woman in labor noticing an insignificant insect on the wall of the room, my father's presence ease up beside me, familiar and concrete, distinctly *him*, and I was too intent to talk, to even react. Part of me watched him watching me as I repeated over and over to myself the most grounding, centering thought that had come to me: that I was seeking a new world, *now*, there was to be no waiting, no clinging, no torn looks back to feed new fears; I am the creator of everything to come.

And I heard his approval and an admission of equality, of brotherhood, sisterhood, and then somehow we switched places and I understood that I was him after his death, caught in this same current of creative energy, left totally alone with the inner God and no hope of salvation except what you can grant to yourself, conceive of, to live in. It was not what he expected, nor I.

I've felt him only once since, the month after I hired a bulldozer, and built myself a magnificent road to the top of the hill, where I will move my cabin. It was Easter morning around 6 a.m., and I had just discovered the redbud in bloom at the top boundary. The dogwood was in bloom too, the forest barely green. The beauty of it just overwhelmed me, and I thought, "I don't deserve this, this is too much," and then I thought, "Of course I do, of course we do, all of us." And in that inclusion, I felt the blessing beamed back at me, by my father.

V

I have dinner with a friend in a busy restaurant on a particularly beautiful Spring evening and hear everything he says with an ear of synchronous experience. His hurt and angry face are my own.

He talks about two of his relationships with friends, their longevity, how much he invested in the relationships and how much he wants friends who can consistently choose to work through any walls between them. One friend has withdrawn, become inaccessible, ignores the bridge the two of them created. And the other, after a recent uprising of old conflicts between them, will not display a shred of vulnerability, not the slightest crack in the door to allow for a new beginning.

His body is tense; he is ready to fight as he talks, even with me, particularly when I tell him to wait — "Don't fight with a stone wall." He answers, "No, I would rather provoke him to anger than endure this cold indifference between us, even if we both hurt more afterwards."

I know, I know. How many times have I tried to blast that wall with sheer force, with anger, for all the "right" reasons, all the evidence on "my side?" How many times have I approached that wall with gentleness, with every tenderness and understanding that there are no personal vendettas, only projected ones, and when the wall did not respond I staggered off, wounded and hypnotized by my own self-pity, imagining this pride to be pure, this dignity of good intentions enough.

It is Kali come home, this territory. Kali — the ancient Hindu goddess of Destruction, sweet hurricane horror with single purpose: to sweep away delusions. I know this place all too well, but it remains an unfamiliar passage, even in its predictability, in the fierceness of the fire, as Kali matches tit for tat, attacks self-seriousness in any form, even under the most tragic of circumstances. She comes in drag, wearing a heavy coat of despair, every imagined loss a looming reality in the fragmented darkness of her eyes.

The truth is forgotten, I am a blind woman on my hands and knees, fingertips following the silk thread through the dark, heart in its season of sorrow, crying "if onlys" and every regret, every denial, hating the moment because I think the light is lost, the beloved gone forever, my confusion the damnation I will be remembered by. It is a short-term hurt for a long-term heal; I suddenly understand, not through some feat of logic but through living alone with the only thing I have ever had or will ever have — the pearl of my Isness. I am not alone, I am the beloved, I am understood, and there is nothing I need ever change.

Starving dog that I am, I refuse to accept the Kali kiss until each time my radar confirms from every satellite signal: yes, this is the way, I can detect no loss, anywhere, in this allowance for everything.

Friends, mates, parents, siblings are separate planets within a larger united universe, not responsible for fulfilling my fantasies of how we meet, or even acknowledging the bridges are there.

My friend's response: "That sounds too hard, to walk in to see him, and not want him to be nice, not want him to want our walls to break down. That means I can't want anything."

"But yes you *can!*" I squeal like an auctioneer taking bids, an excited host on "Let's Make A Deal," urging the lucky lifer on earth to pick a prize! Door number one! Door number two! Or door number thrrreeeee!

My friend sits there looking like a tattered and tired battering ram, his most sensitive side bruised and hidden in the shadows of the curtain behind him. "What can I want?" he says, eyeing me, distrustful of my brand of naivete, my oscillations between arrogant ignorance and innocent ignorance.

"You can want to allow him to come to you when he can, in his own time. You can walk in to see him with that enormous extra freedom, you can walk away knowing you have helped create a space in which he can come to you no more encumbered by the junk between you than exists now, with less fear, a larger opportunity to trust whatever awakens in your meeting. It is an enormous act, the most powerful thing you could ever do, and it is totally accessible as a choice. *You just choose.*"

His face registered it all like litmus paper confirming the emptiest commandment, an intimacy at last earned not through an ego's aggression in the name of love, but through setting someone free.

We sit at the table, food forgotten, the clatter of dishes and dinner conversations touching us as if from very far away. I feel like a lioness, an enlightened animal, intoxicated with unashamed love, ready to roar. It's triumph I feel, for having given voice to the greatest power I know, and for rechoosing it myself. I can't contain my body; it starts to rock in rhythm and I realize, somewhere, simultaneously, I am a black parson preaching primal spirit. I want to sprout a black bush on my head, clutch a microphone and howl like a James Brown banshee at my friend, "Good Godalmighty I LUV ya! CAN'T ya see, I LUV ya!" Instead I laugh helplessly and think, "This is what I live for."

(November 1981)

US/Readers Write About . . .

Amazing Coincidences

Once I had a nightmare that I woke up all frightened from a dream and had run into my parents' room. Now, in "real life" it often happened that my brother would throw a fit at bedtime, insisting that he was too scared to sleep alone and would Pop please lie down with him. After the arguing had settled and Pop had acquiesced, sometimes he'd fall asleep himself and never make it back to his own room. In my dream it was such a night, for Mom was there alone.

I took this in immediately, then leaned over her with a "Mommy, I had a bad dream."

"Ah, I'm sorry," her sleepy voice reassured, but not enough.

"Can I get in bed with you?"

"Sure, honey." But then she didn't move. I waited until, in sickening amazement, I realized she had fallen back to sleep. So I shook her by the shoulder.

"Mommy, I had a bad dream. Can I get in bed with you?"

"Sure, honey."

"Well, move over!" And finally the covers parted.

She must not have realized just how scared I was, for after I'd crawled around a bit she said, "Well, now that you've woken me up, I might as well go to the bathroom." And she left me there alone.

Slow scissor kicks against the sheets, eyes wide and roaming, I waited. The bathroom light came down the hall and bent into the room casting shadows angular and odd. The silence was heightened somehow by Mom's distant noises. More scissor kicks. Familiar objects froze in foreignness. Again more scissor kicks. The room was almost alive now. Mom couldn't be much longer.

And then the shade began to move, quiet lapping against the window. It must just be the wind, so quickly now, I grabbed the shade and pulled.

It rose upon sheer horror. A huge Teddy Bear balloon, some escapee from the Macy's parade, a bobbing, bloated body washed upon the shore, pressed against the window wanting in. I turned to run and simultaneously woke up in my bed. I lay there just a moment, then headed for my parents.

Now, in "real life" it often happened that my brother would throw a fit at bedtime, insisting that he was too scared to sleep alone and would Pop please lie down with him. After the arguing had settled and Pop had acquiesced, sometimes he'd fall asleep and never make it back to his own room. Apparently, tonight was such a night, for Mom was there alone. I understood all this, then leaned over her. "Mommy, I had a bad dream."

"Ah, I'm sorry."

"Can I get in bed with you?"

"Sure, honey." But then she didn't move. She had fallen back asleep. I shook her by the shoulder.

"Mommy, I had a bad dream. Can I get in bed with you?"

"Sure, honey."

"Well move over!"

And then came those dreaded words, "Well, now that you've woken me up, I might as well go to the bathroom."

Slow scissor kicks drew what reassurance they could from the sheets. The bathroom light came down the hall making shadows just as in my dream. And there were those same noises, strangely far away. Objects took on that almost alive distortion.

Then the shade began to move.

I ran. I ran thundering down the hall and bursting into the bathroom. Blinding light reflected everywhere, cold white tiles, thick enamel paint. I grabbed Mom and spilled out my dream: the fear, the repetition, the window, the balloon.

"I can't take it again. Not again. I'd die!"

All this seems long ago now. Twenty years of life with really few regrets intervene. But there is this one which reoccurs. I wish that I had looked. I wish that I'd have had the courage to lift that shade and look. Now, I'm curious. But at the time, there had seemed nowhere else to go, no promise of escape. And maybe that's my real regret. There are always other worlds to wake up into, and only when you don't you die.

Patricia Bralley
Atlanta, Georgia

(January 1981)

Letter From Boston:

Spiritual Fascism in America

Moira Crone

A little more than a year ago, I was involved in a rigorous form of Buddhist practice. I often sat at a meditation center in Cambridge. Passers through — spiritual tourists — came through that center all the time to stay for a while, some of them actually using the book *A Pilgrims's Guide to Spiritual Communities in America* to hop from ashram to retreat center to meditation halls all over the country. I remember a particular fellow who squirmed every fifteen minutes during an all-day meditation. He was dark-tanned, glowing, large, handsome. At every break he went into the kitchen to get himself a super nutrition shake: a double dose of brewer's yeast, tiger's milk, yogurt, acidophilus, soya powder, et cetera. Then he would stand in perfect posture in the doorway of the kitchen and go "AHHH," and go sit

I have never heard a more entire list of The Other Guy's Faults than at the ashram of my friend from college who became a yogi to stop thinking.

back down in the meditation hall and recommence squirming. He was wearing pants with a flap over the front that tied on the sides (nothing so unnatural as buttons or zippers) which gave a loin-cloth effect. His shoes were the Birkenstock flat-molded sandals, that never disturb so much as a cell of the vital skin between the toes. He had something going for every pore. On discussion nights, he always wanted to know how to get high. I wanted to take him and shake him finally, to find out why he was so desperate to feel good.

I remember another one who described to me how he had spent a year with this master, a year with that one, received *shaktipat*, studied kundalini yoga. I asked him what he wanted from it. "I want to be perfect in every way," was his answer. "I want to be every kind of master: I want to make money, I want to have sexual power, healing power, guru power, spiritual power." I thought at the time that so much desire might get in the way of any kind of attainment. He soon dumped that particular style of Buddhism and went on to something else.

Some of the spiritual tourists I am talking about (and I have qualified as one myself) eventually settle down to one path. Once they settle in, they may feel they are fulfilling the desires the fellow above outlined: that is, they mold themselves into something perfect in the terms of a particular movement. They begin to sleep, eat, chant, beg or slop brown rice or curry exactly like the guru says to. And bit by bit, people who don't do it that way seem a bit defiled, unclean, polluted, imperfect. One of the worst days of my college life was when my senior roommate told me she was going into an ashram. "I don't want to think anymore," she said. Seeing her a year and a half later, I think she has successfully stopped. The people around her all believe and eat and say and walk and wear the same things.

The thing is, some people feel they have to go to extraordinary measures these days to feel right and straight and whole and perfect on every plane. By the time they do, given the times, they are respectably paranoid (sometimes) of everything outside their own scene. The paranoia, in some instances, I have it by hearsay, creates its own objective evidence: i.e., arsenals of guns are stockpiled to ward off the Bad Bad Fat Inorganic Middle American when everything comes down and he's on his way to loot the Good Good Ashram (or Retreat or what have you). This sort of thing is a manifestation of what I call the Rise of Spiritual Fascism in America. A collective attitude of superiority (not always with guns, of course, but with a certain brutal attitude of Personal Purity, and of Us-Them) is more pervasive than you might think.

Much of this can be attributed to the people in the movements, their attitudes upon entering ("I want to be perfect on every plane," "I don't want to think anymore") as much as to the gurus. These people are, after all, Americans, from the Land of the Free and the Home of the Brave. Our history-myth is all about people busting ass to remain individual, separate, and "free" in the sense that they get to decide what they want to do utterly independent of one another. Along with the history-myth there are a lot of instances where the big guys gang up on little guys to make sure the big guys keep all their great individual freedoms out of the hands of anybody else (read Cowboys versus the Indians, or Busing in Boston). This latter is also known as acute paranoia.

A problem for anyone deciding to surrender to a Religious Master in our culture is that he can't have every bit of his personal-individual-separated-everything consciousness and be spiritual too. The very critical, skeptical American mentality can't surrender all its pretensions to separateness overnight. So, first they gather into camps, get the team rooting, and take swipes at all the other collective or non-collected consciousnesses around. I have never heard a more entire list of The Other Guy's Faults than at the ashram of my friend from college who became a yogi to stop thinking. The members took swipes at Christians, made ugly pregnant nun jokes, discussed various Buddhist masters who drink, gossiped about the gurus who have a lot of money, and discussed which gurus were sleeping with their consorts among the ones who profess celibacy. There is much converted anger and fear that takes the form of pettiness and tiny-mindedness that goes on under the name of gurus and new religions in this country, Hindu, Christian, and Buddhist alike.

This all ends as an observation, for I think the situation is unsolvable for the time being. A friend of mine who teaches at Naropa Institute told me on the phone from Boulder: the Age is getting more and more collective, people are thinking in groups. Individual conscience and consciousness is waning. That is where it is going, and there is a lot of resistance to that. Yes, there is. Group-think is a very significant feature of the Seventies. On one end there is drug-based and behavioral psychology, on the other end, the T.M. people are getting themselves rounder and rounder. (T.M. people have an intensive meditation practice that they do on retreats called rounding. I get the image from that of a German folktale about a woman who washed her children so much she rubbed the features off their faces. Once they all had faces flat as plates, she couldn't tell them apart.)

Two books with the titles *Beyond Freedom and Dignity* and *The Myth of Freedom* are current — one was written by behavioral scientist, B. F. Skinner, the other by a Tibetan lama.

But we live in a nation whose very identity is based upon freedom of the individual. Group-think is alien to America's ideas of itself. Among many who are involved in current spiritual movements, privacy, individual freedom, personal choice, discriminatory intellect, etc. have lost their meaning or their meanings have been altered immensely. One has a new understanding of privacy, for example, after spending three days sitting Zazen with silent people. You are alone no matter what you do. The fears and patterns underlying everyday distinctions and discriminations can be revealed in meditation. The surrender to a master for religious growth —and with it the loss of certain individual choices —is important for progress on any path. All of this is something I imagined, maybe, and Spiritual Fascism is something sprung from my own paranoias.

But it's not, entirely. We have to have spiritual Fascism in this country because America has always been so radical in the direction of individual freedom. It's inevitable, scary sometimes, startling at others (certain mass rallies come to mind). Maybe in another two hundred years this thing will settle in, and Group-Think will become as everyday as I-Think. Hundreds of religious nations will spring from the union, and the Libertarians (who have made a religion out of individual freedom) will take over Idaho or Nebraska and fight it out among themselves. None of this will seem to make any difference any more. It's the folks today, raised in the Land of the Free, and headed into a time when everything has already been decided, who have the trouble. Crazy lines get drawn. These days, we are utter skeptics, and want to be Absolute believers (all Jimmy Carter says is, "I will never lie to you"). Or we have become Absolute believers, and won't let one ounce of anything outside the particular movement dogma taint our purification. And somewhere in between the new American religious reactionary, and the old line skeptical paranoiac, intervenes that other, unmentioned thing: the pursuit of Happiness, the pursuit of Happiness. . . .

(July 1977)

Lou, Turn Up Your Hearing Aid

Karl Grossman

Birth and death is a continual cycle. Like corn, *you* have a season. You grow, flower, give seed, fade away. But the energy within you keeps going — like the energy of corn. Have you ever been in a cornfield and felt that energy?

No? You say no?

The thing about birth and death is not to have too much of one and not the other. You have to keep birth and death about even in your many lives.

In my first incarnation (at least the first one I can remember) I (or the energy within me) was an Egyptian. I recall this quite clearly.

I was the son of the Pharaoh at that time in Egypt, Pharaoh Irving, and I was being forced to marry my sister, Ethel, who was a creep.

My father, the Pharaoh. I

remember him crystal clear to this day, white silk robe swirling in the Egyptian wind, posing for a statue being carved by 2,000 slaves, screaming at me, "You're going to marry your sister or we'll kill you."

So there I was in bed in my little room in our splendrous palace and a bunch of eunuchs come in carrying Ethel and dump her on the rug in front of my stereo set.

Between birth and death is life. But what is between death and birth? This is the BIG question.

I remember trying to be a famous man in the sixteenth century. I worked forty hours a day, I sweated, I slaved, I became a very rich lawyer and cheated thousands of people, but what did it get me? Fame, yes, but nobody remembers the names of ANY sixteenth century lawyers these days.

In the eleventh century, I met the prettiest woman of any of my lives: Baroness Betty Boomis. She was a very wealthy lady, she had many horses and carriages, and the hugest bust in the village in which we lived, Bayonne. This was a very great life because Baroness Betty Boomis was so dazzling, I didn't think of anything else, her energy was so strong. Which was fine, because let me tell you, the eleventh century was shit.

If you want to remember your former lives, it is quite simple. This is not something you can do while driving your car around or while not being totally, totally serious.

It is best to sit on a box, any kind of box, on the floor of your favorite room. Then recite these words: ktora gozina teraz?

This will usually bring it on. You have to have absolute quiet. Nobody can be running around the house or playing the saxophone or otherwise playing music loud. This would distract you.

When you can see your past lives, you can see your present in proper perspective. I know one man who can trace way back to when he was a cave person.

Of course, I know people who don't remember past lives at all. If this is your case, there are two possibilities: (a) you didn't have a past life, this is your first or (b) there are no past lives for anybody and this whole theory is wrong.

That would mean that this is it, buster.

(April 1976)

On Interviewing Swami Muktananda

Sy Safransky

H e was only another name, another guru, until I read Sally Kempton's article in *New York* magazine. Sally had written for *Esquire* a couple of years ago about her liberation as a woman. Now, she was writing about a different kind of liberation.

Having decided to look for a guru, she chose, in the manner of one looking for a heart specialist, to get the best. Muktananda was said to be a living saint, a perfectly realized human being, a *sadguru* — the highest of gurus. He had the ability, moreover, to give *shaktipat*, to awaken, by touch, or glance, or simply by his presence, the dormant energy in everyone called *shakti* or *kundalini*. Arousing this energy is the goal of all spiritual disciplines. For some, the awakening is subtle; others speak of visions, strong rushes of energy, and spon-

I wondered how a being of Muktananda's obvious evolution could be surrounded by such a scene. Was it naive to be so perplexed?

taneous movements.

Sally's first meeting with Muktananda changed her life. It opened her to a dimension she never knew existed. It was a place her lovers hadn't touched. A place beyond career, and ambition. She gave them up, and joined Muktananda's personal entourage.

I was impressed. Like Sally, I'd heard of realized beings, deathless saints, and gurus who had achieved total self-mastery and merged with God. Only I'd never met one. That there were such individuals fit what I knew about the universe, but so did the far side of the moon.

A week later, I came across a newspaper published by Muktananda's devotees. It featured an article by Paul Zweig, a writer and the chairman of the comparative literature department at Queens College in New York City. A religious skeptic, Zweig was in the company of an old friend, now a devotee herself, when he met Muktananda. The experience was wrenching, tearful, blissful:

. . . walking home along Broadway, in a state between dreamy relaxation and pure aerial energy, I sensed that my system had been overthrown, because what I was experiencing was simply irrefutable. This upheaval didn't need me to prove its reality, just as fear or erotic excitement are tremendous proofs of one's reality.

And there was an article by Muktananda himself. Being a guru, he observed, is popular these days — "you get a lot of food, you are honored and respected, you can charge a fee, you can pass off anything on credulous folks." Of course, he wasn't talking about himself, or the other true gurus in whom the divine energy blazes. Entering into a relationship with such a guru is "the most meaningful thing" that can happen to someone.

Muktananda, it appeared, came from an ancient and unbroken line of Indian Siddhas, or perfected masters. His own powers were developed after years of intensive yoga and meditation. He wandered for 25 years, meeting many saints, before finally accepting Swami Nityananda as his own guru. After nine further years of meditation under Nityananda's guidance, he achieved "God-realization."

"Don't worry," Muktananda wrote, "about finding the right guru. When you're ready, the guru will come and initiate you from within. The moment a true disciple comes into the presence of a true guru," he said, "the guru knows what to give him."

Again and again, in his and other articles, the emphasis was on the guru. True, chanting and meditation were important; once the *shakti* is aroused there is a spontaneous need and desire to meditate, a turning inward to the source of the Self. But without the guru's grace, perfection was impossible. So — sit close to the guru, study his gestures, his words. "It's good to spend as much time with him as you can," suggested the advertisement for the weekend Intensives. One hundred dollars for two days of meditation and chanting, and the opportunity to be touched by Muktananda.

One hundred dollars seemed pretty intensive for two days. Also, I didn't like the syrup. The writing about him seemed obeisant. A little odorous. I was reminded of standing in synagogue as a youth, the men around me extolling God, the Highest of the High, the All-Mighty, the All-Everything, and thinking to myself, flattery will get you nowhere.

I was suspicious. It's one thing to acknowledge that God exists everywhere, in everyone. Did he reside more equally in Muktananda?

But something, somehow, had moved Sally Kempton and Paul Zweig out of their tight and sour sense of themselves, their anxieties and their fears, their prison of ego. They talked about feeling happy. Could I say the same?

My wife and I were planning a trip up North, with our infant daughter, to visit our families. We set up an interview. In our letter, we referred to ourselves as earnest and sometimes confused seekers. Sally, who functions as Muktananda's press agent, wrote back that when she mentioned this to him, he said, in response, "A seeker is confused when he doesn't have a guide."

The interview was for ten o'clock, the ashram an hour away. We left at 8:30. Took a wrong turn. Stopped for directions. Crept along, behind a slow truck, for miles. It was getting late. There was no time to stop for extra film, or a tape cassette. The cassette didn't matter, because the tape recorder didn't work. Our daughter started crying. Her diaper needed to be changed. Sweating, and yelling at each other, we pulled into the parking lot fifteen minutes late.

This is comical in the telling. But we weren't laughing. In light of what was yet to happen, it's hard to chalk it up to coincidence. But what's coincidence, anyway? The tip of an iceberg called reality.

And who can fathom its true dimensions? A guru? Maybe.

The DeVille Hotel, which Muktananda's followers had rented for the summer, had seen better days. Still preposterously elegant, it evoked, for me, the childhood vacations spent with my parents at such resorts. But the four hundred devotees living here were hardly vacationing; they followed a strict and traditional ashram life, getting up at five in the morning to chant and meditate, taking meals together in a huge dining room, and going about their business with an efficient, no-nonsense air. The ground floor was decorated with poster-size photographs of Muktananda and Nityananda, a large, big-bellied man in a loin cloth surrounded by a glowing aura.

The ashram was well organized. There was a reception desk and Sally was on hand to greet us. We were given name tags. Everyone else had them, and there was a profusion of Rohinis, Shantis, and Gautis — the same Esthers and Normans and Davids I'd taken milk and cookies with in the children's dining room in another time, another place, when Hindu names were laughable. Actually, most of the devotees seemed younger than I, in their late teens or early twenties. Their faces were unlined, untroubled — perhaps they were simply untested? I'd come, perhaps wrong-headedly, to associate seasoned spiritual seekers with faces etched by many little deaths and little births, psychedelic upheaval, social uprooting, disappointment, renewal. Maybe the people here had been through it all, and had been washed clean. Maybe all the sour and the sweet of the search didn't matter once you knelt at the guru's feet. Still, I found the air oppressive: the incense, the icons, the photographs, the printed messages to remember God. I didn't want to be reminded at every turn. It crowded me psychically; it made me forget.

The interview room (formerly the card room) was colorfully appointed. Muktananda's throne, a spectacle of velvet pillows and tiny mirrors and peacock feathers, was on a raised dais. On the small table beside him there were three time-pieces, suggesting either a Marx Brothers stage prop or a neurotic obsession. Some dozen devotees, all women, all in long dresses (and well-dressed) sat on one side. They had red dabs on their forehead, symbolizing the third eye which is opened through spiritual illumination. While waiting for Muktananda (we had been fifteen minutes late; he kept us waiting another half-hour), we were told that all of his interviews were tape recorded, in case he said something new. One of the women had a camera and took pictures throughout the interview. Several took notes. All together, it had the feel of a White House press conference, or, more accurately, an audience with a monarch. In the manner of a royal court, his devotees tittered at every joke — for some more politely than genuinely, it seemed to me.

Muktananda came in wearing a saffron-colored robe, a knitted cap, and sunglasses. Sally had written that he looked like a black jazz musician. She was right.

He checked the timers, wound them, fiddled with them. I might have laughed, but I was too nervous, and intimidated. His presence was restrained, but powerful. No piercing looks, no holy air, but the posture of someone totally at ease, and in control. When he took off his glasses, his eyes seemed animated, alternately warm and indifferent.

Sally had urged us — repeatedly, in the protective manner of a press secretary — to focus our questions on his teaching, rather than on topics Sally thought were less important — diet, sex, The New Age. I complied for the most part, although it felt unnatural. I wanted to speak my heart, ask the questions that spontaneously occurred.

Maybe Muktananda's answers would have been more satisfying if I had. As it was, I was disappointed in the interview. I felt that, for the most part, we were asking for, and receiving, spiritual platitudes. From Muktananda's writings, I know he was capable of giving us more. The fact that he communicated through an interpreter didn't help. Nor did the lack of a tape recorder (I wanted to borrow, or buy, their tape; Sally said no, Muktananda required everyone to bring his own. It made me feel like I was in school again, being penalized for some meaningless infraction).

Our infant daughter was with us when we began the interview. Although Muktananda had held, and joked with her, at first, we got the feeling from his disciples that this was no place for a five-month-old baby. When Mara got restless, they took her from the room. A while later, we heard her crying. Priscilla went to get her. After quieting her, she tried to return. Muktananda brusquely waved her away. Sally jumped up and escorted her back outside. She told Priscilla, "You must take care of your own karmic burden."

[Priscilla said that while she was waiting, she spoke to a young woman who related that after being touched with a peacock feather by one of Muktananda's disciples — some of whom act as channels for his energy — she felt a bolt of lightning shoot down her spine. It exploded there and every cell in her body had an "orgasm." Mara finally fell asleep. She was again left with someone and Priscilla was allowed to return.]

The interview was nearing an end. I had heard enough about *shaktipat*. I wanted the experience itself. "How does one obtain the guru's blessing?" I asked. Muktananda smiled and stood up. "You're a good man," he said. He clamped his hand on my head. He pressed his thumb between my eyebrows. He pressed long and hard. Nothing. His hand felt good, strong and reassuring, but no lightning, no orgasm, no awakening. I was embarrassed. I closed my eyes to concentrate. I opened them again. He was still touching me, looking at me. This went on for about thirty seconds. I felt, when it was over, as if I had disappointed him. I wondered if he knew.

He didn't touch Priscilla's forehead at all, but forcefully rumpled her hair for about five seconds. She, too, felt nothing unusual. Then he walked out of the room, his stride long, his body erect, his big belly (big from yogic breath retention, not overeating, it was explained) thrust forward.

We followed him into the lobby. Everything stopped. His movements were studied by everyone, as if each gesture contained a profound message. Hollywood movie stars evoke the same response. So do politicians and other celebrities. Muktananda's followers explain that eventually they let go of their attachment to his physical form. I saw no sign of this while I was there.

We attended the group chanting in the sexually-segregated meditation hall. Nityananda's photograph was suspended in a rectangle of electric light bulbs. It looked more like a tacky Times Square advertisement than a religious centerpiece. I was holding Mara. When she started squirming, I took her to the back of the room, so she wouldn't disturb anyone. One of the devotees came over to me and said, "You're standing on the women's side. You should stand on the men's side."

I was dismayed. Was it more holy to ape the rituals and traditions of another culture than to endure one's own? I wondered how many of Muktananda's followers thought only a year or two before that separate bathrooms for men and women were sexist? If they'd left that behind, they certainly hadn't left with it their impatience. Before the last chant was over, people were already shuffling around and gathering up their things; lunch was next, and the line was long. Priscilla said it reminded her of church.

We decided not to stay for the evening darshan, during which Muktananda receives visitors and bestows blessings. The subtle condescension I'd been feeling all day was making me uncomfortable. By virtue of whatever luck or genius or grace had brought them this far, Muktananda's devotees were on the inside; I wasn't. *Shaktipat* seemed to have become a new kind of spiritual play-money. (Sally had suggested that Siddha Yoga would "sweep the world.")

I wondered how a being of Muktananda's obvious evolution could be surrounded by such a scene. Was it naive to be so perplexed? Naive to think that his touch could wash me, lift me, open me like stars across the sky, and carry me home? Naive to suggest that Muktananda still had ego, a cosmically extended ego, to be sure, huge and powerful enough to imagine that it is God, but limited nonetheless? This was a metaphysical question beyond my ken.

We were pondering it, as we began driving back to North Carolina. We'd left the ashram fifteen minutes earlier. I was at the wheel. I don't remember my exact words. They weren't charitable. Probably something like ego-trip.

That's when the engine blew up.

Nothing spectacular, but efficient. The damage was total. We'd need a new engine.

The van was towed to a crumbling little depot of grease and corruption called a service station, the kind you see in movies about the South. Except this was New York State, where there's no heavy accent to honey the deception.

We called Priscilla's father, who called a friend. In the meantime, Mara started to cry. It began to rain. Finally Tony arrived. He'd arranged to have the van towed to another town, where he knew a mechanic, and he drove us there in his car.

We had just arrived and stepped out of the car when we heard the crash. A car had run off the highway and smashed into the stone overpass 100 yards from us. The car was flattened — and smoking. I ran for the fire extinguisher. Tony pulled out the driver. He was alive, but bleeding.

Were we being told something, and, if so, in what language, and by whose hand? All I have is the question, nothing more.

(July 1976)

Judson Jerome

Psychology Today

My belly joined the Belly Potential Movement.
My brain took EST, my left eye last was seen
swimming with Swami Riva, my right was rolfed.

I'm actualized, if you know what I mean,
transcending, getting ready for the future,
fulfilled with helium, unstressed, piecemeal.

My organs drift asunder above the circus,
each bulbous with capacity to fell —
eastward the nose and south the probing tongue,

each toe afloat and powdered like a clown,
aurora borealis genitalia
higher than acupuncture can bring down.

Why then this aching? Surely not my soul —
for none was found when all was picked apart.
And, strings all cut, who would expect such
        throbbing

from one gland left on earth — my leaden heart?

(December 1979)

The Lazy Man

Thaddeus Golas

Dear Friends,

I am writing this as a letter because I have something I want to pass along right away, without waiting to refine it into an article or a book, just in case Griffith Mountain falls on my head tomorrow. I hope you will find it interesting and useful, since it's an idea that answers so many questions, and it's just a step past what I said in *The Lazy Man's Guide to Enlightenment*. To present the idea clearly, I will start with some things I've said before:

The universe is made of one kind of being.

We are equal beings. Together we are the universe.

Each being has absolute free will and control over his/her/its functions and consciousness.

The consequence of our equality and free will is that the laws of our

What is truly spiritual about you will always be invisible to other human beings. To be spiritual is not to be here at all.

relations must be what they are, and cannot be changed.

Each of us has complete freedom within the law to experience *anything*. That is to say, the law does not limit our freedom: the free will of others does not limit us. There is no need to contradict the law. We cannot and need not contradict what is and how it relates.

When we *do* attempt to contradict the law, to deny the free will of others or ourselves, we experience the necessary consequences, until we again recognize the free will of all beings.

"Free will" and "denial" are not emblazoned in words in cosmic space, but are realized by our actions and concepts.

When we deny free will, we are limited in communication with others, we can no longer tune in. We then see others from outside, so to speak.

When we see others from outside, when we see them as physical space, energy or mass, we are looking at *the operation of the law*. This is a very important point: the law's operation is not responsive to our wishes, it is not "alive" as we see it, we cannot control or change it, it has no significance or value. It is the physical world, seeming to oppose our free will, while having no will of its own. It appears to us whenever we are trying to contradict the law ourselves, denying free will. But what we are looking at is an infinitely large group of us beings relating in lawful ways.

We can, as we human beings do, *manipulate what these beings are already doing*. We can make forms out of matter and try to channel energy, but we can do that only by functioning through material means — a structure like the human brain and body. The entities forming iron atoms or gold atoms, for instance, are not conscious of the use we make of these metals: their conscious experience is free and unaffected.

Now we come to a big little step, the idea I want to tell you about:

In our primary state, our natural state as unique beings, *no evil can exist* — because nothing then exists except the choice of consciousness of each individual, relating to others or not at will. No being can control the behavior or consciousness of another, therefore there is never any *undesired* consequence of any kind. We are free to disagree without denying another's freedom.

However, when we deny free will and begin acting in a physical world, we are then in a context in which events and things persist, a framework in which events happen regardless of what we think about them, in which undesired and unexpected experiences can occur, in which evil can happen.

Thus we have the whole catalog of human history — the persistence of undesired experiences.

The basic truth, our freedom, is lost in confusion. We find more and more "proof" that free will is ineffective, even destructive. We compound our "original sin" by trying to control each other, or asking to be controlled. We try to figure out who or what is controlling this mess.

The answer is that no one is controlling it.

No one can, not God or man. It is the way the operation of the law looks to us when we are denying the law. We are all outlaws.

The possible commentary on this approach is too much even to sketch in a brief letter. For now, I would just like to draw some large clear lines.

Keep clearly in mind that our natural state, the "life of the spirit," is NOT a realm of virtue and goodness. Free spirits are not bound by "the knowledge of good and evil." It's just irrelevant. In a free state, the difference between Yes and No can be experienced as more horrendous than the atom bomb — but it lasts only as long as we wish.

We ourselves, with our passion for our physical forms, are the source of the standards of good and evil on Earth — that is why there are so many, so often conflicting — and these standards have no importance to the spiritual life. Our virtues on Earth will earn us no reward in the spirit, and our vices will not impede us. Our past is worthless and powerless. Whatever it is, we've all done it or could do it. All that matters is what we choose now.

Our basic choice is to be in or out of the Earth experience, and that choice is governed by our own free will. There is nothing on Earth or in heaven that can affect that choice — no faith, no system, no meditation, no virtue, no higher beings, no Brownie points.

But while we are functioning as human beings (which of course we are free to do!), we face a whole set of unusual problems that do not occur in our natural state. While we are making the mistake of seeing the relating of others as something that isn't alive, from outside, then everything we do is limited by that mistake.

Although there is no ultimate good or evil, these standards are still important to us as human beings. In fact, the immediate urgency of values is more pressing than ever, truly a life-and-death question. It's just that we must make them up as we go along, in a puzzling world indifferent to us, with all the confusions that we know so well: Which good for whom? Can we survive better as individuals or in groups? If in groups, how much individual freedom must we give up? How brutal must we be to enforce some peace? And so on.

In human life, the persistence of undesired experiences is only the beginning. We also get innocent beauty disguising evil surprises, and cruelty leading to good — but not always! We are never certain whether to trust our insight and imagination or to depend on learned experience and statistical probabilities. The survival of forms is more important to us than the free flow of life and consciousness. When we try to live with permissive grace, freedom and generosity, the most destructive among us rush to take advantage of it. We are obliged to offend our ideals under pressure of practical necessity. Good intentions are treated with suspicion, out of sad experience.

What can we do?

For myself, I keep in mind this reminder: "Others are free to do as they will, and I am free to relate to it or not." And another: "This is my idea of what's happening." That at least begins to unravel things at the core.

I suggest we adjust our expectations: human life will never be ideal. We are too various. And it is worthwhile to fight for freedom; it is fair to kill the killers. If you don't agree with that, of course, you will be assisted on your way out!

We may withdraw from involvement in earthly affairs, just to reduce our personal chaos and perhaps get glimpses of the free spiritual life, but we should not flatter ourselves that our withdrawal makes us superior to other human beings. If we make special claims to purity and holiness, we're just making ourselves ridiculous in the light of the truth. No special qualifications are required to transcend earthly life: transcendence is our natural condition. Personally, I find the self-congratulation of the virtuous as repellent as the self-contempt of the evil-doers. Questions of good and evil do not apply to the spiritual life, but to earthly experience, and earthly problems must be solved by physical means. Civilization requires people who fulfill their contracts more than it needs saintliness. Religions were most successful when they concerned themselves with practical matters: calendars, clocks and crops. I have never had any patience with the comedy and misdirection that passes for spiritual search, and now I can say why. All of us are spirits, and all that happens is spiritual.

Scientists and technologists quite justly enjoy some success because they are willing to look at the lawful nature of physical events. Of course the use we make of scientific discoveries brings them back into the arena of human choice. In psychology, sociology, and other studies in which we recognize the action of conscious life, it will never be possible to be scientific. It is one of our most tiresome human habits to attempt to borrow the authority of science for areas where it cannot apply.

Since the denial of free will is so crucial a matter, it would be useful to examine ourselves to observe how we might be doing it without realizing it. Exchanging information is a valid human activity, but if we believe that others need our help and rescue for spiritual freedom, we are denying their free will. Status systems and hierarchies have their uses in good management, but if we are blind to our equality with all beings, we are denying our own free will.

As the arts show us, particularly in music, there is much we can enjoy on Earth of our real nature, once we have taken care of the chores. But I do believe we would live more sanely if we realize that the spirit has its limits in solving the problems of physical life. And we can certainly live with more zest when we know that life here is not the only game in town.

This concept has shaken all my thought processes to their roots. I have had to abandon some pet notions, and I must re-evaluate every assumption about the physical world that I took for granted. I am a bit stunned. Therefore I have no idea where this approach might lead.

But I am also confident and satisfied. I understand now why I have lived as I have, often when all reason and common sense told me I was wrong. I find the answer so obvious, so close to us, a part of us, that the wonder is how we ever manage to obscure it at all. Once we enter the condition of not knowing, we are tuned into a whole credible history of ignorance — millions of years of it! It's hilarious!

Now if I could only do something about this flu. . . .

(February, 1980)

Reminders

Maintain the intention to be expanded.

Functions come first.

Your functions must be right before anything else can be right.

Functions happen now, in present time.

Functions are outside consciousness, more than awareness.

Functions come first. As a unique being (a spirit or soul, if you prefer), you have a function: expanding and contracting. Your functions have priority over all ideas, beliefs, concepts and intentions. If your functions are right, the wrong ideas won't stop you. If your functions are wrong, the greatest wisdom in the world won't help you.

You can see how much we have achieved in science and technology just by identifying functions. What I am proposing now is that we identify our functions as unique beings.

Everyone is doing it already, of course, and it seems silly that something so simple should be hard to explain — but that's because functions are independent of consciousness. (That is, there are many times when you are not conscious, but there is never a time when you are not functioning.) When you pick up a cup, you just will to do it, without exactly knowing how your brain works or how your body does it. Therefore, while you are maintaining the intention to expand, you won't have a clear sense that anything is happening, but do it anyway. Keep doing it, and see what happens.

Functions happen now, in present time. You always have full control of your expansion and contractions right now — no matter what others are doing or what else is happening. The only time you *can* function is now: if expanding made you feel good ten minutes ago, that's irrelevant. Maintain the intention. Remind yourself. *Do it now.* I've said this before in other ways: "Pay attention to what you're doing. Love it the way it is. This, too, can be experienced with a fully expanded awareness." Now I have tons of logic for it, but the logic doesn't matter. Don't think about it. Don't take my word for it. *Do it. Expand!*

If you need more reasons, note this: alternating expansion and contraction is energy, which we experience and perceive as "vibrations" and "waves" and so on, but for starters in asserting control it would be better to think in terms of the extremes:

Expansion makes you space. Space amplifies energy and sends it on its way.

Contraction makes you mass. Mass retards energy, and congeals it into form and builds structures.

Now, if you contract to withdraw from "negative" thoughts, guess what form the energy will take? And if, meanwhile, you are willingly expanding only with "positive" thoughts (and creative thinking, high ethics and good morals), your expansion causes all those lovely thoughts to vanish formless into space. (Unless, of course, you get others to resist you!)

I am emphasizing expansion because we are presently involved in the massive contractions of physical life on earth — gravity, etc. — but the goal really is to recover some sense of our freedom to choose our experience.

Postscript to Reminders

The preceding is what I have been passing on to friends on a single sheet of paper, and it would seem that some find it hard to credit the simple advice to do something. What I am proposing is not inspirational or uplifting, which may be all to the good. What I am looking for myself is action with reliable consequence — reliable on all levels of being.

In a cosmic system with a ceiling and a floor, involving functional relations between equal and free entities, it really doesn't matter what names we give to the various processes, how many entities are involved, or whether we measure functions in a complex or simple way. Insofar as our ideas are in agreement with the way we function, we will be successful in choosing our experience, and insofar as our ideas contradict the laws of function, we will fail. Therefore analyzing the spiritual in terms of functions seems to me a fruitful approach; what follows are a couple of examples of this approach.

In Nigel Calder's book, *Einstein's Universe* (Viking Press), he notes that the formulas for acceleration and for gravity are the same. He also notes that Einstein's revolutionary proposal meant that matter does not pull on other matter, but that mass follows a certain course in free fall because *space is warped* by gravity. If I may be so bold as to say it, being as lay a layman as one can be, it appears to me that this just shifts the problem of "action at a distance": instead of matter pulling on other matter, it is now pulling on space.

In my book, *The Lazy Man's Guide to Enlightenment*, I proposed that space PROPELS energy and mass: the greater the contraction and resistance of an entity, the more it is propelled.

Now, in which direction will a mass entity be propelled? It will be propelled in the direction of *other* mass entities: the bigger the blob of matter, the larger the gathering of mass, the greater the propulsion toward it. Why? Because that large contracted mass is not pushing back, it is not pushing outward enough — there is less space there.

Thus we may view gravity, not as a pull, but as an acceleration toward other matter. This would be supported by the equivalence of the formulas for acceleration and gravity. (This speculation can be taken into the Big Bang and out again.)

What has all this to do with the spirit? What this means for us is that any of us, as a unique entity, may leave this earthly mass simply by changing *function*. Nothing is pulling us down. When we begin expanding and cease contracting, we automatically cease being propelled toward matter — we are free in permeative space.

I am sure many of my readers have had the experience of popping out into space, in satori or with psychedelics. Of course you can't take much mental baggage with you at such times, but the next time you're out, try to hold the thought, "I am expanding now."

In any case, this line of thought indicates why I am not interested in making bodies live longer or in taking them out there in space ships.

Am I thinking in terms of survival after death or reincarnation as a personality? No. Thinking in terms of functions leads to other interesting perceptions. For instance, I was watching a TV film about chemosynthesis: a camera had been sent five miles below the surface of the Pacific, and there, where the sun never shone, along cracks in the ocean floor where a little heat from the earth's interior was escaping, there were marvelous and unusual forms of life. Just as plants incorporate sunlight, these forms were responding to heat.

And then it struck me what was happening in photosynthesis: matter will respond to a *slight* increase in energy by organizing itself into self-reproducing and sometimes mobile forms. And once the plants have incorporated energy (which matter in its delusion considers must come from somewhere else — contracted entities hold enormous energy but always plead for more), other forms of life keep on reusing it — animals eat plants and other animals; both animals and plants in death and decay are reused by other forms. (That is why corrupt societies are so creative — there is a lot of loose energy around.)

Now, these "life" forms may be wildly proliferating on earth, and may be incredibly various and ingenious. We may even get a form that considers itself the only consciousness, the apex of creation. But all these forms are still matter, no matter how complex, dissipative and subtle they may be. They will use all the energy they can hold and manipulate, all the information they can absorb — merely to make more forms, more bodies.

ALL material interactions are rooted in contraction. Mass has no future except to be mass as long as it continues to contract. It can only solve the "problems" of material existence by expanding, by ceasing to be mass.

What this means is that there is no way for the spirit to make earthly life work better.

Life on earth is simply its own local system, grounded in the necessities and perversities of resistive entities — anti-space — all trying to tear preformed packets of energy from each other, never using the enormous energy stored within themselves.

Of course space is nothing if not a store of infinitely variable ideas, which would include ideas for manipulating matter in less painful ways. But there is no idealized state of matter — nor of human behavior.

There is no way that enlightenment, or spiritual uplift, or ideals, or varying your consciousness, or any other space-level activity is going to do anything to alter the way matter interacts with matter.

Ecology, saving human bodies, reforming the establishment — all these are *practical* activities, but they are not spiritual.

I am not arguing against optimism and energy in playing with the predictable and repetitive functions of matter. But please, just don't call it spiritual.

Being spiritual, being space, is totally *other*; its rules are the inverse of the rules of mass relations. Space rules are not appropriate in a material context. They just don't work. Enlightenment does not help you run the world better. Remember that space PROPELS energy and mass, and that's all it can do. A mass entity must expand of its own free will to be "saved."

What is truly spiritual about you will always be invisible to other human beings. To be spiritual is not to be here at all. Or to be on your way out in as natural and decent a way as possible. Organize your life so that you need give the minimum of attention to material events.

It doesn't matter what your ideas or actions are — what you do with an expanded self will be spiritual. What you do with a contracted self will not be spiritual.

To emphasize again:

Functions come first.

And, as Nigel Calder noted, the laws of function are the same for all entities everywhere in the universe at all times.

And that is why I am telling you to maintain the intention to be expanded.

(June 1981)

© Copyright 1981 Thaddeus Golas

How Things Came Into Existence

Franklin Mills

Once upon a time long ago in that part of the present that is hidden from general view and which lies in the unreachable future, there were two, only two beings. Where they came from I have no idea and probably they didn't either. Who could have told them? But I am certain that they were named Mr. Nous and Mme. Ordinat. They lived in a place called the Abode of Becoming. I really can't say what it was like, because I've never been there. No doubt, though, it in no way resembled where you or I live.

They were a strange pair — Mr. Nous and Mme. Ordinat — not exactly opposites but definitely very different each from the other. Mr. Nous was a thinker, a muser, an imaginer. Nothing was more pleasurable to him than to spend his day thinking through long and elaborate thoughts.

It was a very long story he told, the longest that will ever be, as big as the universe and all that will ever happen in it. . .

About all that was heard from him from dawn to dusk (if there were the daily cycles then) was "Hmmm!" "Gee!" "I never thought of that before!" "Absolutely fascinating!" His mind seemed to supply all the entertainment he could ever want.

Consequently, Mr. Nous was not much of a doer. And that royally irritated Mme. Ordinat, the kind who's always doing something. Her shadow was threadbare from keeping up with her.

"Don't you realize," she often said to Mr. Nous, "that across the threshold of our Abode lies the whole realm of Existence? And you've never given it so much as a good long look. Why don't you go out there with me now while I do my work. You could use the exercise. It's not healthy to stay cooped up in here, thinking all day."

"What's out there to be seen?" he would ask. "Existence, sure — lots and lots of it. But it's absolutely empty. Nothing in sight as far as the eye can see. No, thank you. I'd rather stay here and think my thoughts than waste my time traipsing about a hollow Existence."

Annoyed at that, Mme. Ordinat would smack her measuring rod on the floor of the abode and then charge out into Existence to do her work.

There was plenty there for her to do. She had given herself the job of measuring that vast realm. Only someone like Mme. Ordinat with a passion for order would have attempted it. Although her measuring rod was very, very long, she could lay it down, one length after another, a trillion times and still find the greater part of Existence lying ahead of her, yet to be measured. The worst part of it was that each day she had to begin all over again; when she took her rod home at night, there was nothing left in Existence from which to continue her measurements the next day. You or I might have given it up as ridiculously futile. Not Mme. Ordinat. Every day she set out annoyed with Mr. Nous and returned every evening completely exasperated by her work. But she never gave up, bless her.

Now one day while she was busy with her rod, Mr. Nous found himself embarked on an especially productive line of thought. What he was thinking about was the universe with its myriad forms and functions, all things and doings that have ever been or will ever be but were then not yet except in his imagination. He thought about stars aflame at birth and old men with stories to tell, about little girls giggling and splashing in mud puddles and the refraction of light in emeralds. He thought of love and hate, rivalry and reconciliation, pleasure and pain, want and plenty, red and yellow, blue and green. He thought what it was like to make something with your hands or to feel the hand of someone you loved turning cold in yours. He thought of redemption. He thought of all these things simultaneously and yet with an appreciation for the separateness of each, the way you might regard polished marbles poured out of a leather pouch. It was by far the greatest thought he'd ever had and it overwhelmed him to silence.

It so happened that this day had been an especially trying one for Mme. Ordinat. Twice she had dropped her measuring rod and quite lost her place as well as her count. And then she had come on a stretch of Existence that wasn't flat like the rest but was instead corrugated like the surface of a huge washboard. How could you really measure it with a stiff, straight rod? If you laid the rod across the humps there were all those rounded valleys between that went unmeasured. She had tried smacking the corrugations a few good ones to straighten them out but to no avail. The way she'd tossed her head had almost ripped the neck of her shadow.

A soft word, it is said, turns away wrath. Mme. Ordinat's required a craven plea for mercy to divert it. When only silence greeted her at the Abode, her rage swelled like an organ's blast in a vacant cathedral.

"Look here," she said, brandishing her measuring rod, "when I say hello to someone I expect a reply! My rod has had enough practice on bumps today to flatten that hollow head of yours if you don't answer me!"

Even had he heard her, Nous couldn't have broken off his thoughts about the universe; they were far too grand and compelling. Mme. Ordinat saw the look of bliss on his face and assumed he was mocking her. The measuring rod came down with a loud smack on the crown of his head.

What a smack it was! Tears shot out of his eyes and over the threshold of the Abode and these were the very first raindrops that fell on Existence. He cried out a thunderous cry that echoed far beyond the abode and this was the very first thunder in Existence. As soon as the passing of pain had let him regain his sight, he noticed something else, something quite extraordinary had happened: Mme. Ordinat had knocked the thoughts right out of his head. They were running helter-skelter all over the Abode of Becoming, up the walls, across the ceiling, everywhere.

"Shoo! Shoo! Get away!" Mme. Ordinat shrieked as she made her stand in a corner, smacking at the whirligigs and fizzpops that played up and down her like tiny frolicsome puppies. "OOOeee!" The more she smacked, the more they capered across her body — the brave little souls. "What are these horrible scudders, anyway?" she cried.

By now the daze had worn off and Mr. Nous stroked his chin to think how he might explain them to her. It was no good telling her how they had existed in his mind, because obviously that was no longer their condition. Luckily, his imagination came to his rescue. He did what many have done since, when their thoughts were running free and needing some order. He did what I am doing now. He began with "Once upon a time. . . ."

It was a very long story he told, the longest that will ever be, as big as the universe and all that will ever happen in it, full of episodes great and small, with plenty of digressions and not a few redundancies. Mme. Ordinat seized the opportunity to rid the Abode of the infestation. As the storyteller went on, she shoved the appropriate subject across the threshold and into Existence. With her measuring rod she prodded each to act out its own story just as Mr. Nous told it. And so will she be doing until the end of time.

One thing needs pointing out. Mr. Nous told his story, as is the custom, in the past tense. That means that the one I have just told is happening actually in the distant future from us. If we ever reach that time — and I have my doubts — we'll find ourselves, it seems, at our beginning. That hardly makes good sense. But then, neither did those corrugations Mme. Ordinat found in Existence.

(March 1981)

Living Within
The Question

An Interview With Reshad Feild
Howard Jay Rubin

Service is one of those code-words I've been contemplating for some time. As the standard work-ethic grows less convincing, there's more appeal in the idea of work as service to others — and through others to myself. I wonder, though, just what it means, and how to make service something more than just another feast for a hungry ego.

Service was the undercurrent of my conversation with Reshad Feild. For Reshad is a Workaholic, and what he considers "The Work" is living in the stream of service — "the stream that leads to the river that leads to the ocean of truth." He sees humility and respect — never presuming one knows the answer but instead "living in the question" — as the door to willing service. And "gratitude," he says, quoting Mevlana Jelal-ud-Din Rumi, "is the key to will." His words conveyed that sense of

> When we commit ourselves to life . . . everything in life will come up, and then we will have the opportunity for the total redemption of what is asked of us.

gratitude, as well as a feeling of deeper respect, as if he were speaking directly to the highest parts in me. They sunk in, leaving me with the sense that not only was Reshad quite honest (in his own foxish fashion), but that he also really knew what he was talking about.

We sat in the living room of his immaculate house in Santa Cruz (even the walls are scrubbed every day), with his pet parrot squawking on his shoulder, engulfed in one of the most powerful conversations I can remember. I was tired, but my concentration was sharp; my mind grew quieter and quieter. It's odd: I felt something special being shared between us — "we're making love," he said at one point, "making love possible in the present moment" — but later, reading the transcript of the interview, it seemed barely to come across. Somehow the words don't do him justice. The talk seemed rambling (which it was), Reshad seemed a bit cocky and grandiose (which perhaps he is), but there's something in him that transcends all that.

I'd read his two books, The Last Barrier and The Invisible Way, and was moved by them. Then, in preparing for the interview, I heard a different tale — of a spiritual teacher whose behavior can be best characterized as outrageous, who sometimes drinks more than others think he should, who had been through two rocky marriages and two tempestuous relationships with his own teachers. But from the moment we sat down together, over a cup of English tea, I felt it just wasn't relevant. He makes no excuses for his humanness, in fact he rather stresses it, but there's a quality in his presence — a wide-open love, an over-extended joy — that needs no excuse. Sometimes he seemed dead serious — almost too serious — but inside I could sense a laugh brewing. After more than two hours, we reached the final question, and Reshad leaned back in his chair with a sigh of relief, toppling straight backward. With a laugh the interview was complete.

So, what does Reshad do? When I first spoke with him he referred to himself as a "retired Sufi," but I've rarely met a man more absorbed in his work. He's an author, an esoteric healer, a sheik of the Mevlevi Dervish order, a teacher, and the founder of more than a half-dozen schools of "alternative education" (spiritual coaxing, though he'd resist the label). He's also a consultant in Geomancy, which he describes as the art of understanding the electro-magnetic field of the planet — others call them ley-lines — and orienting buildings in the right place to produce the most harmony. Put simply, Reshad says, if you put something in the wrong place we're all going to be affected. He's just completed his third book, called

Steps to Freedom: The Alchemy of the Heart, *and is working on another called,* Here to Heal, *which will be released next year.*

Reshad says he was brought up by a Romany Gypsy who was his mother's cook. He spent most of his youth in English boarding schools, and served in the British navy. His first esoteric training was in the Gurdjieff/ Ouspensky work, and then with the Druids. He studied with many other teachers, but it all came together for him in the early Sixties when he met Sufi teacher Pir Vilayat Khan. Pir Vilayat initiated him as a Sufi sheik, and sent him to Turkey to study with a man Reshad calls Hamid, a teacher in the Mevlevi Dervish tradition. "I needed a tough teacher," *Reshad says,* "because I was stubborn, obstinate and big-headed," *and Hamid was just the man.* "He knocked me off my ass when I needed it." *One of the keynotes of Hamid's teachings was trust.* "He used to say, 'Trust, trust, trust!'" *Reshad recalls,* "and I thought, 'Never think that trust means to trust a man.' Trust is a quality of God. And then you know whom you can trust."

The Mevlevi Dervishes are a Sufi order founded by Mevlana Jelal-ud-Din Rumi, the reknowned mystic and ecstatic poet who lived in the thirteenth century. They've become known as Whirling Dervishes because of their spinning dance called "The Turn." "It's a way of completion," *Reshad says,* "not a religion or cult. There is an inner experience with The Turn that no one can speak about. It is a discipline of body, mind, and spirit. We turn to God, who is love, as he turns in us to the world, making himself love in us."* The Sufi tradition is a mystical branch of Islam that emphasizes love and remembrance of God (a practice called* zikr*), more than specific form or doctrine.*

Reshad spent seven years working with the dervishes in and out of Turkey, a period described vividly in The Last Barrier. ("My books are ninety percent underplayed," *Reshad told me.* "If I ever told the whole story, no one would believe me.") *His trust in Hamid waned, and after a major disagreement, they parted, and Reshad returned to the West.*

Here's how Reshad later became the first Western Sheik of the Mevlevi order: "I was running a center in Los Angeles when I got a letter from Suleyman Dede (the head of the order). He wanted to come to America. . . . So we raised the money and flew him over. My wife and I had this tiny little house with only two rooms; we were in one room with the baby and he knocks on the door at 4 a.m.. He didn't speak English, and I didn't speak Turkish. He signalled me to do ablutions. Well, I knew how to do those, so I did. He beckoned me into the room where he spread

out the khirqa, which was the robe, the sikke [hat], his own Koran, and
his prayer beads; he signalled that I was to pray with him, so I did. . . . He
turned around then and said "Taman!" put the robe on me, the sikke on
my head, and said, "Now you're the first Sheik of the West, and I can go
home and die." I didn't even have time to say, 'No.'"

Reshad's reputation as esoteric and Sufi teacher grew, as did a subtle feeling of specialness in his role. "Was I real," he asks, "when I had
3,000 people in England throwing imaginary spears at the sun, all getting
high as a kite? No, I wasn't real. I didn't know what I was doing, and I
didn't help them either. To feel special means you're eventually going to be
crucified on the cross of pride. . . . Eventually I realized that there was
some glamour behind it that I was attached to. Some inner fear that I
covered up with robes and whatever." He let go of the robes, the labels,
and the fear. Now he refuses to call himself a Sufi or anything else.

What's it like to work with Reshad? What I hear from some people is
that it's powerful, and can be trying. Is Reshad-the-teacher a bit of a
bastard? Sometimes. "I'm tough-as-nails," he says. "I have to be." Then
there are the stories. Like the time, late in the evening at one of Reshad's
centers, when he pronounced, "I am not going to sleep until everybody here
loves each other!" So there they sat for a while, groping at each other, trying to figure out what he wanted. "Bring me a chair," he bellowed. And
he was brought a chair. Time passed. "Bring me my mattress." And two
people lugged his mattress down the stairs. More time passed. Finally, one
student turned to the woman next to him and said, in a loud stage-whisper,
"I'm getting terribly bored with all of this." Reshad glared at him.
"Jeremy!" he said. "Turn!" Jeremy performed the Dervish Turn and had
what he later described as "one of the major mystical experiences of my
life." The evening ended.

"The greatest trap is to presume," Reshad says. "We presume
everything. We presume the sunrise, we presume that tree is going to be the
exact same tree tomorrow as today. But it might not be. We presume our
breath, that we just breathe in and it will come out, but actually the
understanding of conscious breath and the rhythm of it is absolutely vital."

He tells of a time when he returned to his Boulder school from a
lengthy trip to England. "People went into fits. 'Reshad's coming back!'
and all that nonsense. There were forty-seven people that night for a special
dinner. I sat down at the table, still suffering from jet-lag, and people were
fawning all over me. I can't stand that, I just think it's ridiculous. I took

one look at them, picked up the bowl of hot soup in front of me and poured it straight over the top of my head. They all went into a state of shock and woke up." What do you do with a man like that?

Reshad is very British, although he says that he's been in America long enough to become bilingual. If there's one thing he's proud of it's a strong sense of inner discipline. "I know how to run a ship," he says laughing, and then proceeds to tell a story from his days as a young naval officer when his discipline hadn't been so good. "I was the navigating officer for two full squadrons of motor-torpedo boats. We were having what they called exercises with the American Navy in the Baltic. So off we steamed, up the Baltic toward Copenhagen. I hear a call coming down the intercom: "Feild!" "Yes, Sir!" "Give me a bearing!" So I was checking my radar instruments and at the same time getting quite seasick. I said, "We're at a quarter of a minute sir. On the port bow twenty degrees . . ." and collapsed again. In a little while I hear, "Feild!" "Sir!" "What were the bearings?" "Well, it's now five minutes past sir." There was an ominous silence, and then, "Feild, on deck!" I get on deck and the commander says, "Feild, stop all engines." So I put on the emergency signal and eight motor-torpedo boats, steaming down the Baltic at nearly forty knots, stop cold. The commander brings me back down below. "Feild, do you know what you've done?" "No, sir!" "You've just navigated two squadrons of motor-torpedo boats three miles into a mine-field! In peacetime!" That was when Reshad ceased to be a British navigating officer.

He laughs easily at the mistakes he's made and the changes he's been through. He considers it par for the course. "If we make our commitment to the Work," he says, "we commit ourselves to change. We commit ourselves, first of all, to allow ourselves to be changed, and then to being an agent for real change to take place in the world around us. . . . It is no good pretending to have committed ourselves if we are not prepared to accept change, and all that it brings with it. It is not useful to put one foot on the path and leave the other on the old road . . . for real change may then come about before we are prepared for all that this entails."

Changes? Reshad has been a racing car driver, an antique dealer, a naval officer, and even a pop-star with a band called Springfield. He's seen his share of struggle. Three times he's contracted cancer and overcome it, though he lost half of his stomach in an early battle.

In healing others he makes use of many different methods, including breathing practices, herbs and flower remedies, dowsing, and an electro-magnetic technique known as radionics. He talks of treating disease as a disturbance of the body's electro-magnetic pattern caused by shock. We spoke at length about this in the interview.

Reshad's days as a performer didn't end with his musical career. Even now, he is a consummate entertainer, playing his parts with majestic style, and more than a little pizazz.

Reshad staged a three-day birthday celebration a few weeks after our interview, marking the end of a seven-year cycle in his work, and more than one hundred people came. It was approaching sundown on the second day when we met on a grassy hill overlooking the ocean. The Royal Stuart bagpipe band was there from Scotland, in full ceremonial array. Some cows looked on curiously from across the field. On that hill, as the sun began to set over the Pacific, Reshad spoke in majestic tones about freedom.

"Freedom is all I have to talk about," he said, "and I'll talk about it until I die. Not freedom from, but freedom within. To live in freedom so that others are freed. . . . We need to have the courage to know that the divine guidance — whatever you want to call it — is there, and you know what to do, you know where to be." His tone grew even grander. "I'm asking you to turn to the highest in yourselves. We are going to make a new world, all of us. We're going on in knowledge. We need the courage to say, 'Yeah! We are going forward for freedom and nothing is going to stop us!' And if you ever lose courage, as we all do . . . remember the sound of the bagpipes — then you cannot help but have courage."

He begins to laugh and beckons the pipers to "pipe down the sun." As the sun sets, a fiery red ball on the water, the pipes play a chorus of "Amazing Grace." Theatre, pure and grand.

This was followed by a feast, accented with eighteen ceremonial toasts that left everyone, especially Reshad, more than a little tipsy. We didn't see him for the rest of the evening.

Perhaps the paradox I felt in Reshad is the same in all of us — our simultaneous divinity and human limitation. It's a high-wire balancing act that Reshad performs well, denying neither. Both aspects of him stand out clearly. He holds the mirror of his being up to the part of me that wants to judge another, and then he points it at the part of me that knows I can't. For this I'm grateful.

—Howard Jay Rubin

SUN: Before we get to questions and answers, let's look at what you mean by "living within the question."

RESHAD: What I try to help people with comes only from my experience. Otherwise it's basically a lie. When I got cancer the first time, I realized that I was living in complete presumption. There was no "question." But mind you, at that point, I didn't have to question anything — everything was given to me on a plate. I had money, and I could always buy my way out of any internal problem. If I felt sick, I'd fly to Switzerland to go skiing. That was my way out, a cheap way. I had no question really. I mean I had a question inside, but I knew intuitively that by asking that question I would cause myself a lot of trouble. So I'd always buy my way out of it.

Years later, in my thirties, I got cancer again. Again I had forgotten. Everything had seemed kosher in every direction. But one morning I woke up, went to the bathroom, and started hemorrhaging through my penis. I was horrified. I had no money and no insurance. Again, I discovered that I'd forgotten to live in the question — I call it the stream of service, the stream that leads to the river that leads to the ocean of truth. After three or four days it was so bad that I was wearing several pair of underpants so nobody could see. I finally went to the doctor. The urologist had one look, took X-rays, and explained that I had a tumor in my bladder and I had to go in right then. I said, "No. Look doctor, I've got enough money for your fee now, but I have not got any money for this sort of operation. Give me three days, and I'll guarantee to you that if it does not stop I'll come back." I telephoned from the hospital and asked some people to pray in the particular way that the Sufis do. The bleeding stopped. I went back to the doctor in three days, he took X-rays again, and there wasn't one trace of tumor. I was very humble and grateful. The doctor said, "I don't know who you are, but I'm going to give you my fee, and you give it to anyone you want."

SUN: So, it wasn't a specific question you were neglecting to ask. Rather, you're talking about a general state of being.
RESHAD: If you're not in the question then you get into the chaos. And if we presume for one moment that we know the answer, we're actually denying God. In Sufism, as well as in the Jewish tradition and many others, one of the names of God means the All-knower. If for one moment we presume that we know, rather than being agents for the knowing aspect of God, then we're not in the question, we're not in the stream of service.

When I work with people, I tell them that I'm not going to give them an answer, except perhaps how to cure their foot-rot. What I try to do is lead them into the question, and once they've gotten into the question they're free of me as a teacher. Then they're in that fastest part of the river, which is also the calmest — dead in the middle.

SUN: Many people who play the role of teacher tend to really eat it up, even while denying it. Do you find yourself enjoying that role and the specialness it implies?

RESHAD: That's a good question. No. But looking back, I suppose that I did about twenty years ago. In no manner do I feel that at all now. I like being an entertainer. I was in show business once. Most people are so damn bored anyway — why on earth not entertain? But I find it personally a tremendous difficulty coping with the responsibility of having been granted a bit of knowledge. You know, I've got three kids to look after, and I feel guilty — I suppose I shouldn't but I do, not giving sufficient time to my family in London. And yet, I know I'm here at the right place and the right time. I know that, yet I'm bound to feel guilty, I'm a human being. No, I don't feel special in any way. I feel embarrassed, and at times frustrated. It's possible to know what the possibility of somebody else is. And you really do know it, and it gets frustrating when you see someone who is still in a denying state to their own mirror, to their own possibility.

SUN: The other night you used the phrase, "It's all done with mirrors." Let's speak about that.

RESHAD: In the inner aspect of Sufism, everyone carries with them a mirror. I used to think when I was with these sheiks in the Middle East that they were being vain — they kept looking at mirrors, at their beards or whatever. Of course they weren't being vain. They were testing the situation. They weren't preening their whiskers, they were seeing how their eyes looked.

The moment is the mirror. We are reflected in the moment, the eternal present.

There are seven levels of the mirror in esoteric lore. The first is seeing myself in you by inwardly addressing the God in you. I may say to you, "Howard," but at the same time time I'm saying "Oh, Thou." And, at the same time, I'm saying how grateful I am that God has made Himself present in you. Then the gratefulness in myself, if it was slightly dead, will come forward.

The second level of mirror is allowing myself to be seen. That's difficult. One always feels ugly in some way, or lazy, or sentimental. So one allows oneself to be seen, and there's an interchange of energy.

The third level of mirror is when the two of us, or a group of us, allow ourselves to be seen by a power, or a world — whatever words you want to use — greater than the one we presently understand.

The next level is going through the mirror. That means going through or beyond the form of energy. In other words, beyond the form of comparison and time as we know it. The being of you, or me, exists before it issues from the womb of the present moment into man or woman, before we issue forth.

The next one involves getting into a whole different level of respect completely. There's no respecting you, or your background, or religion. It is total respect, total humility, complete openness. That is when your realize that you are respected. That word came from *respectare* — to see again. So you see again in a completely different light.

The rest of the levels are too complex to put into words.

SUN: When I first called you, you referred to yourself as a retired Sufi, and later as a snufi. I appreciated your laughing at your own labels. Let's talk about that and about a larger label that we use — whether there's any valid reason to speak of a spiritual path in any way separate from life.

RESHAD: First of all, I haven't called myself anything. I have been initiated into three different Dervish orders and also various other orders. I didn't choose it, though I suppose I did feel special at the beginning — being the first Englishman as a Mevlevi sheik and all that. I'm thoroughly embarrassed by it too. The reason I call myself a retired Sufi is because the word Sufi has become, in many people's minds, almost like a cult. In the Fifties it was Zen, then it was yoga or whatever. I'm not against it because I am trained in it, and I'm deeply respectful to the inner meaning of Sufism, beyond all form. Of that there is no question. But it can be a watered-down version of truth if people attach labels to Sufism. For example, people telephone me and say, "I'm a Sufi." The fact of the matter remains that nobody who was a Sufi would ever say they were, except to be outrageous.

What they say of a Sufi in the Middle East, when he's buried, in my particular tradition, is "And God has blessed his secret." And one respects that because a secret is a secret. I am a retired Sufi only because I do not want to be labeled. I think it is a limitation.

To answer the second part of your question, the average human being is not grounded. And the purpose of life on earth is to get here. I would suggest that a frame of reference is extremely useful. Following the guru may be a good bait, but then, if you catch the bait, you may not like the taste. It's like they say, "If you meet the Buddha on the road, kill him." In one way there is no need for a frame at all. If you and I can talk like this there is no need. But for a lot of people a frame is necessary, because if you take a picture and you stick it on the wall without a frame, you're going to have a lot of frayed edges. For example, in the world of healing, I always recommend to people to get a good frame of reference, become a chiropractic doctor, become a this or that.

SUN: So, the frame then is the concept of spiritual path, or a specific path?
RESHAD: The concept is dangerous and rather slight, isn't it? Life itself is the frame, if we ourselves are grounded enough to accept life, and live out our life. We don't have to explain. When people ask me, for example, "What is reincarnation?" I ask them, "Well, what reincarnates?" They can never answer. They are not yet here.

SUN: You've called your next book *The Alchemy of the Heart*. What if I come up to you and say, "Well, that's a cute phrase, but I've got this pain, I've got this loneliness. How can I start doing this alchemy?"
RESHAD: Well, there are six major steps in the technique of alchemy. The first three steps involve the transformation of base metals — psychologically that means the transformation of all of our "negative" emotions into a vessel, or chalice, to receive the spirit. That's what's called the descent of the purified forces. The way I teach people is very simple. I say, "Look, you've got fear. Turn it into courage. You've got resentment, or grief? Turn it into compassion."

SUN: Sounds easy. . . .
RESHAD: Well, it's hard work, and so is alchemy. Transforming

water is hard work, and we are as you know mostly water. But it's good work because it's the only way we can actually help anybody. Somebody said to me at a public meeting Wednesday night, "Well, what do I do with my negativity?" I gave her some examples, like what do you do when you have an intention and it never works out, and you feel really bad about it? Well, restate your intention, I said, clear your day and get out and do it. Every day is a new day. Of course it's hard work, but you pick yourself up and you do it. In talking about the heart, I'm talking about the inner heart. In the inner tradition of Sufism it's called the very, very secret place. That inner heart becomes your heart, which is no longer really your heart when all concepts of sentimentality and negative emotions are transformed into the stream of service. That is the meaning of the alchemy of the heart. Sufism is often called the alchemy of the heart.

SUN: At this point, what closes and blocks your heart most, and how do you deal with it when it does?
RESHAD: I have not seen my children for two and a half years, and I find it extremely difficult. I still have not faced the fact that in order to really be in the stream of service, you have to give up absolutely everything. For a very long time it blocked my heart. There they are in England and I'm 8,000 miles away, and then I realized that I even had to give up my children, and so my heart opened again. Now I would say that if my heart gets blocked it is only because of a mistake I have made, a judgment upon somebody or something. How I deal with it is through the same practice I give other people. It's called a clearing practice, which I do every evening.

Before going to bed, you decide what time you want to get up. That clears a lot, doesn't it, so you don't get too lazy? Also, you make a decision about something you're going to do the next day, even something simple like cleaning the shoes. You decide when you're going to do it, and visualize how you're going to do it. And do this exercise: lie on your back and relax your whole body. With the attention on the soles of your feet, remember the moment you got out of bed that morning. (In the morning, get *ready* to get out of bed — don't flop out of bed. As the soles of your feet touch the ground, say, internally, "May I be allowed to be of service this day?" And then say a prayer from whatever religious or spiritual background you come from. I say The Lord's Prayer.) Anyway, you lie on your back and put the memory pattern of when you got up in the morning on the soles of your feet, which represent the morning, since that's what hits the ground first. You let the energy come through your body, and with every memory you find, good or bad, you say, "Thank you" — thank you Father, or thank you God or whatever. You bring the energy up the body with the memories from the moment you got up, saying thank you, thank you, thank you, through the top of the head. You're still in the horizontal position. Then you do it again, and you find any other things that you haven't said thank you for. Then you do it a third time, and even if you've forgotten something, you've done a good job. Then you go to sleep, and, as I've said, when you get out of bed in the morning you say, "May I be allowed to be of service this day?" That thank you, that gratefulness, is the key to true will.

SUN: You've set up something called the Chalice Guild. In your description of it you talk of using the knowledge of transformation in your work, whatever your work is. Say I'm a carpenter, or a bus driver. How do I do that? How do I incorporate knowledge of transformation into my bus driving?
RESHAD: First you have to have the knowledge of transformation, don't you? This is the knowledge of the energies or aspects of the one energy, which ultimately is pure love, which are necessary to make transformation possible.

There was a man in England named Max Busby, who was a great alchemist many years ago. Do you know what he'd do? He knew the secret, and knew that it doesn't matter where you put it, in carpentry, in painting, in cooking. What he would do was put it into pebbles. He'd collect the pebbles from the ocean and he'd put it into the pebbles. These were called Busby pebbles. He made them for each individual — like pure Zen art, you never repeat it twice. I use all sorts of things — pieces of paper, glasses of water. He put the ingredient for that particular human being into a pebble, and you wouldn't believe what would happen. I tried it here recently. I had gophers in my garden that were pulling down the plants. I didn't want them there, and I didn't want to kill them either, so I merely took three rocks, stuck them in the right pattern and those rodents left the whole garden.

So you can put it into anything — poetry, making love, cooking, holding hands, anything.

If we are living in the question, undoubtedly we're going to get the answer, whether we like it or not, and often we don't like it. But still we accept it because we gratefully receive what we need to be of service.

There was a man named J.G. Bennett who has written so many extraordinary books, probably the greatest master in the West in our example of how we can get caught in sentimentality. He was about to open a residential school toward the end of his life, with 120 students. It was a superb experiment, with people coming from all over the world. He got sick about ten days before the school was to open. I was so upset and worried. I thought, "This man has given his whole life to serve, and now he'd gotten sick." What ridiculous sentimentality. I sent him some honey and flowers and other things with a note. I got a note back saying, "Dear Reshad, thank you very much for your sympathy but this is exactly what I need for my work. Yours, J.G. Bennett."

In other words, if we're in the question, we'll get everything we need, and not necessarily everything we want.

SUN: Tell me what you mean by living consciously.
RESHAD: At that particular moment you moved your hand from left to right with your pen in your left hand. I watched both eyes, I watched both feet. I was awake to my foot here on the ground, and my other one here on the chair. I was awake to looking through my glasses, to the glass in my left hand — all at once, and being grateful. That's something toward being conscious, that's not being conscious. To be conscious is way beyond that.

Your readers might not accept this as being conscious, but when J.G. Bennett first assembled his tribe of initiates, he had everyone stand up and put their arms up like this (holds his arms straight out, shoulder height, for the next five minutes of conversation). He stood up like that, at the age of seventy-three, in front of all these big, macho Americans, Australians and English, he stood up there for half an hour, forty minutes, until everyone but him had collapsed, half of them in tears. Now what is it that can keep my arms up right now without any trouble whatsoever? It's because I've trained my body to do what it's meant to do, and my emotions also. It may hurt like hell, but I've trained them to do it. That's will — it's not willfulness, but total gratefulness. I've already given my body back before it dies. My body was granted to this person to express the greater "I am," through the lesser "I am," this somebody called Reshad Feild. My arms can stay there an hour. This body must do what I tell it. It's like training a parrot.

SUN: As a retired Sufi, you keep a very busy schedule. Let's talk about some of the work you're doing, starting with healing. Let's speak, in some practical manner, about what esoteric healing is all about.

RESHAD: A great deal of my knowledge of conscious birth, sex and death — which has to do with esoteric healing — is in my last book, *The Invisible Way*. But let me put it to you this way. Esoteric healing is ultimately for one purpose — to know we are loved. *The Invisible Way* was originally going to be called *To Know We Are Loved*, but the publishers wouldn't have that title. I was long finding out, having had cancer and everything. As you know, I'm a laugher now. I laugh at everything because my heart is bubbling with laughter. I see the great joke. I see how you write your own book. I see that you make it up as you go along. And you can't really make it up as you go along unless you know you're loved. You merely make up your ego, and remake it and remake it and go on remaking it. But once you know that you're loved, once this knowledge is present, that, practically speaking, is esoteric healing.

I've been involved with healing for about twenty years. I'll give you a story about it that's a classic in my life. Last year a man came to me who was absolutely riddled with cancer. There was nothing I could do to help his body. He came to me in some pain. Well, the pain went very quickly, once he understood that there was one person who would stand by his side. You can face pain if someone's by your side. He telephoned me later and asked if he could come and see me. Of course I said yes. We were all so moved by him. When he came, he could scarcely get out of the car. I went out and opened the door for him. We came into the house together and he said, "I've come to say thank you, and good-bye." The next day he died, in absolute, complete freedom — because he knew he was loved. That is esoteric healing. If you can love your brother and sister in the present moment, then you're completing the ministry of Christ. That's all esoteric healing really means. As for the methodologies, it's like they say in America, "Different strokes for different folks." If you look in the Bible, Jesus never did it the same way twice. Nor do I. It comes out of my total respect for each individual, for the being of God in each individual.

SUN: In *The Invisible Way*, you said that healing doesn't always mean the body is healed. In fact, in the story of John in that book, healing meant opening to a conscious death. Can you speak about how death can be a healing process?
RESHAD: Death is what you're facing. To face death is to face the mirror, to really see yourself in the mirror. And where is the mirror? It's not a piece of shiny steel. As I sit here, you are my mirror. Can I face myself? Am I being honest? You are my mirror in this moment, so I'm facing my own death. I can remember this moment and everything around it, from the bookshelves to the noise of the typewriter. All at once.

SUN: Do you feel any fear of death?
RESHAD: No. The only fear I have is of pain. I have a very low threshold for it. But, no, I don't have any fear about death. I welcome it as a joyous celebration.

SUN: Let's talk about what you see as the causes of disease, and to what extent we create our own diseases, and create our own healing.
RESHAD: Well, actually we don't create our own diseases. We only repeat a pattern that's been set up. There's a saying in the Mevlevi tradition that expectation is the red death. Most of us were raised in expectation. We're meant to be doing something. That expectation is setting a pattern for our lives. The red death of expectation is what stifles a human being.

If one has knowledge, one does not expect. I don't know what will happen in the next moment, but I don't expect anything. The word expect is very important to look at. I used to be a racing car driver, and when I was racing, I couldn't expect for the motor to fall out, I couldn't expect for the car to crash. All I could do was train my body to train the car to go around the track. That's life.

SUN: So how do expectations influence our diseases?
RESHAD: A pattern. Let me tell you a story about that. A woman

came to me, she was only twenty-seven, I think. She had cancer of the uterus, and they were about to give her a hysterectomy. My work, by the way, is not an alternative to the medical profession. I respect the medical profession. In England I work with a team of doctors, I just add a little bit if I can. So, I did an analysis chart for her — the methods are too complex to go into here — and I discovered that when she was five and a half she had sexual shock. Sexual shock at five and a half? I didn't know how she would know what it was. She had absolutely no memory at all about it. So I said to her, "Suzanne, can you remember what happened at five and a half?" No, she couldn't. Well, I'm also trained to put people into a state in which they can dream consciously. I said to her that I knew I'd been given the correct answer and asked her to dream about it. She called me the next day, and though it hadn't happened while she was asleep, she actually saw it and had a complete recollection about being in the shower with her teen-aged brother. I don't know exactly what happened but the guilt she felt caused her to block that moment of time, what we call tightening around a moment of time. That caused a pattern of shock. Now, that alone wouldn't necessarily hurt. So I said to her, "Suzanne, did you enjoy it?" She said, "Yes." Now, in later life before getting cancer, she had been raped twice. So when I say she brought on her own rape, I don't mean she did it really, but that pattern of attraction drew to her not only the rapes but the cancer. If she was going to get cancer, where would she get it? In the place where she was attracting it from. So I spoke with her and we worked together. In three weeks there was no cancer.

SUN: So, if I'm hearing you right, it's the tightening around a moment of shock that on some level sets up an expectation that can attract a disease. . . .
RESHAD: Right, and what we're actually attracting to ourselves when we tighten is the unredeemed thought-form. I was privileged to spend some time with Krishnamurti, and when we first met he said to me, "You know, a thought-form never dies." That was a very important statement. But a thought-form can be redeemed.

SUN: So, if at this moment I were to receive a shock, say I were to be stabbed in the arm, to react in a way not to set such a pattern I would have to not tighten around the shock. . . .

RESHAD: Yes. If we could see that every experience we are given can be a conscious shock for good, rather than blaming the world for it. . . . If one falls off a bicycle, that can be useful — teaching you to ride a bicycle better next time — even if you break your arm. But if you blame the world for the shock, much trouble.

SUN: What if I come to you and say that I'm in need of some healing. Say I have a problem in my lung. How do I start to release the pattern that might have caused it? What is the first thing you say to me?

RESHAD: The first think I say is, "Thank you." If you come with hemorrhoids I say thank you. If you come with cancer I say thank you. The pain is a visiting card. It's only a manifestation of the problem. I don't purport to be a healer who can put a hand on you and it will be all gone. It's not like that. I say thank you, and let's have a look at it. Where is this coming from? It could be inherent in the physical body, in which case there is probably little I can do. But, on the other hand, I might be able to help. So I then go into the situation of the individual, and tell them that I will take them on for three months. During that time I check them "at a distance" every day and I do my best to clear that problem. There has to be reciprocity. My requirements are that they will come back to me at least every two weeks in that period, communicate with me and state how they are. In that way there is an interplay, like we have talking now. There's healing going on here.

Last year, I started a course on healing which was attended by quite a lot of people, whom I checked every day. There was one day when not one person came up for healing. That was the day when the Americans launched their space shuttle. Why? Everyone was looking up to see what was going on, and they forgot about their pains. I teach people that attitude. I have a tummy ache that I've had for almost thirty years. I got used to it. I look up, too — not to escape from this world, but to see what I have to do.

SUN: How do you help them to unblock their pain themselves?

RESHAD: I would teach people how to breathe properly. The method is tailor-made for the person. If somebody has a sexual problem — an unattended situation — I would teach them one way to breathe. If they had something else wrong I would teach them another way to breathe. So I give them a particular breathing pattern to use, plus the 7-1-7-1-7 rhythm I talked about in my book. That's helpful for everyone. [Reshad described this rhythm, called the Mother's Breath, in *The Invisible Way*, as breathing in to a count of seven, pausing for one count, breathing out to a count of seven, and then pausing for one count before repeating the cycle.]

SUN: Even with your capital letter words, I sense a real lightness and humor in your approach. How do you tickle yourself when you get too serious?
RESHAD: Kick my ass for being too serious. The only way I believe in being serious is when God grants you knowledge and you seriously will put it to good use. You seriously do it, but you still are light. We are a light. We're a spark of the divine flame.

SUN: But in pursuit of spiritual work one often gets heavy. . . .
RESHAD: I can only remember one time in recent years when I was serious. I was in a Tibetan monastery. I was waiting hours for my interview with the lama; I was expecting a whole lot — a burst of sunlight or something to illuminate my soul. He looked at me and said, "You're too ebullient. All you need to do now is to breathe in so that you may breathe out. Now go and do it." I started with six hours a day, then eight, then nine hours a day. And if you haven't got a sense of humor after that. . . .

I was in the meditation hall at one point and this might sound crazy, but I saw snakes and everything I was frightened of. I was petrified. I couldn't move. I got an interview with the lama the next morning and explained to him how everything I was frightened of in the elemental kingdom had come up. He said, "Good! Now continue breathing."

When we commit ourselves to life — and a teacher is very good for that — everything in life will come up, and then we have the opportunity for the total redemption of what is asked of us.

SUN: You've had some fall-outs over the years with everyone from teachers of yours to others for, as you've put it, "not behaving as they expect me to." What gets you in trouble?
RESHAD: I get in trouble because I know — and I say this in great humility — that nobody can lie to me. If people lie to me, then I'm

going to get myself in trouble, because I will not testify to lies, I will only testify to truth. I get in trouble because I am not what people expect me to be. Because they don't want the mirror. If I live in truth, I can see the truth in others. I can see the truth in you, and I know you are honest. I won't get in trouble with you. If somebody comes to me who does not speak the truth, I will cause myself much trouble.

People accuse me of this, they accuse me of that. It doesn't matter to me. It matters to them, and that's their problem. Their problem is merely an unattended situation. They don't have enough generosity or enough compassion, they have too much fear, whatever. To blame me for their problems is not appropriate.

SUN: You also get into trouble when people see you doing things they don't expect you to, like smoking a cigarette or drinking.
RESHAD: I knew you were going to ask that. I wouldn't advocate anybody smoking a cigarette. One day I smoke, one day I don't. It's not going to mean anything to me at all. It's the same with drinking alcohol. We have to have compassion for other people's situations. For example, I can't stand drugs. If I even smell marijuana, I'll run out of the room. Other people might not like me having a raw steak. We have to have compassion. I don't advocate anybody doing anything. All I advocate is compassion. It is not correct to use any method as an excuse for not facing oneself. But I have known people who have done some extraordinary things and still been able to complete their life-cycle.

In writing something like this in your magazine it might sound as though I was saying that you can do anything just for the sake of the moment. No. If I'm conscious I could take alcohol and transform it. If I'm not, I couldn't. There were times that I couldn't. There are times now when I can. But I in no way advocate it.

SUN: I was impressed in your last book with the depth of the romance portrayed between the character you based on yourself and the woman called "Nur." You're not with that same woman now. How do you reconcile it when your romantic expectations conflict with what actually happens?
RESHAD: Many people ask me who Nur is. Nur represents the distillation and ultimately the culmination of my total respect for

woman. So, Penny is Nur. If I let Penny down, I would be quite concerned for my own health. I've made many mistakes, many. Penny of course is Nur, and we've had a relationship for quite some years now which has been incredible. I have made quite enough mistakes. My respect and understanding and love of woman is because the anima in my own heart, in my own being, is at last balanced — it was always greater than my male aspect.

I respect Penny as my mirror. If she roars at me, even if she goes too far, I respect her still. There is nothing that is separate from the truth. There is nothing that is separate from my personal determination to complete the course of my life. If romance, or a better word for it is attraction, steps in my way, first of all I politely ask it to leave. And if it still won't, I yell "Out!"

SUN: In the book, the point was made that it was important to stay with that one woman.
RESHAD: There is only one woman. Until we can accept it we get lots and it causes us much trouble. There is only one woman. There's only one man. There's only one absolute being.

SUN: You've been through a number of marriages and relationships. What makes them work, and what makes them fall apart?
RESHAD: The moment you commit yourself, what we call the denying force comes in. It tests through arguments and whatever. I won't include my first marriage in this, because it wasn't really a marriage — we all make mistakes. I had a great son who was born from it. A child chooses his parents and I don't know why in the world he chose us. How I failed in my second marriage — and I accept I failed — was not doing sufficient homework. After all that I'd been taught by my teacher — of course, there's really only one teacher, God — I hadn't done enough homework about this thing called commitment. By committing yourself you determine that nothing will stop you from completing the course.

SUN: But what if you've committed yourself to the wrong thing?
RESHAD: You must ask first just what you're to commit yourself to. For example, I'm a writer but I avoided it for years. I wanted to be a lot of things, but not a writer. Then, I asked what God was giving me to do, as the manifestation of the frame of service. It may not at

all be what I thought I wanted to do. You ask and you find out. I know I'm best as a writer. When I get behind my typewriter I find my grounding. Your frame is your grounding.

(June 1983)

Tales of Trickster

David Citino

No. 3

Trickster, so life always will have
meaning and there will be more
salmon and trout, ponies and land,
makes himself an invisible fire and visits
the tent of one who's just fallen
and slowly burns away flesh from the muscle
and sinew from the bone, the very marrow
boiling away, to see to it that, while
most children are permitted to become
old women and men, and most of the sick
to become whole again, and most of the women
to remain women and most of the men
men, no matter how many tears fall
from the eyes of parents, lovers, daughters and sons,
no matter how deeply the fallen one's kin gash
their faces, arms and legs,
no matter how many curses and prayers fall
from their lips,
all the dead must stay forever dead.

No. 5:
Trickster Becomes Snake, Smoke, Umbilical Cord

When the daughters of the tribe
come down to the water
to mend nets and wash,
Trickster becomes a long black snake
sinuous in the weedy shallows
wriggling toward their legs,
to make them remember
their husbands and lovers
and run home, hands wild
in their hair, limbs gleaming,
a scream coiling in their throats.
Thus for one more day at least
the nets remain unmended,
the fish untaken.

When the sons of the tribe
go out to the fields to dig
or stalk game in the woods,
Trickster becomes the sinuous smoke
of the cooking fires rising high
above the village, and the scents
of rich loam, mushroom, musk,
to make them remember
their wives and lovers
and go home, clothes tight
around their hips.
Thus for one more day at least
the fields remain unfurrowed,
the deer unfallen.

The daughters and sons of the tribe
come together. Trickster becomes
a hot breeze and enters the tents
to see to it the men become
unyielding as the plow, the arrow,
the women as patient as the net,
pliant as the river. Trickster

shakes the tent poles.
In time, Trickster becomes
a long umbilical cord
joining the women to the new ones.
The midwives enter the tents
and cut him in two.
He dies until the next tale.

No. 6: The Gift of Fire

When Trickster saw that God
fashioned the first woman and man
out of clay with great care,
the pain of his cramped fingers
and the light of squinting eyes,
and that he painted their faces
in his own image
and baked them in his kiln
until they were done
and breathed hot life between their lips,

and when Trickster saw that God
placed them on the teeming earth unclothed
and then sent reckless winds
to snap their limbs
and floods to fill their bellies
with pestilence, and fire to burn away
the insides of bone and breast and lung
and rot their perfect flesh
he had a plan,
and held his sides and laughed,

and Trickster's laughter
became a tree that came apart in time
to nourish a grove
that came apart in time
to foster a great forest
that grew to cover all the land.
And walking in the forest woman and man

found shelter from the reckless winds, a home,
timber to build boats and weather floods,
and blossoming from seasoned wood, a gift of fire.

No. 7

Trickster in the days before
he became Trickster
when he was still a young man

left the tent and fire
of his mother and father
and walked out into the desert

to abstain from love, food and words
and meet God and ask
what he should do with his life.

After a week without women
his penis swelled with hurting
large as a rooster.

After three weeks without food
the pain moved up to his belly,
which bloated large as a calf.

After seven weeks without words
the pain moved up to his tongue,
which grew long as a snake.

After nine weeks of only light and dark
the pain moved up behind his eyes,
which blazed like midnight torchlight,

and he saw the face of God, who
shouted at him from inside his head
"Go home. I'll show you what to do."

When he walked into the village

he looked for women to have intercourse
with and to prepare him food

and he looked for friends
to speak with, and priests,
to describe to them the face of God

but the people feared his
swollen penis, distended belly,
black tongue, burning eyes,

and ran away. And from that day
Trickster became Trickster
and refused to forgive the people

and to this day they know him as
Adultery and Rape, Famine and Lies,
Hallucination and Mirage.

(December 1980)

About 1,000 people turned out for "An Evening With Ram Dass" in Memorial Hall on the University of North Carolina campus. This was a benefit for **THE SUN**. *Not only did Ram Dass have kind words for the magazine, but we raised nearly $4,000.*

Ram Dass is the Harvard professor turned psychedelic explorer turned spiritual teacher. Best known for his association, as Richard Alpert, with acid evangelist Timothy Leary, and, as Ram Dass, for his book Be Here Now, *his message has matured since those early days of the consciousness revolution. As we said last month, "his appeal is no longer merely to hippies and rebels, but to a broader constituency; he wears ordinary clothes again and his beard and hair are trimmed short; his own attachments, lusts, and fears are discussed with a candor striking for any public figure, let alone a "spiritual" teacher.*

Ram Dass' guru — Neem Karoli Baba, or Maharaji (an honorary title that means great king or wise one) — died in 1973, but the spirit of this extraordinary saint lives on in Ram Dass' teachings, and in other ways. In Ram Dass' latest book, Miracle of Love, *he explores his relationship with his guru, and many of the stories he told that night were about him.*

This edited transcript leaves out what words can't convey. There was Ram Dass' amazing chuckle — intimate, resonant, almost sly, as if he were laughing at a private joke (or a cosmic one). There were the silences. Breathing deeply — inner fingers tracing whatever maps he goes by, by whatever light — he'd pause, for ten or fifteen seconds, at the intersection of his world and ours. Then off he'd go — down the broad boulevards and darkened alleys of his own inner struggles. Some of the streets had foreign names, some were as familiar as your own block. After all, part of Ram Dass' appeal is his cultural savvy; he translates Eastern ideas into language Western minds and hearts can hear. He's one of us, reminding us we're One

— Ed.

An Evening
with Ram Dass

L ast night Sy Safransky was driving with me from the air-port. We were actually am-bling along. He's got a Rambler except the R and R are miss-ing. And we were talking, about how wonderful my last book was. It's a book made up of a thousand stories about my guru in India and he said that the quote he liked best was at the end of the chapter about how Maharaji died, or in India we'd say "dropped his body." This was one devotee's estimate of Maharaji: "He did everything ac-cording to nature. A child stays, a young man moves about, an old man stays. He did according to the laws of nature. If he wanted to, he could, but I don't think he changed nature for himself. When he was sick, he asked about medicine. When he was tired, he used to rest. When he got old, he died."

Maharaji had a heart condition and his doctor said, "Take this medicine every day at ten o'clock." So the old women who were talking care of him are told to give him the medicine at ten o'clock, but at ten past ten they've forgotten, and he says to them, "If you don't take better care of me, I'll turn your minds against me." That's a funny one. Because you realize we're the only ones that go away from God. God doesn't go away from us. Our karma is *our* karma, the veil is the veil of our *own* separateness.

Now, Maharaji didn't go around producing miracles, but he was in a universe where there was so little attachment that when he thought of something, it became what he thought. Our own thoughts are so interspersed with other thoughts and ourselves thinking about our thinking, that they have no power, they are not one-pointed like a laser beam. But Maharaji could go somewhere with his thought and find out what was going on and come back and report about it; Maharaji could go there and manifest a subtle body and be there so that people saw him and talked to him, and leave his gross body at home; Maharaji could take his gross body with him. He could walk through walls.

There was an old uncle that was blind. Maharaji was at the house, and the family said to him, "Maharaji, he's blind, but you could heal his blindness." And he said, "No, saints in the old days could do that but nobody can do that anymore, everybody's too impure." And they said, "Oh, you could do it," and he said, "No, no, I can't do it." Maharaji was always yelling for this and that, and he called for some pomegranate, and had them squeeze it, and then he took a drink of it, and he put his blanket over his face. Somebody looking under the blanket saw two red lines coming out of his eyes, probably pomegranate juice, you think. You think blood, but then you think pomegranate juice. Then he gets up and says he's got to go to the train. He says to the uncle, "If by any chance God should heal you, and you should see again, you're an old man and your kids are waiting for you to retire so they can take over the business, they know the business, let them take the business and you spend the rest of your life for God, just devote it to thinking about God," And the uncle said, "Oh, I will, Maharaji, I will."

Maharaji left and went to the train station, and about a half hour later the uncle could see. The doctor arrived and said, "This could not be. Who did this?" See, in the West when something like that happens the doctor says, "This could not be," and then refuses to admit that it is. In the East, he says, "This could not be, who did this?" Somebody said, "It was Maharaji, he's gone to the train." So the doctor ran to the train, and he climbed aboard and fell at Maharaji's feet. Maharaji was hitting him on the back, saying, "This is a good doctor, he's the man that cured his blindness, he's a good doctor, he cured the blindness, he's a wonderful doctor." Three months later the uncle went back to work and the next day he went blind.

I like those kind of stories. I mean, they have a punch to them. You like them and you don't because they're laughing at you. It's like the *Third Chinese Patriarch of Zen*. It's a little booklet. I've been spending about six years with this little booklet. I haven't even gotten through the first four lines yet. Well, you try, before you laugh. I'll just give them to you: "The great way is not difficult for those who have no preferences. When love and hate are both absent, everything becomes clear and undisguised. But make the slightest distinction, and heaven and earth are set infinitely apart." See why it may take you a while?

"For those who have no preferences. . . ." You have preferences. What could it mean? What it could mean is that you cease to identify with your preferences, not that you don't have preferences. T they're no longer *my* preferences, they're just preferences. Wha favorite color? Blue. Who are you? I am somebody whe color is blue. Definition. Definition, to the extent you id limitation. You're already turning off some of the ur is to be full of opinions and attitudes. That's life. sitting in perfect equanimity and spaciousness, an Doing nothing, yet everything gets done. It's so e do is give up being who you think you are — giv who you think you are, because you aren't.

You should see what I'm seeing: twelv "Exit." And I'm thinking there is no exit. T They'll just lead to more of it. You can't get o You'll create it wherever you go. You're everybody's a slide-projector looking for sc nice. . . . I'm listening too, you know. I'd k this evening. I'm not doing this for you. I'r Sy and **THE SUN** although **THE SUN** because this is what I do. Jerry Garcia plays the guitar all day long; that's what he does. In his off-time he plays the guitar; that's what he does. This is what I do. It's not better or worse than what you do; it's just different.

Let's say your occupation is being a mother. It's awfully easy to get caught in mother love, isn't it? There's a great story about Krishna, who is one of these beings that dropped in full-blown. You see, most of us come in thinking that we're babies, but he didn't. He wasn't fooled for a second. There was no karma at all. So he's lying there in his mother's arms and suddenly he opens his mouth to yawn and she looks into his mouth and there are the planets and the stars and the universe, and of course she freaks. And then the line is, "At that moment, he veiled her eyes with the veil of mother love once again." There's an occupational hazard, because who do you think your baby is, anyway? Who your baby is is who you think you are. You think, I'm a mother, there's a child.

It's interesting what you see when you look at other people. You see bodies. Ectomorphs, endomorphs and mesomorphs. Or you see desirable, a competitor for what is desirable, and irrelevant. That's another category system within that domain.

Or you could flip the channel from the physical. You look around and you see the Minnesota Multiphasic Personality Inventory profiles. There's a manic-depressive with an hysteric overtone, if I ever saw one. People in therapy tend to dwell in that plane. Everybody wants something. I need this. I need love. I need. I need. Who are you? I need. Oh, sorry to bother you, you're busy needing, I'll see later. Who are you? I give. Oh, that's interesting. As long as you you're somebody, you've got to have somebody else to comple-. If I think I'm speaking, you've got to think you're listening just a game only one of us is playing. We're all in drag. Oh, I'm receiving. I'm learning. I'm bored. I'm hot. That's a [It was a warm evening, with no air-conditioning.] I'm 's a little righteous. If you were, you probably wouldn't

an flip the channel once more, and you look around e's only twelve people, and various subtle permuta- iously a Sagittarius. I can see it by the way you are

n all these grids of individual differences. For

years, I wished I had more hair. I went around combing it over and around and wishing I had the guts to have a wig. And if you asked me who I was I'd say, "I'm somebody who is balding." If you have a wart and think it's an ugly wart, you're busy being somebody with an ugly wart.

I've got a fellow staying at my house in Santa Fe. He's a beautiful guy. He's twenty-three, he's English and he's very charming and erudite and good-looking and athletic. The only thing is, he's got Hodgkin's disease and he's got a huge tumor on his neck and under his arm which is growing all the time. And he said to me the other day, "You know, I'd really like intimacy with a woman, but I feel so ugly." And I found it so easy to go into it with him. You see how seductive it is? I mean, you can say in the abstract that it's nothing, but when you see him like this, it's hard for the first few times you're with him not to become fascinated with his tumor.

Elisabeth Kubler-Ross once told her audience about a nurse who was twenty-eight and had four children and had more than a hundred operations for cancer already. If you came into a hospital room with her, Elisabeth asked, what would you feel? And everybody in the audience had a different feeling — anger, self-pity, anger at God, sadness, fear, tenseness. She then asked them to imagine that they were that nurse, and what it would feel like. Everyone will be so busy seeing you as a cancer victim that nobody will be with you. Everybody is too busy reacting to your symbolic value.

See how the game would be not to react to the symbolic value? But you can only do that when you're not caught in a symbolic value of your own. As long as you're somebody, all you're going to see out there are more somebodies. If you're physical, you'll see physical; if you're psychological, you'll see psychological; if you're astral, you'll see astral — all in terms of individual differences, to which you will apply the labels "better" and "worse."

If you flip the dial once more, and you look into somebody's eyes, you see another person looking back at you, another being in there. The eyes are the windows of the soul. Are you in there? Far out, I'm in here. How'd you get into that one? And you see everybody packaged in these matrices of individual differences. What trip are you running through this time? Oh, this time I'm a sexy blonde. That's nice. What are you running through? Well, this time I'm a responsible member of the community. Pretty good.

Interesting work.

Imagine somebody has just died, and they were quite conscious. I mean, they didn't die like most people around us die — "Ahh, no! Freeze me! Dry me, do anything, but keep me alive." But this is somebody that died saying, "Well, here we go. Ohh." Dead. Then you're out there, running through your past life, or lives, whatever the case may be, depending on how clear your vision is. You know, my whole life flashed before my eyes — that one. It's a low-level, early stage that you can remember if you happen to be resuscitated. So you look at your karmic scorecard, so to speak, and you say, "Gee, I got a lot of energy. I think I'll take another human birth, a lot of good sandpaper in that." Human births are really good to have, because there's a lot of abrasiveness to rub against, to purify. When you're an angel, it's draggy, there's nothing to rub against, it's all fine, so you can carry karma for thousands of years as an angel. As a human, you get it in your face all the time. So, "I think I'll take a human birth, and let's see, I know what I'll do, I'll be born into the poorest tribe in Africa, that would be great, because that will take care of the time I was a miserable, cruel king. I'll get raped at seven — that'll take care of that one. I think I'll get syphillis at thirteen, I could fit that one in, and then I'll go blind at fifteen and I'll die at seventeen. Okay. Fair enough. Looks like a good one. Cram-packed."

You build a little sign, saying what you are, because you've got to wait for somebody to need you, since we are each other's karma, and kids are parents' karma — so it needs two people, two others who need you like you need them. You wait with your sign and the big computer in the cosmos whirs — it's all outside of time so it doesn't matter — and sooner or later, two beings appear who need you. "Okay, we'll go ahead and we'll call you." And they go ahead and call you, and you say to everybody, "See you around." And you go in. "Waah. Waah!" You've got to cry, because you've got to make it real. If you don't get stuck in it, it's not working out your karma. You've got to stay right on the edge, stuck but not quite. That's the whole secret. But if you don't get stuck at all, you're like Krishna, you're just riding through to say hello and spread a few blessings.

Buddha said we have five hindrances. The first one was . . . I wonder why I don't remember it . . . lust and greed. That's just the first one. All this time we've been treating them as two. Then there's hatred and ill-will. There's agitation, and our old friend sloth and torpor, and the fifth one is doubt. Buddha was pointing out that these are really the stuff of which suffering, or clinging, is made. So, giving you the benefit of the doubt, you have to have at least one of them in some subtle form to be here on Earth, because that's your passport into incarnation, unless you just came to bless us.

Did it ever dawn on you that it's perfect? Oh God, that's heresy isn't it? I mean, every righteous bone in your body is fraught with indignation at this moment. What do you mean, it's perfect. Cruelty, barbarism, starvation. Auschwitz. Hiroshima. The Shah of Iran. God, you really screwed up that time. I mean, if I were making that guy, I would have made him a heavy until the last minute, and then he would have turned it all over to the people. I don't understand what your trip is, God. Some kind of sadist? From what place are you judging God? From your little piece of the rock? Oh boy!

As you quiet down, and empty, and get over the polarities — like good and evil, for example — and start to float around the edge of dualism and non-dualism, you come to a causal plane. The laws of the universe. They're not laws you know with your intellect nor that you can conceptualize, so you never know you know them. You have merely for a moment been them. That's who you are when you are finished being who you think you are. Then you come back into being who you think you are again, and you have those laws as a memory. You keep evolving until you are resting in the law, you are the law, the One, you are also one of the many. Only initially is the game to get high. Getting high is because of the attachment to one's separateness. You want to get out of it, you want to be together, you want a union, you want to co-habit, to transcend your separateness, break through. Surfing can do it, or skiing, or riding a motorcycle, or hang-gliding, or trauma can do it, or drugs, or meditation, or sex, even cooking a bouillabaisse, if you know how to do it.

I hope I'm not irritating you because I'm not more godly. Every time I look around to see what godly is, I am forced to conclude that something isn't, and that fascinates me, so I look at what isn't and it turns into what is. So there you are. It's all the beloved.

When you look into another person's eyes and see the other being looking out at you, you begin to experience that you two are part of another kind of community, a community of the spirit, or of awareness, that doesn't exist in time and space. I remember once in Nepal, Bhagwan Dass was teaching me Om Mani Padme Hum, the mantra, and I did it for two days, day and night, Om Mani Padme Hum . . . [a number of times]. After about two days, in the middle of the night, I stopped to go to the bathroom, and I stopped but it didn't. I started to hear thousands and thousands of voices, like ocean waves rolling in all directions, back in history and out through time, timeless. Om Mani Padme Hum . . . and so I freaked. It wasn't like hearing my own voice, or an imitation of my voice. There were thousands of distinct voices. I went running out to Bhagwan Dass and I said, "You don't know what I'm hearing." He said, "You're hearing the sound of all those that have done that sound purely, have tuned into the sound, have become the sound. A mantra does you, you don't do a mantra. You just pump it up until it starts to do you, and you're cooked when you and the mantra become one. Then you're finished with the mantra, you can use it or not."

Sometimes I get caught in hindrance number one, lust and greed, and I'm feeling lust in which everyone becomes an object that's relevant or irrelevant. Lust has a whole projection system which can only be gratified by something you can use to close the circle of the projection. It has no real people in it, it's just a mind net. You go fishing for something that fits in the net. I see somebody that fits, and I start my tracking behavior, which is, "Hello. I'm Ram Dass. Don't you want to come and see my holy pictures?" It all too often works, but then I'm faced with this predicament that if I should per chance look into the other person's eyes, I see my guru — this fat, tough old bastard looking out of these eyes, laughing at me, saying, "Gotcha that time, didn't I?"

Compassion is to leave people alone to be who they think they are, but if they consider the possibility they aren't who they think they are, you're there to be with them when they think they're somebody different. You're a good environment for people to be free to grow — instead of, "I know you, you're Sam and you've got a nasty disposition." Poor Sam. I mean, if Sam should be happy one day, it's already deception.

We have to stop getting one another in our roles and labeling for efficiency. I want to know who you are, that you're who you were yesterday, so you don't screw up, so I don't have to think about you anymore. You're my father and you're this way. Stay it. Keep cool. You fit in that category. I can't function if I don't have categories.

What happens if I have to look to see who everybody is each time?

Well, you don't. You play within the roles perfectly, but you're always available to step out when somebody wants to dance. I remember being pinched for going too slow in my Buick limousine on a freeway in New York State. I had the trunk out — I was living in the back part of it — and it was a beautiful antique limousine on the outside. He stopped me and said, "License and registration." And I had been driving this big tank for hours and I was doing mantra, and I was so out there I had just enough ground to keep the car going. That's how they always know, because you're going too slow. So he said, "License and registration," but when I looked at him, he obviously was Krishna in drag, he was being a policeman. I saw immediately who he was. I just looked into his eyes. I mean, there was Krishna giving me darshan, right there. How else would he come? "License and registration?" Now I have a choice. I can say, "I know who you are, you're Krishna." But that is not what Don Juan calls impeccable warriorness. So I hand him my license and registration, friendly-like, and he looks at them and he checks me out on the radio and says, "What is in that box next to you?" And I said, "They're mints, would you like one?" And I'm offering this to Krishna, I'm just looking at him with love. And he's being somewhat guarded. I'm sure people have been shot by people who look at them with love. Then he's done, but he hasn't finished with me yet. I can see he doesn't know why, but something's happening. Yet it's a very limiting game because he's a state trooper. He says, "Nice car you got there." That's another gambit you can slide into, another strategy, and you can still be macho in it. "Good car, oh, I mean, back in the twenties we. . . . Once I drove one of these through a snow storm." "Did you really?" "Straight eight, yeah. . . ." "No, it doesn't use oil. . . . Fifty thousand. . . . " "That's amazing." You can play that for quite awhile. All the time I'm looking at Krishna saying, "Come on off it." But I see he's absolutely perfect in his role. Finally, he gets done and says, "Well, be gone with you," which is pretty far out already. So I start to drive away, and he walks to his police car and he turns around and I look in my rear-view mirror and he's waving at me. I was going to stop and say, "You blew it. State troopers don't wave, baby, that's just not the way it's done. Stay in your role. Be impeccable. Glare or something."

If you aren't busy being anybody in particular, you can run

yourself through these different realities, and see if there's anything interesting to catch hold of inside you. You run realities through you to see if you'll grab onto any of them. Walter Cronkite gives you a reality every night. Well *that's* real. Ah, got you didn't he? That's because he thinks he's Walter Cronkite. Imagine if Walter Cronkite didn't think he was Walter Cronkite. Maharaji said to me, "Lincoln was a great president." I said, "Why was that, Maharaji?" He said, "Lincoln knew Christ was president. He was only acting president."

At first we were all trying to get high. We were trying to get to that place where we can look in each other's eyes and say, "Wow, are you there?" That is a place of love and at first you don't know how to get there and sometimes you meet somebody that turns you on to it. They become your connection to the place in yourself where you are in love and you say, "I am in love with you." Meaning, "You are my connection to me exploring the place in myself where I am love" — if you were to say it more exactly. But you say, "I love you," and you focus in on that person because as long as you're with that person that thing turns on in you. But in the course of deepening your awareness, you begin to rest in that place more and more, without the need of an external stimulus. You have certain habits of response when that thing happens to you, and it gets very complicated. You meet somebody and look in their eyes and it happens. You say, "Oh God, I love you, let's build a nest." Then you say, "I'm going out for tofu and yogurt." And you're at the tofu and yogurt store and you're at the check-out stand and you look into the eyes of the check-outer and there it is again. Because you're carrying it with you. If you're Typhoid Mary, every place you look has typhoid. So you say, "Have you ever considered a *menage a trois?*" Where do you go from there? Communes? Adamites? Finally you realize you can't collect on it every time it happens. So you shift gears, and when it happens, you say, "Did you feel what I felt? Wow, I love you. See you around." "Yeah, bye, we'll be together forever." Then you get further out. Because it keeps happening. It gets a little draggy to keep saying that. Finally, you say, "Ah, wow." And then finally you just widen your eyes a little bit with somebody, and they widen their eyes, and it's like dimming your headlights for a moment. It's an acknowledgement that we're here. Like a club. Like a secret handshake.

There's a great story about the king whose wise man came to

him and said, "I'm sorry but all the wheat has been ruined this year and everybody that eats it, everybody in your kingdom, is going to go mad. But what I have done, as your wise man, is put aside a little of last year's wheat, so there'll be enough for you and a little for me, so we don't have to go mad." So the king, in a kingly fashion, paced back and forth. Finally, he said, "What would be the value of staying sane if all my subjects are mad? No, we'll go mad, too." And then he paused and said, "You know, it would be perhaps useful if we could notice this moment. So let's put a mark on each other's forehead so that every time we meet we'll know we're mad."

What are you and I doing in Chapel Hill, North Carolina? What do we think we're doing, being humans on this kind of an Earth? Mad. But I look in your eyes and I see you know it, too — ah, you have the mark of madness. We call it being in love. It's just a widening of the eyes. Finally, you don't even do that. You just meet eyes and go on. As long as the faith flickers you've got to run it through someone else to make sure, to validate it.

Do you need a guru? Well, if you're busy asking that question, you'd never know if one walked up to you. If you just open, whatever happens, happens. You don't need one anyway. You've taken an incarnation that is absolutely perfect to work out your karma. I'll tell you how form-fitted it is. It isn't just some schlock, factory-ready garment. This thing is so tailor-made that every experience in your life — every single one of them, what you felt on the toilet this morning, every one of them — is designed within that game to awaken you, if you want to use it. You're given an entire road map out. Every step you take is another step on it, the minute you see it's a road map. If you don't see it's a road map, you just walk over it like a piece of old newspaper. Which one you do is your karma. It's all in the map. At some point in the map it says, "At this point, awareness becomes aware it's a map." You have to realize that you're in prison. If you think you're free, there's no hope for you at this point. Being in prison means I'm identified with the storyline. I'm busy being the butler in the pantry, instead of the person who's reading the book. Let alone, the person that wrote the book — which is who you are. And you are the book. Once you realize that, getting high is merely a device to release your attachment to the place you thought you were. Then you begin to be fascinated with why you come down. As you focus on why you come down you begin to suspect that you are treating down, down. You're treating it in some pejorative way. Alan Watts was the first one that said it to me: "Dick, your problem is that you're too attached to emptiness. Imagine a microscope, a culture on a slide, and the microscope is out of focus so that when you look into the microscope, you see a homogenous white field. But then as you focus the microscope, you bring the slide into focus and you see the culture. And you see all the exquisite forms that God takes."

He was describing another part of the cycle. Because the cycle is that you go from the many into the One, not to sit in the One, but to come back to play in the many. And it is play as long as you are rooted in the One, and at play in the two. If you are only rooted in the two reaching for the One, the two is all too real and it's not yet play, because there's a lot of suffering. Because you're still attached. Suffering is the result of attachment or clinging.

A truly conscious relationship is two people coming together in order to use the relationship to know the One, to be the One, at which point there is only one of them with two bodies, and they play as two. They go between two and one and two and one. A true bhakti, or devotional, yogi gets it down to almost every breath. It's like being in a sexual embrace in which you go in and out of union with your partner. So now there is somebody enjoying it, and then there are no enjoyers, there is merely, "Unh." It's like, "Here I come here I come here I come. That was great that was great that was great." But at the moment, there's nobody around. See? You go between the moment and the separateness. Like Hanuman, the monkey, who is the perfect servant of Ram, who is God, in the *Ramayana*. Hanuman is kneeling at the feet of Ram. He's found the lost wife of God — Sita. Ram feels very indebted to Hanuman and wants to lift him up and sit him next to him. That means they would merge into Oneness. Hanuman makes himself like stone in order to stay separate, so he can enjoy his beloved. Now that's an interesting one. You enjoy and then you merge and you enjoy and you merge.

Ramakrishna said, "People weep for their children. They weep for their relatives. They weep for their parents. They weep for their money. But who weeps for God?" The only reason for a relationship among conscious beings is to awaken. That's it. The rest of it is just part of the melodrama. How to deal with the melodrama? That was my problem. And then I saw that the game is closing the circle and coming right back into the forms, so you are in the world, but not of the world. Suddenly, the thing to get me to God was learning how to be a good son to my father, a good citizen, an ecologically conscious being, a socially caring human being, learning to remember my zip code, and do my laundry, and having integrity about my being. I had to have relationships, and jealousy and rage and anger. I had to bring it all out of the closet all over again. I was so busy being Ram Dass because I was trying to be out there and everybody was saying, "Come hear Ram Dass, he'll get us out there." Sure it's fine for me to be out there, but I'm also right here. And I've got to stop putting it down and putting it away. I've got to work with it and live with it and love it and honor it and find God in it. [Applause.] You just have to be careful that applause doesn't come out of your attachments.

The final trap about bringing it all home is that you're going to get caught in it. And the one you're going to get caught in, in the last analysis, is righteousness, doing good. It's a real drag. It's a stance. "I do good." Don't get lost in giving and receiving. Because if you're a giver, someone else has to be a receiver, and that keeps you both separate, keeps you within your roles. "You a giver? I'm a receiver. Great." It's the symbiosis of the illusion of separateness.

If you keep meditating through all polarities, and go from dualism into non-dualism, and then come back, you see that all polarities are merely relatively real, including good and evil, and that behind good and evil here we are. I do crummy things, I do beautiful things. Does that mean I'm good or evil? I'm neither. I just am. We will collaborate to create a conscious set of laws to stop the crummy things, and we will help along the good things, within that plane of relative reality. But don't think that's real. It's just relatively real. Once you are rooted in the One, then you can play at the two, and it turns out that you don't kill and you don't steal. I look at you and you are me and I am you. So who am I going to steal from? I put out the six-record album, "Love, Serve, Remember," in a box a while back. It was a beautiful box with a set of photographs and words and six records mail order to you for $4.50. My father looked at it, and he said, "Very impressive." He said, "You know that thing must be worth. . . . You could get fifteen dollars for it." I said, "That's right." He said, "Why are you only charging four and a half?" I said, "Well, it only cost me four and a half." He said, "Wouldn't people pay for it if you charged fifteen?" I said, "Yes, they'd pay for it." He said, "I don't understand you. Are you against capitalism?" I said, "No." I was trying to think of a way to share with him the predicament. I said, "Dad, remember you tried this case for Uncle Henry?" "Yeah." "Was it a tough case?" "Oh, it was a stinker. I worked in the law library weeks." "You must have charged him a healthy fee, because you know you charge good fees." "What, are you out of your mind? It's Uncle Henry." I said, "Well, that's my predicament. Everybody is Uncle Henry. If you show me somebody who isn't Uncle Henry, I'll rip him off."

With the One deeply embedded in your being, you live in the two, in a purely dharmic way, because that's merely the form you manifest in, because who wants new karma? You're just old karma running off then because you're no longer creating new karma — because karma arises from attachment. I use the words "karma" and "reincarnation" realizing that all of these are meta-illusions and that behind it nothing has happened. There is no time and there is no space, there are no forms, as every self-respecting quantum mechanist now tells you. The universe you see yourself to be living in is your own projection of your own karma. Which scenario do you want? How about the scenario that you and I are very, very high beings. We've been waiting around thousands of years for a unique opportunity to take birth in a situation that could be our last incarnation. It would be a particularly fierce one because everything would be destroyed and fall apart. And then finally the paranoia would be so great that somebody would push a button, and there would be a big mushroom cloud, and we would all get enlightened. Do you like that scenario? It's just as real as the others. In that case, "No, no don't push the button. . . . Hey, baby, push the button, come on, we want to get enlightened." The secret is not being attached to any of the scenarios, functioning within all of them.

How do you function within all those different scenarios? Are we these high beings waiting to be enlightened by the bomb? Are we part of the new age that is going to convert the Earth into a beautiful consciousness garden? Are we going toward more and more destruction and paranoia, and ugliness and heaviness, which is finally going to end in just yecchhh? Who could you be if you are trying to live in all three scenarios? Well, you would do just what you came to Earth to do. You would use each experience as a vehicle for awakening out of the illusion of scenarios. And you would find a way to do that perfectly within each scenario by doing what you had to do. You end up being much less attached to what you do. Everybody says, "What do you do? And what will you do then? What are you going to do when you grow up?" Finally you just do what you do. "I'm going to the bathroom now. Now I'm going to wash my hair. Now I'm going to buy a shirt." A river doesn't say, "Now I'm going to turn left. Now I'm going to glisten." A river is mindless in the sense that it's not self-conscious. It's pure consciousness. It's pure awareness. It's pure love. It's pure presence.

One night I was invited by a number of pushers to share in some LSD at Owsley Stanley's house. The ceiling was all decorated psychedelically. And there was the purest acid. It was so pure I took it intravenously. And I had just time to lie down as I went out on an elevator, out into the cosmos. I was having a wonderful trip, just like going to the moon, going to la-la land it's called. As I was soaring out, I felt a tension below. I looked down, and there was one of the young pushers having a bad trip. Owsley was standing next to him with *The Psychedelic Experience,* a manual based on *The Tibetan Book of the Dead* that Tim Leary and Ralph Metzger and I put together. He's reading to him from it. So, I figure I'm getting called. I've got to go to work. I pull myself back into form. I get up, and I walk over, and I fall on top of this guy and I whisper in his ear, "Now that you've got all our consciousnesses, what do you want to do with them?" He turns to me with total hate in his eyes and he says, "I'm going to take my chick, and my motorcycle, and I'm going to get my .38 and come back, and blow your fucking brains out." And I looked into his eyes and said, "If you do that, you'll be killing a really beautiful guy, but if you've got to do it, you've got to do it." So, he got up, and the girl didn't want to leave, of course, so he grabbed her. He headed for the door, black leather jacket, fury. Everybody was stunned. And I said to him, "Well, we're going to stay here because it's nice and warm. We are your friends, but you don't think so, so you go and do whatever you're going to do, but on your way — you obviously don't trust any of us — you could look up at the stars, because they are certainly trustworthy." The door slammed and we all sat there in our own thoughts. After about three or four minutes, the door crashed open. He was sobbing, and he came in, and he fell in the middle of us. We were all through it at that point. He had gotten caught in the reality of a mind projection, but running it against the stars just cleared his head. He heard the message, and he was ready to let go. What we often need are those kinds of mirrors in order for us to see the ways in which we are caught in our mindsets, in who we think we are.

But that doesn't always work. I was with a couple yesterday in Washington State. They said, "Won't you stay at our house? We'll take care of you and we'll love you." I thought, "Well, I usually don't do that, but okay." I came into their house. It was the day they had a terrible fight. So, there are the two of them. She is hysterically rushing around the kitchen cooking. He is sitting solemnly in the corner. The kids are screaming, and I think, "What have I done to deserve this one? Ah God, this is a good one. I thought I was going to get a day off." I realized, as Maharaji said, "You don't have to change anyone, just love them." If it's their karma to fight, then it's none of my business. But I'm there and I love them. Every now and then one of them would come and bounce against me in one way or another. The minute I wouldn't buy into the trip they'd walk away disgusted. Because each one is saying, "This is how it is. You see how it is, don't you?" I'm saying, "Right. And that one, too. Here we all are." "No, you don't understand." And they would walk away.

You've got to want to let go of your trip. If you want to keep it, keep it. Ten thousand births . . . . Go right ahead, no rush. Do you know what kind of a time scale we are dealing with? Buddha describes it: a mountain, six miles long, six miles wide, six miles high. And every hundred years a bird flies over it with a silk scarf in its beak, running the scarf across the mountain once every hundred years. In the length of time it takes the scarf to wear away the mountain, that's how long you and I have been doing it already. You know those bugs that are born in the morning and die at night. Around noon they say, "Boy, this is life."

Finally, compassion is to stop laying trips on each other, to do what you do so impeccably that you are a statement who attracts, just by the nature of your being. Mahatma Gandhi was in a train pulling out of a station with reporters running along the platform saying, "Mahatma-ji, would you give me a message to take back to the people?" The train is picking up speed and Gandhi just had time to scribble on a piece of paper bag which he hands to the guy. The paper says, "My life is my message."

So it is with each of us. Our life is our message. You have to honor all of the individual differences within the way karma manifests. But, in everyone, when done purely, it brings you into such a state of grace that the light pours out of you, and everybody looks. As Ramakrishna says, "When the flower blooms, the bees come uninvited."

There is a wonderful doctor, Larry Brilliant, who is with the World Health Organization. His wife was in India where she met Maharaji. And she came back to America to get him. He was a pretty hip doctor. He was a political activist in Berkeley in the sixties. And he had been in Cuba. [He reads from *Miracle of Love*] "My wife had met Maharaji, had come to get me in America and bring me back to meet him. When we first went to see Maharaji I was put off by what I saw. All these crazy Westerners wearing white clothes and hanging around this fat old man in a blanket. More than anything else I hated seeing Westerners touch his feet. On my first day there he totally ignored me. I began to grow very upset. I felt no love for him. In fact, I felt nothing. I decided that my wife had been captured by some crazy cult. By the end of the week I was ready to leave. We were staying at the hotel up in Nanital and on the eighth day I told my wife that I wasn't feeling well. I spent the day walking around a lake thinking that if my wife was so involved in something that was clearly not for me, it must mean that our marriage was at an end. I looked at the flowers, the mountains, the reflections in the lake, but nothing could dispel my depression. Then I did something that I had never really done in my adult life — I prayed. I asked God, 'What am I doing here? Who is this man? These people are all crazy. I don't belong here.' Just then I remembered the phrase, 'Had ye but faith, ye would not need miracles.' 'Okay God, I don't have any faith. Send me a miracle.' I kept looking for a rainbow, but nothing happened. So I decided to leave the next day. The next morning we took a taxi down to Kenshi to the temple to say goodbye. Although I didn't like Maharaji, I thought I'd just be very honest and have it out with him. We got to Kenshi before anyone else got there and we sat in front of his tucket, the wooden bed on the porch. Maharaji had not yet come out from inside the room. There was some fruit on the tucket and one of the apples had fallen on the ground, so I bent over to pick it up. Just then Maharaji came out of his room and stepped on my hand, pinning me to the ground. So there I was, on my knees, touching his foot, in that position I detested. How ludicrous. He looked down at me and asked, 'Where were you yesterday?' Then he asked, 'At the lake?' He said 'lake' in English, the rest was in Hindi. When he said the word 'lake' to me, I began to get this strange feeling at the base of my spine, and my whole body tingled. It felt very strange. 'What were you doing at the lake?' I began to feel very tight. 'Were you horseback riding?' 'No.' 'Were you boating?' 'No.' 'Did you go swimming?' 'No.' And he leaned over and spoke quietly, 'Were you talking to God? Did you ask him for something?' When he did that I fell apart and started to cry like a baby. He pulled me over and started pulling my beard, repeating, 'Did you ask for something? Did you ask for something?' That really felt like my initiation. By then others had arrived, and they were around me, caressing me, and I realized then that almost everyone there had gone through some experience like that. A trivial question such as 'Were you at the lake yesterday?', which had no meaning to anyone else, shattered my perception of reality. After that I just wanted to rub his feet."

Since you can't be attached to any scenario, you merely work to bring the world back together again, and then how it comes out, it comes out. It's always in the law. Relax, do your part. Don't get freaked about the outcome. It doesn't matter. It's all doing fine. And the way it happens is by living in a world of us. But, you've got to start, first. "Do what you do with another person," Kabir says, "but never put them out of your heart." Do whatever you do, fight them, kill them, but don't put them out of your heart. If you can keep another being with you in love, you can do anything. We used to do parent-child research in psychology. And it turned out it didn't matter whether people spanked their children, or didn't. It was how they did it. You could spank your child in such a way that they just got more and more loving and open and beautiful. You could spank them in such a way that they became neurotic little monsters. It depends on who you thought you were. Were you the lover or the spanker? If you were the spanker you were really creating conditional love. If you were the lover you were creating unconditional love and just straightening up a sloppy act.

There's a couple in Ashland, Oregon. You may have read about it. They had a twelve-year-old girl who went out to play tennis with another girl and both were sexually assaulted and murdered. Somebody sent me the clipping, and said, "These people have read your books and listened to your tapes, and it would be nice if you wrote them a letter." I opened my heart to the situation and the pain was so unbearable. Somebody as innocent and precious as that going through *that* at the last moment of life. The agony was so great I couldn't imagine what kind of a letter I could write. And I had to meditate for hours to get free of the power of that story line. Here's the letter:

"Steve and Anita, Rachel finished her brief work on Earth and left the stage in a manner that leaves those of us left behind with a cry of agony in our hearts, as the fragile thread of our faith is dealt with so violently. Is anyone strong enough to stay conscious through such teachings as you are receiving? Probably very few, and even they would only have a whisper of equanimity and spacious peace amidst the screaming trumpets of their rage, horror, grief, and desolation. I cannot assuage your pain with any words, nor should I. Your pain is Rachel's legacy to you. Not that she or I would inflict such pain by choice, but there it is. And it must burn its purifying way to completion. You may emerge from this ordeal more dead than alive. Then you will understand why the greatest saints, for whom every human being is their child, shoulder the unbearable pain and are often called the living dead. For something within you dies when you bear the unbearable. It is only in that dark night of the soul that you are prepared to see as God sees, and to love as God loves. Now is the time to let your grief find expression. No false strength. Now is the time to sit quietly and to speak to Rachel and to thank her for being with you these few years and encourage her to go on with her work knowing that you will grow in compassion and wisdom from this experience. In my heart I know that you and she will meet again and again and recognize the many ways in which you have known each other. And when you meet you will know in a flash what now it is not given to you to know, why this had to be the way it was. Your rational mind can never understand what has happened, but your hearts, if you can keep them open to God, will find their own intuitive way. Rachel came through you to do her work on Earth which included her manner of death. Now her soul is free and the love that you can share with her is invulnerable to the winds of changing time and space. In that deep love include me too."

The paradox: it is all perfect and it all stinks. A conscious being lives simultaneously with both of those. You huff and puff and you make to appear as if it were real, but you know it isn't. You experience the agony and the ecstasy and behind it you sit, laughing at the moon. It is perfect, and you do everything you can to relieve the suffering, wherever you find it. What else is there to do? And you recognize individual differences — that what is suffering for one person is not suffering for another. Somebody comes to me and says, "You're a yogi. Tell me how to fast." I say, "Don't eat for nine days." "Well, I'd thought of a four-day fast." "No, do nine, it's good." "Can I take anything?" "You can take weak tea." After seven days, the person comes in and says, "I haven't eaten for seven days." "Good, doing fine, two more days." You give a little ego boost. You walk out on the street and somebody comes up and says, "Hey man, you got a quarter? I haven't eaten for seven days." "Good! You're doing fine, two more days."

You only suffer if you are attached. If you think you're young and you start to grow old, you suffer because you're busy thinking you're young. If you're not standing anywhere, where is the suffering? No pain. So, you finally realize it's as if you jump out of an airplane and there's no parachute, but there's no Earth. You could just keep doing it. It's all skydiving from there on in. So, for a person who realizes that, suffering — although you don't go after it because you're not a masochist — isn't pushed because you realize it's teaching you something.

I work with dying people. And the people who seek me out are the people who have said, "I wish to use my death as a vehicle of awakening," which is a *really* select sample. I walk into a room of people, even these people, and I look, and I say, "Oh, I'll come back later, I see that you're busy dying." One woman says to me, "Ram Dass, I've finished my work and I want to die. I want you to help me." She's got a big brain tumor and she's on oxygen and she's very frail. I say to her, "Sounds like ego. How do you know when you've finished your work? Maybe you've got to lose each sense, sense by sense. Take whatever you can get." She reflects on that and she says, "But I'm so bored." I said, "Of course you're bored. That's because you're always busy dying. I mean you're dying and so am I, but I'm not busy dying."

If you try to keep one story line going it's boring. "I'm a husband. Every day. I eat like a husband. I drive like a husband." It gets boring. I wouldn't like to be a husband all the time. I wouldn't like to be anything all the time. I would like to play the roles impeccably, but not get lost in them. To finish her, because that's a good death to share with you, she said, "I see a young child in a tree, frightened, and a menacing man walking around the tree. I think it has something to do with my death, so I've been sending the man good vibrations." I thought about that and I said, "It sounds like one of the first of the ten thousand horrible visions and ten thousand beautiful visons. If you sit around manipulating every one of them you're never going to die." I mean the world does have menacing men and scared children. She says, "But I feel as if everything is pressing in on me." So I went into that space. I said, "That's an easy one. That's because you are busy being a one-quart container where a gallon of water is being poured into you. Because as you start to let go of things you are, you tune into more and more energy. You try to fit that energy into who you thought you were, and it overloads." I remember once I was sitting in front of Maharaji. He was sitting there, and then suddenly he lay over on his side and he started to snore. He wasn't even lying down, he was just sort of on his side, snoring. And when he did that I was focusing on my third eye, figuring this time I'm not going to get sucked into all his talk and movement. I'm going for the inner guru. I'll just use his juice. So, I'm sitting there focusing on my third eye, and I start to shake. I was shaking so badly I thought I was going to break my spine. It was like trying to ride a wild horse in the rodeo. At that point he sat up and he said, "Ask Ram Dass how much money Steven makes." The fellow next to me said, "Well, Maharaji, he's meditating." "No. Wake him up, he's not meditating." And the guy shook me and asked, "How much money does Steven make?" And I heard it from way out, "How much money does Steven make?" Oh shit, well okay, "Thirty thousand dollars." Then I tried to get back out, but then, of course, it's all over. You can't grab a memory. It's like a dead butterfly. It doesn't fly again. So I said to her, "The problem is that you're being a one-quart container. Just expand. Include everything you can hear, smell, touch, taste, feel, or think about. Just go outward." So, we closed our eyes, and I said, "Do you hear the clock ticking? Become the clock ticking. Tick, tick, tick. Hear the children on the street playing? Become the children. Allow it all within yourself."

Feel this hall at this moment. Instead of being somebody sitting in the hall attached to all your sensations, expand outward until all of this hall is within you. Look down within yourself and see all of us sitting here involved with this drama. The Cambodians in the camps on the Thai border, inside us. It's us. Keep expanding. How about the Earth? Can you experience the entire Earth within yourself? Just play. You look on the surface of the Earth, and there's weather, and volcanic eruptions. There's humans and struggles and violence and inhumanity and unfairness and changes. There's floods and tidal waves. And here you are, present, quiet, peaceful, loving, understanding. This is the kind of peace that brings peace to the world, the peace of non-attachment. Keep going out until the entire universe is within you, galaxies, black holes. Everything you can conceive of within form is within you. You are the ancient one. No form, no limit, no time, no space. There is only one of us. You may get lonely if you're busy with your separateness. If you start to experience loneliness, look again to see if it isn't merely aloneness, the great aloneness, the great atoneness, at-oneness, atonement. And rooted in this one you play the dance of the two.

A poem on the Norman Crucifix of 1632: "I am the great sun, but you do not see me. I am your husband, but you turn away. I am the captive, but you do not free me. I am the captain you will not obey. I am the truth, but you will not believe me. I am the city, where you will not stay. I am your wife, your child, but you will leave me. I am that God to whom you will not pray. I am your council, but you do not hear me. I am the lover, whom you will betray. I am the victor, but you do not cheer me. I am the holy dove, whom you will slay. I am your life, but if you will not name me, seal up your soul with tears and never blame me."

We are the One as the many, all of us. And every time we get lost in the many we use it as a vehicle to return to the One. And every time we enter the One we come back into the many to play, and we become impeccable warriors, at service, at love, at relationship, in politics and the arts — in a dance of living and dying. We dance through it, with involvement, but without clinging. When you have become zero, when you have died into the One, when you are fully not my but thy will, oh Lord, then every act, every thought, recreates the universe. But then, who there is to have thoughts that are separate from the law? For at that point there is only one of us left, and we created the dance in the first place. What an extraordinary thing, that you and I can meet on this plane to reflect about this. What extraordinary grace.

You and I chipped in tonight to help pay for **THE SUN** magazine. Why would I do a benefit for **THE SUN**? I mean, of all the worthy causes, why would I do it for **THE SUN**? You know, it's just another magazine. Well, it's an interesting thing for you to ponder. All I can tell you is I am a subscriber. And a lover of the magazine and the beings that put it together, and how it comes together, and the way the spirit manifests through it. There are a lot of little seed things around the country that I just feel love for. **THE SUN** is another dance I feel good in my heart about. See, very often when we go on the spiritual journey we get kind of klutzy and heavy. I realized that I had to honor the totality, and one of the things was aesthetics. What happend to aesthetics? And I went back to playing the cello again, and I play in a trio with a harpsichord and a recorder. You've got to keep it all together.

I'm a part of something called the Seva Foundation Blindness Project, which is a group of people getting rid of unnecessary blindness. I was at the board meeting of the Seva Foundation, and there was an Indian doctor who told us that his mobile eye hospitals were performing operations in India on the kind of cataracts that grew in India because of the diet, and they could perform these operations in four minutes at a cost of five dollars. At this moment there are seven to nine million people who are blind in India, waiting for this operation. Many of them are going to wait the rest of their lives, and some of them are probably thirty or twenty, and they will never get the operation because there is no money or hospital. Five dollars, four minutes. Now, if those people who are blind are "them," then you can use your five bucks to do whatever you want, but if it were your father, for example . . . "Hey, son, daughter, I'm blind, would you mind loaning me five dollars so that I can see again?" "Sorry, I'm going to the flicks." So, we had the annual meeting last year. Larry, who heads the foundation — the doctor whose introduction to Maharaji I read to you — came up to me and he said, "I want you to meet this couple that's given some money. Let them tell you this story." The woman said, "We had set aside two thousand dollars to buy a hot tub, and then I heard one of your tapes in which you said for five dollars a person that was blind could see. And I thought to myself, 'If I give up this hot tub, four hundred people could see. So, we sent you the two thousand dollars.'" The reactions I had to that were both, "Oh wow, what an act, you're a beautiful person," and also, "Oh my God, does that mean I have to give up hot tubs?"

Over Gandhi's tomb it says, "Think of the poorest person you have ever seen, and ask yourself whether your next act will be of any help to that person." Maharaji said, "Be like Gandhi" to me. If I am going to live like Gandhi, I've got to keep that person there all the time as I live my life. Not only that, but I've got my guru, Maharaji, who is laughing himself sick over me. Every time I look at him he's just giggling. So, I have this giggling fool and this poor person starving, looking into my eyes with those big eyes. And I've got to try and live my life? You know, you can't even go to the bathroom. It's like two guys who are given two chickens and told to kill them where nobody can see, and one goes behind the barn and kills the chicken, and the other walks around for two days, and finally comes back and says, "I can't find a place where the chicken won't see." If you really want to get free, you just have to remember, that's all. And it'll do it to you. It's doing it to you anyway. You wouldn't even be here tonight if it wasn't. You don't have to do anything. It's all happening. It's all happened, you've all been had. The Martian takeover is complete. You can go now.

In India when we meet and part we say, "Namaste," which means, "I honor the place in you where, when you're in yours and I'm in mine, there's only one of us. I honor the place of God within you, of peace, of presence." Namaste.

I'm in mine, there's only one of us. I honor the place of God within you, of peace, of presence." Namaste.

After a break, Ram Dass answered questions. On our tape, some were unintelligible. Fortunately, he paraphrased most of them.

QUESTION: What's the purpose of reason and intellect?
RAM DASS: It's an exquisite instrument, just like prehensile ability, to control and master, or tune, or interact within certain planes of relative reality. It's a subsystem. It's a beautiful servant and a lousy master. The minute you are without thought, then you can think as a form of play. If you're attached to your thought, then your thought is your enemy; it's your prison. So, you extricate yourself from thought, in order to play with thought. You cannot understand God. You can only become God. You can't know God with your intellect. But, you can go into that which is beyond intellect, and then come back in conceptualization, and describe the indescribable as best you can.

QUESTION: About mediums. . . .
RAM DASS: I've learned over the years that everybody that doesn't have a body doesn't necessarily know more than I know. What happens is, someone who's a well-meaning pipe-fitter dies. They're hanging around, very attached to the physical plane, not ready to get on with their other work. And they figure, I'll do good for the physical plane, by talking to Uncle Sam, or Aunt Mathilda, and telling them how it is. But all they know is what they know, which isn't much more. Then there are some very high beings that come through to this plane. You can take whatever you can get, and feel it with your heart. You've just got to trust your own heart as to what's useful. Your method can be to use astral help, guides, spirit agents, gurus, all of that. These are all vehicles. You've got to go beyond vehicles finally. But don't throw away the boat until you get across the river, or the ocean, as the case may be. So, if it's useful, use it.

QUESTION: About LSD. . . .
RAM DASS: The first time I went to India I gave Maharaji 900 micrograms of pure acid, and nothing happened. That impressed me. Because I know when you take 900 micrograms of acid, no mat-

ter how fat you are, something happens. So, I came back to America and I told everybody that nothing happened, but then I had the suspicion that he had sort of hypnotized me, and that he'd thrown them over his shoulder instead of into his mouth. I kept worrying about it. When I went back to India in 1971, he called to me, "Did you give me some medicine last time you were here?" I said, "Yeah." He said, "Did I take it?" I said, "I think so." He said, "What happened?" I said, "Nothing." He said, "Well, go away." The next day he said, "Do you have any more of that?" I said, "Yeah." So, I brought it out, and he took 1200 micrograms this time. And he took each one and stuck it on his tongue, and made sure I saw that he swallowed it. Then about halfway through the journey he went under his blanket, and he came up looking absolutely insane. I thought, "Oh my God, what have I done to this poor old man. He probably read my mind and he thought that I thought that he couldn't take the acid and he took it. He didn't realize how powerful it was, poor slob." At the end of an hour he said, "You got anything stronger?" And obviously nothing had happened at all. Then he said, "It's useful. It could allow you to come in and have the darshan of Christ," meaning you could come in and be in the presence of the spirit. He said, "But you could only stay two hours and then you'd have to leave. It would be better to become Christ than to visit him, but your medicine won't do that for you. Love is a stronger medicine than your medicine." I really heard that. I heard that in a final analysis it wasn't the true samadhi. It was a useful vehicle, but finally it wasn't the whole vehicle. I said to him "Should I take that medicine anymore?" He said, "Yes, if you're in a cool place, you're feeling much peace, you're alone and your mind is turned toward God, it could be useful." And I have used it that way about every two years. The last three times were in San Franciso, Bali, and the Mid-America Hotel in Salina, Kansas. And every one of them has been incredibly useful and beautiful. I learned a great deal and honor it. I also know that I don't care if I ever take it again. And I may take it next week. I have no more rules about the games of life. I just listen to my heart. I trust my heart. People say, "Do you take drugs? You don't take drugs, do you?" or, "Do you have sex?" And I say, "I don't have any rules. I don't have any definitions. I'm just open to what is."

QUESTION: About the effects of LSD. . . .

RAM DASS: What kind of effect did it have? I think it had an incredible effect in breaking me out of a kind of reality that I was locked into. It put it into relative reality. I think my first experience with psilocybin did that. And whether or not that would have happened anyway, who knows? You don't have any control over the experiment. It seemed very useful to me at the time. I've learned over time, as I stand back, that things that seemed lke critical events usually aren't. They were critical because you were ready for them. And that has to do with where you were at. Obviously a lot of people have taken psychedelics who don't seem to have awakened much through them. Just the drug itself doesn't do it if your model or your karma is too thick. And I think when your karma gets thin enough a leaf falling off a tree could do it. It well may be that what we needed to blow our brains out with in the Sixties is now anachronistic because the relative realities that we did it to overcome are now accepted parts of the culture.

QUESTION: About dying. . . .

RAM DASS: What has been useful with people that are dying is your work on yourself. You stay so centered and present and loving and uncaught in the whole issue of living and dying that you are right there for that person, so they can get free of the melodrama of dying to be with you in pure awareness. And all you can offer them is your being. Everything you've done and all of your work on yourself is what you offer. And there's no rule of "Do this. Do that." It isn't that way at all. It's be. Be fully present. Be with the death and the life and the healing, whichever way it goes, because you don't know how it's supposed to go. You don't know whether the person is supposed to live or die. There's a great story of Maharaji's in which he says, "Somebody's coming." And they say, "No, nobody's coming." He says, "Yes, somebody's coming." And just then a servant of one of his devotees comes in and Maharaji yells at him, "I know your boss just had a heart attack and he's calling for me, but I'm not going to go." He says, "But he's dying, Maharaji." "I know, but I'm not going to go." And everybody says, "Ah, but he's been a devotee for so many years. Go, Maharaji." "No. I'm not going to go." Finally he picks up a banana. He says, "Here. Give him this. He'll be all right." In India, if the guru gives a piece of fruit. . . . If

you're a ninety-year-old lady and you want to have a baby, you go to
the guru and you say, "I want to have a baby." He says, "Here, eat
this mango." And nine months later you have a baby. So they took
the banana home and they mashed it up and they fed it to him and
he took the last bite and he died. That's the end of the story. All
Maharaji said was, "He'll be all right." He didn't say how.

QUESTION: About love. . . .
RAM DASS: Once you start to tune in to love, then you could fall
in love with everybody, continually, all the time. And obviously,
you have to change your way of reacting to that experience. As you
quiet down, you begin to see that there are various vehicles for
awakening, and you've got to listen to find out what your vehicle is.
Your vehicle may be just taking experiences as they come, letting
them go lightly all the time. That would be a method. Your vehicle
may be renunciation. Go to the mountains. That's a method. There
are thousands of methods. Service is a method. The method that
you may hear might be that of working with a partner to go from the
two into the One. That may be a method. I have my method. My
method is my guru. I'm not looking around for a method. I do what I
have to do. My service is part of my method to my guru. Once
something starts to work for you and you begin to se it as a method,
you lose interest in collecting more because it's just going to com-
plicate the whole stew. And you make decisions: "I could love you. I
could fall in love. We could run away. I feel passion. I feel all this
stuff, but it isn't in the karmic cards because I'm already at work and
it's fine, and I love you and I wish you well." Do you hear that one?
Sometimes, of course, the grass is greener on the other side.
Familiarity turns off the mystery of the romanticism, of the
unknown, and you're suddenly dealing with all of these fascinations.
But, they are just fascinations, and if you keep pursuing them all it's
as if you keep digging shallow wells and you never get the water
because you don't go deep enough. There is a quality when you get
to hate your partner, and you're turned off, and you never want to
see them again, and all that, when it really starts to happen. A
marriage, a relationship — if it is living truth — is right on the line
between cosmos and chaos all the time. The minute it gets too
smooth, forget it. You're probably sleepwalking through it. "Oh,
we're so happy. I love you, you love me, I know who you are. . . ."

Forget it. Because, each of us is changing all the time. As Mahatma Gandhi said, "God is absolute truth. I am only relative truth." As a human being, I see a new truth each day. The commitment is to truth, not to consistency. A relationship that can withstand the changing truths really goes deep. It is a very consuming vehicle. You can't put it on the back burner and go do something else. It really takes a lot of juice.

You find the method that is harmonious with your vehicle and your work with it. So, if you have a physical illness, that's the method. If you have a child, that's the method. If you have an old father, that's the method. If you have a brilliant intellect, that's the method. If you've got a big heart, that's your method. You keep working with your methods.

QUESTION: What role does somebody who is physically disabled play in the spiritual growth of others, and what is happening for them?

RAM DASS: I don't think that I can answer more specifically than that we are each other's karma. When you are with somebody that is disabled, very often this gives you a chance to see your own attachments and fears and particular lifestyle. If you get over seeing one is better than another and just see it as different, the whole game looks different to you. People come to me all bent over with arthritis, in pain, taking a hundred aspirin a day. All I say to them is, "Heavy round this time, isn't it. Heavy work to do." My job is to love and be with the person, not to judge it or anything. Just to honor it and to open to it. I don't know if that isn't the best thing for the person. I don't have to judge God. I just have to be with it. I can feel the functional nature of suffering for people. We wouldn't lay it on each other, we wouldn't ask for it ourselves, but a conscious being uses it. When you are conscious, you are able to see suffering that way, and you create an environment in which someone who is suffering can see it themselves that way if they are ready to see it. There's nothing in you that doesn't allow them to get out of the trap of being somebody suffering. So, when you're working with somebody that is disabled, who is caught in being disabled, your job is not to get lost. With dying people, they're dying at one level. At another level, you're here. I'm here. Here we are. "What's new today?" "Well, I'm dying." "That's interesting. What else is new?"

QUESTION: What is the most easily confused aspect of sexual responsibility?

RAM DASS: The identification with your own sexuality. Sexuality is a part of your being, it is not who you are. The over-identification with it means that you polarize the universe and get into identifying as a relator, rather than that which is the totality. It catches you in the roles, and thus, makes the whole thing dualistic. It comes down to Freudian sexuality, or lust, or subject-object sexuality. The error is getting caught in subject-object, which is merely projecting outward an object to gratify you sexually. Sexual tantra starts from a place of us. It never loses the us, so the sexual arousal doesn't come out of seeing the other person as an object. It doesn't come out of a fantasy projection. It comes out of a natural flow of being together. That's why I usually say to people, only have sex with your friends. And Maharaji says, "Your only friend is God." So, finally, you will only have sex with God. You come to the place where it's us, and out of the us-ness sexuality happens naturally. The problem is, that mechanism is so over-learned, it catches you so strongly, that the minute the arousal mechanism starts, you're busily being a person who has sexual desire or need or being a sexual actor. You get caught in the act in those two levels. And the minute you get caught in the act, you just lost it. Because then the act can only give pleasure, it cannot give liberation. If an act only gives pleasure and not liberation, it increases your karma. There's a way to use sexuality to go beyond sexuality. Or there's a way to use sexuality to stay in it. And most people use sexuality to stay in it, but wanting the rush that comes from identifying with the sexual experience, rather than using it as a vehicle to open, all the time.

QUESTION: About being treated as a sexual object. . . .

RAM DASS: When you feel you're being regarded as a sexual object finally you have compassion for the person who's doing that. Because you know who you are. If somebody hates me, I figure that's their problem; I'm a really beautiful guy. As long as you are using somebody else to tell you who you are, if they see you as a sexual object, that's who you buy. When you finally realize who you are — I *am*, but I'm also that — all you have to do is love them, you don't have to change them. Loving another person is the optimum condition where if they want to let go they can let go, and if not, they see you as an object, and that's just another dance. But you don't buy another person's mind.

QUESTION: About gurus. . . .
RAM DASS: All methods are traps. A guru is dualistic, just as God in form is dualistic, as something or somebody outside, and you use dualistic methods to open your heart, to learn, to listen, until finally you merge. You go through the guru and into yourself and then the guru disappears and you come out the other end. You use the method until it self-destructs. At one point, I was sitting opposite Maharaji in the courtyard and everybody was rubbing his feet and talking to him and I thought, "Why are they all doing that? I'm not going to spend the rest of my life rubbing this old man's feet. That couldn't be my way to God. This is absurd. I don't care if I never see him again." And then I thought, "Gee, this is heresy. I love him so much. How could I not care if I never see him again?" And just as I had that thought, he turned quickly and looked at me and he whispered to this old man, who came running across and touched my feet, which was weird. And I said, "Baba, why did you touch my feet?" And he said, "Maharaji said, 'Go touch Ram Dass' feet. He and I understand each other perfectly.' " And what I heard him saying was, "Don't get hung up on this. You're absolutely right on. Use it, and then let go." And I really feel that. I'm not a guru and I'm not an enlightened being. I'm just somebody on the path, but lest that get confused, I find it really nice to have no students, no ashram, no nothing. I'm just a wandering Jew. I'm just floating around, just growing in the nice soil, here and there.

QUESTION: About spiritual hazards. . . .
RAM DASS: Spiritual occupational hazards, for instance my occupational hazards. What do you do when someone comes up and looks at you as if you are the Light and their doorway through? Oh, Ram Dass! The occupational hazard is that you'll get caught in thinking that you are who they think you are. In other words, how do you deal with the projections, how do you deal with something coming through you? Do you think it's you? Do you get caught in it? Where does your ego buy in? How do you deal with power, because fame is power. And money is power, all this stuff is power. How do you deal with power? Is it your power? Or do you realize you're like a

bookkeeper for the firm and your job is merely to be used as dharmically as you know how. Once you have fame you can gratify yourself much more easily and then you've got to see whether your acts of gratification limit the freedom of another human being. And this would be a misuse of your powers. I don't even see the power anymore. It's just irrelevant. I look at myself as just like you. We're all just here together. I'm just playing my part. I'm no longer identified with the part. It's a Rent-A-Ram Dass. It's much lighter. There are other kinds of hazards of getting caught in spiritual materialism, or getting caught in spiritual myths about who I am. Maharaji used to set me up all the time. He'd say, "Ram Dass is your guru. Follow Ram Dass." And then he'd make a total fool out of me in front of everybody. He'd set me up and then knock me down, and set me up and knock me down. It was great. He was just helping me through.

QUESTION: About grieving. . . .

RAM DASS: The stages of grieving and non-attachment. Don't make believe you're not feeling it. Let the grief happen. You've got to allow yourself to get really lost in it. The minute you push it away, it clings longer. Go through it, and then develop a spaciousness around it, so that there is the grief and there is also that which is aware of the grief. At first there is just a tiny little thread — almost all of you is busy with the grief, and then very slowly the thread starts to develop. Instead of "I am grieving," it's more like, "There's grief. It's a deep grief and I've got to go through it, like I'm walking through a room of grief." But you don't cling, and it comes, and then it goes. It may take years for it to go, but that's okay. There's no rush and it's all a teaching, work with it, just keep working with it, keep bringing spaciousness to bear on it. Then finally you are awareness, not grieving. You finally let go of all the models, even the model of grieving, because the deeper you are aware of your own being, the less you even think anything dies. High beings often laugh when their wife dies, or something like that, because they are so happy she's free, and they're not busy possessing a memory because they're living within the present moment. Maharaji died in 1973, but he sure hasn't gone off the set as far as I can see, so what am I going to grieve about?

(July 1980)

W.G. McDonald

Zen And The Art of Peanut Butter

First, seek the most direct path
leading to the pantry.
Focus on the jar itself.
Reveal the contents
with a reverse spiral motion.
delicately insert the knife.
Delicately withdraw the knife.
As if applying salve
to the infinite being himself,
spread the contents
on the leavened slice.
Attentively lick the remainder
from the blade,
and throw the sandwich away.

(August 1983)

Illustrations and Photographs

I haven't heard from some of **THE SUN's** *contributors in years. I know two of them are dead: Joel Jackson, a fine poet from Raleigh, North Carolina, and Peg Staley, the therapist from Rhode Island who wrote so bravely of her struggle with cancer. Another North Carolina poet has also either died or vanished, according to friends long puzzled by his disappearance.*

Most of them, however, still keep in touch. A few earn a living with words but, for the most part, the writing is a way to earn some understanding. I've always been amazed by the quality of the writing in **THE SUN**, *since we depend on unsolicited material, and haven't been able to pay writers. Thus, everything in this book is also a stunning expression of generosity — the freely-offered gifts of the writers and artists represented here. To my mind, this is something of a miracle.*

—Ed.

Contributors

JIMMY SANTIAGO BACA, who lives in the Southwest, went into a maximum security prison at the age of twenty-two to serve five years for selling drugs. He'd had two years of formal schooling. He'd never read a book and didn't know how to write. He taught himself in his cell. Louisiana State University has published a collection of his poems called *Immigrants In Our Own Land*.

JOE BLANKENSHIP is an actor. When last heard from he was in New York City, waiting on tables between auditions.

ALAN BRILLIANT, with his wife, Teo Savory, runs the Unicorn Press in Greensboro, North Carolina. He wrote recently that "what the world needs is for political activists to become more spiritually aware. And for spiritual inactivists to become more politically aware. Politically aware people tend to become grim and become 'seized' (in Jung's term) by the horrors they witness and long to make others understand. But, too often, those who are joyful in their spiritual exercises use their enlightened attitude and their knowledge that no one but oneself can assist oneself as a way of neglecting the actual and physical responsibilities of a world clenched into a single physical area: a shrinking area. And in the future one's 'space' may well be the result of exploitation of those without space. In short, the combination of the physical and the spiritual within us is becoming mirrored by the world's situation and I believe that some measure of balance can be achieved if we bring together the politically and the spiritually aware. And, it occurs to me, this is what Teo and I have been about, at Unicorn, for almost twenty years now. . . ."

ELIZABETH ROSE CAMPBELL was affiliated with **THE SUN** from 1976 to 1982 as a magazine distributor, typesetter, subscriptions clerk, assistant editor, contributing editor, and flower bed manager. She was infamous for being unable to make good office coffee and being chronically fifteen minutes late but was nevertheless adored. She now lives in upstate New York, where she recently worked on the staff of the Omega Institute for Holistic Studies.

DAVID CHILDERS is a new wave lawyer practicing in Mt. Holly, North Carolina. He is also a student of military history and plays guitar and sings for the rock 'n roll band, Gutwrench.

DAVID CITINO teaches at Ohio State University in Marion, Ohio and is poetry editor of *The Ohio Journal*.

TOM CLEVELAND drew **THE SUN** logo with a Tarot card for his model. Where the monocle came from no one knows. He lives in Chapel Hill, North Carolina.

MOIRA CRONE's "Letter from Boston" was, indeed, a letter to a **SUN** reader, who thought it should be read by others. When last heard from, she was living in Washington, D.C.

NATALIE D'ARBELOFF was raised in France, Paraguay, Brazil, Italy and the United States. Since 1963, she's lived in London, where she's an artist, printmaker, writer, and runs her own press.

RAMESHWAR DAS is a photographer and poet from Amagansett, New York.

THADDEUS GOLAS is the author of *The Lazy Man's Guide to Enlightenment*, a gem of cosmic common sense. "Laziness," he writes, "keeps me from believing that enlightenment demands effort, discipline, strict diet, non-smoking, and other evidences of virtue." An underground success in the Seventies, it's now available from Bantam, and in five foreign translations, and is a superb map through the metaphysical wilderness, plain talk amidst the babble. He lives in San Francisco, California.

ROXY GORDON co-founded *Blackjack*, a literary magazine, in 1973 — it's still published in Montana — and in 1974 he started "a more or less free-form music and pop-culture (though I don't much like that term; I expect culture is culture) tabloid that I edited, published, typeset (my wife, actually, sets type) and pasted-up through twenty-two issues. That thing was semi-successful and even gained a kind of cultish following in Europe (I still write for a somewhat similar magazine in England). But it made almost no money and even as non-commercial as it was, I found myself being drawn much further into the music business world than I cared to go." He now publishes *Art Magic*, which consists of an occasional essay or drawing, "about as free-form as any publishing can get." It's available from 6200 Palo Pinto, Dallas, Texas 75214.

DAVID GRANT is a writer living in Americus, Georgia.

FRANK GRAZIANO lives in Iowa City, Iowa, where he's the editor of the Grilled Flowers Press.

KARL GROSSMAN is a vegetarian who doesn't like vegetables. He does like spaghetti; actually, he loves spaghetti, and eats it several times a week. "Although I'm a vegetarian," he says, "I can, in fact, not refuse meatballs and spaghetti when it is put in front of me, or even nearby." Karl is also an award-winning journalist who writes a syndicated column and teaches journalism at the State University of New York in Old Westbury. He lives in Sag Harbor, New York.

DAVID GUY is the author of two novels, *Football Dreams* and *The Man who Loves Dirty Books*. He lives in Durham, North Carolina.

CAROL HOPPE teaches in the Chapel Hill, North Carolina public schools.

ROBERT HORVITZ is art editor of the *Whole Earth Review* (formerly *CoEvolution Quarterly*).

BRAD HUTCHINSON writes, takes photographs and is an ace bicyclist now living in Peterborough, New Hampshire.

JUDSON JEROME is the author of *Families of Eden* and was one of the founding members of the Downhill Farm Community in Hancock, Maryland, where he moved with his family after twenty years as a professor of literature at Antioch. He now lives with his family in Ohio.

RON JONES lives in San Francisco, California, where he's been a teacher for more than twenty years, often in unusual positions that have inspired much of his writing. Since 1978 he has been physical education director at San Francisco's Recreation Center for the Handicapped. In 1972, he founded the Zephyros Educational Exchange, a non-profit group of parents, artists, and teachers who write, print, and distribute their own teaching materials.

JEANETTE JOHNSON is a singer and an artist who lives in Chapel Hill, North Carolina.

RICHARD JOSTE is the former Art Director of **THE SUN,** and is largely responsible for its simplicity of design and visual openness. He now lives in Palo Alto, California.

JAK KILLEFER is a graphic designer who lives in Chapel Hill, North Carolina.

HARRY KNICKERBOCKER is an artist and poet who lives in Seattle, Washington.

STEPHEN KOONS sells clean water in Durham, North Carolina.

DAVID KOTEEN is a devoted father of three sons and co-founder of Children of the Green Earth, a tree-planting organization. He lives in Eugene, Oregon.

STEPHEN MARCH is a writer and photographer who lives in Chapel Hill, North Carolina.

W.G. McDONALD lives in Durango, Colorado, where he works as a land surveyor.

R.A. MEIER is a photographer who lives in Chapel Hill, North Carolina.

DUSTY MILLER founded and edited *The New Lazarus Review*, a literary magazine, and in his last letter said he was looking for work in Albany, New York.

FRANK MILLS lives in Middletown, Connecticut. Although he was a bona fide priest in a mystical order in San Francisco more than ten years ago, he now finds that his "religious spookiness decreases with the hairs on my head. And I prefer my medicine halfistic from a licensed physician like my father. "

CARL MITCHAM, when we last heard from him, was a member of a small Catholic community called the Families of St. Benedict in New Hope, Kentucky.

LEAH PALMER PREISS bicycled with her portfolio to **THE SUN** office one day, and became our staff artist for the next year. She now lives in Northampton, Massachusetts.

JIM RALSTON is a writer who lives in Western Maryland and teaches at Garrett Community College. He wrote recently that after taking a seminar on "Freedom and the Religious Personality," a wonderful thing happened: "a fifteen- or twenty-year ambivalence fell off my back, as I realized that I was an outsider — and that was my rightful place to be, that was the true *home* of my soul, working on the outside. This realization has made a lot of difference for me — to move quietly to the outside, without rebellion, without anger — knowing that those who work on the inside are equally important in the scheme of things."

JAYA ROBLING lives and works at a yoga and wholistic health center in northeastern Pennsylvania.

JOHN ROSENTHAL is a writer and photographer who lives in Chapel Hill and has the distinction of having written the only piece for which **THE SUN** was ever sued (unsuccessfully). He hosts a local television interview show, "Portfolio."

HOWARD JAY RUBIN is a writer, children's magician, book promoter, typesetter, plant nurseryman, interviewer, **SUN** contributing editor and/or day-laborer, who lives in Durham, Chapel Hill, Mebane and/or Carrboro, North Carolina.

JEROME RUBIN is Howard's father, as well as a photographer and advertising executive. He lives in Englewood Cliffs, New Jersey.

ROGER SAULS is a snow inspector for the town of Chapel Hill. He is the author of *Light* (Loom Press), a book of poems.

MICHAEL SHORB is a writer who lives in San Francisco, California.

DEE DEE SMALL-HOOKER lives in Raleigh, North Carolina and studies ballet "in that strange, nonsensical way those of us do who are too old for professional careers, pursuing it with every fiber."

SPARROW refuses to tell me his real name, though I've never insisted. He lives in New York City and does a lot of his writing on the subway, though "if you write on the subway, people think you're crazy — especially if you look like me. There's a type of Bag Person who writes an endless list of numbers, or a diary, on long rolls of paper, in very tiny print. I am mistaken for this person."

PAT ELLIS TAYLOR lives in Austin, Texas, where she runs the Paperbacks Plus bookstore. She says, "Soon I am going to write the story of my attempt at making enough money to leave town in a van to live as a hermit in the desert eschewing the world of material gain with the security of a few small bills stuffed in my pocket — first selling fireworks the week before the fourth of July and getting hit by lightning, then dressing up as a giant chicken-balloon seller for the Austin aqua-fest where boozed-up cowboys began to cackle, crow and flap their wings when they saw me coming and sometimes threatened to set fire to my crepe-paper feathers."

ENRIQUE VEGA is a photographer from North Carolina.

RICHARD WILLIAMS is the author of *Savarin*, a book of poems.

THOMAS WILOCH is a writer who lives in Westland, Michigan.

•

THE TEXT OF THIS BOOK IS SET IN A TYPEFACE
KNOWN AS GOUDY. THE DISPLAY-FACE IS GOUDY HANDTOOLED.
GOUDY WAS DESIGNED BY FREDERICK W. GOUDY.
HE WAS NOT RELATED TO ANTONIO GAUDI.

THE TYPESETTING WAS DONE BY JOHN COTTERMAN'S
LUNAR GRAPHICS OF CHAPEL HILL, NORTH CAROLINA.

THE SUN LOGO WHICH APPEARS ON THE COVER IS BY TOM CLEVELAND.

THIS BOOK WAS DESIGNED BY DOUGLAS CRUICKSHANK,
PRODUCTION BY SEAN BROWNE.

Ordering Information

This is the first volume of a two-volume set. To order additional copies of this book, or a copy of Volume II, or the two-volume set, fill out the coupon below.

❐ Please send me _____ copies of *A Bell Ringing In The Empty Sky: The Best Of The Sun*, Volume I.

❐ Please send me _____ copies of *A Bell Ringing In The Empty Sky: The Best Of The Sun*, Volume II.

❐ Please send me _____ copies of the two-volume set of *A Bell Ringing In The Empty Sky: The Best Of The Sun*.

    (For each individual copy, enclose $15.95, plus $2 for postage and handling, for a total of $17.95. For each two-volume set, enclose $31, plus $4 for postage and handling, for a total of $35.)

❐ I'd also like a one-year subscription to **THE SUN** for $30 (twelve issues).

_____ Total enclosed.

Please send the book(s) to:

Name _____

Address _____

City _____ *State* _____ *Zip* _____

Send to THE SUN, 107 North Roberson Street, Chapel Hill, NC 27516.